RAVE REVIEWS FOR JULIE KENNER!

"*The Cat's Fancy* deserves a place on any reader's keeper shelf!"

—*Word Weaving*

"Ms. Kenner's debut novel sets the stage for more glorious stories to come. I can't wait!"

—*The Belles & Beaux of Romance*

"Ms. Kenner is an up and coming author with a bright future ahead of her."

—*ReaderToReader.com*

"[Ms. Kenner] is a pure delight, she's fun, she gives readers what they want, a story to take you away and make you forget the rest of the world. [*The Cat's Fancy* is] SPLENDID!!"

—*Bell, Book & Candle*

"Ms Kenner has a way with dialogue; her one-liners are funny and fresh. Her comic timing is beautiful, almost Jennifer Crusie-esque."

—*All About Romance*

MAGGIE'S MAGIC

Keeping her eyes locked squarely on his, she inched forward slowly, doing nothing that might scare him and make him start wriggling and scooting away again.

"Okay, look. I've been really patient. I don't want to seem like a spoilsport, but this has got to—"

She clamped her mouth over his to cut off his protests and suddenly she realized what all the fuss was about. Even with him trying to pull away, something about the way his lips burned under hers made her insides ache. And it was such a good ache. It was better than a belly-scratch, better than the sun on her whiskers. It was even better than a warm lap. More. She had to have more.

Apparently, so did he. With a low groan, his mouth opened for her and she eased her tongue between his lips.

No wonder humans spent so much time in this activity. The shock of his lips against hers, of his tongue wrestling with hers, shot through her entire body. She felt . . . itchy? No. Warm. Warm and tingly. Like air during a lightning storm.

It was magic—just being in Nicholas's arms. Changing from a cat to a human was nothing, a parlor trick, compared to the magic of finally being held as a lover by her Nicholas. She could stay like this forever, floating in a bubble of passion and warmth, lust and desire.

Julie Kenner

LOVE SPELL BOOKS

NEW YORK CITY

A LOVE SPELL BOOK®

August 2000

Published by

Dorchester Publishing Co., Inc.
276 Fifth Avenue
New York, NY 10001

ISBN 0-505-52397-3

Printed in the United States of America.

For all the cats in my life, especially those who seem more than a little human: Madam, Tequila, Tiger, Squeaky, the outdoor kitty commune, Stubby, Garp, Sammy, and my half-brothers <g> Max and Josh.

And to Pam Hopkins and Chris Keeslar—thanks for believing!

The Cat's Fancy

There are people in this world who believe in magic, who search for the possibility in their daily lives. With awe, they open fortune cookies hoping for an omen, and turn over stones searching for fairies. They avoid sidewalk cracks, the thirteenth floor, and the undersides of ladders. Secretly, they believe that Darren was an idiot for not letting Samantha give his career a boost, and hold fast to the conviction that if they keep combing beaches they'll find Barbara Eden in a bottle.

To these people, love is just as magical as a unicorn in your driveway.

Nicholas Goodman was not one of these folks.

It didn't matter.

Maggie found him anyway.

Prologue

"This is what you want?" Old Tom teetered in the crook of the juniper tree, peering down at her with his one good eye.

Maggie pictured her Nicholas. Perfect Nicholas. She didn't hesitate. *"Yes."*

Old Tom cocked his head so that his bad eye, the one covered with the gray-green film, appeared to focus on her. Maggie stood fast. They said he could see things with that eye, he just couldn't see the world. Well, let him look. She had nothing to hide. Nothing to fear, and everything to gain.

As far as she knew, no one had ever asked to do—had never even considered trying—what she wanted. Certainly no one had the nerve to come to Old Tom for help. But she wasn't going to flinch. She wanted this. So much she could feel it in her stomach. So desperately she couldn't sleep for thinking about it.

If it couldn't be done, so be it. But if it could . . . well, Old Tom would know how. Or he could find a way.

"You would do this for love?"

She raised her chin. *"Yes."*

"You understand the consequences? What you would be giving up?"

Consequences? She was asking to be human. Wasn't that consequence enough? Could there be more? *"I haven't . . . I don't . . ."*

"You are . . . special, Maggie. Different. So this yearning you feel does not surprise me. But the consequences . . ." He trailed off, looking toward the sky. When he turned back, his expression was firm.

"Your life. It is quite fine now, no?"

Everything except for not having Nicholas. *"Yes."*

"You are very young—"

"I'm almost—"

"—and this is only your first life. Humans get only one, you know."

"With him, one would be a blessing. Without him, eight more would be torture."

Was that compassion in Old Tom's dead eye? She wanted to look more closely, to explore the enigma, but just then he lifted his head to snarl at a mockingbird cackling at them from the branches above. When he turned back, the eye was flat. Emotionless.

"This love of yours that is so deep, you would give up all you know. . . . Will he return it?" His nose twitched. Could he smell her hesitation?

She turned away. *"He calls me precious. He calls me sweetheart. I make him happy."*

"You haven't spoken with him of this? He hasn't told you how he feels?" Old Tom blinked and the pupil in his good eye narrowed to a slit.

Maggie shrank back. *"He doesn't understand me. I've tried, but he doesn't hear."* How could she make Old Tom understand? She knew how Nicholas felt. He loved her. And if he didn't now, he would. Eventually, he would. He had to.

"Child, you ask the impossible of me."

She struggled to breathe as her world collapsed around her. The stories were lies. He didn't have the power. She was trapped. Trapped in her world, and Nicholas in his. She sank down to the ground, her head resting on the cool dirt, her eyes closed.

Soon Nicholas would belong to that female. And there would be nothing Maggie could do except watch and seethe. She could scratch and spit and howl and claw the furniture, but none of that would matter.

That female would get Maggie's Nicholas.

How could she have such horrible luck? *"But the stories . . ."*

"If there was a bond . . . if he had the hearing,

could understand you . . . But no. Without that assurance . . . no, no, I must not. You are special, Maggie. And I cannot risk being wrong."

Must not? She opened her eyes.

"Oh, please, please, you must. If you love me at all, you must help me."

It was unfair of her, she knew. The members of Old Tom's clan were close, and she knew he loved them all. Still, there was a special place in his heart for her. She'd never asked for favors before, and she knew that her failure to take advantage made him love her all the more. But now, now she would do anything.

"Why now?"

She looked away, ashamed that her thoughts were so vulnerable. *"There is no special reason."*

"Maggie . . ." The compassion was back in his eye, but there was a sternness also. *"I have seen the female. The one in the tall shoes. She touches him as a lover."*

"They are to be married."

"Married? The bonding ritual of humans. You would interfere with this? Why?"

"He doesn't love her. He couldn't love her."

"And you? You would be a better mate? One he does not even know exists?"

Pride straightened Maggie's spine. She lifted her chin and looked down her nose, composed and serene.

Old Tom grunted. *"Hmph. What is it you dislike about this female? Why could he not love* her?"

"She smells . . . unreal." Maggie tried to search

Old Tom's face without looking like she was watching him. They all trusted their noses, but Old Tom more than anyone. Maybe it was because he only had that one eye, the one that she was now desperately searching for a clue.

"If I do this thing, it will be by my rules. Do you understand?"

She nodded.

"You must choose now. Once it is done, only then will you know the rules. But before you choose, ask yourself how well you know his heart. How well do you know your own? Are you sure that he will love you and turn away from his female?" He squinted at her. *"How do you choose?"*

"I choose Nicholas."

"Then it is done."

As he spoke, she felt a tingling in her limbs, like the crackling of the air during a lightning storm, only this was inside her, ripping her apart.

Dizzy. She felt dizzy. *Focus.* Old Tom was speaking. *Must focus.*

". . . The skills you will need . . . but not completely human . . . your soul, yes . . . but not your shape . . . only at night . . . only until All Hallow's Eve . . . by day . . . yourself . . . secret . . . can't reveal to Nicholas . . . forfeit . . . all . . ."

It was no use. She was fading. She was so tired, so dizzy. The sun was setting. Her legs wouldn't support her. Old Tom crouched above her, a silhouette against the full moon.

His words; she needed to understand his words.

"Maggie, child," his tone cut through the fog in

her head. *"He must declare his love for you of his own free will before your time is up. He must tell you. Or you will remain a cat forever, and I will be unable to help you."*

Chapter One

"Maggie, here, kitty, kitty. Maggie?" Nick Goodman dumped the overstuffed bag into the garbage can and took another look around his front yard. Where the hell could that cat be?

Something rustled in the brush that had taken over the vacant lot across the street. "Maggie?" He padded down his driveway, making a mess of his socks in the process, and stood on the curb facing the lot. Nothing.

"Maggie-cat?" As if waiting for his cue, a swarm of birds lifted from the junipers and oaks, flooding the purple sky.

"Nickie? Come back in the house, darling. You look like hell."

Angela's high, nasal tones accosted him and Nick cringed, then caught himself. He put on a smile and turned toward the house.

"I'm putting out the garbage, babe. I hardly think that calls for a necktie." Her eyes met his, then roamed down his body. He knew well enough what she'd see. A paint-splattered T-shirt touting some band he'd never heard play, Harvard athletic shorts that always seemed on the verge of splitting but held together with a fortitude he admired, and dime-store athletic socks. Not *GQ* by any means, but hardly unreasonable attire for a Sunday evening.

She rolled her eyes, then leaned against a newel post wrapped in orange and black Halloween streamers and began to examine the fingernails she'd been fussing over for the last hour. Nick bit back the observation that her fire-engine-red manicure didn't quite match the coordinated leggings and sweater that had probably cost more than his car payment. He didn't give a damn if she was coordinated, and the comment would only piss her off.

He turned back to the trash can. What the hell was wrong with him? This was the woman he was going to marry, after all. She was supposed to be the love of his life, conjure up bells, whistles, fireworks, and all that other stuff. So why was he so on edge every time she decided to stay at his place for the weekend?

Because you're used to being alone. Right. Sure.

Just typical bachelor jitters. Nothing to call Dr. Ruth about.

A yellow Ferrari glided by. Nick raised one hand in greeting to his neighbor, a prep-school type who'd moved to Los Angeles after making and losing a fortune in Internet stocks.

"Do you really think Robert is going to trust his next deal to an attorney who hangs out in his driveway in his underwear?"

"Angie . . ." he said, knowing he shouldn't be annoyed. She was Reggie Palmer's daughter, after all. Killer business instincts were in her genetic code.

"I'm just saying there are certain things that you should keep in mind if you want to get ahead." She arched her brow. "If you want *us* to get ahead."

He glanced down the road, giving the neighborhood one last once-over. The cat was nowhere in sight.

"Have you seen Maggie?"

Her nose crinkled. "I haven't seen the little beast all afternoon."

He sighed, turning back to scan the neighborhood one more time. "Animal control's going to start doing sweeps. They always do around Halloween."

"That's days away. Besides, I'm sure she's not outside. If only I were that lucky. More likely she's in the closet clawing my clothes to shreds. She hates me."

Nick cast a glance skyward. Just what he

needed. A fiancée who was jealous of his pet. "She doesn't hate you."

Angela followed him into the house. "Oh, you're so right. I forgot. I'm the one who detests her."

"I'm not giving up my cat, Angela. Can we not go there again, please?"

"I didn't say a word, sweetie. Really. I'm sure little snookie-wookums is around here somewhere. She'll turn up. She always does. Usually when it's most inconvenient." She flashed him her trademark smile, the one that had practically brought him to his knees the first time they'd met. "Speaking of, do you want me to stay the night?"

"Whatever you want," he said, hoping she'd go back to her place.

"Can we go out to dinner?"

He shook his head and gestured to the pile of SEC filings and other equally dry documents stacked neatly on the coffee table. "Can't. Work."

Angela tapped one of her nails. "All dry. I think I'm going to run, then, sweetheart."

"Sorry if my livelihood annoys you. You liked it just fine when we went to Paris." He immediately regretted opening his mouth. His words had been tacky, true, but mostly he feared she'd change her mind and stay over just to prove him wrong.

It wasn't that he didn't love her. Of course he did. He'd agreed to get married, hadn't he? He just liked having his space, wanted to enjoy it while he could.

She planted a quick kiss on his cheek, then

rubbed the lipstick off with the edge of her thumb. "Ah-ah," she warned, but there was a tease in her voice. "Don't play high-and-mighty with me. You know you want me to leave. Poor Nickie just hates when his routine is upset. I never thought there was anything in the world that could ruffle the great Nicholas Goodman's feathers. At least not until I saw how you reacted when I left my panty hose drying on your shower rod."

"Angela—"

"Now, I'm not criticizing. I think it's adorable. And wouldn't Daddy think it's a hoot? His fireball deal-maker, his secret weapon, brought to his knees by control-top pantyhose and a jar of face cream. You're going to have to get over that after the wedding."

"Angela, of course you can stay. Really—"

She just threw him that I-know-you-better-than-you-think-I-do smirk, grabbed her purse, and headed for the door. Nick didn't try to talk her into staying, and when he saw her turn off his street and onto Laurel Canyon, he felt more relaxed than he had in hours. Maybe that made him a bad person, but the truth of it was, other than her drop-dead good looks, Angela Palmer wasn't exactly warm and fuzzy either.

Hell, they deserved each other.

He wiped his hands on the beleaguered Harvard shorts and wondered what the hell had happened to him in the nine years since law school. No, he didn't really wonder. The answer was plain enough. Youthful idealism and a belief that he could somehow make the world a better place had been trampled like a bug trying to cross a highway at rush hour.

He shoved the melancholy thought aside and took another look around the neighborhood. No Maggie. Now it was after dark, after her supper time. She so rarely ventured outside that he couldn't blame her for wanting to do a little carousing, but now her whole schedule would be screwed up. She'd probably be jumping all over his bed, wanting to play, when all Nick wanted to do was sleep.

"Maggie? Here, kitty. Maggie!" he shouted, knowing it pissed off the neighbors, but not in the mood to care. After watching the lot across the street for any sign of her, he pulled the door shut. He wouldn't worry yet. He'd do that if she hadn't shown up by midnight.

Work beckoned from the living room, and he planted himself on the couch, planning on reading over the stack on the corner of the coffee table. To Angela's credit, she'd left the house exactly as she found it. She'd even straightened his magazines so that the edges were square, and had picked up the wineglasses they'd left on the back patio.

He couldn't help but smile. Yes indeed, Angela was great. Smart, beautiful, well-connected, she was the perfect wife for an up-and-coming lawyer.

He'd told his best friend the same thing not two

weeks ago and, in typical fashion, Hoop had told him that he was only justifying a bad deal he was going to regret. That was the problem with Hoop. He always said exactly what was on his mind. And just because he was often right didn't mean he was on the mark about this.

This time Nick was doing what was right. Settling down, getting married. And getting a good wife in the process. The fact that marrying Angela would lock in what was already sure to be a successful career was little more than a perk.

The phone rang and he said another thank you to the powers that be. Angela had left the cordless phone in the cradle, exactly where it was supposed to be. One of the few women he'd ever dated who did that.

He scooped up the hand set, expecting it to be Angela on her cellular.

"Hey, man, the Ice Queen leave?" It was Hoop.

"Last time I checked, she was still going by Angela."

"No shit? Well, I'll tell you a little secret. I just call her Icey to piss you off." He paused, and Nick could hear him take a swig of something, probably a beer, and exhale loudly into the phone. "Ah, I thought I saw her perky little I'm-a-daddy's-girl Beemer slip past my place a few minutes ago. Can't believe she's leaving a birthday boy all alone."

"That's not until tomorrow, and she hasn't mentioned it."

"Then you're in for it."

"You know this for a fact? She invited you?"

"Are you crazy? She thinks I'm the spawn of Satan. It's just that when a chick doesn't mention your birthday, it can only mean she's pulling out all the stops. Either she's taking you someplace amazing and you're gonna get laid, or she's throwing a surprise party and you're stuck with fifty people you avoid all year wandering through your house making small talk. Considering it's Miss An-gee-la we're talking about, I'd say either way you're pretty much screwed. So"—he paused—"wanna come over for a beer?"

"I'm working."

"Bullshit, man. You're always working. One beer won't slow you down. Besides, you got me sucked into this mess, too, and I've got some news to report."

Some news? Now, that could be interesting. Hoop might be crude and offensive and generally despised by women the world over, but he was a damn good investigator. If Nick managed to pull off the Vision Entertainment deal, no small part of it would be because he had some heavy-duty ammo tucked away. Heavy ammo he hoped Hoop could lay his hands on.

"What have you got?"

"I'll tell you about it when you get here; I don't trust phone lines. Let's just say we all get by with a little help from our friends."

So Hoop had someone on the inside. That was good. If the info was juicy . . . well, who knew how far Nick could milk it? Reggie Palmer would be thrilled, and some of that goodwill would likely rub off on his future son-in-law. And that meant Nick could walk away with a hefty year-end bonus in a couple of months—not to mention making partner.

"You've talked me into it. One beer." He hung up and headed for the bedroom. It never got too cold in Los Angeles, even in late October, but there was a definite chill in the air, and he tugged on the sweatpants that he'd left hanging on the hook inside his closet door. He folded his shorts and placed them back in a drawer, straightened the magazines on his bedside table, then noticed Angela's fingernail polish and manicure tools scattered along the window ledge above the bed.

He ignored a rising irritation. He'd have to get used to sharing his personal space. He could do it. He could leave the miniature nail salon.

Purposefully not looking back, he headed into the narrow hallway between the bedroom and his study. He managed to grab a hooded fleece jacket from the hall closet and then pass through the living room without giving in to the urge to head back to the bedroom and clean up. When he reached the front door, his resolve melted. He trotted back to the bedroom, shoved the paraphernalia into the drawer of his bedside table, and returned to the entrance hall.

"Nick, you're a basket case. Nail polish and emery boards aren't going to rock your world," he told himself.

He was right.

A second later he opened the front door and saw *her* standing there in the twilight: An exotic vision of a woman with close-cropped raven black hair and probing green eyes.

And not a single stitch of clothing.

That was when his world really began to spin out of control.

Chapter Two

The first thought that went through Nick's head was that he was dreaming. The second, that he had died and gone to heaven. But since he didn't remember any pain, tripping over anything, or otherwise meeting his demise, he abandoned that theory. No, there was only one explanation for finding a naked woman on his doorstep at twilight on the eve of his birthday—somebody was playing a really wild joke on him.

And he knew who. Hoop didn't have news. He'd just wanted Nick to open the door and see his birthday surprise.

He pulled open the screen door and tried to grab the woman's arm without gawking. It was more difficult than it sounded. Maybe a monk could have ignored the way her skin glowed in the light of the rising moon or the way her green eyes stayed locked, unblinking, on him. But Nick doubted it. Besides, he was no monk.

He finally managed to grab her wrist and tug her firmly inside. He shrugged out of his fleece jacket and threw it over her shoulders. She stared at him for a moment, blinked, and then slipped her arms through the sleeves. Luckily, the jacket was extra large and she was extra small. It more or less consumed her.

"Didn't anyone tell you that you're supposed to wait until after the birthday boy opens the door before you strip? These mountains may have been a hippie haven during the sixties and seventies, but walking around nude up here now will get you arrested."

Not a word from his little visitor. His eyes drifted down and . . . Oh, Lord, the jacket was unzipped.

Trying not to look at her or brush any of the soft skin he knew lay just beneath his coat, he reached over, joined the jacket's zipper halves, and tugged until the woman was enclosed in gray fleece up to her neck.

Still, she didn't say a word, just grinned at him like the Cheshire cat, some impish maiden who knew a secret that he didn't. Well, he had to admit, that was probably the case.

She opened her mouth and tilted her head forward. The bridge of her nose crinkled and her eyes squinted slightly in concentration. He waited for her to speak. And waited.

Nothing.

"Do you speak English?"

She cocked her head but never took her eyes off him. After a couple of seconds, she nodded slowly, while her perfect white teeth worried at her lower lip. But still no words.

Nick tried again. This whole situation was exasperating. What made it truly odd was that, despite the fact that the woman wouldn't give him a clue who she was, and despite that under normal circumstances he would be throwing up his hands and throwing her out the door, here he was, urging her gently toward the sofa, one arm looped around her shoulder, like she was some poor lost creature instead of a flake who'd shown up naked on his doorstep.

Disgusted with himself, he dropped his arm. She might be Hoop's idea of a birthday bang, but Nick had work to do, and it was screaming at him from the living room.

Having a half-naked woman inches from him was disconcerting, to say the least. Of course, his body didn't seem to think the situation was off the wall. No, sir. His traitorous flesh was reacting quite naturally, with no concern at all for his business concerns. It urged him to relax and enjoy this birthday surprise.

Fat chance. He took a step back. "Look, miss, I'm sorry if you came here for nothing."

Those big eyes held his. They were full of . . .

what? Wonder? Adoration? *Nonsense*. He'd never seen this woman before. Her mouth curved into a smile, not much more than a tease, and she eased toward him. Nick's heart beat a little rhythm-and-blues number. His throat was parched.

He took another step back. She took another forward. And on and on in a ridiculous dance until he managed to back himself up against the edge of his sofa, then fell backward over it, Dick Van Dyke–style.

As vantage points went, the couch ranked up there. His knees curved over the arm of the sofa and his back was stretched out on the seat cushions. His guest stood there, the picture of wide-eyed innocence, with his less-than-innocent eyes about even with the bottom hem of his jacket. For just a second he imagined what he would see if she lifted her arms and the jacket rose just a few inches higher.

He shifted, scooting backward until he could maneuver himself back around into a normal sitting position. She crawled toward him, over the edge of the couch, almost stalking him, her movements agile. Catlike. A smug smile danced on her lips, and her eyes were bright.

No question but that he was her canary. But the thought didn't scare him. On the contrary, every muscle and nerve in his body felt on fire. Alive. Anticipating.

What scared him was the possibility. If he wasn't careful, Nick was afraid he might just end up having the most amazing night of his life.

And if that happened, he knew he'd regret it forever.

"Look," he began, holding up a hand, "you're probably a nice young lady, and this is all very flattering, but this is L.A., and that does mean that nut cases make up the majority of the living, breathing population."

She crouched at the edge of the sofa, balancing on her toes, her slim, muscled thighs ready to pounce. With only the slightest hesitation, she extended her finger and batted at his knee, her fingertips tapping at his flesh before bouncing away, leaving Nick gasping at the current of pure desire that coursed up his thigh. The contact was infinitesimal. But its power was enormous. Any more and Nick was sure he'd die from agonizing pleasure.

Standing was no longer a possibility. Instead, he slid farther down the couch. "I'd feel a lot better about this if I just knew your name. If I wasn't the only one talking. You might find this hard to believe, but strange, naked women rarely jump me in my own house." He was babbling. She'd reduced him to a babbling fool.

But maybe his chatter had worked. She dropped forward onto all fours and started to crawl toward him. Her mouth was open and he could almost hear a whisper.

"I can't hear you." When she said it again, he still couldn't hear, but there was no mistaking the words that formed on her mouth.

My Nicholas.

* * *

Maggie forced air through her throat, trying again to make a noise he'd recognize. What was supposed to be "My darling," came out "Mlg drgly."

From the look on his face, he had no idea what that meant.

So much for having a human voice to go with her human body. Well, that was okay. Sooner or later, she would find the words. In the meantime, if she couldn't tell him she loved him, that she'd done this only for him, she would show him.

She leaned forward on her haunches—*legs, they're called legs*—and tried to lower herself over him.

It didn't work. The superb balance she'd used to have escaped her, and she fell forward onto his chest.

His beautiful body splayed out under her, warm and wonderful. She could feel the rhythm of his heart under her fingertips and hear the trill of his breath in her ear.

With a grunt, he tried to wriggle away from her. Not that it did him any good. She just hung on for the ride.

"I don't know how much Hoop's paying you, but you really need to get off me." Maggie recognized Nicholas's I'm-trying-to-sound-patient-but-I'm-running-out-of-options-here voice. She'd heard it plenty of times when he'd tried to coax her off a bookshelf or out from under the bed.

Good. Maybe he'd quit scooting backward and just give in.

"Miss, I'm not joking around here."

Or maybe not.

Perhaps he just needed some human-type encouragement. Lightning-quick, she zipped in, planted a fast kiss on his cheek the way she'd seen his female do sometimes, and sprang back. Straddling his stomach, she studied his reaction.

She saw nothing. Or, at least, nothing good.

That wild, wary look—like he wanted to run from her, not spend his life with her—still sparkled in his eyes. And he didn't look like he'd cared one whit for her kiss.

She licked her lips and tilted her head, trying to decide whether *she'd* liked it. To tell the truth, it hadn't seemed all that special.

Why did humans spend so much time doing the kissing thing?

Maybe it was an acquired taste?

Then again, maybe she'd just done it wrong.

Okay. Well. The other option was to mash lips. It seemed a little silly—and she'd watched Nicholas with that female enough to know it *looked* silly—but the funny feeling in her stomach suggested that maybe humans didn't think the whole maneuver was all that bizarre.

Time for another go-round.

Keeping her eyes locked squarely on his, she inched forward slowly, doing nothing that might scare him or make him start wriggling and scooting away again.

"Okay, look. I've been really patient. I don't want to seem like a spoilsport, but this has got to—"

She clamped her mouth over his to cut off his protests and, suddenly, she realized what all the fuss was about.

Even with him trying to pull away from her, something about the way his lips burned under hers made her insides ache. And it was *such* a good ache. Better than a belly scratch. Better than the sun on her whiskers. Even better than a warm lap.

More. She had to have more.

Apparently, so did he. With a low groan, his mouth opened for her and she eased her tongue between his lips.

No wonder humans spent so much time in this activity. The shock of his lips against hers, of his tongue wrestling with hers, shot through her entire body. She felt . . . itchy? No. Warm. Warm and tingly. Like air during a lightning storm.

Magic. Just being in Nicholas's arms. Changing from a cat to a human was nothing, a parlor trick, compared to the magic of finally being held as a lover by her Nicholas. She could stay like this forever, floating in a bubble of passion and warmth, lust and desire.

And then the bubble burst.

Nicholas wrenched his mouth away from hers and stared, his face a mixture of shock and . . . something else. Longing? Uncertainty?

"I'm sorry. This is . . . the thing is . . . Hell, I'm

practically married. I don't know you. Who sent you?"

His protests spilled out, and Maggie sighed.

What was that word? Damn? Yes, damn.

Almost in an instant Nicholas recovered, gripping her shoulders and pushing her up and away from him. His legs were moving, too, as he tried to maneuver his way up and off the couch.

All he managed to do, though, was unsettle her precarious position on top of him. When she grabbed ahold of him for balance, they both tumbled off, landing with a thump on the soft carpet.

She couldn't have planned it better if she'd tried.

Nicholas sprawled on top of her, one hand between her legs and his face pressed between her . . . beasts? She thought for a second. Breasts? That was the word. Breasts.

"Are you okay?" She saw the concern in his eyes. They were brown and gold and magnificent.

As soon as she nodded, she expected him to move off of her. When he didn't, she squirmed beneath him, trying to shift herself for maximum contact, wanting . . . what? Something, yes, but she wasn't sure how to get it. The pressure of his body against her had loosed a torrent of sensations. She had only instinct to go on, and instinct told her that only Nicholas could quiet the storm raging inside her.

"Who are you?" He pitched his voice even lower than normal, and its deep resonance teased her as much as his hands had before.

If she could only answer. Old Tom had promised that she would be able to speak as a human, but it took time and some practice, and when she moved her mouth now, nothing would come out even though she could hear the words in her head.

"Can't you tell me?"

She shook her head, the tiniest of motions. Then she leaned in, once again capturing him with a kiss.

This time he did push her away, managing in one motion to move off of her and climb to his feet, leaving her in a heap on the floor. He stood next to the couch, his hands running through his thick, dark hair.

"I can't do this."

He might as well have kicked her. She shook herself, trying to regain her equilibrium. She was falling and wasn't quite sure she would land on her feet.

But you love me? She crawled toward him, hoping he could understand.

He stepped backward even as she moved forward, until the back of his leg bumped the coffee table and he fell, scattering papers all over the floor. Terrified that he'd hurt himself, she sprang up, but he pushed his arm out and held her at bay with the palm of his hand.

"It's not that I'm not interested. Clearly I am." He looked away and she saw him swallow. "Very interested. But I don't know you and you don't know me, and this is not going to happen."

She blinked.

"It's not," he repeated, and she had to smile, sure that this time he was trying to convince himself, and not her.

This was just like hunting birds. Waiting and waiting until just the right time. And then, at the very last moment, when she'd lulled them into contentment, only then would she pounce.

Nicholas just had his guard up. That was all.

He was hers, after all. A little more persuasion and he'd realize it, too. When she finally did pounce, he wouldn't stand a chance.

After all she'd been through, Maggie could bide her time.

With deliberate slowness, she eased back into the deep cushions of his sofa, snuggled his quilt around her, and grinned.

"Just a jacket? And you bolted?" Hoop paced in front of his couch, stepping gingerly around the papers that littered his floor. "Forget magna cum laude, man, that was one magna cum screwup. What are you trying to do? Make a bad name for men?"

Nick was in no mood for Hoop's unique brand of humor. "If you sent her, then 'fess up. The woman was all over me like a cat in heat. I've gone way beyond the ordinary limits of willpower here." Nick took a slug of the half-assed American beer Hoop had pressed into his hand, managing to down about half the can in one gulp.

"I wish I'd thought of it, but she didn't come

from me. Maybe someone from work?"

Nick didn't even bother to respond, just half-glared at Hoop, who had the decency to look sheepish. "Sorry. Forgot you spend your day slumming with the personality challenged."

"They just have better things to do than think up stunts like this. You're the only one I know who'd get his jollies sending naked sexpots my way." He finished the can with one swallow.

"Like I said, the whole situation is definitely worthy of the Hoopster. I'm ashamed I didn't think of it." Hoop propped his feet up on a piece of plywood balanced over two milk crates that now did double duty as a coffee table. "I can see it now—well-buttoned Nicholas Goodman and the voluptuous vixen. This has vaudeville farce written all over it."

"Thanks, pal. You're really helping me out here." Nick wiped crumbs out of his friend's threadbare recliner and sat down.

"She must have really rattled you."

"What makes you say that?"

Hoop waved his hand in Nick's direction. "You're here, aren't you? And some naked chick is alone in your house." He leaned forward, a wicked leer on his face. "But she may not be robbing you blind, man. Maybe she's just trying on your underwear and prancing around your living room."

"Great. Thank you. You're being very helpful."

"You're really not worried about her ripping you off, are you?" His friend sounded shocked.

That the thought hadn't even entered his mind worried Nick more than the possibility that she was a burglar. "She's not a crook." He held up his hand to ward off Hoop's protest. "Don't ask me how I know, I just do; she's not a thief. But she could still screw up my life."

"And that's why you're planning to sleep on my couch."

"Right again, my friend."

"So why not just toss the chick out on the street? Sleep in your own bed?"

Nick shook his head. No way. No, sir. If he went back into that house and she was still there, and he faced her, somehow he knew—he just *knew*—that no matter what his intentions, he wouldn't be sleeping alone. Not that he was going to explain any of that to Hoop. "Look, can I crash here or not?"

Hoop shrugged, then got up and moved the television off the old army trunk that doubled as a table. He opened the trunk and pulled out a stack of wrinkled linens, tossing them to Nick.

"If I was really your friend, I'd kick your ass out of here. I'd wait just long enough for you to get home and for your vixen to coax you into bed. And then I'd call the Ice Queen and tell her to get over to your place. You'd be pissed at first, but you'd thank me later."

"Wouldn't work. I'd just go to a hotel." Nick cast a purposeful gaze over Hoop's living room and kitchen, decorated in what he called early Post-apocalyptic decor. In other words, it was a mess.

"If I'm willing to risk contracting some new strain of disease by sleeping here, don't you think I would sleep anywhere rather than go back to my place?"

Hoop just laughed and pitched him a pillow.

"Besides, all of this is your fault," Nick said, grabbing another so-called beer from the ice-filled tub under Hoop's makeshift coffee table.

"How do you figure?"

"I was all settled for the night, ready to tackle a mountain of briefs. I wouldn't even have opened the door if you hadn't called." Nick popped the top on the beer. "So give. Either you really had news or I was right and you did send the girl."

His friend lit up at the change of subject. "I've got news, all right." He paused. "Know any models? Actresses?"

"I'm not setting you up, my friend."

"I've seen the women you date," Hoop shot back. "I'll fend for myself."

Nick held up his hands. "So, why are you asking about actresses?"

"Vision Entertainment is in the market for a new late-night hostess."

"It's been a long day. You're going to have to run that by me again."

"You need inside info to keep the Ice Queen's daddy happy—"

"To get the best deal possible for the client—"

Hoop waved Nick's correction away as if shooing a gnat. "Yeah, right. Whatever. Point is, they're now minus one on-air hostess. She quit last week to take some job at a network. If we can fill that slot, you'll have someone on the inside."

Nick pondered the idea. Over the last few years, Vision Entertainment had grown into a respectable company that did most of its business producing infomercials for such mind-numbing products as veggie slicers and stain removers. But it was Vision's foray into programming designed to air on the Internet, instead of television, that had attracted the attention of corporate investors such as Angela's father, Reggie Palmer. Trouble was, Palmer wasn't the only one who was interested, and Vision's management wasn't talking to anyone.

If Nick wanted to get a foot in the door, he needed dirt, something that would up his negotiating potential. And if that meant putting his own Girl Friday into the place as the key personality, well, he had to admit it was a brilliant plan.

"There's no way we can ensure our girl will get the job," he pointed out.

Hoop shrugged. "Auditions are Wednesday. We've got until then to find a woman with unflappable charisma who'll work for cheap and report to us."

Nick couldn't help but grin. "Well, when you put it like that, what's to stop us?"

"Maybe we should audition your naked sex kitten," Hoop said, a challenge in his voice.

"Thank you, no. With any luck I'll go home and she'll have gotten fed up and gone back wherever she came from. The last thing in the world I need is to be coordinating this deal and planning a wedding with Angela, all the while fending off a sex-starved, possibly demented beauty with the hots for me."

Hoop reached down to grab yet another beer, and Nick was pretty sure he was hiding a grin.

"What?" Nick asked.

"Nothing." Hoop looked up, the corner of his mouth twitching. "It's just that I don't think I've seen you this flustered over a woman since . . . well, never."

"I'm not flustered," Nick said, resisting the urge to reach up and feel if his nose was growing.

"The hell you're not. Who would've thought? Good ol' hospital corners Nicholas Goodman lusting after some sweet young drifter." The twitch turned into a smug smile. "You know, your life could use some shaking up, and she may be just the lady to do the job."

Nick shook his head, holding fast. "I wouldn't bet the ranch," he said. No matter what else he might think of her, a fling with the rather off-beat woman would be a huge mistake. Personal-wise, career-wise, and most certainly mental-health-wise.

Chapter Three

"Ob-sess-ion." Maggie took another breath and looked at the magazine she'd left open on Nicholas's couch. She'd picked the page on purpose. In smaller letters at the bottom, it said "for men."

There you go.

She was obsessed with Nicholas. Nicholas was a man.

Beyond that, she didn't know what she was supposed to do. And the page she was staring at wasn't helping at all.

At least with the television she could practice talking and have some idea how she was doing. After about an hour practicing words like "must see" and "improved" and "dealership blow out," she'd turned the thing off and dug a magazine out of the basket by the coffee table.

Still, despite its noise, the television had given her some useful information. Thanks to the people on the screen, she knew that she shouldn't leave home without American Express, and that Visa was everywhere she wanted to be. She needed to trust her thirst, use Kodak paper, and just do it. The magazine might be quiet, but it wasn't much help.

Scowling at the page, she curled back up on the cushion. Old Tom had given her the ability to understand human language and to make words out of these funny symbols, but that didn't mean any of it made any sense.

If she'd been smart, she would have paid more attention to what was on the television back when she'd been a cat. Had any of these programs made any sense to her then? She didn't think so. She could remember lounging on Nicholas's lap, his strong hand stroking her fur, and the noise from the machine in the background. But she hadn't been able to make out words, hadn't even tried to look at the pictures.

She sighed. How wonderful it would be to already have some of this knowledge instead of having to learn everything all at once. But there was no sense in crying over spilled milk. It was doubtful that she'd have been able to understand anything had she tried. Most likely it would have just been gibberish.

Well, that lost opportunity only meant that

Maggie had no time to waste now. Some of Old Tom's rules might have whooshed right over her head—how did he expect her to concentrate with her body pulling and squeezing and shaping into a human's?—but she'd heard him say she only had until All Hallow's Eve. *That* part was unmistakably clear.

She wasn't exactly sure when that was, but she knew it was soon. No matter what, Maggie had no time to waste.

Okay, one more try. "Obsession," she said, faster this time. She didn't trip over the word as she had an hour ago, so maybe this practice was going to pay off after all.

The person in the picture was thin. Like a stray who hadn't eaten for a month. Was she supposed to be as thin as that picture? She hoped not. The woman in the picture—at least Maggie thought it was a woman—didn't really have any breasts at all. Maggie ran her hands over her chest, feeling the curves of this new body. Unlike the magazine girl, she had an ample supply.

Maybe Old Tom had messed up. Maybe she was a freak, some weird hybrid between a cat and a human. Like one of those monsters she'd seen when she was pushing the buttons on the television.

Maybe that's why Nicholas ran away. Not because he wasn't madly in love with her, but because she was a horrible human-cat-beast and he was fleeing in terror. Maggie would simply get Old Tom to fix his mistake, present herself to

Nicholas again, and they'd live happily ever after.

She just needed to see what she looked like.

Somewhere in the living room was a big reflecting space. She used to sit for hours at night and watch herself. She turned a circle in the room trying to remember, but only managed to get herself dizzy.

She became so woozy that she had to drop to the floor to clear her spinning head. But that wasn't really so bad, because suddenly the world was back in its usual perspective. From about eight inches above the ground, everything once again looked familiar. She rolled around, looking at everything, and then noticed the drapes. Of course!

When she stood up and inspected the curtains, Maggie found a pull string. She gave a tug and the curtains parted, revealing the wall of glass that reflected the inside of the room onto the night. She unzipped Nicholas's jacket and dropped it at her feet, then stood sideways, looking at her reflection.

No monster-cat-beast stared back at her. Actually, she wasn't too surprised. If she'd been a beast, surely he would have turned and run at the very beginning. He wouldn't have let her steal a kiss—wouldn't have shared a kiss of his own—if he thought she was a monster.

Still, she didn't look like the magazine girl, either. Breasts definitely clung to this new chest. And hips flowed from a tight little waist. The magazine girl had none of that. But Maggie's hair was short, and so was the girl's.

She ran her fingers through her short black hair and fluffed it up. It was nice of Old Tom to let her keep it the same color.

Maggie frowned at her reflection. Even though she wasn't a monster, what if Nicholas didn't like her body as a woman? Maybe that's why he'd gone away.

No, that probably wasn't right. As much as she hated to admit it, this new body looked a lot more like the female Angela's than it did the magazine girl's. And Maggie already knew that Nicholas liked the way Angela looked. So Maggie had to at least be on the right track.

The truth was, Maggie already knew why he'd walked out. Nicholas wasn't rejecting her, not really. At first, the possibility had troubled her, but the truth of it was, she knew better.

Humans were just different.

If Maggie wanted something, she took it. If she wanted to sleep somewhere, well, that's where she slept. But she'd watched a lot of humans, especially recently. And they all did things backward. Humans danced around everything. Nobody ever seemed to come out and say or do what they wanted.

But Maggie had. She'd pounced on Nicholas.

No wonder he'd run away.

Nibbling on her lower lip, she snuggled against the sofa cushions and hugged her knees to her chest. This whole thing wasn't turning out the way she'd expected. First of all, she hadn't known she'd be so clumsy. How did humans stand it? Bumbling around on only two legs, trying not to fall over when they walked around on these long, gangly sticks. Really, what a cumbersome way to get about. She wanted Nicholas to fall *for* her—she didn't want to fall all over him.

That he hadn't immediately fallen in love with her had been her other big surprise. She'd stood outside his door just as confident as a cat, knowing he'd do exactly what she wanted and let her in, just like he always did.

That had been a major miscalculation. Apparently kitty treats and belly scratches were one thing. Falling head over heels in love with a woman? Well, that was something entirely different.

But she'd expected it, she had to admit it. She'd played the scenario in her head while she waited for him to open the door. He would open it, see her, and then . . .

Well, the specifics of "and then" escaped her. All she knew was that Nicholas would say he loved her, that he'd take her in his arms, and that she'd stay human with him forever.

Too bad reality interfered, and Nicholas had run away.

But none of that mattered, Maggie told herself. The end result would still be the same. She would make him love her. And the television would be the perfect teacher. In no time at all, she'd know exactly what she needed to do to make Nicholas hopelessly, madly, completely in love with her.

Outside, Maggie heard birds twittering as they greeted the pre-dawn light that her new human eyes couldn't see. Then she heard a rattling at the front door.

Nicholas.

What better time to start convincing him than the present? She practiced his name as she stumbled to the front hall. "Nich-o-las. Welcome home, Nicholas." She grinned. She could talk to him!

When she reached the hallway, her legs cramped up, and she fell. The doorknob turned. Maggie tried to move forward. Her muscles knotted, tightened.

Nicholas stepped into the hallway, and she called out his name, the word gliding off her tongue.

The sound hung in the air as she finally remembered the last thing Old Tom had said—only at night. She'd only be human at night.

Nicholas smiled down at her.

"Hey there, Maggie girl. How'd you get back in here?"

She rolled on the tile, letting him scratch her belly.

"Meow," she said again, but this time she knew he wouldn't understand.

Sleep stalked him like a tiger, creeping up. Slowly . . . slowly . . . then pouncing when he least expected it.

"Goodman? Goodman?" A hand on his shoulder. "For Christ's sake, Nick, wake up!"

Nick's head shot up, and his hand immediately went to the back of his neck, rubbing the crick he'd developed from tossing and turning on Hoop's sofa.

"Sorry. What?" He shook his head to clear out some of the grogginess.

Larry, Nick's assistant for the last two years, plopped down in one of the chairs under the Wall of Fame, the repository of all Nick's diplomas and academic awards. He'd wanted to gag when Mitchell Dryson, Dryson & Montgomery's senior partner, had insisted he display them like little trophies. "You have to let the clients know what they're paying for," Dryson had said. Ridiculous pretense, Nick had thought.

But Nick hadn't argued, even though he'd much rather look at one of his sister Deena's bizarre paintings of sprites and fairies. Dryson signed his paycheck, so Dryson called the shots. Nick had managed to squeeze some personality in, though. Among the Harvard J.D. and the U.C.L.A. diplomas, laced in with the State Bar licenses and the academic award certificates, Nick had sneaked in his kindergarten diploma, nicely framed with a forest green matte to complement the dancing green alligator.

Most clients didn't notice, and the ones who did tended to at least crack a smile. And Dryson was none the wiser.

Not that the office artwork mattered that much

to Nick. Considering the hours and intensity of the job, he rarely got the chance to kick back and contemplate the decor. And now he barely noticed the damn diplomas—River Rock Kindergarten or Harvard Law.

Larry grabbed a mint out of Nick's candy jar. "Rough night?" He plastered on a leer. "Or a really, really good night?"

"Couldn't sleep. Insomnia." Brought on by erotic images of a lithe beauty whose kisses had worked him into a frenzy.

"Yeah, well, if you know what's good for you, you'll wait 'til tonight to catch up on your *z*s. Dryson's on his way down, and I don't think he's coming to tuck you in."

Nick grinned. "You're probably right."

"I saw the Bullfrog poke his head in and leave a couple of minutes ago. Since he only stayed a minute, I thought I should check on you."

Jeremiah Kennedy was a rotund little brownnosing, back-stabbing creep who was an insult to frogs everywhere. Soon, Bullfrog and Nick would both be up for partnership in a firm that typically made only one partner per section each year, and left the reject to either quit or languish for twelve more months, wondering if he'd be passed over yet again.

Jeremiah also never shut up. So if he was in and out of Nick's office, odds were good he was up to something.

"Thanks for looking out for me."

Larry shrugged. "I hadn't seen you leave, and I

couldn't imagine Frog-face getting through a conversation in under an hour. Plus he looked a little too smug when he left. Like he could just smell that partnership. Thought I ought to check in on you before Dryson made it down here."

"Like I said, thanks." Larry might be the most high-maintenance legal assistant Nick ever had, but he was also the most loyal.

Larry pushed himself up out of the chair and grinned. "Just looking out for number one. You get promoted and suddenly I'm the assistant to a junior partner."

"Well, if it was just personal interest, no reason to remember this at bonus time . . ."

Larry bit his thumb, a purely Shakespearian insult that wasn't the least bit out of character. "Just remember who sorts your mail. It'd be hell if an SEC filing just never made it to the post office. . . ." He drifted out of the office, leaving Nick to grin at the empty threat.

Nick leaned back in his chair and put his feet on his desk. Too bad Larry was one-of-a-kind at Dryson & Montgomery, a staid law firm with what seemed to be a carved-in-stone policy to only hire the personality challenged.

He chuckled. Hoop's vocabulary was seeping into his brain. Of course, Nick was an eight-year veteran of D & M. What the hell did that say about *his* personality?

Mitch Dryson's voice echoed from the hall, and Nick pushed the thought away. Nick's personality was doing just fine. He had a good job, a house in the Hills, a fat bank account, and a gorgeous fiancée. The people he worked with might lack color, but personality wasn't what had paid college tuition for his sister, or kept her from getting evicted when her art wasn't selling.

Nick swung his feet off the desk, hunching over his papers as Dryson strolled in.

"Good morning, Nick. I had breakfast with Reggie Palmer. He sends his best." Dryson's voice was clipped, even more formal than usual.

Nick looked up, wary. "Oh?"

"I'd hoped you could join us. I called this morning at about five."

Here it comes. Nick waited for the other shoe to drop. The shoe that would be planting itself on his backside to shove him out the door right after Dryson asked who the woman was who'd answered his phone. The woman in his house in the middle of the night who was absolutely, positively not Reggie Palmer's daughter.

Why, she's no one, sir. Just a naked, gorgeous brunette who knocked on my door and whose memory kept me awake imagining all the things I wanted to do with her.

Dryson dropped casually into one of Nick's office chairs. Nick had the feeling he was being toyed with. Batted about like a furry toy mouse.

"I must have been in the shower. I didn't get the message that you'd called."

One wave of his hand and Dryson dismissed the problem. "No matter. It was a last-minute arrangement." Nick took a breath. "It just never hurts to remind Palmer of all the reasons he loves this firm—not the least of which being that our very own golden boy is soon to be his daughter's husband."

Nick let the "golden boy" comment slide. Until the committee picked him over Bullfrog to be the next corporate partner, he didn't feel too golden. "Sorry I missed it."

"Any more news? If we don't pull this Vision Entertainment deal together for Palmer, he'll go shopping for new counsel. And losing billion-dollar clients gives me indigestion."

Nick's head was swimming. One minute he was the Anointed One who could do no wrong, and two seconds later he was about to single-handedly bring on the demise of the entire firm.

"I wouldn't worry about it, sir. Everything's under control."

"How? Whose control?"

"Mine, sir," Nick said, his polite smile masking gritted teeth.

Dryson pushed himself out of the chair. His head tilted down and his brow arched as he looked at Nick over his half-glasses. "Let's hope you're up to your usual high standards, Nicholas."

If that wasn't damning him with faint praise . . .

Nick kept the smile plastered on as Dryson nodded and headed out into the hall to continue spreading his morning cheer.

Tapping a rhythm on his desktop with a cheap ballpoint pen, Nick leaned back in his chair and considered Hoop's proposition. Much as he hated to admit it, Hoop's idea had rattled around in his head all night. Get their own girl in as Vision Entertainment's spokesmodel. And rattling right along with that thought was the memory of the girl on the doorstep.

The way she'd glowed when she looked at him. The way his skin had burned from her touch.

She'd been on his mind all night and all morning. Over and over he'd played back images of her through his mind, wondering all the while who she was and where she'd come from. And despite having told Hoop that there was no way in hell he'd hire the little vixen to audition for the Vision spot, when he'd gone home that morning, part of him had been ready to be convinced he was wrong.

Get a grip, Goodman. You're engaged, remember? Remember? How could he forget. He was engaged all, right—to his job security.

He heaved his pen across the room and watched it bounce off the plate-glass window.

The last thing he needed to be thinking about was the mysterious girl from last night. And he sure as hell didn't need to dwell on how disappointed he'd been to find her gone.

Chapter Four

Her whiskers twitched. Twilight was approaching, and she paced in front of the glass door, edgy and unsure.

Why didn't she feel the change coming yet? She laid back her ears, worrying. What if she'd missed her chance? Maybe since Nicholas had run away the spell was broken.

No, no, that couldn't be. She had time. Surely Old Tom hadn't lied to her.

She pawed at the glass, trying to urge the sun to set faster. But despite her coaxing, the sun continued to move at the same lazy pace, apparently unwilling to do even the slightest favor for one nervous cat sitting in a living room longing for sunset.

She felt, rather than saw, the exact moment when the sun finally dipped below the horizon. Felt it in her head, her belly, her blood. The same queasy wonderfulness she'd felt yesterday. Wonderful because it meant change. Wonderful because change meant arms and legs and breasts and kisses.

Kisses with Nicholas.

The metamorphosis seemed to pass faster than it had before. She opened her eyes, and the human Maggie looked back at her from the glass door.

A naked human Maggie.

She frowned. Yesterday, the first thing Nicholas had done was yank his jacket around her shoulders. Her lack of clothes hadn't bothered her any. Not yesterday. But today . . .

Today Maggie wanted something to cover her new body. She scanned the floor, looking for the fleece jacket she'd discarded before changing back into a cat at dawn. Nowhere. Not too surprising. Her Nicholas wasn't the type to keep things on the floor. Not unless she mewed for something to play with or sleep on.

And this morning she'd ignored the jacket entirely, not bothering to roll around on it, or sleep on it, or pounce on it. Instead, she'd followed Nicholas into the bedroom and watched as he'd dressed for work. She'd purred more than usual, somehow more appreciative of his tight thighs slipping into the suit slacks. Nicholas hadn't seemed to notice her intent stare, though. He'd just scratched her head and slipped back out into the hall. She'd followed at his heels, intending to follow him back to the front door, but had been distracted by the plate of tuna he'd put down on the floor for her.

She'd been ravenous. It hadn't occurred to her to look for food when she'd been human. By the time she'd finished her breakfast, Nicholas was already out the door.

Since she'd been gorging herself on tuna while he was leaving, she hadn't seen where he'd put the silly jacket, so she tried to remember where Nicholas kept his clothes. Funny, but she'd never really paid attention to that before.

She wandered back into his bedroom and tried to picture what he did every morning while she was curled up on the fluffy comforter that smelled faintly of birds. A dark wood dresser caught her attention and a flash of memory grabbed her. That was where she'd seen him pull out the short pants that he wore under the long pants.

She pulled open the drawer and examined the muted rainbow of fabric. A red bit of material here, a blue-striped garment there. Despite all the colors, the pants boiled down to two types. Really short ones that looked a lot like what the magazine girl had been wearing, and longer pants that looked looser. More floppy.

She stepped into a pair of floppy pants with

light blue and white stripes. She rolled over the waist a couple of times to keep them from falling down. Except for a funny little hole in the front, the pants pretty much covered her.

Now she just needed something to cover her breasts. She rooted around in the drawer, pulling out the rest of the short pants and throwing them onto the floor and the bed. There was nothing for her top half.

She tried another drawer, clawing and digging, but all she found were the funny cloth tubes that Nicholas put on his feet.

In the next drawer, she found success. She pulled out a soft shirt and read the writing on the front—Harvard Law, *Res Ipsa Loquitar.* The first two words she could make out. She'd heard Nicholas mention his school enough. The last three words didn't make any sense, and she wondered for a second if Old Tom had forgotten to give her all the language skills she'd need. She shoved the thought aside. Nothing she could do about it now, anyway.

The shirt hung down almost to her knees. Soft and cozy, the material smelled vaguely of Nicholas, and she pulled the neckband up over her nose and sniffed. A clean, soapy smell filled her head. That was the way Nicholas always smelled, clean with just a hint of musk. She wrinkled her nose, trying to find the subtle smell of Nicholas in the air. Without her cat's nose, she had to concentrate harder, but she found his scent and breathed deep.

She looked out the window into the recent darkness. Nicholas would be home soon, and she wasn't ready at all. She scrambled over the pile of clothes on the floor and headed for the living room.

Last night, the television had taught her how to talk.

Tonight, it would teach her how to catch—and keep—a man.

"Now, don't eat too much, Nickie."

Nick took a sip of the restaurant's house Merlot and winked at Angela. "Guess the surprise party's being catered, huh?"

She leaned back and pouted. "You knew! When did you figure it out?"

"I didn't. Hoop did. Man's a hell of an investigator."

Angela wrinkled her nose. "He's a ruffian."

"A *ruffian?* Where'd that come from? Your bridge club renting word-power tapes?"

"I don't know why you hang around him. Really, Nickie, he's so . . . so . . . base."

"Really, Angie, that's so . . . so . . . snobbish."

She glared at him, and Nick decided to drop it. He'd been putting up with Angela's set-in-concrete ideas about people—and Hoop in particular—for the three years he'd known her.

"So, I take it Hoop's not on the guest list."

A smug smile crossed her face. "Of course not. But Michael Ferrington is." She finished her wine and searched his face, clearly pleased with herself.

With good reason. Michael Ferrington owned Vision Entertainment, the current focal point of Nick's professional life. And since his professional client was his fiancée's father, that made Vision the focal point of his personal life, too.

"Ferrington never socializes. How'd you manage that?"

"My natural charm, Nickie. How else?" She held up her wineglass in a toast. "Aren't you going to thank me? You need the goods on Ferrington if you're going to get his company for Daddy. What better way to do that than to get in with Ferrington himself?"

"The goods? Angie, all I'm trying to do is negotiate a deal to buy Vision for your dad. This isn't *Mission Impossible*. I'm not doing espionage."

"No?"

A waiter approached and Nick was glad for the distraction. The truth was, some days he did feel like three years of training at Quantico would have been more useful to his practice than three years of law school. But the need for all that cloak-and-dagger stuff was why he had Hoop on retainer. And that's why Hoop wanted him to find a perky, cute woman to take a job at Vision. They needed her to infiltrate the company, to get the kind of dirt on Ferrington that would persuade him to sell. To sell cheap. An image of the naked brunette in his living room flashed in his mind. Hoop was right—a woman like that could make a man do anything. Say anything. She could make a man give up all his secrets.

With a shake of his head, he pushed away the thought. It was too dangerous to let his mind wander in that direction.

The fact was, Angela was right. Somewhere along the line he'd abandoned the traditional practice of law and replaced it with . . . what? Espionage? No way. That sounded romantic, worthy. James Bond, saving the world, all that jazz.

But Nick was no James Bond. Not at all. Instead, he'd given up his career to be a snoop and a snitch. His life wasn't what he'd expected. But then, what ever was?

"Another bottle of wine," Angela said, and Nick looked up to see their waiter nod and move away.

"More wine?" Nick asked. "What, won't you be able to get alcohol at my surprise party?" he said, teasing her.

"Very funny. We're going to sit here and have dessert and coffee, too. I have to keep you occupied until at least nine."

"Ah, keep me distracted while they set up and everyone arrives. Where're we going, anyway?"

"The Covington, of course. I rented the ballroom."

He should have guessed. The Covington in Los Angeles rivaled the Plaza in New York. Only the best for Angela.

She reached across the table and took his hand. "You're not going to let on you knew about the party, are you?"

"Afraid I'll spoil everyone's fun?"

She dabbed her mouth with a napkin. "What would people think if I threw a surprise party and the guest of honor wasn't surprised? I'd be a laughingstock."

Nick sighed. "Don't worry, babe. Your secret's safe with me."

"I pulled off quite a coup, didn't I? Getting Ferrington to the party? Now you can work your magic, find his secrets, and . . . um . . . convince him to sell Vision Entertainment to Daddy."

"Convince? Are you under the impression I'm packing heat?"

"Just persuasion, sweetheart."

Nick cringed. In only eight years he'd moved from relying on brains, advocacy, and his negotiating power to being a corporate strongman who looked under rocks for dirt. It was not the conventional path for an up-and-coming lawyer, but if he was reading the signs right, he was well-positioned to climb the career ladder—all the way to the top.

A thriving career. Money. A beautiful woman. Everything he'd worked so hard for was right there in his grasp. He should be thrilled, exuberant, proud.

So why did he feel like he had a hole in his gut?

Maggie's head swam. After "The Brady Bunch" she'd watched "The Jerry Springer Show." Then something called "Melrose Place." She'd gone from sweet kids and parents pecking each other on the cheek to amnesiac sisters who slept with their husband's brothers to people who seemed to do nothing except kiss and mate.

The amnesiac women held the most fascination for her. Aside from the fact that they kept yelling and slapping each other and pulling out handfuls of hair, they still seemed a bit lost. Out of place. Unsure.

Exactly how Maggie felt.

Not that watching the amnesiacs helped a lot with her immediate problem of grabbing Nicholas's attention and keeping it, but that's where the other shows came in. She grabbed a pillow and practiced sloppy kisses on the rough material while a buxom blonde on the television did the same with a fair-haired boy probably half her age.

Her intimacy with the pillow wasn't nearly as satisfying as the night before with Nicholas had been. But, of course, the pillow just sagged beneath her. Nicholas, on the other hand, had kissed back.

The memory warmed her, the tingly sensation starting at her toes and working its way up her body to settle in her belly. It was a nice feeling. Like coming home.

Then she remembered the gusto with which Nicholas had trotted out of the house, and the warm feeling cooled considerably. Once again she was left to doubt how she would ever manage to pull this off. She faced the pillow again, gripping it by the corners with determination. Two nights of television might not have taught her everything, but one thing was certain—if she wanted to catch a man, a mind-numbing kiss was a good starting point.

Once she got that technique down, she'd work on the rest of her feminine repertoire. Things like flirting and cooing and dressing the part.

Oh! She'd forgotten all about dressing. Nicholas's baggy pants and shirt didn't even come close to hugging her curves the way the clothes on "Melrose Place" or even "Jerry Springer" did. How was she supposed to get new ones? For that matter, where did clothes come from, anyway?

The rattle of a key in the front door startled her, and she dropped into a crouch, wriggling her nose before she remembered what and where she was. Nicholas was home much sooner than she'd expected. But that was okay. She'd been practicing since twilight. She was ready.

She gave the pillow one last enthusiastic smooch to warm up, then bounced over the back of the couch toward the entry hall. She made the maneuver without falling and congratulated herself. Yesterday she'd been a klutz in this new body, but now she'd gotten used to the way these arms and legs moved, and some of her old agility was returning.

The doorknob turned. Maggie adjusted the shirt and straightened the short pants, looking down to make sure the hole in front was modestly closed, one of the tidbits of information she'd picked up watching the television.

The door pushed open just slightly, and the yellow glow from the porch light streaked into the hallway. Maggie itched to move forward but held herself back.

Then she saw a foot, a hand, and—

"Deena!" Maggie called out, recognizing Nicholas's sister.

"Oh, my God!" Deena's voice cut through the dark room and just about scared Maggie to death. Deena *never* yelled at her.

"Do I know you?" Deena tentatively stepped forward, looking just about as unsure as Maggie felt. "What are you doing in my brother's house?" She took another step forward and Maggie took another step back. "Are you his housekeeper?"

She kept approaching, faster than Maggie could navigate backward, and finally Maggie fell to the ground and started to scramble away on her hands and knees. This was a nightmare. Just awful. She'd been all set to talk to Nicholas, to seduce him with soft words and kisses, to make him fall in love with her.

But she had no idea what to say to Deena, who'd never yelled at her before and always brought treats, scratched her ears, and brushed her fur for hours.

"Oh, wow. Oh, gosh. I'm so sorry. I scared you. I didn't mean to. You just startled me." Deena towered above Maggie, one arm outstretched to help her up. Maggie hesitated, but the soft tone was back in Deena's voice. She sounded like Nicholas's sister again, and that was a woman Maggie liked very much. She grabbed hold and let Deena hoist her to her feet.

Maggie followed Deena to the living room and plopped down on the far end of the couch, her knees tucked up under her chin, waiting for the interrogation to begin.

When Deena didn't jump right in with a flurry of questions, just looked at her with a strange expression, Maggie began to wonder if maybe she should tell Deena the whole story. She'd always been incredibly nice to Maggie, staying in Nicholas's house whenever he left town for a few days. And she never failed to bring a snack or a toy when she came over, so Maggie knew that Deena liked her.

She cocked her head. Nicholas's sister didn't seem to have brought anything today, which was too bad, because Maggie was getting awfully hungry.

If she was going to tell anyone the truth, Deena would be the person to tell. Also, Deena didn't like the female, Angela, any more than Maggie did. She'd told her brother that plenty of times, but Nicholas had always managed to change the subject—usually by teasing Deena about her own beliefs, like fairies and the like. Nicholas always called her a free spirit. And wasn't that just the kind of help that Maggie needed?

She opened her mouth, planning to spit it all out—Old Tom, the magic, the television lessons, and her real identity—but Deena spoke first.

"Okay. I figure you aren't the housekeeper. So who are you?" She bounced on the cushions. "Oh, oh, I know! Please, please, please tell me he dumped that bitch, Angela."

Maggie opened her mouth, but Deena cut her off in an embarrassed rush. "Oh, no. Did I just say something stupid? Is the bitch your sister or something? Are you in town visiting and she put you up here? Or maybe she's your best friend."

"No—"

"Well, I gotta tell you the truth, even if she is, I just really can't stand her." She leaned back against the armrest and crossed her arms over her chest. "That's just the way I feel. So let me have it, baby. Just lay into me for being a reverse snob myself."

Maggie swallowed. "I—I don't like her either."

Deena practically launched herself across the couch and planted a kiss on Maggie's cheek. "Baby doll, you just made my day." She settled herself back in place, hiking her gauzy skirt up so she could curl her legs under her. "Well?"

Maggie just stared, wide-eyed and unsure. *Well, what?* "Um?"

"So are you the new girlfriend? Lord, I hope so. Please tell me old Angela's out of the picture. She's hardly sister material."

"Um, yes and no."

Deena looked wary. "You're not telling me my big brother's two-timing the smarmy witch, are you?"

"Oh, no. Nicholas would never do that. He's too . . . too . . ."

"Dull?" offered Deena.

"Honorable," Maggie announced.

"You think he's honorable?"

"Oh, yes. He's perfect."

"I'll admit he's a great brother. Hell, he's practically a parent for that matter. But perfect? What a crock. I'd snort, but my brother raised me to be ladylike."

Maggie frowned, not at all sure what she was supposed to say to that. True, she was new to being a lady, but she was pretty sure that Deena was missing the target by slumping on the couch, her skirt arranged not nearly as modestly as Maggie's revealing pants, spouting the kind of language Maggie had only recently come to associate with television.

But if she was a lady or not, Maggie liked Deena. A lot. If anyone could help make Nicholas fall in love with her, his sister could. And nothing in Old Tom's rules prevented her from telling the truth to Nicholas's family. She just couldn't tell Nicholas himself.

Once again, Deena spoke before Maggie had the chance. "So, you said 'yes and no,' but you're not his part-time plaything. So who are you, honey? And why are you running around the house in boxers?"

"I'm Maggie," she said, sitting up a little straighter. "And I'm in love with Nicholas."

"Maggie! Oh, my goodness. I completely forgot." She scooped a huge canvas tote off the floor, turned it upside down, and dumped the contents on the couch between them. Immediately, the cushions were covered by cosmetics, paint brushes, crumpled menus, various scraps of paper, a dozen or so pens, earrings, and, there in the middle, a bag of tuna-flavored chewy snacks.

Maggie's mouth watered.

"Do you know where the cat is? I brought treats."

"I'm—not sure," Maggie finally said. On second thought, she wasn't completely sure about Old Tom's rules and didn't want to push her luck. More than that, she was afraid Deena wouldn't believe her. Or, even worse, that she *would* believe her—and would hate the idea of fixing her brother up with a woman who was not really a woman.

Deena pitched the kitty snacks onto the coffee table and started stuffing the junk back into her tote bag. "Well, she can't have gotten outside. She's probably hiding somewhere." Deena smiled at Maggie. "She's not too crazy about strangers."

"Really?"

"Mmm." Deena shifted around in her corner of the couch, settled down, and stared at Maggie. "So what were you saying? Your name's Maggie, and you're in love with my brother?"

Maggie nodded, not really sure what else to say.

Deena stared at her for what seemed to be an eternity. Just as Maggie was sure Deena was going to tell her to get out and go bother someone else's brother, a huge grin split the woman's face.

"Well, you've got at least two things going for you."

"I do?" Maggie asked, her voice barely more than a whisper.

"Sure. You've got the same name as that cat he loves so much. And you're not Angela. In my book that makes you okay."

Nicholas loved her. She'd known all along, but to hear it from Deena made it so much more real. A tentative smile tugged at Maggie's mouth. "Thank you."

"But how do you know Nick? And how'd you get in his house?"

Oh, my. She really hadn't planned this out very well. Maggie wracked her brain, trying to remember all of Nicholas's little details. Something about Hoop coming inside one day . . .

Then she remembered. "Nicholas keeps a key on the back patio. For emergencies."

"He told you about that?"

"He showed me," Maggie said, dodging the question.

"So you're in love with him, huh?"

"Oh, yes. So much."

Deena smiled. "Yeah, he's a good guy. He needs a vacation like you wouldn't believe. But he's a prince, my big brother is." She shifted in her seat, rested her elbow on her knee and her chin on her fist, and squinted at Maggie. "So what's your story? You're here in Nick's boxers. You sure I didn't wander into a secret little love nest?"

Maggie shook her head, trying to find words, but Deena was so fast and so loud, she wasn't sure her words could be heard over all that energy. "I'm . . . he's not . . ."

She took a breath and tried again. "He doesn't know I'm here."

"Aha! Yes! The old secret-love-from-afar. This is great. So how did you meet him?" Deena's leg was tapping out a rhythm on the cushion, and her head was bobbing up and down along with it.

Maggie leaned over and grabbed the kitty snacks off the coffee table. She wanted something in her hands so she wouldn't fidget with her fingers. Deena was so perceptive, she'd probably be able to tell right away that Maggie wasn't used to fingers. And then the gig would be up.

"Well," Deena pressed, "come on, girl. Give. It's not every day I find some stray female in my brother's apartment." She leaned forward and lowered her voice to a conspiratorial whisper. "And the fact is, I like you. You may think I'm just the loud sister from another planet, but that's not the case. Bottom line is, I like you and I don't like Angela. So help me out here. Tell me your story and let's see if I can't help you catch my brother."

"You'd do that for me?"

"Like I said, I like you. When were you born?"

The change in topic confused Maggie. "Um . . . in the fall. Right around October. Three years this week, actually."

"Cool. Practically a Halloween baby."

Maggie gulped. *Halloween?* "When is Halloween? Exactly, I mean?"

"Next Sunday. A week."

One week. Her body went slack, and she leaned back again, letting the soft cushions comfort her. She'd known the day was fast approaching, she just hadn't realized how soon. And she still had so much to learn, so much to do if she was going to convince Nicholas that he loved only her.

"Let's see," Deena said. "That makes you a Scorpio."

Maggie steeled herself, determination rising. There was enough time. There had to be. Old Tom wouldn't grant her request only to see her fail. She just had to use her time well. Halloween was a special day for black cats, after all. This one would be even more special because this time . . . this time Maggie would be a woman, and she'd spend the night—and the rest of her days—in Nicholas's arms.

"And you were born in the Chinese year of the—" Deena stopped. "Did you say *three years?*"

Oh, my . . . had she really said that? Sweat broke out on her upper lip, and she leaned forward on her legs, ready to spring up and run away if Deena found out her secret.

But Deena didn't seem too concerned about her slip-up. "I usually just say twenty-one. I'm stuck there until I get wrinkles and gray hairs. 'Course, after I tell people I'm twenty-one, I always tell 'em I'm lying. And then I have to tell them my real age so they won't think I'm thirty or something."

When she paused to take a breath, Maggie did the same. The woman was exhausting.

"Fact is, I'm twenty-six. You're about two or three years younger, right?"

"About that." In fact, she was twenty-four in cat years, but she wasn't going to get into specifics.

"Okay. So you're both Scorpios. That means the sex should be good, at least. Lord knows I doubt he's getting fireworks and rockets with her royal highness, Miss Angela of the Snot-Nosed Class."

Maggie nodded. "Mating with Nicholas should be wonderful. When he kissed me yesterday, I thought I might shrivel up and die when he stopped."

"Mating?"

Maggie frowned. "That's bad?"

"No. No, I've got nothing against mating. It's just a rather, well, *odd* turn of phrase."

Already she was messing everything up. She'd never be able to keep the secret from Nicholas. Not even five minutes of conversation with his sister and she'd already come close to ruining everything. "What should I say? I don't want to sound funny."

Deena shrugged. "It's no big deal. I shouldn't have said anything. I'm just used to hearing more colloquial terms, you know? Sleeping together. Making love. Hell, even screwing. I don't think I've ever heard anyone say 'mating' except that French guy I dated for a few months in college." She cocked her head to one side. "Say, you're not a foreigner, are you? Just learning English?"

Maggie hated lying to Deena, but she didn't know what else to say. Unless she told her the truth—*"Well, Deena, I'm actually the four-legged Maggie and, by the way, thanks for all the kitty treats"*—anything she said would be a lie.

Unless she didn't say anything at all . . . Maggie bit her lip. Yes, that was good. It just might work.

"Maggie? Is that it? Are you from some other country?"

Maggie glanced toward the television, made up her mind, then let out a sigh. "I don't know. Maybe."

"You don't know? What's that supposed to mean?"

Maggie just shrugged and looked at her hands.

Deena scowled at the strange young woman who'd appeared in her brother's apartment. Man, oh, man. Until fifteen minutes ago, this had been a dull, unremarkable day.

For a nanosecond, she longed for dull. But almost as soon as the thought left her head she took it back. God forbid somebody might actually be listening to her prayers, formal or otherwise. She'd learned a long time ago that wishes were potent. Besides, she didn't really want to call off the extraordinary part of this day. It had been a long time since something really extraordinary had happened to her.

Maggie might be a little whacked out, but so was half the population of Los Angeles. And so long as Mags here had designs on Nick, that meant Angela might just lose her slot as the Queen Bee.

And that possibility suited Deena just fine. Besides, she kind of liked this girl.

"Okay, Mags—can I call you Mags? Here's the thing." She took a breath, not really waiting to see if Maggie cared about her name being butchered, then hurried on. "I have to be in Beverly Hills in an hour and a half for Nick's birthday party. But I'm not going anywhere until I know your story. The problem is, I don't plan to be late for the party. So talk fast, okay?"

"Okay."

Deena waited a good ten seconds, but Maggie didn't say anything else.

"Maggie!" The woman jumped. "The story," Deena prodded.

Maggie's eyes flicked back to the television, and Deena was just about to scream that a muted episode of "Charlie's Angels" didn't have a plot, much less the answer she was asking for, when Maggie finally opened her mouth.

"I think I have amnesia."

Deena blinked. That was one comment she wouldn't have expected in a million years. "Amnesia?"

Maggie nodded, but didn't volunteer anything else.

"An hour and a half, remember? You wanna give me a little bit more to work with here?"

"I . . . I don't remember how I got here or where I came from."

Sounded like amnesia, all right. Not that Deena was any sort of an expert or anything, but she'd seen her share of movies and TV shows. Anyone past nine years old these days knew at least the basics of amnesia.

"Did you get hit on the head?"

"No."

"Well, what do you remember?"

"Just my name, and that I love Nicholas. And that I came here yesterday to tell him that."

"And what did he do?"

The girl took a breath, and when she looked up, her eyes glistened with tears. Deena's stomach clenched. If her brother had been a prick to Mags, she'd read him the riot act.

Maggie snuffled, wiping her nose with the back of her hand. "He . . . he ran from me."

Deena almost snorted. Wasn't that just like Nick? Running from anything that didn't fit squarely into the square little world he'd molded for himself. Lord knows he'd run far and fast from some of the doozies she'd laid at his feet over the years. "Did he know who you were?"

"Oh, no. He'd never seen me before. But I knew he'd love me as much as I love him. And when I kissed him, he kissed me back. But then he pushed me away again and ran out of the house." A single tear slid down her cheek. "I was so sure he'd love me. I guess I was wrong."

Before Deena had time to consider that she might be comforting a possible psychopath, she leaned over and patted Maggie's hand. "Hey, kiddo. Maybe he's just not in love yet. Or maybe he doesn't realize he's in love. Or maybe he's just being a guy. They're scared to death of love, you know."

Maggie sniffed. "They are?"

"Oh, yeah. Guys never really make it past fifth grade. You know—girls have cooties and all that. You have to really pound love into their heads. But"—she winked—"once they finally do fall . . . Well, let's just say that a guy in love is as tenacious as a . . . a . . . oh, hell, I can't think of anything. But you know what I mean."

Deena wasn't sure Maggie *did* know what she meant. Instead of nodding or agreeing, Mags just stared at her as if she was nuts. Deena shut her eyes and pressed her fingertips to her forehead. Hell, maybe they were both nuts.

The really weird thing was that even though they were pretty close in age, and although they'd only met less than an hour ago, Deena already felt like Maggie's big sister, and she had to admit she liked the feeling. Ever since their parents died, Nick had been smothering her with brotherly affection. Not that she would have wanted it any other way, but the bottom line was that she was always the nurtured, not the nurturer.

When she opened her eyes, Deena noticed Maggie's outfit again, the T-shirt and boxers so familiar from all the times Nick had guilted her into doing the laundry.

"Uh, Mags, this is just a shot in the dark, but what were you wearing yesterday when you got here?"

"Nothing. Although that did seem to bother

Nicholas. He put a jacket around me."

Deena almost had to physically restrain herself to keep from laughing at the image of her brother—the virtual choir boy—and a naked girl. She'd have to tease him mercilessly about that. Of course, knowing Nick, he had probably fled to Hoop's house. And unless Nick broke from his usual pattern and kept a secret from his best friend, Deena figured Hoop had already administered the teasing of a lifetime.

None of that, of course, helped out with the Maggie problem. This gal seemed to be totally smitten with her brother.

If she were a more analytical woman, Deena would probably have spent some time thinking about whether this somewhat clueless, absolutely quirky woman, who had shown up at her brother's house, was really someone she should be bonding with. But no one had ever accused Deena of being analytical.

She'd spent her whole life trusting her feelings, believing in things she knew she shouldn't and going with the flow. She liked this girl. And she had a feeling Maggie would be very good for her brother.

She only hoped Nick would realize it, too.

"Sweetheart, don't you worry about a thing. If Nick's the man you want, then I'll help you get him."

She took Maggie's hand and squeezed it. "I think Nick's party is going to be a surprise in more ways than one."

Chapter Five

"Um . . . Mags? Are you hungry?"

Deena frowned at Maggie's lap, her upper lip curled and her nose wrinkled. Maggie looked down, then realized she'd ripped open the bag of tuna treats and had been munching away. As they'd talked, she'd devoured about half of the crunchy snacks.

She licked her lips. Tuna treats, it seemed, were off limits for humans.

"Um . . . maybe a little hungry."

"I guess so. Gross, girl. That is really nasty. How 'bout we go get some real food?" She reached over and patted Maggie's arm. "My treat, okay? We'll get a Big Mac or something."

Maggie had no idea what a Big Mac was, but if she hoped to pass as human, she'd better find out soon. "Okay."

"All right. My kind of girl." Deena winked. "I'm pretty much the fast-food queen, so if I try to cram too much down your throat, just kick me and we'll find some tofu or something."

"Tofu?"

"Yeah, I know it's nasty, but they say it's healthy and I figure I need all the help I can get to counteract the grease-fest I've got going."

Big Mac? Tofu? Grease-fest? Maggie only nodded. Since she'd never heard of any of those things, she didn't know what to say. Hopefully between tofu and a Big Mac, she'd find something that tasted good.

She started to reach for the kitty treats, wondering if she could smuggle them out without Deena noticing. No, too risky. The last thing she needed was Deena wondering why Maggie preferred cat food to a Big Mac, whatever that was.

Deena stood up and hoisted her tote bag onto her shoulder. "Okay. So we're off to the mall to get you the perfect party dress, then we've got a party to go to."

"Are you sure I should go to Nicholas's party?" Even as she said it, Maggie knew she had to go. Time was running out. She was already several hours into the second night, but still no closer to winning Nicholas over. She needed to spend as much time as possible with him, and if that meant parties . . . with humans . . . well, she could do that.

"Hey, don't worry. He's gonna be bowled over by you. You're a total knockout. Besides, until I met you I was sure this party was going to be as dull as . . . something," Deena said, waving her hand in the air. "But now I expect this'll rank up there in the party hall of fame."

Maggie bit her lip and and followed Deena toward the entryway.

"Oh, hell," Deena sputtered, stopping short and nearly tripping her. "I've got to find you something to wear until we can get you some real clothes." She dropped her bag in Nicholas's recliner. "Hang here for a sec while I go see if I've left anything here. You're about three sizes smaller than me, but maybe there's something."

As Deena disappeared, Maggie heard the front door creak open. She opened her mouth to call Deena back, then shut it when she heard the voice.

"Yo! Anybody here? Hey, funky naked chick?"

Maggie almost clapped with delight when she recognized Hoop's voice. She took a step forward, then remembered that he didn't know her as a human, and yet he seemed to be looking for her. She wrinkled her nose, then stepped backward into the shadows by Nicholas's bookcase.

Hoop clomped over the tiled entry toward the living room. "Hey, girl, are you still here? I've got a proposition for you."

"That you, Mags? I found some of Nick's sweats you can pull on. You'll just need to tighten the drawstring." Deena's voice carried from the back of the house. "And I grabbed a pair of my sandals. A little big, but you can shuffle around in them."

Hoop stepped into the living room just as Deena came in from the study, tossing Maggie a handful of gray fleece that smelled like Nicholas. In fact, Maggie was so intent on burying her nose in the material and inhaling his wonderful scent that she didn't notice the shoes Deena had pitched until they landed at her feet.

"You're battering the girl with flip-flops?"

"Hoop!" Deena pulled herself up short and Maggie was pretty sure she saw a blush color her cheeks.

Interesting. Maggie sniffed, trying to catch Deena's scent from across the room.

Deena coughed and looked down. "Hoop. Hi. Wow. Uh . . . what are you doing here?"

He waved toward Maggie but kept his eyes trained on Deena. "Looking for her."

Maggie tried a weak grin. Her second night as a human was turning out to be really, really complicated.

"For Maggie? You know her?"

"Y—" Maggie began, then clamped her mouth shut.

"No," Hoop said, then grinned. "Let's just say I know her by reputation only. Like I know she makes one damned entertaining entrance. And I sure as hell didn't know Nick's little vixen had a name."

Maggie swallowed. "It's Maggie."

"So I gathered. Just like the cat's. Convenient.

Less to remember." He looked around the room. "So where is that cat? Nick couldn't find her last night."

She bit her lip and took a step backward, shaking her head.

Deena stepped forward, leaning sideways so that she was in Hoop's line of sight. "Forget the cat, all right? She's probably under a bed or something. But we've got to run, so you wanna tell us why you're looking for this Maggie?"

"Sure thing, sweetheart. Hell, you're as tenacious as your brother."

"You have no idea."

Hoop turned to Maggie. "So what's your story, babe?" He raised his brow and spoke directly to her, though tilting his head just slightly in Deena's direction. "You some stray the flower-child here picked up on Venice Beach?"

"I am not a stray." *The nerve.* Old Tom had worked hard—really hard—to make sure she belonged to a human. And all the mewing and howling lessons had finally paid off when Nicholas had found her in the vacant lot almost three years ago.

"Hey, hey. Don't get your panties in a wad. I didn't mean anything. It's just that if you're hard up for cash, I know of a little job you might be interested in."

Maggie perked up. *A job?* If "Melrose Place" was right, men liked women with jobs. If a job would impress Nicholas, then she wanted one very much.

"A job?" Deena repeated. "You've never even

met her and you're offering her a job?"

Hoop turned his toothy, crooked grin from Maggie to Deena, and once again the color rose in Deena's cheeks. Maggie put her hand to her own cheek, wondering if her skin took on that pretty pink flush around Nicholas.

"I'm not offering," Hoop said. "The job's not mine to give away. I just know about it."

Deena rolled her eyes and shook her head. "Hoop, you're a loon. Always have been. Always will be. Why my brother puts up with you, I don't know."

Hoop clutched his hands over his heart. "Deenie, baby, you wound me." He took a step toward her. "Come on. Admit it. You love me, don'tcha? I mean, hey, what's not to love, right?"

"Would you like me to give you a typed memo? I could alphabetize your faults if that would help." She leaned over to pull up her tote bag and knocked it over instead.

When Maggie rushed over and helped Deena scoop all her junk back into the bag, it didn't escape her notice that Deena's cheeks seemed even pinker than before. And the scent. Faint, but familiar. The smell of attraction. Of lust.

Yes, it was all very interesting.

After they'd collected the brushes and snacks and little pieces of paper, Deena hoisted the bag onto her shoulder and stood up. It fell off. She rolled her eyes and pulled it back up. "Ready, Mags?"

Maggie grabbed Nick's sweatpants off the floor

and stepped into them, pulling them up over her floppy pants and tightening the cord tight around her waist. Then she hurried forward to stand next to Deena, who had her hands on her hips and a stern look on her face. She seemed to be concentrating on breathing in a regular rhythm.

"Here's the thing, Job Boy. Tonight, my buddy Mags isn't looking for a job, she's looking for a lover. And that means we've gotta shop for a party dress. So, we'd love to stay and chat, but we've got to get going."

Deena headed for the front door, but Hoop matched her every step of the way, and Maggie had to hurry to keep up. When Deena reached out to grab the doorknob, Hoop put his hand on her arm.

"A lover?" He looked over his shoulder at Maggie.

She nodded. *Oh, yes. She wanted Nicholas to be her lover.*

"Well, maybe I'll do some shopping with you," Hoop said. "Maybe we can come up with a mutually beneficial arrangement. And by that I mean a deal where no one gets screwed but Angela."

He winked at Maggie. "Not counting you and Nickie-boy, of course."

By the time they got to the mall, Deena was a nervous wreck. First, she'd told Hoop he'd need to take his own car, since they were going straight from the mall to the party, but he'd just grinned that grin of his and told her that he'd find his own way home. Then she'd told Maggie to sit up front, but Maggie had put on her little-girl-lost face and climbed into the backseat of Deena's Mustang.

So she'd ended up in close quarters with Hoop all the way from Nick's house to the Beverly Center. To make it worse, they'd spent the entire drive talking about how Maggie had shown up. So words like *naked* and *kissing* and *love* kept popping into the conversation.

The situation was almost enough to make Deena scream. After all, how much could a girl tolerate? She'd had the mother of all crushes on Hoop ever since Nick's sophomore year of college, back when she was still in high school.

Instead of lessening as crushes often did, this one had just managed to get stronger, until finally, like right now, Deena felt like she was twelve years old, instead of twenty-six. It was appropriate, of course, since Hoop still thought of her as a flighty kid who argued with him and needed her big brother to take care of her.

She maneuvered the car up the parking garage ramp, barely listening to Hoop's gentle interrogation of the woman in the backseat. Lady Luck threw them a bone in the form of a primo parking spot near the mall entrance, and Deena pulled into the space.

So Hoop still thought of her as a kid. Well, why wouldn't he? She frowned at the dashboard, killed the engine, and opened the door. She owed her brand-new convertible to her brother's generosity. Not to mention pretty much everything else she owned.

She'd never asked Nick for help—hadn't even told him she'd been out of work now for almost three months—but somehow he was always there.

As she headed across the parking lot to the entrance, Hoop and Maggie filed in behind her, still chatting.

"So you've got amnesia?" Hoop's voice jerked Deena back to herself, and she turned to see Hoop walking backward facing Maggie. He turned back to Deena, quickening his step until he caught up with her. "She's really got amnesia?"

"How should I know? She can't remember. Sounds like amnesia to me."

"Mmmm. Could be. Or maybe she remembers just fine and doesn't want to tell you."

Deena shot him a wary look as the escalator carried them up. "What?"

"Maybe she's a spy."

She gaped at him. "You're thinking she's come to set Nick up somehow? Please. The girl snacks on cat food. She may be a little flaky, but she's not out to sabotage Nick's deals."

"Hey, just an idea. You're probably right. She's not out to screw Nick—not in the business sense, anyway. So maybe she does have amnesia. Or maybe there's some other explanation."

"Such as?"

"How the hell should I know? Maybe she's the cat. You're the one who said she was going to town on those kitty treats. Her name's Maggie. And nobody's seen the damn cat."

"Oh, for cryin'—," Deena stepped off the escalator and turned to Hoop, planning to lay into him good for coming up with such a harebrained idea.

He crooked a finger at her and pulled an imaginary trigger. "Gotcha."

"Great. You're a real laugh riot. I'm trying to figure out where she's from and you're making up "X-Files" episodes."

"The truth really *is* out there."

Deena scowled, then scanned the crowd behind her. *Oh, shoot.* "Maybe the truth is, but Maggie's not."

Hoop stared at her. "What?"

Panic raced through her gut. *Dammit, she was always losing things. You'd think she'd at least be able to keep track of a person, even if she could never find her keys.*

"Oh, God, this is a nightmare." She turned to Hoop. "I don't get the feeling Mags is the comfortable-in-crowds type."

He laid a rough hand on her wrist and gave it a slight squeeze. Deena's breath caught.

"Don't get all bent out of shape, kid," he said in a soft voice that lacked the sharp edge she'd come to associate with him. "She can't have gone far. She was right behind us."

They exchanged glances, then raced back down. Deena took the traditional descending stairs two at a time, and Hoop crammed and pushed his way down through hordes of surly teenagers on the up-side.

Two floors later Deena found her. At first, all she noticed was that the up escalator opposite her was log-jammed near the top. But, just as she was wondering what all the commotion was about, Deena saw Maggie standing wide-eyed in the middle of the throng, ignoring all the pushing and shoving around her, but still managing to look as if modern technology was something that was all brand-new to her.

Deena chuckled. Even only knowing Maggie for a few hours, she should have known better than to take her eyes girl off the girl for even a second. Especially around a funky machine like an escalator.

She flew the rest of the way down the stairs, then rammed her way through the cluster of pissed-off people until she ended up right behind Maggie near the top of the moving stairs. She looked down and had to laugh again.

Every time the escalator came to the top, Maggie took a step backward. Hell, if Mags kept this up, she'd never need to join a gym. Why climb on a stair machine when you've got mall access?

"Um, Mags? You've gotta get off sometime this year."

"Where does it go?" Maggie whispered.

"Up. It goes up."

Maggie bit her lip and shook her head, then stepped back yet again. "No, the step. It disappears. But it always comes back." She looked up at Deena, and they both moved back in unison. "What if it swallows you up?"

Surreal. The entire afternoon was becoming surreal. "Work with me here, okay? Do what I do." Deena grabbed Maggie's arm, then stepped forward onto the solid flooring.

Maggie hesitated and then mimicked her, turning to look over her shoulder at the mechanism disappearing into the metal landing.

"You've never seen an escalator before?"

"I . . . I don't think we have such machines where I come from."

"Then you come from the wilds of Africa, kid. Escalators are everywhere. They're harmless. A lot easier than climbing the stairs, you know."

"Ss-ka-lay-ter." She beamed at Deena. "I can remember that."

"Great. I'm thrilled. Ready to tackle the next one?"

"Oh, yes, please. This is fun once you get used to it."

"Ride 'em cowgirl! Yee-ha!" Hoop's voice filtered down from the next set of escalators. Contorted from obvious laughter, he was bent over at the waist, facing down, and holding on to the handrail as the staircase moved him steadily up to the next level.

Deena raised her eyes to the ceiling, then focused on Maggie as they rode up to the next level. "*He's* Nichoas's best friend. In case that gives you any clue what you're getting into."

She followed Maggie, who stepped gingerly onto the polished floor that opened up onto the mall. " 'Course, if my brother can pick a best friend like the Hoopster, he sure shouldn't have any problems with your quirks."

"Quirks?"

"Never mind. I didn't mean—"

One look at Maggie's face and Deena snapped her mouth shut. The woman's gaze darted back and forth, taking in every possible inch of the super-chic shopping center. Her mouth hung open, two fingers resting lightly on her lower lip, looking for all the world like an art student getting her first in-person view of the Sistine Chapel.

"Never seen a mall before, huh?" Deena asked, for some reason keeping her voice at a whisper.

"No. I mean . . . I don't think so."

Deena gave Maggie's elbow a quick tug. "Well, then, you're in for the ride of your life today, kid."

"Hell, yes, she is," added Hoop. "Deena's got her big brother's credit cards. Gonna be a hot time in the old town tonight."

Maggie followed in silence, not sure what a credit card was or what Hoop meant by a "hot time." She was certain of only one thing—that this building called a mall outshone any place she'd ever been in her young life.

Each surface seemed to be made of glass, marble, or polished metal. The floor gleamed. Vibrant colors splashed out from behind crystal-clear windows. Sweet fragrances caressed her, riding on the waves of cool, processed air.

She'd ridden the metal staircase up, only to find herself lost in this building that seemed a thousand times bigger than Nick's house. Except for Deena and Hoop, nothing she saw seemed the least bit familiar.

For the first time, Maggie wondered if she wasn't in over her head.

Being human might turn out to be a lot more complicated than she'd expected.

"If that outfit doesn't catch Nick's attention, then my buddy's a dead man. You are one hot number, Mags."

Hoop's voice echoed through the boutique, and about ten women who looked even better than the ones Maggie had seen on "Melrose Place" turned to stare. She watched in the three-way mirror as he approached, each of his long strides bringing him closer to her reflection.

"Just ignore him," Deena said. "You look great. Very classy."

Maggie didn't know about classy, but she did know that for the first time since they'd come to this place, a tiny portion of her confidence had come back. They'd been in and out of shops for the last hour, ducking in whenever Deena or Hoop saw some flimsy little dress that one of them thought would make Nicholas fall madly in love with her.

But Maggie hated them all. Nothing felt comfortable; every garment was either too tight here or too loose there. And dresses . . .

For some reason she just didn't like dresses.

And then she'd seen the tight black thing on a strangely immobile plastic human, and had stopped cold in front of the display window.

"It's a cat suit," Deena had said.

Maggie's heart skipped a beat. "A cat suit?"

"Yup. Pretty sexy, huh?"

Oh, yeah. Even if she had all the clothes in the world to choose from, she couldn't get any better than this. And it was called *a cat suit.* Well, that just had to be—what did they call it?—serendipity.

The solid black outfit completely hugged her body, fitting so close that when she stood on her toes in front of the mirror, she could see ridges from the muscles in her human legs. Skin-tight, it hugged the curves of her waist and breasts.

Hoop looked her up and down while Deena leaned against a nearby clothes rack, her arms crossed over her chest.

"Are my breasts okay?"

A lump rose and fell in Hoop's neck. "Excuse me?"

Maggie ran her hands over her chest. "These breasts. Are they too big? The girl in the magazine at Nicholas's house—"

"They're fine," Hoop said, his voice tight.

"Nicholas will like them?"

Deena's lips pursed and her eyes twinkled. She looked like she could use help breathing. Hoop ran both hands through his hair before finally answering.

"Nick'll love 'em. Trust me on this one." He turned to Deena. "Cat suit, huh? Fitting. *Maggie the Cat*. I'll be damned."

He knew! How could they know?

"Maggie? You okay? Is the neck too tight?" Deena came forward and slid her finger under the tight collar. Maggie turned to look in the mirror. All the color had drained out of her face.

"C-c-cat?"

"Ignore him. He's just being a guy. Tennessee Williams and *Cat on a Hot Tin Roof*."

"I don't . . . I don't understand."

"From the play. The star is a woman called Maggie the Cat, but I don't remember why. She's who Nick named his cat after. And she's a sexy little thing. Like you."

Maggie realized she'd been holding her breath.

"Trust me, Maggie," Hoop added. "You ain't no cat. From the view over here, all you are is one-hundred-percent, all-American woman."

"You're sure Nicholas will like this?"

Deena and Hoop looked at each other.

"Oh, yeah."

"Damn straight."

Maggie smiled. "Then I would like to keep it, please."

"That's why we brought credit cards."

Maggie followed Deena to a counter. Hoop hung back, his eyes glued to the various women who kept popping in and out of the dressing rooms, often in clothes that looked to be a few sizes too small.

"Can she wear it out of the store?" Deena asked a dark-haired woman.

"Sure, honey." She stepped out and gestured to Maggie. "Come here, sweetie."

Maggie hesitated until Deena nodded, then stepped forward. The woman tugged on the back of the outfit, then clipped something off and returned to the other side of the counter.

"You know, I think when Nick sees you in this outfit, he may actually think about something other than work for a change. And Lord knows Angela's mouth will drop wide open. She couldn't pull off this outfit in a million years."

"Sure she could," Hoop volunteered begrudgingly from across the room. "Angela's a babe. She's a bitch. But she's still a babe."

Bitch. That word kept coming up, and Maggie was beginning to figure out what it meant.

"You wanna say that a little louder? I don't think they heard you in the food court," Deena said.

"Sure thing, sweetheart." He took a backward step and sucked in a chunk of air. "Ang—"

"Never mind. Forget I said anything."

Hoop chuckled and wandered over. "Well, what do you know? I think I was on the verge of embarrassing the unflappable Deena Goodman. Maybe I should try again."

"Or not."

Hoop held his hand up. "All right. Besides, Nick's not brain dead. He'll notice our little Maggie." He flashed her a smile and winked. "After all, it's his party. There's no way for him to sneak away to his office like he usually does."

"Cash or charge?" the boutique cashier asked.

Charge?

"Charge," said Deena, rummaging around in her bag. Maggie figured a charge was something like bartering.

Deena turned back to Hoop. "He may not be able to slip off to read files, but he can suck up to Ferrington. That's work. Or Nick thinks it is."

"Who is—"

"Ferrington?" Hoop interrupted. "Michael Ferrington? He's going to be at the party?"

Maggie watched as Hoop stepped closer to Deena, ending up less than an arm's length away. Maggie sniffed, wondering if maybe the man was . . . But the perfume samples on the counter overpowered Hoop's scent.

Deena pulled a wallet out of her bag and held it up triumphantly.

"Ferrington?" Hoop prodded.

"Angela snagged him. Swore me to secrecy last week. I guess she's planning to surprise Nick."

"Who's Michael Ferrington?" Maggie asked.

"He's the key to *your* gainful employment."

She didn't understand, and her confusion must have been obvious, because Hoop tried again.

"The guy with the job I was telling you about."

"She's not looking for a job. She's looking for a romance." Deena signed something, thanked the lady, and took a bag that Maggie saw now held the sweat pants and shirt she'd worn into the store.

Hoop followed as they walked toward the entrance. "Yeah? Well, Ferrington is Nick's biggest concern right now. If Maggie gets in with that man's staff, then suddenly Nick's got one more reason to stay as close to her as possible."

Maggie stopped, then turned around. A reason for Nicholas to stay near her? That would be useful. "What reason?"

He held up a finger. "Not just a reason. Several million reasons. And each with a portable portrait of George Washington."

He brushed her cheek. "And since I really want you to get that job, looks like I just invited myself to Miss An-ge-la's party."

Deena's eyebrows soared. "Not dressed like that you can't."

He was wearing light brown shorts, heavy boots with socks, and a ripped T-shirt. Maggie thought he looked fine—casual and comfortable, like Nicholas looked on those mornings when he lazed around the house with her.

He looked down, shrugged. "Whatever you say, chief. Get our little ingenue some shoes while I track me down a new party dress."

The party practically screamed "Angela," which was Nick's first indication that it wasn't going to be a hell of a lot of fun. Instead, perfection and pretense would be the buzz words for the evening.

A jazz band that Nick remembered seeing on the Tonight Show jammed in the far corner. Tuxedoed waiters strutted through the ballroom offering alcohol to all takers. Professional photographers trailed after couples, snapping wildly. Angela circulated through the crowd, her smile bright, her well-exercised social skills operating at full capacity.

Nick hovered over the buffet, trying to look interested in the unfamiliar food decorating the linen-swathed table. He didn't recognize one thing, unless he counted the caviar. But since Nick hated caviar, he wasn't about to count it as a recognizable food product. He liked his eggs scrambled, thank you, not in gelatinous mounds.

Even the crackers seemed odd and unappetizing, more for decoration than for eating. As for the old stand-by—a colorful fruit plate—not one apple, orange, or melon ball existed in a three-mile radius. Instead, Angela's culinary slaves had tracked down fruits so exotic they seemed more artistic than appetizing.

The real kicker was Nick's birthday cake. Forget German chocolate. No way was Angela going to sink so low as to actually serve Nick his favorite cake at his surprise party.

Nope. Instead, each of the one-hundred-plus guests and the birthday boy would get to indulge in some award-winning vanilla hazelnut cake with cream cheese and raspberry icing.

Award-winning being the critical word.

Forget that Nick hated raspberries and ranked

cream cheese icing down there with lemon meringue pie.

He couldn't stand meringue and wasn't that crazy about lemons, either.

All in all, Nick had to say the party was just dandy.

His assistant wound his way through a nearby cluster of folks. "Well, birthday boy, how're you enjoying this little shindig Angela's thrown together?"

"What do you think?"

"That you're pretty much hating life right now."

Nick swept his arm to encompass the entire room. "Look at this. She knows I hate these parties. I don't even know half these people."

"These folks are the Los Angeles elite. Don't you read the society pages? *Variety? Los Angeles* magazine? It's networking time, buddy boy."

As if to prove his point, Larry waved at two men who walked by, deep in a conversation that Nick would bet involved stock options.

Nick plucked one of the more normal crackers off the buffet, sniffed, and took a bite. It was bitter and dry. He made a face and forced himself to swallow even though he wanted to spit the mess out.

"You remember networking, right, Nick? It's what everyone else in L.A. does to get ahead."

"That's not how I work."

"Sure, I know. But it looks like your intended wants to change that." He cocked his head toward the far side of the ballroom. "You saw she managed to get Ferrington here?"

"It seems she thinks I'm going to perform a Vulcan mind meld, get his secrets, and strong-arm him into selling."

"Silly of me. I thought pretty much the same thing."

Nick grinned. "Oh, I'll get Ferrington, all right. But I don't play the strong man at parties. And Hoop's the one with the mind melds."

"Speaking of, did Angela invite him?"

Nick barked a laugh. "You're kidding, right? Hoop could be the last man on earth and Angela wouldn't even invite him to a barbeque."

Larry stabbed something orange on the buffet and gestured toward the main ballroom doors with his fork. "Then he must've crashed. Looks like he convinced your sister to smuggle him in."

Nick spun around. Sure enough, Hoop was stepping over the threshold with Deena at his side. A wave of almost parental pride swept through Nick. Dressed in a casual-chic dress made out of some flowing, gauzy material, Deena looked both elegant and down-to-earth.

Hoop was another story. Wiry and unkempt on a daily basis, Hoop even looked rumpled in an Armani suit, as if his pores oozed antibodies against tidiness.

The two of them looked around the room, their search finally stopping when they found Nick. He waved and headed toward the parquet dance floor.

When Deena stepped forward, Nick just about had a heart attack. His mystery woman glided into the room, a stretchy black body suit clinging with such tenacity to her curves that Nick was pretty sure he was going to need oxygen. What might seem tacky—even cheap—on another woman, on this one seemed like nothing more than understated elegance.

An appreciative hush fell over the room, and Nick knew that every other man's body was doing the same little number as his. But she didn't seem to notice. Or care.

Instead, she turned slowly, as if she was scanning the room, and when her eyes found his, she stopped. A smile lit up her face and Nick found himself returning it—sincerely.

Only one day before this gorgeous, sexy, enigmatic woman had been naked in his living room, and he'd run screaming into the street.

Well, Hoop was right.

Nick knew he qualified as a full-fledged idiot.

Chapter Six

"You been keeping secrets from me, boss man?"

Nick blinked and turned away from the girl to stare at Larry. "What?"

"The sex kitten. You know her?"

"Not exactly."

"Looks like she wants to know you."

Nick glanced again at the girl and had to agree. Lust, longing, *something* burned in her eyes. And that something was aimed smack dab at him.

The realization affected him more than he wanted to admit. "I'm beginning to wonder if she does know me." He took a step forward, unable and unwilling to resist the pull of those eyes.

"Come again?" Larry asked. "I thought—"

But he just walked away, letting Larry's voice mix with the din of the party as he crossed the ballroom toward her. The woman smiled, then said something to Deena. When she took a step toward him, Nick stupidly felt like his self-worth had just increased tenfold. All because some nameless, mute beauty seemed infatuated with him.

Nick did a double take and stopped in the middle of the dance floor. Wait a second. Wait just a damn second. She had just *said* something to Deena. As in words. Had he really seen that? He'd thought she couldn't talk.

Dancers swirled around him as he watched the pair. Yup. The girl's lips moved, and Deena nodded. The mystery girl started walking toward him.

And all he'd managed to coax from her the other night had been a grunt or two. He shook his head, marveling at the depths his sister would sink to. This whole thing had been a joke. A scam. Just like he'd thought all along. He'd just pegged the wrong culprit.

It hadn't been Hoop who'd set him up. It had been Deena.

His sweet, innocent, compelled-to-always-butt-her-nose-into-his-business sister had hired one of L.A.'s umpteen million actress-slash-model wanna-bes. Or maybe she'd hired—*please, God, no*—a prostitute.

One look across the room and he nixed the prostitute idea. She seemed too innocent for that. The little actress hovered on the other side of the dance floor, nibbling on her lower lip. Her sexy, impish face reflected intense concentration mixed with a touch of terror. Although he doubted she realized it, she swayed with the music, every once in a while stepping forward with the beat, then springing back whenever a couple whooshed by on the polished floor.

For about half a second, he wondered why on earth Deena would want to send such a befuddled beauty his way. Correction: a befuddled, *naked* beauty. True, his little sister usually came up with some pretty original birthday presents, but harem girls didn't seem to be her style. Hell, maybe this mysterious woman really was just someone who had the hots for him. . . .

Then Nick noticed Angela playing hostess in the corner. The proverbial lightbulb flashed over his head, destroying any lingering fantasy that the new woman in his life was there for any reason other than an elaborately concocted birthday hoax. And this scam had a dual purpose; it had been aimed not only at giving him a prurient thrill, but also at getting Angela's goat.

"Damn it, Deena," he muttered, quashing a wave of disappointment. When Deena had given Angela the cold shoulder on Thanksgiving, it had been tacky but expected. *Accidentally* losing her luggage when the three of them had traveled together to Manhattan had also been tacky but amusing. This time, however, his sister had gone too far, and Nick intended to lay down the law.

First to this mystery woman, and then to his kid sister.

He stepped onto the dance floor, fully intending to push through the throng and confront her. The beauty had other plans, though, and she derailed him with a single flash of her brilliant smile. Nick's heart beat a little mambo in his chest, drowning out his resolve to set the lady straight.

Dancers in soft focus swirled around him, melting into the music. They were undefined, *nonexistent.* Except for her. She filled him up, made him forget where he was. She took his breath away.

Like Tony gazing upon Maria while Jets and Sharks rumbled around them, he moved forward. She did the same, her movements fluid and graceful. By the time they met in the center, he was completely and totally bewitched.

Palm touched palm, fingers caressed fingers. They swayed to the music as he memorized the star pattern in her emerald irises. She matched his gaze, never blinking, an enigmatic curl playing at her mouth, as if she knew all his secrets. If the eyes really were the window to the soul, what did this woman see? The heart of a man so entrenched in his career that he would marry simply to ensure his success? Or could she see past the last eight years? And if she could, Nick wondered, was there anything worthwhile left to be found?

He bit back a curse. His birthday and his upcoming wedding were making him melancholy. And this beautiful woman had knocked him off kilter. He pulled his hands away and concentrated on keeping his arms at his sides.

"Nicholas."

He looked up, not sure he'd really heard her. "What? Did you actually say something?"

She bobbed her head, her eyes bright. "I said 'Nicholas.' "

He swallowed. "That's me." The words scratched past his suddenly parched throat. *Damn it, Nick. You're not some seventeen-year-old meeting a Playboy bunny. She's the hired help, remember? Take the upper hand.*

Her gaze dropped to the floor, and he looked down as well. She wore flat black sandals and her toenails were painted red. He closed his eyes, trying to remember if she'd had red toenails the night before. Try as he might, he couldn't recall, and the gap in his memory frustrated him, so sure had he been that he'd locked a complete image of her in his mind. *So much for taking the upper hand. Even her memory drove him to distraction.*

She played her foot back and forth on the polished floor but didn't speak. When the silence grew awkward, he cleared his throat. "Well, you know me, but I don't know you." He stiffened his arm at his side, forcing himself not to caress her smooth cheek. "I'm not sure I like being at such a disadvantage."

When she looked up, the intensity reflected in her eyes startled him. "Disadvantage? You could never be at a disadvantage with me, Nicholas."

Nicholas again. "Why do you keep calling me Nicholas?"

She licked her fingertips and smoothed a strand of raven-black hair behind her ear. "What else would I call you?"

"Nick. Most people call me Nick." *But you can just call me crazy.*

"I'm not like most people."

No kidding. The more he talked to her, the less inclined he was to confront her charade. As soon as he admitted to knowing about Deena's birthday scheme, the gig would be up. And that meant she'd be out of there. It was not a thought he relished, even though every fiber in his body screamed that if he didn't get as far away from her as possible—and soon—the window of opportunity would be lost. And so would he.

A flash of lacquered blond hair caught his eye. It was Angela, moving his way fast. It was now or never.

"Who are you?" he pressed.

Angela pushed past a couple swaying nearby. She'd be there any second.

"I'm Maggie," she said, as if they'd known each other forever.

"Maggie?" The near-black hair, the sparkling green eyes. For just an instant, rational thought abandoned Nick and he thought of his black cat, curled up in his lap. The image faded, and he pictured this girl's head resting on his thigh, his hand stroking her hair, soft music drifting through the house, and a feeling of contentment like he'd never—

"Nick, sweetheart, I've been looking everywhere for you. If you're going to stand in the middle of the dance floor, at least have the decency to dance." Angela grabbed his elbow and tugged him toward the edge of the floor.

She was tugging him away from the girl. He jerked his arm back. Angela pierced him with a sharp glance.

"I was talking with someone," he said.

"Who?"

Nick frowned as he scanned the dance floor. She'd disappeared. Hadn't Angela seen her? "She was right here." He tried to remember whether the woman had still been standing there when Angela had grabbed his arm. True, his mind had been wandering, but surely he would have noticed as she'd walked off. Wouldn't he?

There was no question; he was losing it. And everything tied back to his nutty sister. "I've got to find Deena."

Angela's pursed her lips. "Your sister is persona non grata today, darling. She brought *him*."

"*Him* happens to be my best friend."

"That's not the point. The point is that I specifically told her that Mr. Hooper wasn't on the guest list. I'm sure she invited him only to defy me."

Nick opened his mouth, then shut it again, remembering the first rule of getting out of holes—quit digging. Truth or not, Angela's mood wouldn't improve with the knowledge that she ranked so low on his sister's list that Deena wouldn't waste her time thinking up ways to defy Angela.

Nick, on the other hand . . .

Him, Deena would defy in a second.

He took a tentative step away. "I'm sorry she irritated you, Ange. I'll say something when I find her."

She pulled him back, eradicating what little progress he'd made toward the far side of the ballroom. "I've got *people* here I want you to talk to."

"Deena's a person."

"Dammit, Nick! Have you forgotten what I told you at dinner? Michael Ferrington is here. This is the perfect opportunity."

Aspirin. He craved aspirin. Or tequila. Or aspirin washed down with tequila.

He leaned over and pecked her cheek. "Sweetheart, it's just a party, remember? Not a board meeting. Not a networking luncheon. A party."

She squinted at him. "Never waste an opportunity. Aren't you the one who told me that? Isn't that the motto of the great Nicholas Goodman?"

"That doesn't translate into 'Accost potential corporate targets at birthday parties.' That's not my style. And this is my game, babe. Don't start telling me how to play it."

"Your game? In case you've forgotten, Palmer Enterprises is your biggest client. And I happen to own a significant block of voting stock in that little company. Not to mention that I'm wearing your engagement ring. So I think I have just a little bit of a say-so in how you play the game." She pressed her lips into a thin smile. "Darling."

He bristled. "No, Angela, you don't." Every inroad he'd forged in the last eight years, every deal he'd made, every dollar he'd earned, it all had come from his hard work. His creativity. His instincts. There was power in self-reliance. Safety. And he didn't intend to change the game now.

He put a finger over the perfect *o* her startled lips had formed. "The day you get a law license and start signing my paychecks, we'll talk. Until then, I do my job my way." He slid his hand down to cup her chin and urged her head up until he was looking deep into her eyes. "I'm going to go talk to Deena now. And after that, if I see Ferrington, I'm sure I'll chat with him. But if you're insisting that I even hint that he sell Vision to your father's company, then you need to find yourself a new attorney."

He almost said *and a new fiancé*, but the words wouldn't come. This would be a good marriage, provide him a secure future. And he couldn't risk her calling his bluff and walking away.

Angela needed him, true. But he needed her as well, along with Palmer Enterprises.

"Ma'am, there's a line forming."

Maggie nibbled on her lower lip, unable to decide. Hunger and thirst gnawed at her gut. The Big Mac had been tasty. Unusual, but tasty. Still, it hadn't been very filling. And now her throat was dry. She'd considered just getting water, but that didn't seem sophisticated. She needed to be sophisticated to compete with Angela.

She wrinkled her nose. Trouble was, nothing behind the bar smelled . . . well, good.

A polished woman eased around Maggie. "Look, while she's deciding, will you pass me a kahlua and cream?"

The bartender nodded and poured brown liquid into a glass full of ice, then topped it off with something Maggie actually recognized—thick, rich cream. She inhaled the fragrance, her mouth watering. "I'd like one of those too, please."

A smattering of applause sounded from the line behind her, and a look of extreme relief washed over the bartender's face. "Whatever the lady wants."

She took the drink and sniffed it, then took a tentative sip. Not bad. She licked her lips and took another sip. Pretty good, actually. She tilted the glass up and swallowed the rest of the drink, letting the thick cream coat her sore throat. All this talking had taken a toll.

"Lady?"

"I'd like another please."

"I'm not sure—"

"What are you, the drink police?" Hoop's voice interrupted, and Maggie turned as he sidled up next to her. "Just get the lady another. In fact, why don't you make it two?"

She smiled at Hoop, who took both drinks and

passed one to her as they walked away. "Where's Deena?" she asked.

"Saw Nick heading her way, so she took the chicken's way out and ducked into the john."

Maggie considered asking who John was. She took another sip of the drink, then decided it didn't matter. "I need to go find Nicholas again. Is *she* still with him?"

"Hold your horses there, kid. Let's run down your strategy first. Okay?"

Maggie frowned, then finished her drink. "My strategy?"

Hoop looped his arm around her shoulder and led her toward a free table just off the dance floor. He pulled a chair out for her, then sat himself on the tabletop, one foot on the floor for balance. He took a sip of his drink, then pushed the glass toward her. "Here, kid, you need this more than I do."

When Maggie blinked, her eyes stayed closed just a little bit longer than necessary. The chair swayed beneath her, and she held on to the edge of the table with her free hand. She opened her eyes, saw Hoop's precarious position, and stifled a laugh. She could laugh later. Now was the time to get serious. It was time to get Nicholas. "What did you say about a strategy?"

"A plan, Mags. You gotta have a plan if you're gonna catch our boy Nick." He crossed his arms over his chest. "So lay it on me."

"Lay it . . . ?" *What on earth was he talking about?*

"The plan, babe. What's your plan?"

"I don't have a plan. I love Nicholas."

"Hoo-boy." He slid off the table and plunked himself into the other chair.

"That's bad?"

"It ain't good, sweetie. What do you think? You're just gonna walk up to our boy and say, 'Hey, Nick, I love you, let's go roll in the sack'? Me, that might work on. But ol' Nick's just gonna run like hell."

Maggie thought of Deena. "That would work on you?"

"You changing targets, babe? 'Cause if you are, let me know. I mean, I'm doing my damnedest here to be a gentleman. But, well, look at you." With a broad motion, he gestured up and down.

She gave him a quick kiss on the cheek. "But you don't love me."

"And you think Nick does?"

"Oh, yes. I'm sure of it."

Hoop slumped in his chair, gave her an odd look, then drummed his fingers on the tabletop. Then he shrugged. "What the hell? I mean, who am I to say otherwise? But Mags, even if you're right, are you sure that's enough?"

No, not anymore. When she'd first gone to Nicholas, she'd believed in what humans called fairy tales. But such stories and magic weren't enough for humans. So now she had her television repertoire. But what if that was wrong, too?

"Mags?" he prodded, interrupting her thoughts. "What are you going to do?"

"'Melrose Place,'" she confessed. What had that television man said? *Vixens*. The women on television were *vixens*. Well, she could be a vixen, too.

"Stand up."

She did, standing tall while Hoop's eyes roamed from the top of her head down to her toes.

He let out a low whistle. "Okay, you can sit."

"I look okay?"

"Mags, you look better than okay. The thing is, I think you've already tried the 'Melrose Place' routine. I mean, showing up at his house naked. Hell, back when it was on prime time, that coulda been a Sweeps Week episode." He took her hand. "But it didn't work, did it?"

"No."

"Thing is, our boy Nick's got his own little code. He's engaged to the Ice Queen, and he's not gonna dump her just 'cause you show up dressed like Emma Peel. So you've got your work cut out for you."

"Emma . . . who?"

"'The Avengers'; she wore a leather body suit." He waved a hand in the air. "Point is, he's a committed guy. To Deena. To his job. Even to Angela. Or, at least, to his promise to marry her."

"He doesn't love her." Of that, Maggie was positive.

"Who the hell knows with Nick? He's got a boatload of issues, and she's got Palmer for a parent. That would make any woman a raving bitch from hell. Either way, they've both got career tunnel vision."

She bit her lip, and he took her hand.

"Look," he went on. "I don't think he loves her. Not really. But it don't matter. Either way, the hell of it is, he's committed to her."

Maggie bristled. "But he loves *me*."

"Maybe. The point is, you need to make sure Nick ends up being more committed to you than he is to Angela."

"How do I do that?"

He ran his fingers through his hair, causing tufts to stick out in every direction. Maggie stifled the urge to groom him. "Hell if I know," he said. "Main thing is to just be around him. All the time."

All the time! How could she manage that? She only had half as much time around Nicholas as Angela. Except . . .

An idea flitted through her mind. If Angela had twice as much time, then Maggie would have to work twice as hard during the time she was human. As for the rest of the time . . . well, Maggie the cat would just have to see what she could do about keeping Angela away from Nicholas's house.

She sat up straighter. If she had her tail, she'd twitch it. "Okay," she agreed. "All the time."

"Good. And play up this amnesia thing. Nick's a sucker for a hard-luck case. And try and fix it so that he needs to be around you as much as you want to be around him."

"All right." She tilted her head and squinted at him. "How?"

"That job. Remember? You get in good with Michael Ferrington, and Nick's gonna want to get in good with you."

Of course. She'd forgotten about the job. "So now I have a strategy?"

"For what it's worth. It's the best I can do on short notice." He paused, once again looking her up and down. "And flirt. Hell, flirt a lot. If you can keep my man Nick on the edge, you've got a definite leg up over Angela."

Flirting and Ferrington. So that was her plan.

She shrugged. As far as she knew, it was the best plan ever. She might as well get started.

After taking the last gulp of her drink, she pulled herself out of the chair and scanned the room. "Which one is Michael Ferrington?"

Hoop nodded toward the buffet. Maggie saw a rather round man chatting with Angela. His glasses slid down his nose and he shoved them back up, all the while keeping a polite smile plastered on his face.

"Might as well wait 'til he's out of the Ice Queen's clutches. In the meantime, you should go give Nick a dose of feline flirtation."

Her head shot up. "What?" she croaked.

"Flirting. Nick. Remember?"

"You said 'feline.' "

"Wouldn't want that cat suit to go to waste." He looked at her, a question in his eyes. "I was just kidding around. What's the deal?"

They'd been just words. She took a breath. Really, she had to quit being so jumpy or someone would figure her out. "I'll go now." Hesitating, she licked her lips. "Hoop? Will this work?"

"I don't know, kid. Just do your best."

She nodded and scanned the room for Nicholas, finally finding him near an archway. Staring at his watch, he seemed oblivious to the party. She started toward him, then turned back to Hoop.

"Why are you helping me?"

He spread his hands wide. "Hey, I'm a hopeless romantic. Can't you tell?"

She cocked her head, considering. "Yes. I can." Surprise flashed across his face, and she smiled at him before turning away.

Hoop caught her elbow and pulled her back. "You barely know the guy. And if what you say is true, you don't remember half of what you do know about him. But you're really in love with him, aren't you?"

She nodded.

"Why?"

How could she explain to Hoop the way Nicholas made her feel? The way he cared for her. The way he protected his sister. The way he smelled. The way he laughed. She didn't really have the words. "Everything about him, all put together," she finally said. "I tripped."

"Tripped . . ." Hoop's face cleared. "You *fell.* You fell in love."

"He saved me. I'm going to save him back."

Chapter Seven

The big hand passed the nine, and Nick sighed. Fifteen minutes. Either Deena had contracted some dreadful stomach disease, or she was hiding out in the ladies' room.

He'd lay money on option number two.

A few more minutes ticked by. Nick counted ten different types of flowers in the pattern of the nearby wallpaper. No Deena. He wondered how the tuxedoed waiters kept those trays balanced on one hand. Still no Deena.

Well, hell. Ladies' room or not, he'd just have to go in after her.

Right. Sure. He could do that.

After one quick glance to make sure no one was

looking, he grabbed the polished brass handle, yanked the door open, and ducked inside.

He entered a parlor. The place was nicer than most people's living rooms, and it sported a solid wall of mirrors, baskets of potpourri, big comfy chairs, and a couch. There was even a basket of magazines. No wonder women always went to the rest room in groups. They were escaping to Oz, having tea at the Ritz, and getting the hell out of Dodge. And to think, in the men's room he felt lucky when the paper towel dispenser was stocked.

The lushly carpeted, L-shaped parlor opened up onto a tiled area. He didn't have the full view yet, but he'd gamble that around that corner lay more familiar bathroom territory. Muted voices filtered toward him and he cringed. Voices meant people, and people meant Deena wasn't alone.

So maybe this wasn't the greatest idea after all. He eased back toward the door, hoping nobody would walk in and catch him. Headlines flashed through his head—LOCAL ATTORNEY ARRESTED FOLLOWING BATHROOM BRUHAHA.

"Well, well, well. If it isn't my brother the Peeping Tom." Deena appeared from around the dividing wall, then leaned back, her arms crossed over her chest, amusement dancing across her face.

"We need to talk." He headed for the door, then looked over his shoulder. She hadn't moved. "Deenie, you want to get a move on, here?"

"Um . . . let me think." She tapped a finger

against the corner of her mouth, frowning. "Nope. Definitely not." She glided over to one of the chairs and sank into the overstuffed cushions. "I think I'll just stay here."

Heels clattered on the tile, the sound preceding two women—a redhead and a blonde—who headed through the room, then stopped dead when they noticed Nick.

He held up a hand and tried a polite smile. "Hi, there."

The redhead giggled furiously and dragged her friend toward the exit. They both took one last peek his way before the door swung shut. Nick pictured them circulating through the party, telling everyone in the room that the birthday boy was hiding out in the ladies' lounge. He shut his eyes. This was a nightmare. A total nightmare.

"So, brother mine. What's up?"

It was time to get a grip. He wasn't about to let his baby sister know she'd thrown him for a loop. He'd conducted negotiations in 747s, over grease-stained tables in barbeque joints, in smoke-filled basements, and in intimidating, mahogany-paneled boardrooms. If he could do that, surely he could cope with the ladies' room.

With determined casualness, he picked up a basket of wrapped mints and headed for the other chair. "I should be asking you what's up."

She waved a limp hand toward herself. "*Moi?* Whatever do you mean?"

"Maggie. I mean Maggie."

"I like her, Nick. She's got all the qualities Angela doesn't. Including a personality."

"Very funny."

The door opened and an elderly lady stepped in. Nick held out the basket. "Mint?"

The woman didn't bat an eye. "No thank you, young man," she said, then disappeared toward the stalls. Nick grinned at Deena, and they both laughed.

Nick cast a glance toward the door. No way was he having this conversation in Grand Central Station. He got up and hung the CLOSED FOR CLEANING sign on the outside of the door. That oughta hold 'em for a while.

"Look, kid," he said when he'd returned. "I just want her out of my life, okay? Send her back where you found her. Now."

Deena squinted at him. "Back where I found her?"

Why was this so hard for her to comprehend? "Yes, dammit. Get her out of here. It was funny for about five minutes, but the show's over. Pay her and send her back where she came from."

A slow smile spread over her face. He knew that smile. That smile meant trouble. "What?"

"Nothing," she said, but the smile stayed. "I'll take her back right now." She pushed herself out of the chair.

Nick grabbed her skirt as she passed by. "Hold on." She took two steps back. "Where did she come from?"

"Your living room, as far as I know."

The single square knot in his stomach morphed

into a sheepshank. "What did you say?"

"Your liv—"

He held up a hand. "Never mind. I heard you. Where'd she come from *before* my living room?"

"Beats me." She linked her fingers together and stretched out her arms, a delighted little smile playing at her mouth. "I got the impression you guys knew each other, at least a little."

"Why on earth did you assume that?"

Deena blinked, then started to tick off reasons on her fingers. "Let's see. She was in your living room, in your clothes—"

"She was wearing clothes?"

She shot him an amused look. "Yeah. I wasn't lucky enough to get the *au naturel* encounter."

He shrugged, and she returned to counting off her reasons. "She knows a hell of a lot about you, and I'd have to say she likes you." She broke eye contact and focused on something over his shoulder, a diabolical grin spreading over her face. "Don't ya, Mags?"

Nick spun around, and sure enough, there Maggie was, a beatific smile on her beautiful face.

"Hello again, Nicholas."

She still had that little-girl-lost look about her, and he stifled the urge to gather her into his arms and rock her back and forth until he'd made it all better. He shook his head. All she had to do was come near him, and he got all bent out of shape, as if her body cast off pheromones designed specifically to drive him crazy.

Not this time. He wasn't going to lose his focus.

Once and for all, Nick intended to get to the bottom of this.

Deena moved toward the door.

"You, stay," Nick ordered, shooting her a warning glare. He turned to Maggie. "And you, sit."

As Maggie sank into a chair and curled her feet up under her, Nick positioned himself between the two women. "Now, does one of you want to tell me what's going on?"

He looked first at Deena. She shrugged and examined her fingernails. He glanced at Maggie. She sat a little straighter and held his gaze, her eyes bright. "Okay, you first. Maggie, right? You want to tell me what you're doing here?"

Her gaze darted to Deena and then back to him. "Celebrating your birthday?"

"Not *here* here. In my house, here."

"Oh." She licked her lips. "Looking for you."

Nick tried to stay patient. "Okay. Why?"

"Because I lo—"

"Lost her memory," finished Deena, dropping into a chair.

As Nick whipped around to look at his sister, he caught the tail end of Deena's hand motions in Maggie's direction. The word *cahoots* popped into his head, and he sighed. "Okay, then you tell me what's going on."

Deena nodded. "Well, it seems that Maggie here's got amnesia. 'Bout the only thing she does remember is you. Right?"

He glanced over his shoulder at Maggie, who nodded.

"But I don't know you." His mind reeled. For some reason, he'd been pegged as the central figure in this enigmatic beauty's life. But he'd never seen her before, he felt sure of *that.* No doubt he would remember meeting someone as sensual and exotic as Maggie.

Okay, so he'd never met her. Why, then, did some little demon in the back of his head keep whispering that she was familiar?

He shook his head. Forget whether he knew her. The point was, she didn't know herself. He grabbed an overstuffed footstool and dragged it in front of Maggie's chair. Settling himself on it, he took her hand. "Let's see what we can figure out about you, all right?" She nodded, her eyes full of absolute trust. He fervently hoped it wasn't misplaced. "How do you know me?"

She looked down at their intertwined hands, then back up at him. "I don't know. All I know is that I'm supposed to be with you."

He savored her voice, light and sweet, like an aperitif in which he could never overindulge. "But the first time I saw you was yesterday. I'm sure of it." He stood up and walked around the small room, not wanting either woman to see the pleasant memory of finding Maggie naked at his door reflected on his face.

Oh, God, she'd been naked.

That had made sense when he'd thought she was a stripper. Now, though . . .

Now he imagined the worst.

He faced the girls. "Have you called the police?"

Maggie squirmed in her chair, looking like she'd happily fade into the upholstery.

Deena gaped at him. "What on earth for?"

"What for? She showed up naked. That's what for."

His sister leaned forward, striking her I've-got-an-argument pose. Then she stopped and fell back against the cushions. "Oh."

"That does it. I'm calling the cops." He reached into his jacket for his cell phone and flipped it open.

"No!" cried both women.

He shut the phone and crossed his arms over his chest. "Why the hell not? Well, Maggie? You're the one with no clothes and no memory. You want to tell me why I shouldn't try and get you some help?"

She bit her lip and her eyebrows tilted into a little *v* above her nose. "How would they help me?"

"Exactly," shouted Deena, propelling herself out of the chair and pacing the room. "What would the police do? She's not hurt, are you?"

Maggie shook her head. "I'm not-hurt. I just lost my clothes."

"Lost?" He wondered if Maggie realized just how absurd that sounded.

A toilet flushed, and they all turned, waiting for someone to appear. The old woman who'd turned down the mints shuffled into the room. "Don't mind me." She grabbed the handle, turning back to Maggie before opening the door. "I lost my clothes once, dear. I found them a week later. Check the formal dining room. That's as likely a place as any." Then she pulled open the door and was gone.

Nick looked at Maggie and grinned. She smiled back, and for a second he was sure he recognized her smile. But the moment passed before he could latch on to the memory.

"If someone's reported Mags missing, we'll see it in the papers," Deena continued, not missing a beat. "Otherwise, all they'll do is put her in some county hospital and let some shrink have a whack at her."

Maggie stared at Deena, her eyes wide, terror playing across her face.

He hastened to tone Deena down. "We don't know what they'd do—"

"Even if it's not that extreme, they're still gonna take her away. And how's that gonna help? Huh? Tell me that?"

"Well—"

"It won't," she continued before he could think of anything to say. "All it'll do is take her away from the one link to her memory—you." She sat down as if to emphasize the point, then rested her chin in her palm and waited for him to respond.

He didn't have a clue what to say. Hell, maybe Deena was right. Although he doubted Maggie would end up in Nurse Ratched's ward, the thought of her in any sort of hospital made him queasy.

For some reason, Maggie had focused on him.

Him, of all people. Other than Deena's teenage years—when he'd been raising her all alone—he'd never been the center of anyone's entire world. The feeling was kind of nice. All the more so because it was Maggie who needed him, and without a doubt she was a woman he wanted to know better.

He banged his forehead with the palm of his hand. What the hell was he thinking? He could help her, sure. But get to know her? Have warm, fuzzy feelings about her? No way. Why? One word. Fiancée. Fee-on-say.

Angela Palmer. Job. Security. Wedding. Marriage.

Fiancée.

With a mental sledgehammer, he pounded the word into his brain. Fiancée, fiancée, fiancée.

Okay. Okay, he was calm. He turned back to the women, both of whom stared at him as if he'd lost it. Well, he more or less had.

"Problem?" Deena asked.

"No problem."

"You won't take me to the police?" A tremor laced Maggie's voice, and he rushed to reassure her.

"No police. I promise."

"Then what are you going to do?" Deena prodded.

"Good question." He moved to stand in front of Maggie, cupping her chin and tilting it up so that he could see into her eyes. Sentimental and sappy, maybe, but he wanted to be sure she realized that he'd do everything possible to help. "Let's start at the beginning. What exactly do you remember about me?"

Her face tightened, and Nick tried to imagine what it must be like to lose yourself. How terrifying to have people poke and prod into your memories. No wonder she looked like a cornered animal.

"The key," said Deena, moving to stand behind Maggie. "Tell him what you told me about the key."

"Oh, yes. I'd forgotten." She gave him a crooked smile and dropped her eyes.

"The key," he prodded.

"You showed her where you keep the spare," Deena answered. "That's how come she was inside when I got there."

"The spare," he repeated. He stood up slowly. This could be bad. This could be very, very bad.

"What?" Deena asked.

"Only you and Hoop know where I keep the spare."

"Well, obviously that's not the case, because Maggie knows."

"That's my point. How does *she* know?"

"You told her."

"No, I didn't. So I have to wonder if maybe I wasn't a little bit hasty in my promise not to get the police involved."

"What . . . what do you mean?" Maggie asked.

He shot her a look over his shoulder. "Just that maybe you've been watching me for a long time.

Maybe that's why you know me, but I don't know you. Hell, you could be a stalker for all I know."

"I'm not!"

"How would you know? You've lost your memory, right?"

"Nick, calm down. Maggie's no stalker. And you're scaring her."

"I'm scaring her? Didn't you ever see *Fatal Attraction*?"

"I never left."

"What?" He whipped around to face Maggie. "What did you say?"

"I said I never left. After you let me in. I stayed. I fell asleep in that little room with all the books. And then I heard you come home in the morning, and I was scared. So I stayed quiet. Then I heard you leave." She shrugged. "I just waited in the house until Deena got there."

"The spare key?"

"I wanted Deena to help me, so I pretended that you'd shown me where you keep your key." She tilted her head up and looked at him with pleading eyes. "I'm sorry I stayed in your house, Nicholas. But I didn't stalk. I would never hurt you."

God, he could see the turmoil in her face. Without thinking, he took her hand. "It's okay. I believe you. I'm not mad." So help him, he did believe her. And for all the world he didn't know if that was good—or a whole hell of a lot worse.

"See, I told you Maggie's not a stalker."

"Score one for you, Deenie," he said, with a wink to Maggie, who still looked tight as a spring and ready to bolt. "So now take a guess at what you win."

"What?"

"A roommate."

"Are you crazy? Maggie can't move in with me."

"Why not? You two seem to have hit it off." He turned back to Maggie. "Don't worry. She's impossible to live with. That should give you some incentive to get your memory back real soon."

Maggie leaned forward, her hand reaching out and her green eyes imploring. "But I want to live with you."

"Yeah. Why can't she stay at your place? You're the one with a house."

He glanced at Maggie, trying to ignore her silent plea, desperate to stay on track. "I'm also the one with a fiancée. Angela, remember?"

He would have sworn that Maggie tensed at the mention of Angela's name, but he shrugged off the thought as simply his own nerves. Angie would have his hide if he invited strange women in to camp out in his guest room.

Not to mention the effect that having her there—in his house, all day and all night—would have on his already frayed control. Just the memory of the way she looked, the way she smelled . . .

No, it was for the best that she not take up residence at his house.

"Okay, then," he said. "That's settled." He stood up, an absurd feeling of relief flowing through him. One mini-crisis under control. Now if the rest of the evening would just keep to an even keel . . . He'd had about all the birthday surprises he could handle.

The door opened and Hoop sauntered in. "Escaping from your own party, Nick? Tacky, tacky." He pointed toward Maggie and looked over his shoulder at his companion—Michael Ferrington. "I told you I saw them traipse in here." He turned to Maggie. "Hey, Mags. Got someone here who wants to meet you."

A pudgy little man, it took Ferrington four strides to reach Maggie. He pulled out a handkerchief and mopped his forehead, then tucked it back in his breast pocket before holding out his hand. "My dear, I've been watching you all evening. My name's Michael Ferrington, and when you have a moment, I'd like to talk to you about a job."

When she took Ferrington's hand and flashed her sweet smile, an absurd wave of jealousy washed over Nick. "I really don't think this is the time or the place to talk about giving the lady a job," he said.

Ferrington grimaced. "Well, I don't usually conduct business in the ladies' room, but it's best to keep an open mind about these things, don't you think?"

"I think this is getting a little out of hand," Nick said.

"No, Nicholas. It's all right. I'd like a job." She smiled at Ferrington again, and Nick's stomach dropped to his knees.

As Ferrington started to describe to Maggie the

thrills and chills she'd experience as a spokesmodel, Nick glared at Hoop, trying to telegraph both confusion and annoyance. The whole idea was to secretly install a spy at Vision. Preferably a girl with some sort of investigative background. Not a nymphette like Maggie, who occasionally showed up naked on doorsteps. And certainly not a girl who might as well be wearing an I-Know-the-Attorney-for-Palmer-Enterprises T-shirt.

Well, if Nick hadn't already decided that trying to get Maggie in as their Girl Friday was the stupidest idea since New Coke, this little stunt would have sealed the decision.

Hoop just shrugged and glanced toward where Ferrington was fawning over Maggie, apparently unconcerned with Nick's irritation.

He ran a hand through his hair. So much for his hope that the birthday surprises had drawn to a close. He sighed. Well, at least the evening couldn't get any more bizarre and complicated.

When the door to the ladies' room swung open and Angela sashayed in, Nick realized just how wrong he was. She turned slowly, her eyes seeking him out. "There you are, darling."

His first instinct was to bolt, but he managed to stay rooted firmly in place by reminding himself that running would only make him look guilty. *Guilty? Guilty of what?* Automatically, his eyes found Maggie.

Oh, yeah.

Angela glanced pointedly at Ferrington, then

back to Nick. "Unusual place for a business meeting. Anyone mind if I join in?"

"It's not a meeting, Angie. I'm just having a little one-on-one with my sister."

Angela looked with disinterest at Deena and Maggie, then aimed her million-megawatt smile directly at Ferrington, managing not to let any of its shine bounce off Hoop. "My Nickie hates to admit that he mixes business with pleasure." She leaned closer and lowered her voice. "But the fact is, he's ever so good at both."

Ferrington took a half-step backward. "I'm sure that's true, Ms. Palmer. But so far he has nothing to admit. I think I'm the only one sneaking a little business in. I was about to suggest that Ms. Goodman's friend audition for a job on my show."

Like a hawk suddenly realizing it was hovering over a field mouse, Angela turned her focus to Maggie. One ring-laden hand extended toward the girl, and Nick was struck by the dichotomy between these two women who, for the moment at least, played a huge role in his life.

"We haven't met," Angie crooned, as Maggie tentatively grasped her hand. "You are . . . ?"

"Maggie," she said, her voice stronger than Nick expected. "I'm Maggie."

"And I'm Angela."

"I know. You're the bi—"

"Birthday boy's fiancée," Deena rushed to put in.

Nick turned to his sister, and she gave him a sheepish grin. He stifled a chuckle.

"Right," said Maggie. She looked toward Nick and rewarded him with a self-satisfied smile.

"And you're a friend of Deena's? How sweet."

"We just met."

"Oh." Her social chit-chat going awry, Angela deflated a bit. "I thought he said . . ." She trailed off, looking to Ferrington for help.

Time for a rescue. "Mr. Ferrington's mistake was quite natural," Nick said with a glance toward Hoop. "I imagine Mr. Hooper may have overstated the situation."

Hoop shrugged and hoisted himself up on the antique vanity near the door. "Just calling 'em how I see 'em." He leaned against the wallpaper, his arms crossed over his chest.

"Well, then, whose friend *are* you?" Angela demanded.

Maggie's gaze darted to Nick, then back to Angela.

Ferrington stepped up to the plate. "Forgive me if I intruded in a private matter." He took Maggie's hand. "When you're finished here, find me if you're interested." He kissed the back of her hand and headed for the door, stopping short of the threshold. He turned back. "I am curious about one thing. Have you ever been in front of a camera?"

"A camera?" She nibbled on her lip. "Oh! Yes. I think so. Yes."

Ferrington looked to Nick, pushing his glasses up on his nose. "I knew it. The camera would have to love her." He pulled open the door. "The audition's yours if you want it."

The door swung shut, and Angela turned on him, her eyes flashing and color rising in her cheeks. "What the hell were you thinking?"

"Me?"

"You embarrassed him. No wonder he left. Really, Nick. What happened to your finesse?"

He kept his mouth shut. No sense telling Angela that he had a hard enough time maintaining self-control around Maggie. Actually finessing a meeting was way out of the question.

Hoop jumped off the vanity and strode to the middle of the room. "I can't believe I'm saying it, but for once I'm gonna side with the Ice . . ." He swallowed. "With Angela." He plopped down on the arm of Maggie's chair. "I mean, he's the one coming after Mags, here. He's doing all the hard work for us."

"She can't work for him."

Angela put her hands on her hips. "Why not?"

"Because we just had this cozy little tête-a-tête." He turned to Hoop. "Not that I wanted to use Maggie as our girl in the first place, but what were you thinking? Even if he was to hire her, it wouldn't do us a damn bit of good."

"What was I doing?" Hoop repeated. "Cleaning up her mess, that's what I was doing." His finger pointed accusingly toward Angela.

"Me?"

"Yes, you. You want to acquire Vision for

Daddy? I suggest you leave the maneuvering to the professionals."

Angela turned to Nick, her mouth set. "Would you like to tell me what he's talking about?"

His answer to that would be no, because Nick was just as clueless as Angela. He turned to Hoop, hands out to his sides, silently begging an explanation.

"Just hiding out in the open," Hoop explained, a bored expression on his face.

Angela's brow arched toward the ceiling.

Hoop sighed, shifting on the armrest. "Miss Priss here gets all gung-ho and invites Ferrington, right? Okay, that's cool. Except my number-one draft pick's also at the party. And my buddy Nick's talking and dancing with her, and Ferrington's watching the whole thing and practically drooling."

Nick nodded, following Hoop's reasoning.

"That makes no sense whatsoever," Angela said. "I'm completely confused."

"Babe, I'm not at all surprised."

Angela glared, but Hoop just grinned.

Nick started to jump in with an explanation, but Deena beat him to it.

"If Maggie had just shown up for the audition, Ferrington would have suspected something was up since he saw her with Nick. But since Hoop went out of his way to introduce her, he's gonna figure it's all innocent." She shrugged. " 'Cause who'd be stupid enough to introduce your target to your spy?"

"Deenie, my love, there's hope for you yet," said Hoop, and Deena began to intently study a worn patch on the carpet. "Plus, since Ferrington was the one who noticed her and asked for an intro, I figure the odds of him suspecting Mags are pretty slim."

Angela clapped her hands together. "Well, it's perfect, then."

"So, I can have the job?"

Nick put his hands to his temples. "No," he said to Maggie. He turned to Angela. "It's not perfect. Maggie is not going to be our mole."

"What now?" Angela asked.

He almost shrugged as he searched for a reason that sounded sane. Because if Maggie was working for Ferrington, that would mean he'd be working with Maggie, too. Behind the scenes, trying to glean whatever information she learned on the job. In other words, he'd be working *closely* with Maggie.

His mouth went dry and he shoved his hands into his pockets, grappling for a reason and thrilled when an idea finally came to him. "Because she doesn't even know who she is. Maybe she already has a job."

"Well, whoop-de-do. Hell of a lot of good it'll do her now. What's she supposed to do? Stand in the middle of Wilshire Boulevard, flag people down, and holler, 'Hey, do I work for you?' "

Nick glared at Hoop. "Maybe she should be concentrating on getting her memory back, instead of running around trying to earn a buck?"

But he knew it was a lame excuse. What was she supposed to do, sit cross-legged on the floor saying "omm" and hoping some inkling of memory seeped back into her brain?

"Nickie, you're being silly. She'll be on television. Maybe her family or friends will see her. That would be the best thing for her memory. Not sitting and waiting for some recollection to spark."

"We're seeing history being made here, folks," Hoop said. "That's the *second* time old Angie here's said something that makes sense."

"All day?" Maggie squeaked, still curled up in her armchair. She licked her lips and looked down at her feet. "Oh, dear."

"What?" Deena asked.

Maggie looked up, pushing her short hair off her forehead with the back of her hand. "A job would be during the day, wouldn't it?"

"That's the traditionally accepted time period," Deena said. "Personally, I think the nine-to-five routine is a total downer. But, hey, to each his own. Me, I'm a night person."

Maggie rubbed her teeth lightly along her knuckles but didn't say anything.

"Maybe Ferrington should be recruiting Deenie," Hoop said. " 'Cause this gig's at night." He looked up at Nick. "Remember? Vision lost their *evening* hostess. The show airs from eight to ten, I think. One of those live call-in things."

Suddenly Maggie was all smiles. "Oh, well, that will work just fine, then." The smile she flashed

Nick warmed him to his toes. "You could say I'm a night person, too."

"Lovely. That's settled, then. She'll audition."

Nick smiled at Angie, glared at Hoop, and tried not to look at Maggie. "Fine. Great. She auditions. How wonderful. Couldn't be better."

The hell of it was, it really couldn't be better. Without even trying, Nick's crew had managed to get this girl a coveted audition. The girl seemed to have a thing for him, so he shouldn't have any trouble convincing her to share what she learned about the company. And Ferrington liked her, so the odds were good she'd get the job.

She'd get the job, Nick would get his information, and Palmer Enterprises would acquire Ferrington's company. The perfect setup.

Except that Nick would be working closely with this woman who scratched him in places he never knew itched. And his fiancée would be looking over his shoulder the entire time. Just perfect.

He mentally kicked himself. He was a professional. She was an informant. A witness. Nothing more. In fact, he didn't even have to deal with her. Hoop could handle her. Sure. He'd leave it all to Hoop.

But then Nick looked at Maggie and saw her feet tucked under her on the chair, her chin resting in her palm, her delightful green eyes soaking up every inch of him. She looked adorable. Innocent. Sexy.

A finger of something suspiciously close to possessiveness crept up his spine. No way Hoop was getting his paws around this gig. No way at all.

He shook his head. What the heck was he thinking?

Nick backpeddled. That wasn't what he'd meant at all. No, he'd meant that he knew Maggie wouldn't cooperate with anyone but himself. He had no choice, no other option but to be in on this investigation. Because of Maggie, he didn't have the luxury of waiting for Hoop's reports from the trenches. Though if it were up to him, he'd sit back and let Hoop run the show.

Really, he would.

He caught Maggie's eyes, and she smiled. He looked away, swallowing. Purely professional. They'd keep the whole thing on the up-and-up. He'd meet with her for an hour or so every night after she left the studio. Debrief her. Nothing big, nothing intimate. And then they'd both go about their lives. He'd get the company for Palmer. He'd get the promotion at work. He'd marry Angela. Life would be good.

He clapped his hands together, a gesture designed to work up his own enthusiasm. "Okay, I guess we've got a plan." He focused on Maggie. "Why don't you go work out the details with Ferrington? Then you and Deena should go home. She'll help you with clothes, makeup, whatever you need." He turned to his sister. "Won't you?"

"No problem. Hell, I took some acting classes. I'll teach you those vowel things you do to work out your mouth." She opened her mouth wide and took a breath. "Oh . . . you A, E, I, O, U," she said, stressing every syllable and making the string of vowels sound like an insult.

Maggie stared at Deena like she'd lost her mind.

Nick rolled his eyes.

Deena shrugged.

"I don't want to stay with Deena," Maggie said. "I want to stay with you."

She was staring right at him, a victorious little grin playing at her mouth. Well, she could just wipe that look right off. No way she was moving into his house. No way, no how.

"Pardon me?" Angela looked up from the fingernails she'd been inspecting. "You want to move in with Nick?"

Well, hallelujah, Angela. Who would've thought his fiancée would be the one to rescue him from his . . . well, from Maggie?

"I think that's a great idea," Deena said. "I'm a little cramped for space."

"I'm gonna side with Deena and Mags on this one. The kid should stay with Nick." Hoop winked at Angela. "Sorry, babe. But two out of three ain't bad."

Ignoring Hoop and Deena, Angela turned to face him, her hands on her hips. "That is really *not* acceptable. People might talk."

So much for the fantasy that she might be even the slightest bit jealous. Nope. Angela was just worried about what the neighbors would say. He chuckled, remembering Maggie standing on his front porch, naked as a jaybird for all the world to see. Poor Angela. If she knew, she'd probably have a coronary.

"Would you like to tell me what's so funny?"

He shook his head. "No. No, I think I'll just let it go."

"I mean it, Nicholas Goodman. I won't have this arrangement turned into a farce." She turned to Maggie. "You can stay at his sister's," she announced before turning back to Nick.

"No."

Angela craned her neck to look over her shoulder at Maggie. "What did you say?"

"I want to stay with Nicholas."

"Not possible."

"Then I don't want that job."

"What?" Nick said.

"What?" Angela said, at exactly the same moment.

Deena snuggled back into the cushions, mumbling something about this "being good." Nick didn't even look toward Hoop, afraid his friend's glow of pure amusement would blind him for life.

"I said that I don't want the job unless I can live with Nicholas."

"Look, Maggie, you'll have a lot more fun with Deena, really. She—"

"Why on earth do you insist on staying with Nickie?"

With watery eyes, Maggie looked from him to Angela and then back to him. He was afraid she'd burst into tears before she could explain. And he really wanted to hear her explanation. Some little part of him even hoped it would be convincing.

"Because he's my . . . I want . . ." She stopped, and disappointment washed over him. Without a good reason, he could hardly offer her his guest room. Not with Angela standing there ready to spit nails.

"For cryin' out loud, Nick. You're the kid's touchstone."

"Excuse me?" said Angela, voicing exactly the question Nick had intended.

"Her touchstone," repeated Hoop. "Her amulet. Secret weapon. Whatever. Point is, you're Mags's only link to her memory. You stick her over in Deena's place, she may never remember who she is. She'll end up wandering the streets, eating out of dumpsters, just one more Maggie Doe for the rest of her life."

"That's right," Deena chimed in.

"They have a point, Angie," Nick added.

"I could care less about the little minx's memory. I need her in that studio with Mr. Ferrington." She glared at Maggie who, he noticed, looked rather like his cat after she'd succeeded in begging tuna fish from him.

When Angela turned back to Nick, she wore her I'm-above-all-this social smile. "Fine. You win." She twisted her head to include Maggie in her gaze. "Happy?"

Maggie didn't move a muscle, and Nick exhaled, relieved that she had the presence of mind not to push her luck.

"Hell, yes." Hoop, it seemed, wasn't as concerned about pushing Angie's buttons. "Come on, Deenie. Let's leave the little ménage à trois alone and go raid the buffet."

Deena practically flew across the room. She and Hoop slipped out the door and past a crowd of women gathered outside, probably on the verge of storming the door.

"A word, Nickie." Angela grabbed his arm and propelled him as far from Maggie as possible.

"There's no reason to be jealous," he said, silently assuring himself that he was speaking the truth. Not that there was any real question. Sure, he found Maggie attractive, but he was an engaged man. And he had no intention of compromising that commitment.

"Jealous? Oh, Nickie, please." It was the same tone of voice Nick would've expected if he'd up and told her he was joining a punk-rock band. Or getting some intimate part of his body pierced. "I'm willing to accept this because it looks like it's the best arrangement for Palmer Enterprises, and that's my priority—*our priority*—right now."

She patted his cheek and his chest tightened. "So you do whatever's necessary to make sure your little houseguest shares any secrets she learns about Ferrington. But at the end of the day, you just be sure to remember who it is who's wearing your engagement ring."

Chapter Eight

Maggie snuggled back against the couch, a mug of cocoa topped with whipped cream in her hands, waiting for Nicholas to return. He'd told her to relax while he made up the bed in his guest room. Silly man. She should have told him they wouldn't be needing two beds. One would do just fine.

Tonight she intended to jump-start her plan. She would make Nicholas love her above all others.

Tonight, she intended to make him her mate.

"That about does it," called Nicholas, stepping into the living room.

She used the tip of her tongue to steal another

taste of the cream. Heaven. She smiled at Nicholas, silently thanking him for this new human treat. With her tongue, she outlined the rim of the cup, making sure she didn't miss any of the marvelous confection.

She heard the whisper of a moan and looked up to see Nicholas clutching the edge of the bookshelf, his eyes trained on her, burning through her. Their gazes locked, and she curved her mouth into a smile. He did the same and took a step toward her, one hand outstretched. She held her breath, wanting his kiss but afraid to wish for it in case her wish didn't come true.

His hand brushed her nose and she shivered at the gentle touch.

"You've got cream on you," he said, his voice deep, hypnotic.

"Oh. I . . ." She trailed off, leaning forward, wanting to lick the last bit of cream from the tip of his finger. Closer. And closer still.

But then he blinked and stepped back, breaking the spell. He cleared his throat and glanced around the room, looking at walls and furniture, anywhere but at her. After a few moments, his brow furrowed and he frowned. She realized he'd switched from avoiding her eyes to searching for something specific.

"Nicholas?"

He crouched down to look under the buffet. "Have you seen my cat?" he finally asked.

"Me?" She stiffened. "Ah . . . seen your cat? No." She knew she was tripping over words, but she couldn't help it, too terrified that if she said the wrong thing or looked the wrong way, he'd realize who she really was. And then he wouldn't want her.

"This is so odd. She doesn't usually disappear for this long." He stepped into the entrance hall and opened the front door. "Maggie? Did you get outside, sweetie? Come here, Maggie-girl."

Maggie tensed, fighting the urge to leap toward Nicholas every time he called. "Maybe she's hiding under the bed. She doesn't like strangers, right?"

He looked over his shoulder at her, one eyebrow cocked. "Now how do you know that?" Before she even had time to back out of her mistake, he went on. "Do you have a cat?"

She licked her lips, not sure how she was supposed to answer that. "I don't . . ."

"I'm sorry," he said. "I wasn't thinking." He shut the door and moved to her side, sitting on the arm of the couch and taking her hand in his. "You probably don't remember, do you?"

His hand engulfed hers, and she felt a warm, tingly sensation start at her fingertips and spread through her entire body. She looked away, fighting the urge to tell him everything, the whole story, and hear him say that he loved her no matter who or what she was.

But if she did that, she would risk everything. So instead of telling him the truth, she had to continue to be one of those amnesiac women like she'd seen on the television. It didn't seem fair, though. He was taking care of her because he thought she needed him. And she did—oh, how she needed him. But not in the way he thought.

She sighed. The least she could do was keep her lies to a minimum and not take advantage of Nicholas's good heart.

"I don't think I have a cat," she said. "But Deena told me your Maggie doesn't like strangers."

With his other hand, he traced the outline of her fingers. "Are you a stranger, Maggie?"

Her heart picked up its tempo, but before she could answer he pulled away, gently removing her hand from his. He stood up and ran his fingers through his hair, making little tufts stand awkwardly on end. Without thinking, she licked the side of her hand, then moved toward him, intending to smooth down the wayward hairs. At the last moment she caught herself and pulled back, tucking her legs under her as she sat back down. Sighing, she balanced her chin on the arm of the sofa, never taking her eyes off him, memorizing the way he moved.

He paced in front of the couch, pausing occasionally to straighten a magazine or throw pillow before finally stopping in front of her. His gaze raked over her body before he glanced away, clearing his throat and looking toward the television. "Do you need anything to sleep in? A shirt or something?"

Maggie restrained a groan. She had to wear these restricting garments even when she was asleep? There were some definite disadvantages to being human. "I don't really want—"

With a wave of his hand, he cut her off. "That's okay," he said, meeting her eyes. "It's probably best you don't tell me the details of what you sleep in."

She bit back a smile, recognizing the same spark in his eyes that she'd seen the last evening when she'd kissed him. *He wanted her*. She was certain of it. So what should she do? Pounce on him? Capture his mouth in a kiss? Would he run? Or would he stay and kiss her back?

The memory of his lips on hers teased her, and she sighed. Yes, a kiss. She needed his kiss.

But just as she started to push herself off the couch, he turned back toward the hallway.

"Wait here a sec. I'll grab one of my robes for you."

Maggie had no intention of waiting a sec. She left her cocoa on the table and padded down the hall behind him. When he stopped abruptly at the door to his bedroom, she slammed into him, then sprang back, surprised and unnerved by how much the feel of his body against her chest affected her.

"Dammit, Deena," he said, taking a step into the room. "I can't believe she did this."

Maggie leaned forward and stuck her head through the doorway. Bed. Furniture. Clothes. Everything looked pretty normal. "What did she do?"

"This." Nicholas gathered some of his short pants off the bed—the ones she'd flung there earlier when she'd searched for clothes—then shoved them back into a drawer. He pointed at the clothes piled on the bed, littering the floor, and hanging out of the drawers. "And this." He pulled open a drawer, shoved the clothes that were spilling out back inside, slammed it shut, then bent down to grab some more clothes off the floor.

Oh, dear. She'd completely forgotten how tidy Nicholas liked his house. She licked her lips. "Um, Nicholas?"

He looked up, his face bland, as if he'd forgotten she was there. Then half his mouth lifted into a grin and he chuckled. "I'm overreacting, aren't I? Sorry." He sat on the floor, his back against the bed, and looked up at her. "It's just that hurricane Deena can walk through a perfectly clean house and in five minutes it'll qualify for FEMA aid."

Maggie frowned, not sure what a fema was. But she remembered the junk that had cascaded from Deena's tote bag. True, Deena was a little messy. "But, Nicholas . . ."

He met her eyes as she trailed off, a dimple forming in his cheek. "Well," he said, "I just wish my sister wasn't Hoop's female counterpart."

Maggie bit back a smile, tucking that tidbit of information away. Nice to know Hoop and Deena were so compatible. But Hoop and Deena weren't her problem right now. The mess was. *Her mess.*

"I did it," she blurted before she could stop herself. Then she took a step backwards, pressing her shoulders against the doorframe, hoping he could still love her even if she'd made a mess, wondering if she'd destroyed her chances of losing herself in his arms.

"You?"

She nodded. "I was looking for clothes."

"Looks like you found some," he said, kicking at the mess that was spread around him on the floor.

She met his eyes, relieved to see amusement reflected there.

"And if I didn't mention it earlier," he said, his voice low, "you looked fabulous tonight."

Her new body hummed as his eyes traced her curves under the thin black material. "I'm . . . thank you."

His gaze lingered a moment before he shook his head and pulled himself up. "I don't suppose Deena thought to buy you any other clothes, did she?"

Other clothes? She recalled those horrible dresses. Surely she didn't have to wear those things. "Can't I just wear your floppy pants?"

"Floppy . . . ?"

She cocked her head toward the chest of drawers. "With the hole in front."

The muscle in his jaw twitched again and she saw him swallow. "Is that what you were wearing earlier? My boxers?"

"Boxers," she repeated. What a funny word. "Yes." She glanced up at him, then back down to study the pattern in the plush carpet. "Is that okay?"

"Sure. No problem," he said, his voice sounding a little strangled. "But I think I'll have Deena take you shopping tomorrow afternoon, okay? We need to get you something for your audition, anyway."

The afternoon? She frowned, trying to figure out the best way to avoid this new complication. "I can't . . . I don't . . ."

"What?"

She sighed. There was no easy explanation. "Can't I just wear your clothes?"

"Tell you what," he said, getting up. He pulled open his closet and removed a white robe. "We'll let you and Deena figure that out tomorrow."

"Okay." What else could she say? If Deena came after dark, Maggie would go shopping. But if she came during the day . . . well, that night Maggie would just have to tell another little lie and say she'd gone looking around the neighborhood.

She ran her teeth over her lower lip. Old Tom's rules were turning out to be quite a burden.

"Well," he said, handing her the robe, "I suppose we ought to get to bed." He coughed. "To sleep. I mean that we should go to sleep."

"Now? Is it almost morning?" She needed him to stay up with her. She certainly couldn't win his heart if he wanted to sleep the night away. Not if that was the only time she was allowed to have with him.

"Pretty near. It's getting close to two."

She slipped the robe over her clothes as she tried to recall what time the sun rose in the morning. If he went to bed now, she'd lose a huge chunk of prime together-time. "Just a little longer, please. I'm . . . I'm afraid to go to sleep." It was only a little lie. She *was* afraid. Afraid that she'd lose the battle to Angela, who could be with him any time she wanted to.

"Afraid?" He stepped toward her and cupped his arm around her shoulder. She snuggled against him, breathing in the wonderful smell that was Nicholas. "Don't worry, Maggie. I promise I'll help you get your memory back." He coaxed her toward the bed and sat on the edge, urging her down next to him. "Do you trust me?"

Wordlessly, she nodded. How could she not? Every day, she trusted him with her life. He'd given her a home. He'd saved her. And he loved her. He just didn't realize it.

She tilted her head back so that she could see his face. "I trust you, Nicholas."

When he stroked her hair, she closed her eyes and tried to purr, but only managed to make a strange gurgling noise in the back of her throat.

"Do you want to talk about it?" he asked. "How you got here? I haven't brought it up because I thought you might need some time. But if you want to talk . . ."

"No. I just want to stay here. With you." She looked deep into his eyes, hoping that, like Old Tom, he could see into her heart. "I'm safe with you."

He pulled her close against him. "Do you want to talk about last night? I've never been greeted by a naked, beautiful woman on my doorstep. And I don't think I've ever met a woman quite so intent on kissing me." He kissed the top of her head. "Do you want to tell me what you remember? How you know me?"

She shook her head against his shoulder, her face pressed against his crisp, clean shirt, her eyes closed.

"Well, Maggie, what *do* you want?"

His words were little more than a whisper, his lips so close that they brushed her ear when he spoke. She shivered. *Had she won?* Something told her that Nicholas was hers now, that he wanted her as much as she wanted him, and all she had to do was go to him, lose herself in his arms. Then she remembered that he still belonged to Angela, and suddenly the winning became a little sad. She pushed the melancholy away. She wasn't going to let quirky human emotions keep her from her goal. She'd won.

"You, Nicholas," she murmured. "I want you." She stretched to meet his lips, hungry for another kiss like she'd discovered last night. At first his mouth was firmly closed beneath hers; then his lips parted and she trembled when they shared breath and soul.

He pulled her close, crushing her against him, his hand under her clothes and stroking her back. She arched against him, the sweet memory of past caresses fading under the onslaught of his skin against her human flesh.

With a groan so low it was almost a growl, he

pushed her away and stood, his back to her, running his hands through his hair.

"I'm sorry, Maggie." He turned to face her, regret lining his face. "I can't do this."

She studied her fingers, still unfamiliar and new. "I understand." She stood up and looked up at him, relieved and happy and sad all at the same time. She blinked to keep the wetness out of her eyes. "Good night, Nicholas."

Only when she was across the hall and into the spare bedroom did she dare take a breath. She wanted Nicholas so badly she ached in every part of her body. But somehow she'd known he wouldn't mate with her tonight, and some tiny part of her had even hoped she was right. Not now. Not with Angela wearing his ring. Hoop had told her that Nicholas wouldn't go back on a commitment, and she'd known that was true.

Just as she'd told Deena only hours ago—Nicholas was honorable.

She climbed onto the bed and curled up into a tight ball, human feelings running wild and loose inside her, mixing her up. Being a woman was turning out to be terribly complicated. And not just because the language, clothes, and food were new and odd.

No, somehow her whole world had changed.

Only yesterday she had wanted him to ignore the other female and turn to her, would have begged him if she could have found her voice. Now, though, something was different. She still wanted Nicholas, of course. But now she understood more *who* Nicholas was. He wasn't like the men she'd seen on television. She'd always known it. Now she understood. Her Nicholas would do the right thing. And the truth was, she loved him all the more for it.

She only hoped that before her time was up, the right thing for Nicholas would be loving her.

Through a fog of sleep, he felt her warm body press against him, and Nick knew he must be dreaming. He had to be. He'd turned her away, kicked her out of his room, conjured up every ounce of his strength just to keep from easing her back on the bed, pressing her shoulders into the mattress, and kissing her senseless. The effort had nearly killed him, but he'd managed it.

So there was no way that Maggie could be snuggled up next to him. He was just dreaming, fantasizing. Hoping.

He rolled over, burying his face in her hair, inhaling the earthy scent of her shampoo.

Her scent? Her hair? He stiffened. This was no dream. Holding his breath, he opened his eyes, then exhaled, relieved. "Maggie," he said, stroking her fur. "Where've you been, girlie-girl?"

His imagination must have been working overtime. He hadn't inhaled his houseguest's scent, or felt her body pressed close to his. This was just his cat. Which only proved that the presence of the other Maggie was making him a little goofy.

His white terry-cloth robe had fallen to the floor, and he stooped to pick it up, then paused.

Hadn't he lent it to Maggie last night? He shrugged and stood up. Maybe he'd given her another one. After all, he had more than a dozen of the damn things, all neglected birthday or Christmas presents, hanging in pristine condition in his closet.

Before stepping into the hall, he slipped on the robe and tied the belt around his waist. He hardly ever wore one, but, under the circumstances, it was probably best not to parade around the house half-naked. He glanced at the clock. Already past seven. Great. He never left for the office this late. Dryson was going to have a fit.

"Come on, Mags. Let's get you and your namesake some breakfast so I can get out of here."

Maggie mewed and stretched, rolling onto her back and presenting her belly for him to scratch.

"Hey, you," he said, bending over and rubbing her fur. "Aren't you listening? I'm late. If you wanted attention, you should have come out from hiding last night." She batted at his hand, and he pulled away. "Ah-ah. No time for playing."

Her mew of protest changed to a twenty-horsepower purr when he scratched her ears.

"Okay," he said, giving her one final pat and heading for the door. "It's breakfast time."

In the hall, he paused in front of Maggie's room and rapped on the door. "Maggie? I've got to run. Want some breakfast? Do you drink coffee?"

No answer. He tapped again. "Maggie?"

His cat intertwined herself between his legs, and he leaned down to scratch her head. "Just a sec, sweetie-cat. We need to feed our guest, first." One last, quick tap at the door. "Mags?"

Still no answer. Well, she was probably exhausted. Not surprising. In the space of one day she'd lost her memory and her clothes. If the poor thing wanted to sleep past seven, who was he to criticize?

He opened a can of fish-flavored food and scooped it onto a china plate for Maggie. Then he picked up her bowl, and filled it with fresh water. He put both dishes back down on the Josie and the Pussycats place mat Deena had given Maggie last Christmas.

While his cat sniffed at her food, he started the coffeemaker and plunked a box of cereal onto the kitchen table for Maggie. A cereal like Cap'n Crunch or Froot Loops seemed more her speed, but generic corn flakes was all he had. Well, she could make do.

Just in case her loss of memory extended to food preparation, he pulled a bowl out of the cabinet, grabbed a spoon from the dishwasher, and wrote a quick note telling her to help herself to the milk in the fridge.

For himself, he poured a glass of orange juice and downed a megavitamin, then rinsed the glass and left it in the drainer next to the sink. He'd have some coffee when he got out of the shower. *Breakfast of champions.*

With Maggie at his heels, he headed for the shower. She tried to paw her way into the room, but he nudged her back with his toe. "What's up, little girl?" With the side of her head, she rubbed his foot, and when he reached down to scratch her ears, she rolled over and demanded that he pet her all over.

He indulged her for about a minute before getting back up and shutting the bathroom door, firmly keeping her out. "Crazy cat," he muttered, having a sudden premonition that today wasn't going to be any more normal than yesterday.

Leaning on the marble counter, he stared at himself in the mirror. He was thirty-three years old, had a hell of a good job, a gorgeous fiancée, a house in the Hills, and plenty of money. A week ago, he'd thought he had it made.

But today . . .

Today his cat was sticking to him like glue, his houseguest had the hots for him, his fiancée expected him to be unfaithful at the drop of a hat, and his job security depended on getting a woman who didn't even remember herself to dig out hidden secrets and reveal them to him. Not a typical morning in the old Goodman house.

Rubbing his hands over the shadow of his beard, he chuckled. Despite all that, he felt more alive than he had in months.

And he'd be damned if he was going to shave today.

The key rattled in the lock and Maggie scrambled to the front hall, the pads of her feet slipping on the tile. She peered at the door, fearing it was the Angela female. The door moved inward, and she sniffed the air, ears back, poised to leap. Ready to shred nylons.

And then . . .

A man's shoe. It was Hoop. She relaxed, purred.

"Yo? Anybody home?" He leaned down and scratched the back of her head. She arched up on her haunches to better meet his hand. "Hey there, girl. Where you been hiding?"

She mewed, and he laughed.

"Sorry, kid. I don't speak cat."

He headed into the kitchen, and she followed at his feet, twisting and turning in figure eights through his legs. At the table, she hopped up onto a chair and then onto the tabletop.

"Oh, man, look at this junk." He picked up the box and shook it, then opened the top and stuck his nose in. "Gag me." He looked at Maggie. "Do you like this shit? What kind of food is this?"

Maggie curled up on the table, her tail twitching, and watched, amused, as Hoop poured a bowlful of flakes, then added milk. He took a bite, made a face, then took another.

"Hello?" Nicholas's voice carried from the back of the house. "Maggie? Is that you?"

She pricked up her ears and mewed.

"What's with the health food?" Hoop asked, as he swallowed a spoonful of flakes. "Haven't you got anything decent to eat? Pop-tarts, Lucky Charms, anything?"

"Don't you knock?" Nicholas crossed the living room and joined them in the kitchen, his tie hanging loose around his neck and the top button of his collar open.

"Why knock when you've got a key?"

Maggie stuck her head in Hoop's bowl and lapped at the milk. It was not as good as cream, but better than the stuff on the floor.

"Maggie!" Nicholas scooped her up and dropped her in front of her dish. "You know she's not supposed to be on the table. And what are you doing sharing your cereal with the cat, anyway?"

"I'm surprised she'll eat the stuff. Now if it was an Egg McMuffin . . ."

Maggie sniffed her food, then reached her paw out and pretended to cover it up. She looked back at Nicholas, hoping he'd notice and offer her something a little more appetizing.

"See, even Maggie doesn't like your cooking," Hoop said.

Nicholas bent down and stroked her back. "It's your fault. This was her favorite food until you decided to introduce her to cereal." He grinned. "And she seems to like corn flakes, so I don't know what you're complaining about."

Hoop eased another chair out from under the table and kicked his feet up onto it. "Well, sure she likes it. By comparison it's dinner at Spago's." He tilted his head, indicating the floor. "What is that junk, anyway?"

Nicholas picked up a can and read the label. "Ocean whitefish in a yummy aspic gel."

Maggie wrinkled her nose, sure that yummy aspic gel didn't compare to kahlua and cream or to the little cheese puffs she'd discovered last night.

"I rest my case."

Nicholas shrugged, then poured a mug full of coffee and passed it to Hoop. "I can't argue with that," he said, pouring more coffee into a tall plastic cup and screwing on a lid.

Since he seemed to agree that Hoop's food was better than hers, Maggie hopped onto Hoop's lap and then back up onto the table. She sniffed the bowl, looked toward Nicholas, then lapped at the milk.

Hoop took a sip of his coffee as Nicholas buttoned his collar. "So where's your little friend?"

"She's still asleep."

"Really?" Hoop waggled his eyebrows. "You two must have had a hot time last night, eh?"

"Oh, you're a regular laugh riot this morning. She's in her room," said Nicholas, knotting his tie. "Where she's been all night. Alone. I didn't have the heart to wake her up just for breakfast. Figured I'd let her sleep until Deena gets here."

"Nick, my boy, you disappoint me."

"Yeah? Well, if it's any consolation, I had to work damn hard to disappoint you."

Maggie almost meowed with delight. She'd been right. He had wanted her. The thought was comforting, and Maggie began to purr, low, almost unnoticeably.

"No kiddin'?" Hoop said. "Sexy, beautiful, and practically throwing herself at you? I would have thought she'd have been easy to resist."

Nicholas laughed. "I definitely wouldn't say it

was easy. For that matter, I'm not sure that *easy* and *Maggie* are two words you should even use in the same breath."

"Fair enough." Hoop nodded at Maggie, still on the table lapping up both the milk and the conversation. "Speaking of Maggies, you're not supposed to be up here," he said, scratching behind her ears.

She tilted her head and watched Nicholas, ready to leap from the table if he scolded her.

He ran his fingers through his hair and sighed. "I suppose it's okay this once." Then he stroked his chin, and she noticed his jaw seemed darker than usual. "I'm living on the wild side today."

"Way to go, Nickie-boy." Hoop slapped his palm against the wood, and Maggie jumped. "Loosening up already. Hot damn. Maybe she didn't get in your pants, but it looks like our little Maggie managed to work some magic after all."

Maggie purred and rubbed Hoop's arm until he noticed and scratched her ears. She hoped Hoop was right. When she'd gone to bed alone last night, she'd felt a long way from working any magic. At least not the kind of magic that could keep her human. But this morning, when she'd crawled into bed with him right before the change, she'd pressed close, letting her human body mold against him. In sleep, he'd draped an arm over her, and she'd felt safe and warm and loved.

She wanted that feeling to last forever.

For that she needed the kind of magic Hoop saw.

And she needed it fast.

Chapter Nine

From her sun-drenched perch on the coffee table, Maggie heard the door to her room slam shut, followed by feet tromping into the living room. Deena stopped in front of the television and glared at Hoop.

"You wanna step aside, babe? You're blocking the view."

Maggie wished she'd move over, too. For the last twenty minutes, she'd been camped out, watching what Hoop had called "those damn boring soap operas." So far, they weren't boring at all. In fact, so long as she was stuck in the house, she was really interested in what was happening at that hospital. She mewed and rolled sideways on the table, trying to see around Deena to the screen.

"The view?" Deena repeated, foot tapping, hands resting on her hips. "You expect me to believe that you're engrossed in 'All My Children'?"

" 'General Hospital.' Where've you been?" Hoop kicked back and put his feet on the table, one sock-clad toe chucking Maggie under her chin.

"Where have I been? I've been looking for Maggie. Who, I might mention, isn't in her room."

Hoop chugged some soda and wiped his mouth with the back of his hand. "No kidding?" He leaned over, obviously trying to see the television, only to give up when Deena stepped sideways and casually blocked his line of sight. "Hey, I'm relieved the girl's outta here. It's already past noon. If she were still asleep, I'd feel guilty for not calling the paramedics or something."

Maggie looked from Deena to Hoop to the television, finally deciding that the show in the living room was a lot more interesting than the one on the screen.

Deena turned around and hit a button on the television and the screen faded to black. "So what are you going to do about it?"

"About what?"

"Hello? You lost Maggie. Or hadn't you noticed?"

"Whoa, whoa, whoa, there, kid." Hoop swung his feet off the table and leaned forward. "How come I'm the one gettin' in trouble?"

"You were here, weren't you? You're the big-shot investigator, aren't you? What kind of detective manages to lose a girl who's right there under his nose?"

Hoop rolled his eyes and tilted his head back so he was staring up at the ceiling. "Maybe she went out for bagels."

Scowling, Deena ran her fingers through her hair, the bouncing curls catching Maggie's eye. Her paw itched to reach out and swat one, but she bit back the urge. She was human now—more or less. She needed to try and act it.

"Oh, that's funny," Deena continued. "Like she's going to walk down the canyon to Studio City." She swept her arm up and down, indicating him. "And look at you. Just hanging out watching the soaps. Nick's going to kill you. Hell, *I'm* going to kill you."

"Slow down. Man, you're wound up tighter than the Ice Queen. You're gonna give yourself an ulcer." He grabbed her hand and tugged her toward the couch. "Now, you just sit down here and tell Doctor Hoop all about it."

Maggie watched as Deena almost sat on the couch but sprang back up even before her backside hit the cushions. Hoop was right. Deena *was* all wound up. And Maggie had a feeling she knew the reason why.

"Hey, come back here." Hoop grabbed a handful of skirt and tugged Deena back toward the couch. "What's with the hysterical female bit?"

"I'm not hysterical."

Hoop grinned. "Glad to hear it. But send me a

memo if you ever are, then. I wanna be sure and be far, far away."

Deena rolled her eyes. "Sorry. I'm just . . ." she twisted her hand in the air. "It's just . . ."

"Maggie's a sweet kid and you're worried about her."

Pleased, Maggie started to purr.

"Listen to that," Deena said, twisting her thumb toward Maggie. "She thinks we're talking about her."

"Yeah, well, you're sweet, too, aren't you, Maggie-cat?" Hoop said, leaning over to ruffle the fur on top of her head. He turned back to Deena. "I'm right, aren't I?"

"It's not just that," she said, licking her lips. "What if she doesn't come back?"

Hoop shrugged. "Why wouldn't she? Where else is she gonna go?"

"I don't know," she said, her voice screeching like a mockingbird. She stood up and circled the table, and Maggie rolled over to keep her in view. "That's not the point."

"So what is the point?"

Deena splayed her hands. "It's just . . . I don't . . ."

"You think she's right," said Hoop, and Maggie rolled back to look at him.

"What? Who's right?"

"Not right as in *correct.* Right as in *the one.* Perfect." He shrugged. "That's it, isn't it? Maggie's just plain *right* for our boy." His tone was calm and reassuring, totally unlike any voice Maggie had heard Hoop use around Nicholas.

Blinking, Deena nodded. "I like her, Hoop. She's a total space cadet, but I really like her. And I don't want Nick to end up with Angela. He deserves better. Hell, I think he wants better. He's just too stubborn to admit it."

"I'm with you, kid," Hoop said.

Maggie almost meowed with joy. They were on her side! They were really and truly on her side. With a huge effort, she forced herself not to leap off the table and run circles around the house. Instead she just rolled around on the coffee table, letting the slick magazine covers slide under her fur as she writhed in pleasure.

Hoop glanced down at Maggie and raised his eyebrows but didn't comment on her antics.

"Well, then, why are you just sitting there? We need to find her. Call Missing Persons or something."

"She's a big girl, Deenie. And the cops aren't going to consider a person missing for at least twenty-four hours."

"But she has amnesia. Can't we at least try?"

Hoop shrugged. "Won't do any good."

Deena cut through the living room to the kitchen and grabbed the phone. "Well, if you're not going to do anything, I am. Nick told us to take care of her today, and all you're doing is sitting there like a lump." She snatched up the handset.

"Hold on." He fumbled in his pocket, then

pulled out a rumpled card. "Call this guy. He's a buddy of mine from LAPD."

"Thanks," she said, snatching the card. She disappeared back into the kitchen, and Maggie heard her punch numbers on the phone, then, "I need to report a missing person. . . . Maggie . . . Hooper told me to call you and . . . Huh? Hoop? Yes, he's here . . . Hold on a second."

She came back into the living room, her forehead creased, two little lines above her nose. She passed the handset to Hoop. "He wants to talk to you."

He took the phone as Deena sank into the recliner. "Hooper here . . . Hey, Doze. What you got for me? . . . Well, hell . . . Nah. That's okay. Just let me know if something turns up." He clicked the phone off and dropped it onto the couch.

"Who's Doze?" asked Deena, voicing the question Maggie wanted to ask.

"Like I said, an old buddy. Name's Roger, but he's built like a truck, so we call him Bulldozer."

Deena pulled her legs up into the chair and smoothed her skirt. "So, how'd he know about Maggie?"

Hoop grinned. "I already called him this morning—when *I* realized our Maggie'd flown the coop. He got a couple of his buddies to help canvas the area, ask at the convenience store on the corner, cruise the neighborhood." He flashed her a weak smile. "Sorry, kid. No news."

Maggie realized she was purring again. Somehow she'd known Hoop was taking care of her.

Not that she needed to be taken care of. She was right there. They just didn't know it. She got up, stretched, then jumped from the table to the couch and curled up next to Hoop, kneading the upholstery with her front paws.

Deena returned his smile. "Thanks for checking."

"No problem." His grin expanded. "Now, come on, Deenie-baby. You never really doubted me, right?" He spread his arms. "I mean, babe, you wound me. How could you doubt the Hoopster?"

Maggie looked up to see Deena laugh and blush at the same time. Then she looked down at her fingernails. "I'm, uh, going to go get some coffee or something. Want anything?"

Hoop shook his head, and Deena scurried to the kitchen, leaving the potent scent of desire in her wake.

Oh, yes, Maggie had been right about Deena. She ratcheted her purr up a notch. The question was, did Hoop feel the same way? And if not, what could Maggie do about that?

Of course, until twilight, she was stuck in her feline body. So there wasn't a whole lot she could do—for Deena and Hoop, or for herself. Not that it was all that bad being a cat again. For that matter, it was kind of nice to take a break from all the novelties of being human. The mall, for example. Lights and noises and smells coming from all directions. And the party. A whirlwind of new sights, new sounds. And Nicholas, even Nicholas. It was nice to have a break from the tingly, tight, *anxious* way she felt every time she thought about Nicholas.

Stretching every muscle until she took up the width of the couch, she dangled her paws off the edge while Hoop idly stroked her belly. As a cat, she *knew* she loved Nicholas. She felt warm and nice and safe in his lap. Her cat feelings weren't all jumbled and confused. Her love was there, and it was strong. But it was mostly in her head.

But as a human, her love for Nicholas burned through every bit of her—her head, her heart, her body. And the feelings weren't calm at all. No matter what else she was doing, her human body, her human soul, longed for Nicholas. Waiting for his touch. Imagining his caress. As a human, she knew in her head that she loved him. But she experienced it with her being, too.

As a cat, the way she felt when he scratched or brushed her, the way his warmth spread through her when she curled up on his pillow at night, didn't come close to comparing to the sensation of being around Nicholas as a woman. She wanted, needed, the way he made her feel. But at the same time, being human—loving Nicholas—scared and confused her. Confused her so much that she hadn't pounced on and kissed him last night, hadn't begged him to forget Angela and love only her. Instead she'd stood back, not crying out and demanding what she wanted as if it was tuna fish or a furry mouse toy.

Human emotions were all mixed up inside her. But scary as it was, she couldn't bear the thought of only feeling safe and loved as his cat, of never feeling passion, or the giddy tease of his touch against her human skin. That just felt *wrong*.

She rolled out from under Hoop's hand and stole away to the far side of the sofa, curling up into a ball in the corner. What torment had she brought on herself? If she didn't make Nicholas love her, she'd stay a cat forever. Nine lives spent knowing what she was missing, never again able to experience that wonderful, magical touch of love. She closed her eyes tight, wishing upon whatever stars could hear. She had to make him love her. She had to.

But even that wouldn't be enough. Not really. Nicholas had to do more than just love her. He had to tell her that he loved her. And Nicholas was too honorable to do that while Angela was around.

Thinking of Angela, Maggie hissed.

"Hey, Maggie-girl. Calm down." Hoop reached over to smooth her fur as Maggie sulked.

Eight more lives with no Nicholas. All because of Angela.

With a twitch of her tail, she uncurled. That simply wasn't acceptable. Time to get moving. Days—and nights—were slipping away.

She slunk back over to Hoop and stretched out next to his thigh, trying to think. The only question was, what could she do to make Nicholas love her more? Or to otherwise solve the Angela problem?

Hoop again ran a hand along her back, then

wiped his fingers on the sofa. "Jeez, Mags. Where's your brush? You're shedding something fierce."

Shedding? She rested her head across his thigh. Shedding. What a perfectly delicious idea!

When he reached over to give her another pat on the head, she nipped his thumb. Just a little love bite to let him know she appreciated the help.

Then she hopped off the couch and, tail held high, headed for Nicholas's bedroom. If she remembered right, the Angela female kept quite a few clothes hanging on the bottom rod in the closet. And Angela did like fur coats. So maybe it was time to bless Angela with the wonderful gift of cat fur.

Nick wasn't himself.

He wasn't real sure who he was, but the fellow sitting in his office, wearing his clothes, and staring at his computer screen was definitely not workaholic, organized, always-on-top Nicholas J. Goodman. He gave a quirky grin. Maybe he'd been kidnapped by aliens and no one had bothered to tell him.

But no, that was the easy explanation. The real reason was about as off-the-wall as aliens, but a lot more difficult to accept—Maggie. Somehow, when he wasn't looking, she'd sneaked into his head and taken up residence there.

All afternoon he'd been trying, without success, to concentrate. He'd logged onto his computer and pulled up the latest SEC filings of a company he was investigating, but something in the dull little rows of numbers and paragraphs of notes reminded him of her, and he had to put the project aside. After lunch, he'd walked down the hall to the library, half-expecting to find her spread across the table like some sultry piano bar singer. By the time he turned the corner and realized that no Maggie would greet him, he'd forgotten what he needed.

In the eight hours since he'd arrived, he'd only billed two hours to a client. The rest of his day was pretty much a write-off. Certainly no client was going to pay him to daydream about his houseguest.

Then again, one client did have a vested interest in him keeping Maggie happy—Palmer Enterprises. For a split second, he wondered just how much leeway Angela really would give him in the quest to keep Maggie smiling. Lord knew, he'd had no doubt last night about how to reach that goal.

His body tightened as he remembered the way she'd looked, lips parted, eyes bright. What would have happened if he'd taken her mouth to his, run his hands along her back, pressed her body close to his own? He shifted in his chair and groaned, then began to list the companies on the NASDAQ, hoping such mundane thoughts would cool his rising body temperature.

"You okay, Goodman?"

Nick looked up to see Larry frowning at him from the doorway.

"You look a little pained."

Shaking off the last remnants of his Maggie thoughts, Nick picked up a stack of documents and banged it lightly against the desktop to straighten the edges of the pile of papers. "I'm fine. I'm getting nothing accomplished today, but I'm fine."

Larry's shoulders rose and his face lit up, as if he'd just discovered that the more he played on the Internet during office hours, the bigger his bonus would be. He dropped his satchel in the doorway, then balanced on the arm of one of Nick's chairs and leaned forward, eyes wide. "So? Tell. Don't leave me in the dark. What tidbit of gossip have I missed out on?"

"No gossip." Nick glanced around his desk for a way out from under Larry's scrutiny. He spotted the telephone. "Just call after call and no time to get anything done."

"Uh-huh." Larry slid off the arm and landed with a plop in the seat of the chair. "Larry's rule number one—never con a con. Rule number two—never try to pull one over on the man who answers your phones. It's been quiet as a tomb here today."

Nick held up his hands. "Well, you caught me."

"It's that girl, right? The one from last night who kept eyeing you across the dance floor. What happened? Get lucky?"

Interesting question. "Not in the way you think." But somehow, Nick felt lucky just having met Maggie. He groaned and pushed his chair back, wondering when this warm, fuzzy, sentimental side of his personality was going to release control of his brain. "I'm not getting a damn thing done." He nodded at Larry's satchel. "You on your way out?"

"Yeah. It's getting near five, and I want to beat the worst traffic. Plus, they say it might rain. Millions of people crammed into this godforsaken town and not a one of 'em can drive in the rain."

An image of Maggie standing in the pouring rain filled his mind. With uncommon clarity he pictured her, arms out to her sides, head thrown back. Her short hair would be drenched and stuck to her head, streetlights reflecting off droplets that coursed down her face. She'd twirl in the rain and laugh, splashing in puddles and soaking her shoes. And she'd look at him and smile with the wonder of it all.

Nick frowned at the papers on his desk and the blinking cursor beckoning from his computer monitor. He knew he should stay. He also knew he wasn't going to. "Give me a second and I'll walk down with you."

They were waiting for an elevator when the Bullfrog passed by. Nick stepped behind Larry and stared at the call button, hoping Jeremiah wouldn't notice him.

"Calling it a day, Nick?" the Bullfrog croaked.

Damn. "Hey, Jeremiah," Nick said, turning around. "I've got some things I need to take care of."

The Bullfrog cocked a finger toward him. "Right. Well, then, you just go ahead. Me, I'm heading downstairs to chat with Dryson about a few things." He aimed a sugar-coated smile toward Nick. "Maybe I'll mention that I bumped into you."

Wonderful. Nick tried not to imagine what Dryson would say if he came in to find his golden boy had cut out early for the afternoon. The thought was almost enough to make him head back to his office and dig in for a few more hours. Then he pictured Maggie. *Almost.* But not quite.

"That's a great idea," said Larry, his voice overflowing with enthusiasm. "I told Nick he should tell Dryson, but you know how modest Nick can be."

Larry nudged Nick with his elbow, and Nick glared at him, sure that his assistant had finally fallen off his rocker.

Crevices appeared in the Bullfrog's pudgy face as he scowled. "Tell Dryson what?"

Larry bit his lip. "Well . . ." He glanced at Nick. "Should we?"

Nick shrugged, clueless, but hoped he didn't look that way, because he had a feeling Larry was on to something.

Larry nodded at him. "You're right. It's Jeremiah, of course we can tell him." He took a step forward, then bent slightly at the waist, urging the Bullfrog closer. As soon as Jeremiah was within whisper distance, Larry spoke up. "It's the Vision deal."

That did it. Jeremiah shot straight up, his face wearing the look of a man seeing his partnership potential evaporating. "You got the company for Palmer?"

Nick couldn't let that rumor live. "No. Not that." He looked at Larry, hoping the kid wasn't going to dig Nick's grave.

"A hot lead," said Larry, then made a zipping motion over his lips. "Can't say more than that. But Nick's appointment is pretty key, if you know what I mean."

The corners of Nick's mouth twitched, and he had a hell of a time not laughing. Just nodded sagely. "We really need to go," he said.

Jeremiah's mouth was open. "Right. Yeah. Well, good luck."

The elevator dinged and the doors slid open. Larry and Nick stepped on, then Nick held out a hand to keep the doors from closing. "Oh, Jer, on second thought do me a favor and don't mention this to Dryson. I'd like it to be a surprise when it all pans out."

Silently, Jeremiah nodded as the doors slid shut.

Nick collapsed against the elevator wall, laughing. "Perfect. Larry, that was perfect." No way in hell would the Bullfrog report on Nick's absence now that he thought it had something to do with Vision. The simple fact was, if Nick could pull off this deal, everyone knew he'd have the partnership all wrapped up and the Bullfrog would be spending another year as an associate—with an associate's salary and without a partner's prestige.

It wasn't until he was almost home, turning off Sunset Boulevard and heading into the canyon, that Nick realized that Larry's little ploy was more than just perfect. In his plot to craft the perfect excuse for Nick, he'd stumbled across a half-truth. After all, Nick was going home to spend the evening with Maggie.

And Maggie was their secret weapon.

Persistent rays from the setting sun filtered through a light mist that hung in the air, casting a greenish tint over the neighborhood. He turned onto his street, passed Hoop's house, then pulled into his driveway. Deena was leaning over, pulling something out of the trunk of her Mustang, when he pulled in next to her.

He stepped out of the car into the damp air just as she slammed the trunk. Turning, she grinned at him, two shopping bags dangling from each of her arms.

"Well, well. You look like my brother Nick, but that's not possible. He hasn't been home in time for dinner in years." She held out a hand for him to shake. "Deena Goodman. And you are . . . ?"

He took her hand, trying not to grin. "No one in particular. Just an alien who abducted your brother and stole his identity."

"That's pretty much what I thought," she said, handing him a bag.

The sun slipped below the horizon, and his porch light automatically turned on, lighting their way to the house. With his sister following, he headed for the cover of the front patio. "I'm guessing Maggie has a new wardrobe."

"Good guess."

"So where is she?" He paused in front of the door and looked back, hoping the anticipation of seeing Maggie again wasn't reflected in his voice.

A shadow crossed Deena's face and Nick's throat tightened. "What's wrong? She's okay, isn't she?"

Deena pressed her lips together. "She's—"

"Nicholas!"

He turned just in time to catch Maggie, still wearing her black body suit, as she launched herself from the doorway into his arms. Laughing, he caught her around the waist and spun her in a circle before realizing that Deena was staring at him, arms crossed over her chest, a smug little smile playing at her lips. He set Maggie down and stepped back, taking in her welcome presence with his eyes.

"Hello, Nicholas. Welcome home." Her eyes shone and she was grinning like a kid on Christmas morning. Nick knew he was the source of her pleasure and the knowledge warmed him. Except for Deena, he couldn't remember anyone ever looking quite so happy to see him.

"Hi, Maggie." He held up the bag. "How come you didn't go shopping with Deena?"

Her tongue darted out, sweeping the corner of her month. "Shopping?" She glanced at Deena, who was looking down her nose in a pretty good imitation of a schoolmarm.

Deena stood with perfect posture, Doc Martin

sandals tapping a rhythm on the wooden porch. "Yeah, Mags. Tell Nick why you didn't go with me and play dress-up."

Maggie's eyes widened, and she looked from Deena to Nick and back to Deena again. "Dresses?" she said, her voice low, almost disappointed.

Waving an arm in Maggie's direction, Deena's perfect posture slumped. She glanced at Nick. "You just can't stay mad at her. It's the most amazing thing." In two long strides, she was next to Maggie, her gauzy skirt fluttering behind her. She swung an arm around Maggie's shoulder. "Don't worry. I remembered. No dresses." She headed through the door with Maggie in tow. "Come on. I'll show you what I bought."

As soon as they hit the living room, Nick stopped dead. A Hoop-shaped lump covered his sofa, soda cans littered the end table, and the magazines from his coffee table were spread out across the floor. Hell, the place was approaching meltdown. He cupped his hand around his forehead and massaged it.

"Sorry. We'll clean it up," Deena said, reading his mind.

He turned, laughing at her kid-caught-in-the-cookie-jar expression. Pigsty or not, there was no denying the grin that remained firmly pasted to his face. "Don't worry about it." Her face lit up, and he held up his hand. "Clean it up, yes. But don't worry about it."

The lump groaned, and Hoop emerged from

under a quilt, sitting up and rubbing his hands over his face. "Is it night already? What're you doing here?"

"I live here. What are you doing?"

"Waiting for Mag—"

She smiled and wiggled her fingers at him from the hallway.

"For Maggie," Hoop repeated, scowling at her. "Where the hell did you come from?"

She opened her mouth, but no sound came out.

"Where did she come from?" Deena said, jumping in before Maggie could speak. "You mean you didn't even know she was back?"

"How would I know? I was asleep."

"That's my point. Why were you asleep when you were supposed to be waiting?" Deena put her hands on her hips and looked down her nose at Hoop.

"What difference does it make? All I'm doing is sittin' here. It's not like I'm gonna miss something."

Deena pointed at Maggie. "You missed her."

Hoop ran his hands through his hair. "She's here now, isn't she?"

"No thanks to you. You didn't even know—"

"Children." Nick held up a hand. "She's here. Let's drop it."

"But—"

He gave his sister his semi-parental glare.

She shrugged. "Okay. Fine."

"The important thing is, she's here." Of course, for God only knows how long, she'd been somewhere else. His stomach churned as he pictured her wandering down Hollywood Boulevard, every hustler, pimp, and two-bit drug dealer from miles around tagging along after her. He turned back to Maggie. "Just where were you, anyway?"

Maggie's eyes widened even more, and she glanced from him to Hoop to Deena. "Out," she said, in the smallest possible voice, the word almost a question.

Deena's arm hooked around Maggie's shoulder. "Nick, you're scaring her."

"I'm scaring her?" He focused back on Maggie and took a deep breath. "Where, exactly, is 'out'?"

She pointed toward the door. "There. Outside. Around the houses."

"Well, congratulations, kid," said Hoop from his nest on the sofa. "You must have a knack for blending in, 'cause my cop friends have been patrolling this neighborhood since this morning and not a one of 'em saw you."

Her pink tongue moistened her lips and disappeared again. "I was thinking. Trying to remember. I remember better outside."

"Did you remember anything useful?" Deena asked.

Maggie shook her head. "No. But I think I should walk around outside every day." She looked up at Nick. "During the day. For my memory."

In Nick's mind, the drug dealers and pimps from Hollywood suddenly relocated to his secluded little street. "I'm not sure that's such a—"

"Nick! It's her memory."

Between Deena's indignant defense and Maggie's silent plea, Nick knew he'd been beaten. Especially since Hoop wasn't helping. He was still on the couch, looking more groggy than interested.

Maybe best to try a middle ground. "Well, we don't have to decide tonight." He fixed Maggie with his best authoritative glare. "But tomorrow you stay in. Please."

Her brow furrowed. "Tomorrow?"

"Your audition's tomorrow night. Sleep in, and Deena can come over in the afternoon and work with you. Okay?"

She stared at the ground.

"Maggie?"

"Okay, Nicholas." When she lifted her head, she looked him straight in the eye. "I'll sleep in tomorrow morning."

Nick nodded. He was absolutely sure that she was telling him the truth. But at the same time, he had a sinking feeling that he was missing something.

"Can I show Maggie her new clothes *now?*" Deena asked, in a tone better suited for someone who'd missed three canceled flights on Christmas Eve.

"You gals gonna give us poor slobs a fashion show, or do we just get to sit out here, bored out of our minds, watching prime-time television?"

The grin that split Deena's face was one of pure delight. "What do you say, Maggie? Want to show off the Maggie Fall Collection?" She smiled at Nick. "Considering what I bought, I guarantee the boys won't be bored."

Maggie graced Nick with the tiniest of smiles, blushed, then nodded.

Nick swallowed. "Great."

From the time she could walk until she started to drive, Deena had loved to play dress-up, traipsing through the kitchen to model her latest creation while he struggled over homework. Nick had always been amused.

With Maggie doing the modeling, however, amusement was the last thing he expected. Arousal was more like it. Not that getting him turned on would be any great trick. Hell, he was already halfway there just being in the same room with this woman.

"We gonna get any refreshments with this show?"

Deena smiled at Hoop. "Actually, you are. I stopped at MacGuire's on my way home and put in an order. Should be here any minute."

Hoop clutched his chest. "Deena, my darling, I think this is true love."

For a second, Nick thought his sister actually blushed, but he chalked it up to the lighting. Deena Goodman simply wasn't the blushing type. And Hooper could hardly be called a ladies' man.

"Hold that thought," said Deena, looking up from the floor. "You may change your mind when I tell you that I didn't have any cash. So the food's coming C.O.D."

Hoop shrugged. "Can't let money come between true love." He waved a hand toward Nick. "Pay the man when he comes, will you?"

Deena actually giggled. Another something she never did. If she could giggle, maybe a blush wasn't that far off the map. Nick tried to catch her eye, to see if he could read a clue on her face, but she was busy bustling Maggie off to change for her runway debut.

So he looked instead at Hoop. His best friend's hair shot out in about twelve different directions, he was slouched on the couch wearing a T-shirt that had probably started out white but had been washed with something very red, and a pile of debris had already gathered around him. He was like the messy little guy from the Peanuts cartoons, only older.

No, he had to be imagining things. Most women ran screaming from Hoop. Then again, Deena wasn't most women. *Interesting.* He caught himself wondering what Maggie thought, and smiled at the image of him and Maggie curled up on the couch, chatting about Deena's latest antics, Nick worrying like a fiend and Maggie absolutely certain that whatever Deena did would turn out okay. It was a scenario that appealed to him. And one he couldn't even imagine with Angela.

When Deena had insisted that Nick quit paying her rent, he'd tried to talk to Angela about his sister, explaining that he worried about her selling her art from a pushcart on the Santa Monica

Promenade. Angela had agreed wholeheartedly. Not because she was afraid Deena would get mugged walking to her car late at night. No, Angela thought it was beneath Nick to have a street vendor in the family.

That was the last time he'd tried to talk about Deena with Angela. He'd certainly never told her about Deena's bizarre childhood insistence that fairies had promised her everything would be okay after their parents had died. He'd been terrified then that she was going to lose it—that the stress would somehow suck her under and he'd end up losing the only family he had left.

She must have picked up on his fear, because she quit talking about the fairies and started painting them instead. But sometimes—every once in a while—he'd see her hunched over in the flower garden, and he'd wonder what she thought she was doing. On even rarer occasions, he'd join her, giving in to some secret, jealous part of his heart that wanted to see through his sister's eyes. None of which would make any sense to Angela, but he had a feeling Maggie would completely understand.

The doorbell rang, interrupting his musing, and Nick's mouth watered like a dog at suppertime. Knowing Deena, the food would be heavy on taste and low on health, with ample portions of the grease and carbohydrate food groups. It would not be what he would order for himself—ever—but since she'd gone to the trouble of providing dinner, it would be rude to complain.

He opened the front door, expecting to see the MacGuire's Deli delivery boy holding a bag of fried chicken, mashed potatoes, biscuits, and a hot apple pie.

But there was no boy, no biscuits.

Just Angela.

Chapter Ten

Looking at Maggie, Deena knew one thing for certain—if her brother's eyes didn't pop out of his head, then Nick Goodman was dead. Decked out in her new duds, Maggie would turn the head of any male within a ten-mile radius. And any female, too, for that matter. Maggie was one of those women who clothes were made for, the kind of girl other women loved to hate.

But with Maggie, even a tinge of envy was out of the question. Just one look at her—staring at the mirror, eyes bright, fingers tracing her hips in black capri pants—and any green-eyed monster who might consider nipping at Deena's heels immediately dropped dead.

For one thing, Maggie was just too sweet, too unaware of her own appeal. How could Deena be jealous of someone like Maggie?

Not that Deena would ever compare herself to Maggie, anyway. After all, there was no way in a million years that Deena would go out in pubic wearing painted-on pants and an itty-bitty, sailor-striped, midriff-baring top. But in them Mags looked perfect—casual and sweet and not even the tiniest bit like a streetwalker. Which was a good thing, especially considering Deena's shopping spree had mostly focused on stretchy pants, clingy tops, and open-toed sandals, all of which were now laid out like a rainbow on the bed.

No one could call Deena Goodman a fool. No, sir. After seeing the way Nick's eyes had roamed over Maggie last night, Deena had aimed Nick's credit cards like tiny smart bombs, ending up with a trunkload of the stretchiest, perkiest, *sexiest* clothes she could find.

And if she did say so herself, she'd done a damn fine job.

"About ready? Nick's gonna die when he sees you."

Maggie whipped around to stare at Deena, her eyes huge, her finger pressed against her open mouth. "Die?" she whispered.

"No, no, no," Deena said, holding up a hand and stepping toward Maggie. "It's just a figure of speech, Mags."

Relief practically oozed off Maggie. "Oh." Her brow furrowed. "What does it mean?"

Deena leaned back against the door, arms crossed over her chest. "You know, I'm beginning to think amnesia's not your problem at all. I think maybe you're from another planet."

Maggie shook her head. "Oh, no. I'm sure I'm from here." She glanced at the floor and back up at Deena. "You're positive Nicholas won't die? I wouldn't like that at all."

"Don't worry. I just meant that he'll be blown away, knocked off kilter."

"Painful," Maggie whispered.

Deena gave herself a mental shake and reminded herself that patience was a virtue. "It means he'll love it, Mags." She walked behind the girl, grabbed her shoulders, and turned her to face the mirror. "He'll think you're hot stuff, totally sexy, and he'll want to jump your bones." Maggie bit her lip, and Deena sighed. "That means he'll want to make love with you. Okay?"

Maggie smiled and nodded. "Oh, yes. That sounds nice." She turned around to face Deena. "Thank you for the clothes." She picked at the Lycra-blend material clinging to her thigh, pulling a little tent away from her skin and letting it spring back. "They're like my cat suit."

"Yeah, well, you can't argue with success, and my brother obviously liked your cat suit, too." She walked to the door and put her hand on the knob. "Okay, let's go show you off for my brother and Hoop."

"Wait."

The word came out as a plea, and Deena turned back around. "What's wrong?"

"I'm not sure how to flirt."

"Flirt?"

Maggie nodded. "Hoop said I needed a plan. Flirting and Ferrington. That's the plan."

"Ferrington? You mean the job?"

"Yes, but that's tomorrow night's plan. Tonight I need to flirt because "Melrose Place" doesn't work. I already showed up naked and kissed him, and Nicholas still doesn't love me."

Deena opened her mouth but closed it again, unsure what to say. She took a breath and tried again. "Hoop told you this?" *Amazing.* Deena tried to imagine Hoop and Maggie having a conversation about how to lasso Nick, or about Maggie naked. Or even about reruns of syndicated shows with sexpots. She tried a moment longer. Nope. She could imagine Hoop telling Maggie to just jump Nick. But flirting? That she couldn't picture. "Hoop really told you to flirt?"

"Yes. But I forgot to ask how. I thought I knew." Maggie's eyes welled with tears and her chin started to quiver. "But now I'm not sure, and I'm afraid if I don't get it right, Nicholas won't love me. And he'll stay with Angela, and I'll stay a ca—"

"A what?"

"What?" Maggie repeated, looking like a teenager caught stuffing her bra.

"You were going to say something. That you'll stay . . . something."

"Oh. Yes. I'll stay here with Nicholas. That's what I want."

Deena massaged her temples. Maggie had been planning to say something else, and she was dying of curiosity. But the girl's lips were zipped tight. Well, it had probably just been some lustful thought about Nick, and Maggie was too embarrassed to say it out loud.

"Deena? Will you teach me how to flirt?"

Considering that Maggie already hung on Nick's every word and looked at him in abject adoration, Deena wasn't real sure what more Hoop thought she should do. Pout? Make inane small talk? Giggle? Surely Hoop didn't think Nick would fall for that kind of transparent nonsense.

"Hell, Mags, I'm no expert. But it seems to me the whole point of flirting is to let the guy know you like him."

With her lips pressed together and her brow furrowed with concentration, Maggie nodded. "I can do that."

"There's nothing to do, kid. That's my point. If Nick hasn't already figured out that you've got the hots for him, then my big brother's running a few brain cells short of a full set. Just be yourself. Be yourself to the max."

"Myself . . ."

Deena nodded toward the door. "Ready?"

Maggie turned back to the mirror, then licked the side of her hand and smoothed back her short hair. Deena made a mental note to buy Maggie some hair gel.

"Ready."

"Here we go." Deena pulled open the door and tried to make the sound of a drumroll. "Welcome," she boomed, "to the First Annual Deena Goodman Fashion Extravaganza, featuring Maggie the Model."

"Wait a second, Deen." Nick's voice filtered back to her.

No way, José. If she stopped now, Maggie might chicken out, and Deena was dying to see Nick's face as Maggie paraded past him with the hip-swinging runway walk Deena had taught her. She started clapping wildly, leading Maggie down the short hall to the living room.

But when she reached the threshold, she stopped dead, and Maggie plowed into the back of her. No Nick. No Hoop. Just the enemy, sitting right there on the couch, legs crossed, hands primly settled on her knee.

Well, if that didn't beat all. Her brother and her favorite person had both vanished, leaving her least-favorite person sitting alone in the living room looking a lot like a spider queen surveying her web.

Wasn't that just dandy?

Hoop raised his eyebrows as Deena's laughing and clapping died abruptly. "Told you she wasn't just going to stop. If you want someone like Deena to listen to your orders, you're gonna have to train her better."

He slapped the top of his beer bottle down

against the edge of the counter, neatly popping the cap, and, fortunately, not dinging the Formica.

"They've invented this thing, you know. Marvelous device. It opens bottles." Nick opened a drawer and pulled out a bottle opener. "Let me demonstrate." With one quick motion, he popped off the cap. "See? It's all in the wrist." He took a swallow.

"Fine. Don't listen to me. You're the one with a catfight about to erupt in your living room—and it's hell getting blood out of white carpet."

Despite Hoop's definite lack of housekeeping abilities, he had a point. "I'm going to go keep the peace." He gestured toward the bags MacGuire's had just delivered.

"Gather up the grub, will you? They say food calms the savage beasts."

"That would be Angela, right?" Hoop said, as Nick stepped around the corner and into the living room. Deena was standing just inside the hallway. Maggie was pressed behind her, her fingers latched onto Deena's shoulders.

"Hello, Angela," Deena said, sounding vaguely like Jerry Seinfeld greeting Newman. "What are you doing here?"

"Apparently I'm here for a fashion show. And it's so nice to see you again, Maggie," she added, her voice saccharine sweet.

Maggie shrunk back, using Deena as a human shield between her and Nick's fiancée.

When Angela had arrived five minutes ago,

Nick hadn't felt the urge to explain why he'd left work early. But now, he felt compelled to tell Maggie that he hadn't invited Angela over.

He frowned at the thought, telling himself that the impulse didn't mean anything. Of course not. He just wanted to protect her. She thought she'd be showing off her new clothes for friends. And though Angela might think Maggie was the cat's pajamas if she could get Ferrington to spill some secret they could use, that didn't make Angela Maggie's friend. Not by a long shot.

He took a step forward, his heart lifting a little when his eyes met Maggie's, and her mouth curled up in a smile. "Angela dropped by my office and heard that I left early."

Angela turned toward Nick. "Jeremiah explained that you were working on Daddy's deal. I certainly didn't expect a fashion show."

Nick moved to stand behind Angela. "Deena bought Maggie some new clothes. She has the audition tomorrow."

"Of course." She leaned to the left, looking around Deena to Maggie. "But you should have asked my advice. I'm not sure that beachwear is the best costume for a television hostess."

"Thanks for the tip, Angie," Deena said, with the sugary-sweet voice that always meant trouble. "But I also bought some cute little overblouses. So don't worry. Maggie will look just fine. And I'm sure Ferrington will have some idea of what he wants for a wardrobe, anyway."

"I'm sure he will. I just don't want to risk losing

this opportunity." She smiled at Nick. "That's why I came by. To make sure everything was going according to plan."

"What's the matter, Angie-baby?" Hoop said, coming into the living room. "Afraid your little Nickie's not man enough to take care of the plan?"

"Of course not. I—"

"Or maybe you think he's plenty man enough to take care of Maggie."

"Hoop," Nick warned.

Angela flipped her hair over her shoulder. "Don't be absurd. Nickie would never do anything like that."

Last night he had been sorely tempted to do something exactly like that. But he hadn't. It had taken every ounce of his strength, but he hadn't. And now, he had to admit that it was kind of nice to realize that Angela trusted him.

"Nickie wouldn't dream of doing anything that jeopardizes Daddy's business."

Disappointed, Nick exhaled. He should have known that Angela didn't actually trust him—just his business acumen. His eyes drifted to Maggie. From the moment he'd met her, she'd made no secret that she trusted him. Hell, she trusted him with her most important possession—her economic survival.

"Daddy's business? How romantic," Deena said, deadpan.

"Marriage isn't necessarily about romance." Angela paused just long enough to wink at Nick.

"Though Nickie and I do just fine in the bedroom department."

"Way to go, hotshot," Hoop muttered behind him, his voice low enough that Angela couldn't hear. "Maybe a little more hanky-panky would thaw that Popsicle heart of hers."

"Gag me," said Deena, in a voice plenty loud enough for everyone to hear.

Nick ignored both of them. Apparently, so did his fiancée. In fact, about the only one paying any attention at all seemed to be Maggie. She took a tentative step around Deena and crawled over the arm of Nick's leather swivel chair. She crouched in the seat, balancing on her heels, never taking her eyes off Angela.

"If it's not about romance, then what is it about?" she asked.

Business. Nick knew exactly what she'd say.

"Business, of course," said Angela.

That's what Nick had told himself when Angela had suggested they get married. Only foolish sentimentalists marry for love, he'd admitted. And considering the sky-high divorce rates, the sentimental saps didn't have a very good track record.

All true. And with a hefty career carrot dangling in the distance, it had seemed like such a good idea at the time.

So why did he feel like he was missing the bigger picture? Why now, when he was so close to partnership—to everything he'd ever dreamed of—that he could almost taste success?

"Marriage is a compromise, like any partnership," Angela went on. "Each partner brings something to the table." She smiled at Nick. Not her trademark flash of pearly white teeth, but a real smile that even held a hint of pride. "Nickie's a brilliant attorney. A woman would have to be a fool not to marry him."

Nick's heart twisted, and for an instant, he was reminded of the way he'd felt when he and Angela had first met. Back before he'd realized that the only things they had in common were their goals. Nick had wanted to be successful enough that he never had to worry about where Deena's next meal was coming from. Angela had wanted to head up her father's corporate empire. They were two compatible goals. It had seemed to make sense that the people would be compatible, too.

Until this week, he hadn't seriously questioned the wisdom of that conclusion.

Deena ran her hand along the edge of the bookcase. "Well," she finally said. "I won't argue that Nick's brilliant. But if that's the case, then why are you here checking up on him?"

Angela glanced at Maggie, then moved her shoulders in a dainty shrug. "All businesses need a little quality control."

Nick laughed. "The audition will go fine, Angela. I promise." He aimed his smile at Maggie. "Do you still want to do a fashion show?"

She looked from Angela to Nick. "No. Thank you."

Hoop ambled over and leaned against the back of the couch. "Tell me this—do all the clothes

Deenie bought for you look pretty much like this?"

Without losing her balance, Maggie reared up a bit on her legs, arched her back, and looked at her own outfit. Then she sat back on her heels. "Yes."

"Well, hell and damnation, Angie-baby. Look what you're making me miss out on."

Deena laughed, then slapped her hand over her mouth.

"Nick, too," Hoop went on. "I mean, the man's only human."

"How about dinner?" Nick suggested, glaring at Hoop.

"Just calling 'em as I see 'em."

"Maggie? Deena? Angie? Food?"

Maggie licked her lips. "I'd like food, please."

The fact was, she hadn't eaten since that morning, when she'd finished Hoop's cereal. In the late afternoon, she'd picked at the ocean whitefish in aspic sauce that Nicholas had left on the floor. He was right. It had used to be her favorite. Today, however, she hadn't even been able to abide the smell.

And now . . . now the mouthwatering smell of chicken was wafting toward her from the cartons spread out on the kitchen table. Her stomach rumbled. She'd have to remember to hide some real food in her room tonight, so that tomorrow she wouldn't have to eat fishie food and tuna treats during the day.

"Come and get it, then," Nicholas said.

Maggie sprang from the chair and headed for the kitchen, more than ready for food.

"Wait a second, dear."

Angela's red claws reached for her, and Maggie slunk back, out of reach.

"You have tags hanging off of you," Angela said. "Let me just cut those off."

Maggie glanced at Deena, who shrugged. She moved one foot toward Angela, paused, then pulled it back. Then she frowned, realizing she was being silly, and darted forward, ending up right in front of Angela before she could stop herself.

"Such enthusiasm," Angela said. She reached out and fingered the little paper tag hanging from the waist of Maggie's pants. "Not bad," she said, looking at Deena. "I'm surprised you even knew how to find the designer sections."

"I'm just full of surprises," Deena said.

"Really? Your outfits are never a surprise. Though they are always . . . unique."

Deena's eyes narrowed and her hands fisted, but she didn't say anything, just stared at Angela.

Maggie didn't understand at all. Deena's gauzy skirts had always been one of Maggie's favorite things. Whenever Deena sat in a chair and let the multicolored material flow down, Maggie would sit under her, the edges of the material draping over her neck and ears. And if she was bored, she could always swat at them. But Angela seemed to be saying that she didn't like Deena's skirts.

She looked at the outfit Angela wore. Navy blue

cuffed pants and a jacket with shiny buttons. It was a lot like something she'd seen one of the magazine girls wearing. But Maggie couldn't figure out why her clothes would be better than Deena's.

"Can we run through the worst-dressed list later?" Hoop said. "I'm ravenous over here."

"We certainly wouldn't want to keep you from the trough," Angela said. She took a little pair of scissors out of her purse and cut off the paper hanging from Maggie's clothes. "There you go."

"Food?" Maggie said, her eyes on Nicholas.

He grinned. "All your walking around work up an appetite?" At her vigorous nod, he laughed. "Well, come on, then. Let's eat on the patio."

"The patio? Nickie, it's raining," Angela said.

Maggie looked at Nicholas, not sure what that had to do with eating.

"The porch is covered," he said.

"It's humid."

"Your fiancée's worried about her creases decreasing and her hair falling," Deena said.

Falling? Maggie cocked her head and stared at Angela's hair, wondering why she hadn't noticed before that this woman also shed. But her hair was always perfect and her clothes were always neat, so she must not shed very much, unlike Maggie and her earlier antics in the closet. Then, she'd managed to shed quite a bit. She concentrated on not smiling, all the while wishing she could tell Deena or Hoop. Surely either one would appreciate her efforts.

"Her hair? Is that what she's worried about?" Hoop asked. "I thought she was worried about melting."

"The patio was just an idea, Angela," Nicholas said. "We can eat inside."

"No, no. I'm happy to defer to the majority." She smiled at Hoop, a big smile, showing two full rows of gleaming white teeth. "Besides, if I don't, Hoop might think that all it takes to get rid of me is to douse me with a bucket of water."

"Great. So it's settled," Nicholas said.

Maggie squirmed, not wanting to take Angela's side—even for a little bit—but agreeing that being drenched by a bucket of water wouldn't be any fun at all. She recalled the one time Nicholas had given her a bath after she'd discovered his fireplace. She'd been wet and cold and extremely unhappy. And then she'd hid under his bed for six hours, until he finally coaxed her out with fresh tuna and a litany of sweet talk and apologies.

But sitting on the patio during the rain wasn't anything like being submerged in water, and watching the rain had never made her shed, so she didn't understand why Angela wouldn't want to go outside.

Angela stood up. "But I'm certainly not going to sit outside in the damp wearing this outfit," she said, and Maggie tried not to smile at the thought of Angela going back to her home. "I'm going to go change."

Maggie froze, trying to keep her face innocent and her eyes on the ground. Angela walked past her toward the hallway, and Maggie shifted from one foot to the other, waiting for the ruckus she knew would come as soon as Angela noticed her clothes.

Nicholas nodded toward Deena. "Grab some plates and things, will you? And there's some wine in the fridge." He grabbed a sack off the kitchen table, then held the door open.

"Nicholas Goodman!" Angela's voice echoed from Nicholas's bedroom. "Where is that damn cat of yours?"

Maggie jumped and considered climbing on top of the bookcases. She shook herself, remembering that wasn't an option, then looked at Deena, Hoop and Nicholas, hoping they hadn't figured out that she was the culprit. Nicholas was holding the door open, and she bolted through it, desperate to get outside before Angela came back, even though she reminded herself that Angela couldn't know she was guilty.

The moment she stepped out of the house and onto the patio, Maggie's nose twitched. The heady odor of damp soil and grass assaulted her senses, and the pitter-pat of raindrops on the metal roof enticed her. She crept to the edge of the patio and poked at the dripping water. Immediately, her finger was soaked. She jumped back, knocking against Hoop.

"Whoa there, kid." He hooked an arm around her shoulder and held up a bag with his other hand.

She bit her lip, a reminder that she shouldn't

swat at the bag, grab the chicken, and run off under the bed. No matter how hungry she was, that would be a mistake.

Hoop looked at the bag, then squinted at Maggie. "Hungry?" At her wordless nod, he smiled. "Then let's eat."

Nick watched as Angela picked apart her chicken breast with the fork she'd insisted Hoop bring out to her. She took a dainty little bite, then wiped the corner of her mouth with her napkin before looking up and catching his eye across the table.

"I mean it, Nick Goodman. Your cat hates me."

Beside him, Maggie spilled her milk and Hoop snickered.

"Cat's got taste," Hoop muttered into his napkin.

Nick ignored him, glancing instead at Maggie, who dropped her napkin over the puddle and started sopping. Then she gave him a weak smile, held a chicken leg up to her mouth, and took a bite, her adorable mouth closing over the well-seasoned skin.

The rain continued to fall, beating a rhumba on his recently replaced patio roof and creating a curtain of water where it sluiced over the side. Beyond the waterfall, the yellow tint of his landscape lights lit the redwood deck that highlighted his postage-stamp yard. Earlier, he'd imagined Maggie in the rain. Now he imagined her running barefoot across his grass, hopping up onto the deck, and twirling in the downpour.

"Nickie! Could you at least pay attention when I'm talking to you?"

He blinked, fighting off a wave of guilt, and gave Angela his full attention. If he was going to imagine any woman dancing in the rain, it should be his fiancée. He bit the inside of his cheek to keep from laughing at the idea of Angela frolicking. The image was absurd anytime, but especially right now, when she was still wearing her perfectly tailored navy pantsuit, fresh from her last shopping trip on Rodeo Drive. "You're welcome to wear my sweats, Angie."

"I don't want to wear your sweatpants, Nicholas, darling. I want to wear my own clothes. I spent an entire weekend coordinating the wardrobe to leave at your house. I have perfectly good clothes right here that aren't made out of fleece and held together by a drawstring."

Nick shrugged. "Just offering. You're the one who didn't want to get your outfit damp."

"My outfit would be hanging neatly in the closet right this very second, every crease still perfectly pressed, if it wasn't for that cat. She did this on purpose, Nickie. She's never liked me."

"Who can blame her?" Hoop asked, then waggled his eyebrows when Angela glared at him.

"Hoop . . ." Nick warned, wondering why he even bothered trying.

Deena reached into the bucket and came out with a chicken wing. "Come on, Angela. She's just a cat. She doesn't like you or not like you. She was just doing cat things."

Out of the corner of his eye, Nick watched Maggie systematically lick each one of the fingers on her left hand, her tongue sliding over her skin. He groaned, looking away when she started on the right hand.

"Just a cat," Angela repeated. "Just a cat? The little beast methodically pulled down every piece of clothing I have hanging in that closet. And she must have spent an hour rolling around on them. I don't think I've seen more cat fur in my life."

"I'm sure she didn't do it on purpose," he said, not really sure at all. Angela definitely didn't make Maggie-cat's top-ten humans list, but he couldn't imagine a cat planning and carrying out a premeditated furring. Most likely, Maggie had been playing and gotten a little carried away. Still, his cat knew she'd been a bad girl, that much was sure. Usually he could find her if he looked hard enough. But fifteen minutes of solid searching had turned up no sign of her.

"The hell she didn't." Angela waggled a finger at Nick. "I swear, Nick, you need to figure out a way to control that little monster. You should get her spayed or something." She looked away from Nick. "And what are you staring at? Do you know anything about this?"

He turned to see Angela aiming an icy gaze across the table at Maggie, who was nibbling on a biscuit, her unblinking green eyes matching Angela's piercing blue gaze.

"Angela . . ." Nick said, his voice low.

"Attacking your foot-in-the-door at Ferrington's shop?" Hoop said. "There's a real smooth move."

Angela scowled, then pasted on her best smile and aimed it at Maggie. "Sorry. I'm just a little frustrated. Nickie's cat and I go way back, and I have to say she detests me. Fortunately, the feeling's mutual."

Maggie's face never changed. For that matter, she didn't even blink. "I like the cat. I like her a lot."

"You've seen her?" Nick asked. "Tonight? I haven't seen her since breakfast."

Maggie licked her lips. "When I got back. Hoop was asleep. I saw her then."

"Maybe Maggie knows where her namesake is hiding. Why don't you see if you can find her, since Nick and I had such terrible luck?"

With her nose crinkled, Maggie just stared at Angela. Nick was pretty sure he even saw her ears twitch. He had the feeling that if Maggie'd had claws, the catfight Hoop had predicted would be starting just about now.

"I'm thinking that changing the subject would be a real good idea," Deena said. She turned to Maggie. "Nervous about your audition?"

Moving only her head, Maggie turned from Angela to Deena. She smiled, then nodded.

"Just be yourself, kid," Hoop added. "That's all Ferrington wants."

"You'll do great," Deena said.

Angela caught Nick's eye. "This isn't over," she

whispered. "We're going to do something about that cat."

"Later, Angela." He looked again at the wet wonderland that had taken over his backyard. "Want to go dance on the deck?" He told himself he was asking in jest, but part of him wanted her to say yes, to surprise him. To give him just an inkling that they were even the tiniest bit compatible in ways that didn't involve sharks and chum and corporate America.

One eyebrow arched. "Are you insane?"

Okay. Seems tonight wasn't his night for surprises.

Deena bit her knuckle but didn't say a word, and Hoop eyed him as if he was nuts, which made one more thing about which Hoop and Angela agreed.

"I'll dance with you, Nicholas."

His chest constricted and he turned to Maggie, planning on telling her no. The thought of walking into the rain—into his fantasy—with her was too enticing. Too dangerous.

But when he saw her face, innocent and open, he stood and held out his hand. "M'lady."

Her fingertips burned against his palm as she stood up, her eyes darting to the curtain of rain and then back to him.

He glanced down, planning on telling her to take off her shoes, but saw that she wasn't wearing any. He was, and he slid out of his loafers. In his socks, he moved to the edge of the patio, urging Maggie along with him.

She stuck a finger into the waterfall from the roof, then pulled it back as if burned. When she looked up at him, he saw wonder dancing in her eyes. Could amnesia have made her forget the rain? She was acting like she'd never walked out into a rainstorm before.

"You've been in the rain before, right?"

Her teeth worried over her lower lip, and she poked at the water again, this time keeping her hand under the cascade. "Oh. Yes. Of course. Somehow it just seems . . . new."

"Maybe she's from the desert," Hoop said.

"Maybe the rain had something to do with why you lost your memory," Deena offered. "A torrential rainstorm. A car speeding down Mulholland Drive. There was a crash, the squealing of brakes, and then—"

"Deena!"

Maggie's eyes were wide, and she'd stepped back from the water.

She shut up. "Sorry. I get a little theatrical sometimes."

"Sometimes?" Hoop rolled his eyes. "Don't worry, Mags. For one thing, this is the first storm we've had in months. And for another thing, I already called in some favors and checked out accident reports, and I seriously doubt you were in a wreck. At least not one around here." He looked around at the others. "Besides, she doesn't have a scratch on her anywhere. Does she, Nick old buddy?"

Nick ignored Hoop and turned back to Maggie. "Ready?"

She nodded and started to step through the downpour to the series of stepping stones leading to the deck.

"Really, Nick", Angela said. "This whole thing is ridiculous. What's come over you? You're going to ruin your suit. And Maggie's clothes are brand-new. Entertaining the girl is one thing, but I think you're taking the role of good host a little too far."

Maggie pulled back, putting her wet foot down. She picked it up, saw the wet print, and put it down again, then smiled up at Nick. His heart leapt at the mischievous joy reflected in her eyes.

"Get a grip, babycakes. Unlike some people, I don't think either Nick or Mags is gonna melt."

Angela's jaw stiffened as she stared at Hoop. "Melting wasn't one of my concerns, Mr. Hooper." She pointed at Maggie. "Those clothes are brand-new. And *that,*" she said, shifting her aim to Nick, "happens to be an Armani suit."

"No," said Deena, scooting her chair closer to Hoop's. "*That* happens to be my brother. Who happens to be wearing an Armani suit. And if he doesn't care about drenching it, why should you? It's not like it's the only one he owns."

"Trust me, Angela. My clothes will survive."

With her mouth closed, Angela ran her tongue over her front teeth, causing her mouth to bulge out in a not particularly attractive manner. "This isn't like you, Nick."

He had to agree with her on that. It wasn't like him. Not usually. But tonight . . .

Well, tonight he thought it was very much like him.

"The lady wants to dance, Angie," he said. "And it's certainly not like me to disappoint a house-guest."

Angela rolled her eyes. "Fine. I think I'm going to go home now and take a long bath. You don't mind if I leave?" She didn't wait for Nick's affirmative reply. "I already feel damp and sticky enough. You'd think *I* was the one dancing in the rain."

"Wait a little longer, Hecuba. If you're picking up that much moisture, maybe we'll get to that melting stage after all." Hoop leaned back, balancing his chair on two legs, and chuckled. Then he sent the chair crashing down on all four legs again. "What the hell am I saying? Go. Go now. Your bath is calling."

Ignoring him, Angela stood up and buttoned her jacket. She nailed Nick with her stare. "We'll talk tomorrow."

He held his hands up in a what's-a-guy-to-do manner. "Tomorrow," he repeated. As soon as she was back in the house, he turned back to Maggie. "Ready?"

When she nodded, he took her hand, and they stepped through the curtain into wonderland.

Chapter Eleven

Maggie was drenched.

No matter which way she turned or how much she squirmed, she couldn't escape the water. It was clinging to her skin, soaking through her clothes, rolling down her back, plastering each hair to her head.

It was everywhere.

She tilted her head to the side and considered her predicament. She really didn't like being wet. At least, she'd never liked it as a cat. But all in all, it wasn't nearly as bad as she'd expected. Especially with Nicholas there, a little-boy grin on his face, his free hand held out in front of him to catch raindrops.

Still, she was awfully wet. Might as well try to get a little of the water away from her skin. She stopped on the path and stood still, tensing all her muscles, concentrating on getting the water off. Then she shook all over. Or tried to. Her human body didn't seem to be designed for the hearty kind of shake that would send the water flying. All this shake did was make her jiggle all over.

But if the way Nicholas was staring at her was any indication, jiggling might not be a bad thing. He ran his hands up on either side of his face, then slicked back his wet hair. "Too wet?" he asked, his voice hoarse. "Do you want to go back inside?"

"No." To prove it, she tilted her head back and closed her eyes, letting the droplets land on her forehead, her eyelids, her lips. The drops streamed down her face, and she stuck her tongue out, catching the liquid.

She opened her eyes and saw him watching her, desire pooling in his golden brown eyes. A hint of a smile touched his lips.

"Come on," he said, before he turned away and continued on the path.

As Maggie followed close behind, she wondered if there wasn't something magical in the backyard that night, hiding in the rain that danced between them or in the lights that shimmered like fairies in the dark. Night magic. And she needed all the magic she could get if she was going to win Nicholas.

"Maggie?"

She looked up to see Nicholas, his hand held out to her.

"Second thoughts?" he asked.

Never. She shook her head and started to scramble toward him, then stopped. Running pell-mell into his arms was hardly graceful and feminine.

Keeping her head high and her back straight, she moved through the drizzle toward Nicholas, closer and closer, until she could feel the warmth of his body.

"Hold me, Nicholas," she whispered, curling her arms around his neck. "I want you to dance with me," she whispered.

With a soft moan that turned her insides to jelly, he pulled her close, wrapping his arms around her waist. Every movement of his body sent warmth coursing through her, making her entire body hum.

They swayed together, the air between their bodies charged, almost crackling with passion. He groaned, sliding his hand over her lower back, the gentle pressure enticing and exciting, his touch as eloquent as a thousand words of love.

Heaven. She wanted to stay like that, secure in his arms, forever.

"Maggie," he murmured, his breath hot against her ear. "I can't . . . we can't . . ."

"Shh." She leaned back just enough to reach up and press a finger against his lips, not wanting to hear what he would say. She already knew he wouldn't mate with her, wouldn't love her. Not tonight. Not so long as Angela remained his female.

Right then, though, none of that mattered. Angela didn't even exist. The one real thing in Maggie's world was the rhythm of his heart matching hers as they moved as one together in the dark. She was in his arms and he belonged to her. She knew it. Deep in her soul, she knew it.

In silence, they held each other, Nicholas turning them in slow circles on the deck, moving to a melody Maggie couldn't hear. The rain dwindled and finally stopped. Pressed close to Nicholas, Maggie looked out over the yard. Every leaf and blade of grass sparkled, and in Maggie's mind, nature was congratulating her on a job well done. Deena too, for that matter. When Maggie looked toward the old wooden swing hanging between two sturdy trees, she saw Deena sitting there, her feet dangling, her hand held out toward Maggie with her thumb raised high and a goofy grin on her face.

Over Nicholas's shoulder, Maggie returned Deena's smile. As his arms tightened around her, tender and possessive, she sighed and snuggled closer.

The last thing she noticed before she pressed her face against his shoulder was Hoop, making his way through the wet grass toward Deena on the swing.

She smiled to herself. She'd been right. This night really was magic.

* * *

Outside, the rain still pattered against Nick's roof, the rain and humidity increasing the frizz factor of Deena's hair exponentially. Inside, she sat on the corner of Nick's coffee table, kohl pencil in hand, enough makeup around her to stock Wal-Mart, a half-dozen magazines scattered across the floor. With her toe, she pulled one of the magazines closer and peered down at it, trying to figure out what color eyeshadow the dark-haired model was wearing.

Behind her, Nick shuffled some papers, switching the pile that was next to him on the couch with a new pile from the coffee table. To her surprise, he hadn't said one thing about the pseudo-salon she had going in his living room. At the very least, she'd expected a lecture about not spilling foundation or powder on his ivory carpet. But so far, not a word.

Maybe her high-strung brother was finally loosening up. It was hard to believe, but, then again, a lot of things were changing. Like Nick making it home for dinner. That was enough of a miracle that Deena had considered calling the Pope. But the fact was, divine intervention didn't have a thing to do with Nick's new—and, in Deena's opinion—improved behavior.

Instead, the reason was sitting right across from her, perched on a footstool, waiting for Deena to pick yet another look for the audition. So far, nothing had worked out quite right, but Deena was having too much fun to stop now. She'd already tried the Ivana Trump heavy-handed method. Now it was time to try a little of the Kate Moss barely there routine.

"Okay, let's try this." Deena leaned forward, eyeliner ready, feeling a little like Molly Ringwald in *The Breakfast Club.* Except the girl Deena was making over looked just fine without blush or eyeshadow. Still, the camera lights would wash her out, so they needed to figure out what kind of cosmetics looked best.

And, to be perfectly honest, playing big sister was loads of fun.

"One more time, Mags. Just close your eyes and lift up your eyebrows. Like this," she said, demonstrating again how to get just the right amount of tension so the eyeliner would swoosh on without glopping.

"Oh, that's attractive," Nick said.

Maggie giggled.

Deena opened her eyes and frowned at her brother. "We're doing girl things over here. If you can't sit quietly, I'll have to send you to your study."

He winked at Maggie and she practically preened under the attention. "My sister's sure that men just don't understand the art of makeup."

"Well, you don't."

Maggie looked from Nick to Deena. "I'm not a man. But I don't think I understand it, either."

Nick laughed. "There. It's not just a guy thing."

Deena stuck out her tongue at Nick, then turned back to Maggie, her hand pulling the soft skin under her eye taut. "Look up," she said, then carefully outlined Maggie's lower lid when she complied. "What about it, Mags? Aren't you having fun?"

Maggie started to shake her head, but Deena held her in place as she moved to the other eye. "Oh, no. I'm having fun. I'm just not sure why we're doing this."

"Because you'll need to wear makeup for the cameras," Deena said, leaning back and examining her handiwork. Not bad. The kohl matched her raven-black hair and accented the deep green of her eyes. "You know, I think I started out all wrong. With you, less is definitely more."

Maggie swiped her hair back with the side of her hand, then started to run her hand over her eye.

"Whoa, whoa," Deena said, grabbing her wrist. "You'll smear."

With big eyes, Maggie just stared, her mouth forming a little *o*.

"The makeup. If it smears, you'll look like a raccoon and Ferrington will never hire you. Okay?"

Silently, Maggie nodded. Then she moved her hands to her sides and sat on them.

"Okay. That'll work." Deena rummaged around on the table until she came up with a deep red lipstick. The color was dramatic, but she had a feeling it would have the effect she wanted. Once she'd applied it, she turned to glance at her brother, who seemed to be a lot more interested in Maggie than the work he claimed to be reading.

Good. Maybe she could get him even more interested.

She passed Maggie a tissue. "Blot." Maggie just stared at her. "Pucker up and press your lips against the tissue."

Maggie's head drew back slightly, as if Deena had just made the most off-the-wall request ever. But then her shoulders moved in the slightest of shrugs. With a sideways glance toward Nick, she pressed the tissue to her mouth and came away with a perfect red kiss.

"I don't think you've ever worn makeup before, Mags."

"Why would she have?" Nick asked. "She looks perfectly fine without it."

"Does Angela wear makeup?" Maggie asked.

"Are you kidding? Angela's practically the poster child for every cosmetic company on the planet."

"Oh." Maggie shifted on the footstool, turning to face Nick. "Does Angela look perfectly fine without it?"

A lump rose and fell in Nick's throat.

"If he says yes, he's just being polite. The woman's got nothing on you, Mags. Does she, big brother?" She smiled, knowing Nick would probably kill her by morning. "I mean, Mags wins hands down in all the major categories and has a personality to boot. Not that Angela's even in the running for Miss Congeniality."

"Deena . . ."

With a casual gesture toward Maggie, she

moved in for the kill. "This is the look we're going for, don't you think? Innocence, with just a hint of sex appeal? Desire, mixed with danger. Ferrington will love it." She smiled at Nick. "I mean, what man wouldn't?"

When he fumbled and dropped his pen, she gave herself a mental pat on the back.

He shifted on the couch, finally dropping his papers back on the table and standing up. With his eyes aimed only at Deena, his arm swept the room. "You girls clean up this mess when you're through. I need to go check a few things on the Internet."

Instead of walking between them, he circled the couch, taking the long way to the hall. But Deena wasn't about to let him off that easy. "Here, Nick," she said, holding out the tissue. "Why don't you take Maggie's kiss with you?"

He gave her The Look, but took the tissue. Then he swallowed again. "I mean it," he said, as his gaze moved between the two of them, his jaw set in stern lawyer mode. "I want this room clean."

But as he stepped out of the living room, he folded the tissue and put it in his pocket. In her mind, Deena did a little touchdown dance.

Maggie watched Nicholas leave, then turned to Deena. "Why did you give him the tissue?" Deena had been throwing the soft tissues in the garbage can all night, so Maggie wasn't sure why one was suddenly worthy of Nicholas.

"Lipstick kisses." She shrugged. "Some folks think they're romantic."

Kisses? That wasn't like any kiss she'd shared with Nicholas before. Still, the idea that Nicholas held her kiss in his hip pocket pleased her. "Have you given a lipstick kiss to Hoop?"

A blush crept up Deena's face, deepening until even her hair seemed to turn slightly pink. "Why would I have done that?"

"You like him. I can sme—I mean, I can tell that you like him." She nibbled on her lip, worried that Deena had noticed her mistake.

But Deena just seemed flustered. "You haven't said anything to him, have you?"

Maggie shook her head, and Deena sighed.

She moved from the coffee table to the couch, letting her head fall back against the armrest as she looked at Maggie. "Good. It's nothing, really."

"Why don't you give him a lipstick kiss?" After all, if Deena thought it was good enough for the man Maggie wanted, surely it was good enough for her own crush.

Deena shook her head, sending her curls bouncing. "I don't think the Hoopster's exactly the romantic type, you know?"

Maggie just smiled, recalling the look of surprise on Hoop's face when she'd agreed that he was a hopeless romantic. But Nicholas? Was *he* romantic? She remembered the look in his eyes at his party, the way he'd swung her around when she'd greeted him on the porch, the way he'd held her in the rain. Then she recalled the late hours he kept, the work he brought home, the beautiful days with birds singing and the sun shining where all he did was sit in his study and work while she watched from the windowsill.

She shifted on the stool, then decided to move to the recliner. Perched in the chair with her legs curled up under her, she wrapped herself in her arms, breathing in the smell of Nicholas. He'd offered her the oversized shirt to replace her wet clothes, and she'd rushed to borrow it, anxious to stay close to Nicholas in every way possible.

"You look confused."

Maggie nodded, trying to put her thoughts into words, trying to figure out the secret to loving Nicholas. All the pieces seemed to be right there, but nothing quite fit. And until it did, Angela would win and Nicholas would never tell Maggie he loved her.

"I thought Nicholas didn't want romance. Isn't that what Angela said?" And Angela should know, since she—not Maggie—had Nicholas. The trouble was, Maggie couldn't be like Angela, not even for Nicholas.

She couldn't even come close.

"Angela's gotta say that because she couldn't be romantic even if a rabid Cupid bit her on the butt."

Maggie grinned. She wasn't completely clear on what a cupid was, but she knew what rabid meant. And she liked the image of a little dog like the terrier next door sinking his teeth into Angela's backside and hanging on.

"So what should I do?"

"Do? I think you're doing just fine." Deena

smiled. "I mean, it wasn't Angela who asked him to dance, right?"

Maggie sighed, the memory of Nicholas's strong arms around her waist almost physical.

"Trust me," Deena went on. "My brother may think he needs to run his life like one of his balance sheets, but he's not immune to a little romance. I've been trying for over ten years to get him to look at the world from a different perspective. To be open to possibilities." She shrugged. "You may have managed in a few days what I couldn't do in a few years. I mean, if the way he's taken to you is any indication, he's just dying to be somebody's knight in shining armor. And," she added, "I get the feeling he wants that somebody to be you."

The numbers swam in front of Nick's eyes, and he put down the memo he'd finally managed to digest, an internal report drafted by one of his very first clients. Dryson had pawned off most of Nick's other work to other attorneys in the firm, leaving him more time to focus on Palmer, but Nick still had one or two smaller matters to handle. And he didn't intend to let those clients suffer while he was playing with the big dogs.

Yawning, he ran his fingers through his hair. Next to him, Maggie was curled up on the couch. Deena had crashed on the couch in his study, too tired to drive home. All the magazines were back on the table, neatly stacked in the top left corner. With his feet propped up, Nick was trying to catch up on his reading. Just a typical two o'clock in the morning at the Goodman house.

Except that it wasn't typical at all.

Even though he might be going through the motions of reading, the letters and numbers were making about as much sense as hieroglyphics. And the Maggie dozing beside him wasn't his cat, she was his—what? Nick didn't know. All he knew was that he couldn't get her out of his mind.

He couldn't believe he'd only known her for three days, because it seemed like she'd been with him forever. She occupied his thoughts, filled his senses. No matter where he was, he had only to close his eyes to see into the emerald-green depths of her gaze, had only to breathe deep to catch her sultry, earthy scent.

Feeling a bit like a sappy romantic, he slid his hand into his pocket and pulled out the tissue with her lipstick kiss. He folded it into a near perfect square, then absently rubbed it over his lips.

For days, he'd ached to touch her, hold her close, feel her body crushed against his. Their kiss after his party had tempted him almost beyond belief. But tonight, dear God, tonight had nearly been his undoing, and all they had done was dance.

All they had done? He groaned, leaning back against the firm cushions and staring at the ceiling. No, no, no. To the casual eye, perhaps they'd only swayed in the rain, but Nick knew better. Somehow, they'd danced with Deenie's fairies, and they'd shared something magical. A something that Nick wanted to explore, even as he wanted to run from it.

With a drowsy murmur, she stirred on the couch, stretching out like his cat, then curling back up as she snuggled against a pillow, her toes just grazing his thigh.

Nick froze. Or perhaps he melted. Either way, he forced himself to remain perfectly still as the electric current her touch generated flowed through him, thrilled him. Aroused him.

He fisted his hands, sure that if he didn't, they would move of their own accord to caress her legs. Even though she now wore his sweatpants, rolled over five times at the waist, the image of her well-formed calves shoved its way into his mind.

He'd known that letting her into his house would be a mistake, and he'd been right. By welcoming her into his home, he'd let her into his heart. And, God help him, he didn't know what to do now. Except fight—to keep his head on straight, and his hands to himself.

She shifted again, rolling onto her belly, the friction of her feet against him sending waves of lust roiling though him. When she finished adjusting, she snuggled back against her pillow, her hair mussed, a tiny smile gracing her lips. Her toes now dangled between his legs. Her ankles caressed the curve of his thigh. And right there, so close he had only to move his hand, the perfect curve of her rear tormented him.

Only when he gulped in air did he realize he'd

been holding his breath. Knowing he was playing with fire, but unable to help it, he reached for her. His hand grazed the fleece, barely touching, but Nick was sure he could feel the warmth from her body. He longed to be consumed by that heat. *Her* heat.

Like the box did Pandora, Maggie tormented him. He longed to touch her, stroke her. More than anything, he wanted to hear her whisper in his ear—*Nicholas*—and know that he'd brought her to the heights of passion. But this all was a box he just couldn't open.

With a little yawn, Maggie woke, her head turning as her eyes sought his, delight evident in her deep green gaze. She nibbled on her lower lip, and then her mouth curved into a smile. "Do I look funny?"

Nick laughed. "Hardly. You look beautiful."

Her forehead crinkled as she frowned. Then she rolled over and swung her feet to the ground, reaching for a hand mirror Deena had left on the coffee table.

"You're sure? I really don't look funny?" Maggie asked again, peering into the hand mirror.

Funny was the last word Nick would use to describe her. Beautiful, exotic, wild. But not funny.

She ran the edge of her finger under her eye and scowled at her reflection. "I'm all smeared."

"Well, I'm no expert, but you're not supposed to sleep in makeup." He couldn't hide the amusement that laced his voice. She was right—she was smeared. But even with eyeliner spread under her eyes, she looked amazing.

"I fell asleep watching you."

Nick laughed. "Now there's a rousing endorsement for my potential as a fun date." He regretted the words the instant they left his mouth. No way should he be thinking about her as a date.

"Are you fun?"

Nick sighed, shrugging off the question. The sad truth was, he hadn't thought about fun in a long, long while. Hadn't had time for it. What little fun he'd had in the last year or so he'd stolen from his sister, or from Hoop. Except for one or two working jaunts to London or Paris, his last real vacation had been five years ago, and even then, he'd insisted that the hotel set him up in a suite with a computer and a fax machine.

So no, the Nick Goodman who'd framed his kindergarten diploma, the Nick Goodman who used to play on the Barristers softball team, the Nick Goodman who at one time had actually sung in a karaoke bar—that Nick didn't hang much around these parts anymore.

But that wasn't something he wanted to admit to Maggie.

"Nicholas?" When he looked up, she continued. "Thanks for coming home tonight."

"Where else would I go?"

"Early, I mean."

"What makes you think tonight was early for me?" It's not like she knew him well enough to know his habits, and, Lord knew, he hoped his idiosyncracies weren't that transparent.

"Nothing, Nicholas," she said, but her mouth twitched as if she had a secret. "It's just a . . . um . . . hunch. I would trade money that you usually don't come home until very late."

What was she talking about? "Trade money?"

"That's wrong?"

"That's bizarre." Inspiration struck. "You'd *bet*. Is that what you mean?"

Grinning, she bounced a little on the sofa cushion, clearly delighted that he'd understood her. "Yes. I'd bet."

"Well, you'd win that bet." That's for sure. Nick was probably the one person in Los Angeles who thought the traffic was a breeze. Even on the 101, there just weren't that many cars on the road when he usually went home.

"That's what I mean. Thank you for coming home early." She leaned forward, her hands and knees on the sofa cushions. Keeping her gaze locked on his, she crawled forward until she was right beside him. Then she laid down, her cheek pressing into his thigh, the back of her head tucked against his hip.

Somehow, he managed not to jump simply from her touch, but every cell in his body ignited. Forget two a.m., he was wide awake.

Knowing he probably shouldn't, he stroked her hair, his fingertips trailing over her smooth cheek. He both felt and heard her sigh of contentment, so deep and rhythmic it was practically a purr.

"Thank you for dancing with me, Maggie."

"Thank you for letting me, Nicholas." She rolled over, so that the back of her neck curved against his thigh and her green eyes looked up at him. "It was fun, wasn't it? Dancing, I mean."

His stomach twisted. To say that dancing with Maggie had been fun was the understatement of the year. It had been splendid, erotic, sensual, silly. Every emotion he shouldn't feel toward this woman, all wrapped up in one wet night. And try as he might, he couldn't conjure any regret.

But if she wanted to call it fun, who was he to argue? "Yeah. It was a lot of fun."

"Will you dance with me again, Nicholas?"

His conscience screamed at him to say no, to nip in the bud—right then, right there—whatever was building between them. He even opened his mouth, planning on spouting negatives and platitudes. "Of course I will," he said, every effort to be reasonable and controlled running south of the border.

"You should come home early all the time."

He laughed. This woman just didn't understand how much work it took to get—and stay—where he was in his career. "I don't think my job would last too long if I did that."

"Is it worth it?"

"What?"

"Your job." She rolled over again, no longer looking him in the eye.

"Of course it is," he said, without hesitation. If it wasn't for that job, Deena wouldn't have an apartment, much less a college degree. Working in the district attorney's office for a year after law school might have been challenging and fun, but it had hardly paid enough to cover the bills, much less make sure his sister was okay. And Deena had been his responsibility ever since their parents had died without a dime of insurance during his first year of college.

The second he'd realized Deena couldn't get into a good art program without some financial help, he'd quit working as a prosecutor and taken the obscene salary D & M had offered. It wasn't the kind of work he'd planned to do, but he'd never once looked back.

From the time Deena was eleven, he'd never let her down. And he wasn't about to start now. They'd suffered through food stamps, welfare, and a year of Deena living illegally in his dorm room. No matter what, Nick was going to see to it that his sister never lacked for money.

"Yes," he repeated, more to assure himself than her. "It's definitely worth it." He smoothed her hair. "Why all this interest in my *job?* are you worried about your audition?"

She rolled off the couch, then climbed onto his coffee table, sitting cross-legged on top of the sturdy antique, pushing the magazines onto the floor as she got settled. Nick pressed his lips together, quelling the urge to ask her to get off the table.

"Why wouldn't Angela dance with you?"

Nick shifted on the couch. Comparing Angela

and Maggie was a dangerous game. "Angela is Angela. She's got her little eccentricities just like everybody." He shrugged. "I can hardly fault her for not wanting to ruin a five-hundred-dollar pant suit."

"Do you love her?"

Nick cringed, not at all surprised by her straightforward question. Maggie might seem a little lost at times, but she didn't seem the type to beat around the bush. "I'm going to marry her, aren't I?"

It was a cop-out answer, and he knew it. And, if the satisfied little smile on her face was any indication, Maggie knew it, too.

"We've got a lot in common," he added, somehow compelled to justify his pending nuptials. "She's got an incredible mind for business. Got her M.B.A. at twenty-four and was running two divisions of her dad's company by twenty-six." He coughed. "We'll make a good team."

He recognized the little crease that appeared above Maggie's nose as she processed his homage to Angela.

"I don't know anything about business, Nicholas," she said, her green eyes locked on him. "But I think I know about you."

Swallowing, he tried to look away, but something compelled him to watch her. Fear, perhaps. The fear that she was right, and that somehow he'd managed to get his life completely off track, even while he was telling himself that he had everything he'd ever wanted or needed.

Her gaze drifted to the patio door. "Sometimes, I look outside and think that there's nothing in the world I want to do more than rush out of the house, run in circles, and climb a tree. Then I want to lay back in the grass and let the sun shine on me as I count the clouds in the sky."

He smiled, picturing Maggie running ahead of him through a field of flowers. He imagined him catching her and falling to the ground, his arms braced on either side of her, as he lowered his mouth to hers and lost himself in her kisses.

Maggie's unspoken question hung in the air—would Angela ever do anything like that? The answer, of course, was no.

"Do you ever feel like that, Nicholas?"

"Truth?"

Maggie nodded. "Yes. Please."

"The truth, Maggie, is that I feel that way almost every day of my life. But the way things are, there's not a damn thing I can do about it."

Chapter Twelve

Under the bed, Maggie held the chicken breast down with her paws and took a bite. Thank goodness she'd remembered to leave herself a secret stash. This morning, Nicholas had fed her that canned concoction again, and she hadn't been able to eat a bite. She'd swatted at his blueberry muffin, trying to explain that she wanted a taste, but he never got the message.

Earlier, her hidden cache of chicken had satisfied her rumbling stomach. Now, she wasn't actually hungry. But eating calmed her nerves, and battling the cumbersome chicken breast gave her something to think about other than Nicholas. She had only a few days left to make him realize—

and tell her—that he loved her. But how?

Deena had told her to be herself. The problem was, she wasn't sure what that meant. As a cat, she'd always been graceful, confident, secure. If she wanted something, she simply demanded it. Either that or she'd rubbed and coaxed and mewed until he gave her whatever she wanted. And if that hadn't worked, she'd stared out the window with her tail curled close, the picture of an aloof and independent feline, ignoring Nicholas. That maneuver had always won his attention.

She licked her paw, considering.

Could the answer be so easy? She was becoming more used to her human body, so being graceful shouldn't be a problem. As for secure and confident—well, being human was a little awkward. But, after her initial fear that Old Tom had completely messed up, she really was sure she looked good. If Hoop hadn't said so outright, she would have known simply from the way Nicholas looked at her. Plus, she was certain that the people who liked her as a cat still liked her as a woman.

Most important, she knew with absolute confidence that she loved Nicholas and he loved her. He just didn't realize it yet.

Just like the women on television, Maggie had to go after what she wanted. She'd done it as a cat, and she could do it as a woman.

And what she wanted was Nicholas.

Unlike the women on television, she had more

going for her than just feminine wiles. She could rely on her feline wiles as well.

Turning away from the chicken, she rolled onto her back and stared at the slats supporting the mattress. She wasn't sure what time it was, but from the dwindling light, she was pretty sure twilight was approaching. And that meant her audition was drawing near.

Absently, she swatted at a piece of material that hung over the side of the bed. Last night had been wonderful. Nicholas had held her close, and it had taken all the willpower she possessed not to kiss him, hard, and insist he kiss her back. But she hadn't wanted to risk shattering the moment.

Now, though, time was running out. She needed to be around him as much as possible, and one way to do that was to get this job. If she didn't, someone else would. And that someone else would spend hours with Nicholas every evening, going over what she learned from Michael Ferrington.

No, Maggie had to win Ferrington over at the audition.

She yawned, stretching her body out from her claws to the tip of her tail. When she hadn't been eating, she'd spent most of the day sleeping. After staying up all night with Deena and then with Nicholas, she'd needed the rest.

A noise from outside cut through the stillness in the house, and she tensed, twisting her ears to hear better. There came a squeal of tires, the hum of an engine. All sounds she recognized.

With a mew of delight, she started to run out into the hallway, intending to greet Nicholas at the door. But as her tail brushed the underside of the bed, she realized that probably wasn't such a good idea. She could change at any moment, and changing in front of Nicholas would be a very bad thing. So instead of running to the door, she sat next to the bed and silently urged the sun to set faster.

A key rattled, followed by the creak of the front door.

"She'll appreciate you going with us tonight," Nicholas said.

"Are you kidding? After shopping for her and staying up 'til the cows came home working on poise and voice and makeup and all that junk? I wouldn't miss this for the world." She paused. "Is Hoop going?" she asked, and Maggie heard the clear attempt to sound casual.

"Haven't asked him," Nicholas answered.

"Oh." Disappointment. Maggie would have to see if she could do something about that.

"Maggie?" he called, his voice closer than before.

She slunk back under the bed, terrified he was going to enter her room.

A tap at the door. "Are you still asleep? We need to get going if we want to grab some dinner before the audition." He paused. "Maggie?"

"Not there?" Concern laced Deena's voice.

"I told her to rest, but maybe she went for a walk after all."

Maggie stretched out, hoping to feel the familiar tingle in her limbs.

Nothing.

"Go on in," Deena said.

From her vantage point under the bed, Maggie saw the door swing open and Nicholas's loafers move toward the bed.

"Do you smell that?" he said.

"What?" Deena's bare feet caught up with Nicholas's shoes.

"I'm not sure. Chicken, maybe."

One knee dropped down to the floor, followed by another. When the sheets rustled, Maggie tensed even as her limbs began to flutter with the setting sun.

Then Nicholas's head appeared, his eyes scanning the area under the bed.

She yelped, a strangled mewing sound, and took off, all four legs pumping as she tore past Nicholas, past Deena, and into Nicholas's bedroom.

Nick watched the cat zoom by, jumping back as she zipped past, then losing his balance and landing on his ass. "Maggie!" He looked at Deena. "She's been stockpiling chicken under the bed."

"Huh? Who?"

"Maggie."

Deena blinked. "Which Maggie?"

That was a good question. He ran his hands through his hair. "Hell, I don't know. The cat, I assume. She must have got in the trash last night and dragged a snack under Maggie's bed."

He stood up and looked around the room. The bed was still perfectly made. He frowned and exhaled noisily. Today of all days, he'd wanted Maggie to rest during the day. She had to be ready for the audition.

"Maybe the chicken's Maggie's."

"Why would she eat chicken under the bed when I've got a perfectly good kitchen?"

Deena smirked and Nick shrugged, remembering Deena's story about the kitty snacks. His heart twisted with the realization that when his Maggie got her memory back, the memories might be so unpleasant, she'd just as soon forget them. "At any rate," he said, "we won't know until we find her."

"Want me to go walk the neighborhood?"

He nodded. "I'll catch up with you after I find Maggie cat and make sure I didn't scare her to death."

"Scared *her?*" Deena laughed. "The way she ripped past me, I thought I was gonna have heart failure right then, right there."

"Where'd she go?"

Deena gestured toward his bedroom. "I'll meet you outside."

In his room, Nicholas checked under his bed, looking behind and between the boxes that stored paperbacks he no longer had time to read but couldn't bear to throw away. "Maggie? You there? Come here, sweetie."

No cat.

He stood up, looking around the room, his gaze moving from the top of the bookshelf to the windowsill to the dresser to the closet door, still slightly ajar.

Finally.

He pulled the door open and saw—

"Hello, Nicholas."

—Maggie. The decidedly human Maggie. Sitting right there on the floor of his closet, her legs bare, apparently wearing nothing but one of his white button-downs.

With his heart beating an unsteady rhythm in his chest, he gazed down at her, trying to remember what he was doing, trying to think of anything other than how amazing she looked.

"Have you seen the cat?" he asked, then rolled his eyes at the absurdity of the situation.

"That way," she said, pointing out of the closet toward the bed. "She went that way."

He didn't bother to look, just continued to stare at Maggie. "Maybe this is a strange question, but what are you doing in my closet?"

His mouth went dry as her tongue swept over her lips. For just an instant, her face registered confusion. Then her expression cleared. "I was playing with the cat," she said, a mischievous smile tugging at her mouth.

"In my shirt?"

"Yes, Nicholas. In your shirt." As she moved to stand up, the neck gaped open, confirming what he already suspected—she was wearing his shirt and absolutely nothing else. A wave of longing swept through him, and he gripped the door-frame for support, pretty sure that his fingers would leave indelible marks in the hard wood.

She pulled herself up to her full height and tilted her head back so that her gaze collided with his. There was no mistaking the hunger in her eyes, and he beat back the urge to curl his arm around her waist and pull her close to him.

With a knowing smile, she moved forward, placing one hand on his chest as she stood up on her tiptoes. With her free hand, she beckoned, and he leaned forward, unable to do anything except what she asked.

"I like to wear your clothes, Nicholas," she whispered. "Is that okay?"

Mute, he simply nodded.

She stepped back, her hands going to the top button. "Or should I give you your shirt back now?"

"No," he said, blurting out the word. "That's okay. Maybe you should just go change for tonight."

Before he even realized what she was doing, she lifted up on her toes and planted a kiss on his cheek. Then she darted from the room, his shirt barely skimming the soft swell where her thighs met her rear. The material might be hanging just low enough for modesty, but not low enough to keep his imagination from kicking into overdrive.

With one hand, he touched the spot on his cheek where her lips had burned against his skin. What would have happened if he'd pulled her close, running his hands up under the slightly starched cotton to caress the back of her thighs, feeling her smooth, hot skin as he trailed his fingers upward, tempting and teasing her until she—

He shook himself. His thoughts had no business going there. Not now, not later. Not ever.

He needed to calm down, needed to think straight. Taking a deep breath, he mentally recited the formula for calculating a stock's price/earning ratio.

And in case that wasn't libido-quelling enough, he ran down the closing prices of the top ten stocks in his portfolio.

"Hard to choose, isn't it?"

Blinking, Michael Ferrington poked at the console until the image of a blonde with bright red lipstick froze on the monitor. He shoved his glasses back onto his nose and looked up at Tony. "What?"

"Choosing a new girl. I don't know how you think you're gonna decide. I mean, it's not like any of them are from Dogsville."

Michael frowned. "Did you sleep through the feminist movement?" Tony might be extremely talented with a computer, but political correctness was completely beyond him.

"Feminist-scheminist. These gals are here 'cause they look good and they know they look good."

With a wry grin, Michael swiveled his stool

back around to face the monitor. Tony was right. Beauty and poise weren't an issue for any of the women who'd spent the day streaming through the studio. They all looked fabulous. And they were looking for a foot in the door.

And if they couldn't manage a foot, then a toe would do nicely. In Los Angeles, any job that provided a screen credit and air time was desirable. City of Angels, Land of Opportunity, and all that.

Lord, he loved this town. Where else could a former high school geek who'd started out in cable access end up with his own production company and a hefty income from infomercials? Not to mention his latest coup d'etat—innovative software that should make Vision a leader in direct-to-Internet programming.

With a sweet deal like that just around the corner, not just any girl would do.

"None of these are right. I know the girl I want." And he was damn frustrated that she hadn't shown up. He pushed away from the console and stood, sending his stool scuttling backward, its hard plastic wheels clattering on the vinyl flooring. "I'm looking for enthusiasm, not a pretty face. I want an innocence mixed with sex appeal. A girl people want to tune in to see but are inclined to trust."

"Hell, Mikey, I think Mary Tyler Moore's all booked up."

Maybe Mary was, but that Nick Goodman's little friend was in the market for a job. He paced between the editing bay and the refrigerator, casting a quick glance toward the clock. Eight-thirty.

"Give it up, Mikey. She's an hour late. That should be a little hint that she's not coming." He gave Michael's stool a shove, sending it rolling back toward the bay. "Besides, hiring that Maggie woman wouldn't exactly be your smartest move. Didn't you tell me she's in tight with Angela Palmer and that lawyer dude?"

Michael ignored Tony. At eighteen, he'd come to California with fifty bucks in his back pocket. Now he had a house in the Hills and a bank account so stuffed he had to pay someone money to look after his money. It was a perverse truth, but one that made him incredibly happy. And he'd gotten there all by himself. So he certainly wasn't going to start taking advice from Tony now.

He straddled the stool and scooted up to the bay, letting the tape scroll forward as he watched the silent screen tests. Not one spark among them.

"Palmer's not a problem and neither is the girl," he said, somehow believing that if he talked about her enough, she'd waltz into the studio. "I asked her to audition. Giving her the job was *my* idea."

Tony shrugged. "Doesn't change anything. Palmer's hungry for this company."

"I'm not selling."

"Yeah? Well, tell that to Westside Online. Palmer Enterprises bought them out three months ago, and Nick Goodman closed that deal. Word on the street was, Westside's owner thought it was more prudent to sell than to let Goodman or

Palmer go to the newspapers with some interesting tidbits they'd dug up about a certain call girl's little black book."

"I don't doubt it." In fact, he rather admired the maneuver. Business was no place for the squeamish. "But the fact is, I don't have any secrets." He frowned, then reached into his pocket and pulled out his handkerchief. "More to the point, I can't believe our fresh-faced Miss Maggie would be seeking them out," he said, mopping his brow.

Tony looked over his shoulder at the monitor. "She may not seek, but she may find."

"Thank you, Confucius," Michael said, in no mood for jokes.

"I just mean that your little innocent flower might be just that. But that doesn't mean Goodman or Palmer won't be using her to get information they might find useful."

Michael shoved his glasses up his nose, then ran the handkerchief over his face one more time. As much as he hated to admit it, Tony had a point. But the problem was easy enough to solve. He could test this girl. He just needed some bait—something tender and juicy and completely false.

He smiled, realizing the perfect setup was hanging on the dressing room wall.

"The picture," he said.

"Huh?"

"That charity benefit. Remember? The one where I actually put on that dress and did the skit with those two other guys."

Tony shrugged. "Yeah. So?"

Michael grinned. "There you go. That's my deep dark secret." And that was how he would test Maggie. If the bait made it back to Goodman's ear and the bargaining table, then he'd know for sure they were pumping her for information.

Assuming, of course, that she ever made it to her damn audition in the first place.

With a jerk, Nick shifted the car into park and pulled up the emergency brake. "Okay, everybody out." He looked at his watch. Nine o'clock. "An hour and a half late. Hell, he's probably already cast the part and shot a month's worth of footage."

"Get a grip," Hoop said. "If he wants our girl, he'll wait."

Nick shot his friend a warning glare. "You're skating on thin ice, considering you're the reason we're late." He slid out of the car and opened the back door for Maggie. Behind Hoop, Deena was scrambling out as well.

"Wait, Mags," Deena yelled, holding a tube of lipstick out like a weapon and skirting the back of the car. "Just one more coat."

Hoop's door slammed and he circled the sedan, finally lounging against the trunk. "My fault? How do you figure? I was completely vegged out watching *Mad Max* and catching up on my beer sampling when you called."

Nick shrugged, enjoying baiting his friend. "Maggie wanted you along, but I'm sure as hell not gonna blame her for being late. So I'll blame you. Though why she'd want a wild card like you along is beyond me."

Hoop grinned. "You're an ass, Goodman. You know that?" He fingered imaginary lapels. "I'm a veritable fount of moral support. Of course Mags wants me around." He pointed toward Deena and Maggie, who'd already reached the far side of the parking lot. "You wanna blame somebody, blame the traffic report queen. Shortcut, my Aunt Fanny."

"I heard that," Deena called. "How was I supposed to know they'd closed off a lane?"

Hoop grinned at Nick. "I just love baiting her."

From what little he'd seen, Deena was pretty keen on being baited—if it was Hoop doing the fishing. On a normal day, in a normal week, in a normal month, Nick would have been suffering heart palpitations merely from the idea of his sister cozying up to a man whose idea of planning for the future was sticking a box of Twinkies under his bed. Deenie needed stability. Sense. Normalcy. Today, however, Maggie's audition took precedence over Deena's love life.

"Hurry up, Nicholas!"

"I'm coming," he called, rushing to catch up with the girls.

No, it wasn't just Maggie's audition that was distracting him. It was Maggie herself. Little by little she was unraveling the fabric of his life. That alone he could have handled. He could have used the craziness as a shield to keep her away from his heart. The problem was, she kept managing to knit the strands back together, and the end result was so much warmer and cozier than the life he'd had before she'd appeared on his doorstep a lifetime ago.

With a grin, he realized that he was already planning on asking her if she'd noticed anything developing between Deena and Hoop. Maggie might have an innocent perspective on the world, but she also called things like she saw them. And she was honest. With her there was no game-playing and no backhanded maneuvering. She wanted him, and she'd told him so. And, though she hadn't exactly taken no for an answer, she seemed to at least respect his decision. She was easy to talk to. She was funny. She was . . .

Special.

He sighed. No two ways about it. Maggie was one special woman.

He pulled the door open, then followed Maggie and Deena in as Hoop hustled up the steps.

"If she doesn't get this job, we're back to square one," Hoop said.

Nick nodded. Worse than that, without this job, Angela would throw a fit if Maggie continued to stay on at his house. And Nick had no intention of letting Maggie stay anywhere else. Not anymore.

His stomach twisted at the mere thought of midnight rolling around without Maggie beside him on the couch. She'd get the job. If he had to get down on his knees and beg Michael Ferrington, Maggie would get this job.

* * *

"She's a natural. I just knew it." Michael Ferrington slapped Nicholas on the back, and Maggie jumped when he almost fell into the camera.

"I knew she would be," Nicholas said.

Maggie sat up straighter at the compliment. When Michael—he'd insisted she use his first name—had told her to act natural, she'd felt awkward and unsure. Especially since she wasn't wearing her cat suit. She'd wanted to, but since Deena had spent an entire day buying outfits, it seemed only fair to wear one of them. Still, she'd opted for all black, taking a tiny bit of comfort from that piece of familiarity.

As soon as Michael had started talking to her, though, she'd known it would be okay. He'd told her to pretend that the furniture on the platform was her real house, and to read out loud the words on a card near the camera. It had seemed silly, but she'd obeyed, telling Nicholas and Deena and Hoop all about something called a Veg-E-Fryer. It wasn't until after she'd finished reading the card that she realized she'd crept from the chair to the little couch. It probably had not been a very human way to get from one place to the other, but Michael seemed to like it.

"So I was okay?"

"My dear, you were more than okay. You were astounding. A bright light in the dim night of infomercials."

She blinked, not at all sure what he was talking about.

"She's what?" Deena asked.

Michael laughed. "Forgive me. I get a little carried away sometimes." He stepped up onto the platform and joined Maggie on the little couch. "She's perfect. And she's hired." He took her hand. "That is, if you want the job."

She looked at Nicholas, who gave her an encouraging nod. "Yes, please."

"Wonderful. Wonderful. Welcome to the Vision team." He walloped her on the back, and she scrambled to keep her balance, her fingers clawing into the cushion.

Michael pulled a small leather book out of his front pocket. "I want to start you on Sunday. I've got a little something planned. In the meantime, we'll do a little bit of orientation, some rehearsal. Sound good?"

"That's Halloween," Deena said, stepping onto the platform and plopping down in one of the chairs.

Maggie swallowed. Her time was flying by. She nibbled on her lip, wishing they were away from the studio so she could be alone with Nicholas.

Michael closed his little book. "Actually, I've got a little Halloween idea I'd like to try." He gestured for Hoop and Nicholas to join them. Nicholas crossed the platform in four long strides, finally settling next to her on the armrest of the couch. When he put a light hand on her shoulder, she turned her head and smiled, her eyes meeting his warm gaze. She bit back a contented sigh. *Progress.*

Hoop clambered up the steps and planted himself in a chair all the way across the fake living room from Deena. This time Maggie swallowed a sigh of frustration. What was that saying she'd heard on the television? One step forward and two steps back? Obviously, she still had work to do.

"What's on your mind?" Nicholas asked as soon as Hoop was settled.

Michael looked at each one of them, finally stopping at Maggie. "Children's programming," he said, then leaned back against the seat cushions, apparently waiting for someone to praise him.

"What's that got to do with Mags?" Deena asked, voicing Maggie's question.

"That's the beauty of it. A personality like Maggie's shouldn't be wasted on slicers and dicers." He lowered his voice. "No matter how much money that rakes in for the company."

He leaned back, slapping his palms against his thighs. "Just think of it—children's programming on the Web." This time he practically bellowed, and Maggie shrunk back, pressing even closer to Nicholas. She both heard and felt his soft chuckle. His hand closed over her shoulder, his caress soothing and calming her. She liked Michael, she really did. But he could certainly be loud.

"I'm still not sure how Maggie fits in," Nicholas said.

"Or Halloween," Deena added.

His hands spread wide. "A storybook hour," Michael said, after a dramatic pause. "Vision's going to throw a Halloween party, and we'll tape Maggie telling stories to the kiddies."

"Know any good stories, Mags?" Hoop asked.

She licked her lips. She was living one very good story, but she wasn't sure she could talk about that. Still, if she made it sound like one of the human fairy tales . . .

"I know a story about an enchanted cat," she said.

Deena raised an eyebrow but didn't say anything.

Michael clapped her on the back. "Great. Wonderful. And we'll pull some more together for you to read." He pulled out a handkerchief and mopped his forehead. "You're all invited, of course. It's gonna be a hell of a party."

The strange expression still lined Deena's face. Maggie cocked her head, wondering what Nicholas's sister was thinking.

The couch cushions shifted as Michael pushed himself out of his seat. "Okay, then. Bring your Social Security card and driver's license tomorrow." He looked at her over the rim of her glasses. "Unless you have them on you? We can take care of the paperwork today, if you'd rather."

Panicked, Maggie opened her mouth, trying to make a sound. Nothing. Somewhere in the back of her mind she registered that he wanted legal papers. Documents proving she was a woman. She turned in her seat and gazed up at Nicholas, sure that her face registered pure terror.

"Just so happens I brought all her paperwork with me." Maggie whirled around to stare at Hoop. He nodded toward Deena. "Wanna run to the car and grab my backpack?"

Deena looked about as surprised as Maggie felt, but she just nodded and caught the keys Nicholas tossed to her.

"Glad you remembered to bring all that stuff," Nicholas said. "It didn't even cross my mind."

"What're friends for?" He turned back to Michael. "I brought a passport, driver's license, and Social Security card for Miss Margaret Perdue. I figure that ought to do you good."

Michael looked half-bored. Not surprising, since he was probably wondering why the energy in the room had increased tenfold just because she suddenly had papers. "Sure. That's great. I'll make a copy tonight." He turned to Maggie. "Perdue. That's a lovely last name."

"Thank you," she said, unable to think of anything to add.

"Isn't it, though," Hoop added. "Her family's French, you know." He winked at Maggie. "It means lost."

"In that case, maybe you should think of a stage name," Nicholas said.

She looked back at him, returning the gentle smile playing at his mouth.

"Because you're not lost anymore, are you?"

She shook her head, the tiniest of movements, her eyes never leaving his. "No, Nicholas. I'm not lost at all. In fact, I'm very, very found."

Chapter Thirteen

Drumming a rhythm on the steering wheel, Nick watched as the last link between him and self-control slid out of the car.

"Don't do anything I wouldn't do," Hoop said, ducking his head back in through the open door.

Nick grimaced. *That was the real trick.*

Maggie leaned over the seat and planted a quick kiss on Hoop's cheek. "Thank you for going with me."

"No problemo, babe." He turned to Nick. "Catch you tomorrow." Then he stepped back and slammed the door, leaving Nick alone in the car with Maggie.

Nick rubbed his palm along his khakis. If he'd

been smart, he would have suggested that Deena crash at his place. After all, she and Maggie had spent the drive to Deena's apartment huddled together in the backseat, whispering about who knows what, and going over the brochures Ferrington had loaded into Maggie's arms. It would have been a natural step to suggest they continue their gab session at his house.

So why hadn't he?

The answer nagged at him, but he tried to push it away. In truth, he wanted to spend time alone with Maggie. Best he not analyze that little fact too closely. This wasn't one of those situations where the truth could set him free. More like the truth could chase him, catch him, and throw him to the wolves.

He glanced in the rearview mirror and caught Maggie's eye. Their gazes locked, and then she smiled, slow and confidently. He groaned, his stomach leaping and fluttering with the same sensation that had plagued him the night he'd asked Mary Beth Marker to go with him to the school dance. His first date. That's how he felt tonight. Nervous as a schoolboy.

A schoolboy who'd just lost his chaperone.

With sudden resolve, he hit the button to roll down the passenger window. "Hey, Hoop," he called.

His friend had already made it to the front patio, but he stopped and turned around, the yellow glow from the porch light casting a halo around him. Considering it was Hoop, the effect was more 1950s comic swamp monster than Clarence the angel.

"What?"

Taking care not to look at Maggie, Nick gestured for Hoop to come back. He obliged, finally sticking his head through the open window.

"I thought you might want to come over. Maybe rent a movie."

Hoop didn't look like he was buying it for a second.

"A movie?"

Nick shrugged. "Or a beer."

"Anyone ever tell you that you're transparent as hell, Goodman?"

Nick frowned. "I'll take that as a 'no.' "

Hoop ignored him, turning toward Maggie. "Do you want me to come over and watch movies?"

"No, thank you, Hoop. I want to spend tonight alone with Nicholas." Her words reached out from the backseat, stroking and caressing him.

His throat went dry and his body began to thrum. Nick had serious doubts he'd survive the night.

"There you go, Nick. Straight from our little sex kitten's mouth. I'm not wanted." He turned back to Maggie. "I'm counting on you to keep our boy entertained."

"Hoop . . ." Nick managed, forcing the word, his voice gravelly.

From the backseat, Maggie nodded. "Don't worry, Hoop. I promise I'll stay very, very close."

And from the sound of her voice, Nick had no

doubt that she meant what she said. The realization both excited and terrified him. It also confirmed what he already knew—where Maggie was concerned, he was in over his head and out of control.

With a devious grin plastered on his face, Hoop headed back to his front door, leaving Nick and his libido in the car, scrambling frantically for some semblance of self-control.

"Well," Nick said, as soon as he was confident he could form a word, "why don't we head on home?" He gave himself a mental pat on the back, pleased that he'd not only been able to utter a word, but he'd followed it with an entire sentence. Would wonders never cease?

She started to climb over the bench seat but stopped midway, ending up stretched across the leather upholstery, looking a bit like a gymnast resting on a balance beam, her chin on her hands. She waited there, her breath tickling his ear, until he shifted in his seat to face her.

"Comfy?" he asked.

A smile tugged at her mouth as she nodded.

"Any particular reason why you're straddling the seat?"

The slightest of shrugs lifted her shoulder.

"Because you look a little like you're stalking me." *Or trying to seduce me.*

"Maybe I am." Her grin expanded and she reached out, swiping a strand of hair off his forehead.

He fought the urge to take her hand and pull

her forward, over the seat and into his lap. He hadn't "parked" since high school, and never with a woman as tempting as Maggie. Just the thought of her in his arms, molding herself to him, snuggling up close—

He groaned, trying to ignore the fire that coursed through his body. Pressing his eyes closed, he pictured Angela, Hoop, Deena, and even the Bullfrog. Anything and everything to cool him down and get his mind off Maggie.

Almost as if she understood his predicament and took pity on him, she slid the rest of the way over, settling herself in the passenger seat, her body turned just enough to look at him. "I don't want to go home, Nicholas." She pressed her lips together, then looked down at the seat cushion.

"It's late," he said. "Don't you think we should call it a night?"

She lifted her head so that he could see her green eyes peeking out under her lashes. The seductress was gone. She was just Maggie now, beautiful, innocent, and a little bit shy.

And sexy as hell.

"I want to share the night with you."

Or maybe she wasn't so innocent after all. He stifled a groan, his mind bending and twisting her words, erotic images dancing through his head.

"I've got work tomorrow," he finally said, forcing himself back to reality. "I should get some sleep."

Not exactly true. He hadn't been to bed before "Letterman" in years. But if that's what it took to get some distance and quash the steady stream of erotic thoughts . . . well, it wouldn't hurt him to get a few more hours of shut-eye.

She tilted her head, a mischievous gleam in her eye. "You never go to sleep this early."

"Never? A handful of nights and you know my sleeping habits?"

"Yes," she said simply.

He sighed. Hell, he couldn't argue. She was absolutely right.

He glanced at Maggie, still watching him, waiting for his response. "What do you want to do?" he asked, knowing that he'd agree to anything just to spend the time with her.

"Show me the city. I've never seen it." Her brow furrowed. "I mean, I don't remember it. And the beach. I want to see the ocean."

"The ocean?"

She nodded, her hand reaching out to rest on his thigh. "I thought last night was fun. I liked being wet."

Oh, dear Lord. Nick tried to stay sane, but he was pretty sure that her last comment had melted every bone in his body. He slid closer to the door, pulling his leg out from under the sweet torment of her fingers.

"Please, Nicholas."

He should say no. If he was smart, he'd go home, call Angela, and bury himself in his work. What he should do was put the car in reverse, back down the driveway, careen down the block to his house, race up the sidewalk, run through the house, and hide in his bedroom until whatever spell Maggie had cast over him wore off.

Trouble was, she hadn't really bewitched him at all. It was worse than that. All she'd done was open his eyes.

Voices and laughter danced on the wind. Lights twirled through the sky around them, burning brighter than the wishing stars above them.

Maggie squeezed Nicholas's hand, unafraid because he was with her, excited by the sights and sounds around them.

She tilted her head back, losing herself in the velvet blanket of sky, the stars just pinpricks of light shining through. Her stomach twisted, and she held on to Nicholas as they moved forward, the little box they sat in swaying as it crept through the air.

"What did you say this was called?" she asked, leaning against Nicholas.

He let go of her hand and slid his arm around her shoulder. "A Ferris wheel. Do you like it?"

She nodded and smiled, not sure she could find words to tell Nicholas how wonderful it felt to be flying through the night with him.

The boardwalk rose up to greet them, and their little box bounced to a stop. A bearded man with a long braid draped over his shoulder opened the gate for them, and Nicholas helped Maggie out.

"Where to now?"

With her arms spread, Maggie turned in a slow circle. Her nose twitched as sights and sounds and smells wafted nearby, enticing her. Everything was fresh and new and wonderful, but nothing more so than simply being with Nicholas.

He held out his hand. "Come on."

Walking side by side in silence, he led her past the people selling food and funny-colored toys, then back up the pier to the buildings and lights of what Nicholas had called Santa Monica. She frowned. He was leading her back toward where they had left his car.

"Are we leaving?"

"Not yet."

A woman in a tight red dress stepped in front of Nicholas, holding out a cylinder stuffed with a rainbow of flowers. "A rose for the lady?"

"No, tha—" He stopped, turning to Maggie, an unreadable expression in his eyes. Then his familiar half-grin lit his face, and he nodded. "Actually, yes. I think the lady would like a rose. A red one."

Nicholas gave the woman some bills, then plucked a perfect red rose from the woman's container. Maggie didn't say a word, not certain why he was giving her a flower but somehow knowing that it was important. The moment he handed her that flower, everything would change. And she'd be one step closer to staying with Nicholas forever.

He held out the flower. "A perfect rose for a perfect evening."

With her eyes closed, she lowered her nose to the bloom and inhaled the fragrance. His fingers brushed her cheek, and she opened her eyes to find herself looking deep into his gaze.

"Thank you, Maggie."

"For what?"

For a moment, he didn't answer. He just took her hand and continued down the pier. "For suggesting this," he finally said. "For a fun date."

She smiled to herself, grabbing the *date* word from the sky and holding it close to her heart. "Do you come here a lot?"

"I used to," he said, leading them off the boardwalk and onto a sidewalk. Ahead, she saw a row of cars, and beyond that, the moonlight glinting off the froth of waves that crashed onto the beach. "But that was years ago. I don't have the time anymore."

"Why not?"

"My job, my life." He shrugged. "Dull stuff you don't want to know about."

"But I do want to know," she said, taking his hand. "Tell me, Nicholas. Why do you do what you do?"

"Because I have to."

"Why?"

"Security. Deenie." He hesitated, swinging their hands between him. "Everything."

"Deena?"

Nicholas nodded. "Our parents died when she was just a kid. I pretty much raised her."

"Oh." She frowned, not sure she was completely following. "But you're not raising her now, right?"

He shook his head, a grin tugging at his mouth.

"Sometimes it feels like I still am. I just mean that I'm responsible for her. I need to make sure she's safe. Deena's . . ." He trailed off. "Well, Deena's special. In a lot of ways she's fragile."

Fragile? Deena was a lot of things, but Maggie wasn't sure she was fragile. She must have looked confused, because Nicholas kept explaining.

"She reacts . . . funny . . . to stress. To bad situations."

"Funny?"

Nicholas sighed, then turned to stare out at the ocean. "It's only happened twice." He looked at Maggie. "She's not nuts or anything—don't get me wrong."

Maggie chewed on her lower lip, wishing she could jump up and down and make Nicholas hurry up and tell her whatever this funny thing was about Deena.

He sucked in a breath. "Right after our parents died, she said she talked to a fairy. And then again when I fought to keep custody."

She watched him, waiting for the big news. Nothing came, and she finally clued in. "Oh." She frowned. "That's bad?"

Nicholas raised an eyebrow. "Well, it sure isn't good."

"Was it a bad fairy?"

"Why am I not surprised that this doesn't shock you?" He glanced at her, then away, a muscle in his cheek twitching. When he looked back, he was grinning. "At any rate, this whole magic thing's really a non-issue anyway. I mean, if I can keep her safe and educated with a roof over her head, then everyone's happy, right?"

"Everyone?" Maggie asked.

Nicholas cast her a sideways glance.

She licked her lips, needing to understand him. "Your job. Do you like it?"

The corner of his mouth turned up. "Some days I like it a lot. Others, not at all."

"The thing with Michael. What am I supposed to do? Exactly, I mean."

They walked a few more steps in silence, then Nicholas stopped, rubbing the palm of her hand with his thumb. "Well, you just need to keep your eyes open and remember what you see and hear. Then every night we'll talk, and you'll tell me what you learned."

"And then what?"

He shrugged. "Hopefully, you'll learn something that Vision doesn't want the general population to know. Then I can convince Ferrington it's in his best interest to sell."

Maggie frowned. "That doesn't sound very nice."

He began to walk forward again, stepping off the sidewalk and onto the parking lot. "Don't think about it in terms of nice or not nice. It's just business."

"What if Michael doesn't want to sell?"

"I get paid to convince him he does."

"Oh." That didn't seem at all like the kind of thing her Nicholas would do. "Do you like that part of your job?"

He seemed to bristle. "It's necessary."

"I don't understand."

He maneuvered them through the parked cars to the edge of the sand, then turned to face her. "I'm in a unique position. Because of Angela, I mean. And the firm knows that. So pretty much they've cleared my plate. Except for a few minor matters, Palmer's my only client. If I screw up, I'm out of a job."

She grazed her teeth over her lower lip, wanting to know more—to resolve the riddle of the Nicholas she knew and believed in, compared to the Nicholas who wanted her to spy on Michael and who would marry Angela even though he didn't love her. "But aren't there other jobs?"

"Not for me, not making that kind of money." He pulled his hand free and shoved it in his pocket. "I'm a senior lawyer without a corral of clients to bring with me, so who's going to want to hire me? Plus, I'm on the verge of making partner. Even if I could find another job, I'd be an idiot to jump ship now. Or to screw up and get fired." He smiled but looked a little sad. "I'm pretty much stuck."

She stepped onto the sand, a few grains slipping into her sandals. "Have you always done that job?"

The corners of his eyes crinkled as he smiled. "For a year, I worked in the DA's office."

That she understood. "Like on television? Did you catch burps?"

"Perps," he said, laughing. "They're called perps. It's short for perpetrators, and I just put them away. Hoop caught them." He smoothed her hair back. "Does that seem like a more honorable way to earn a buck than the job I do now?"

Nodding, she glanced down at her toes, embarrassed that he could so easily read her mind, wondering how he could feel honor bound to Angela and yet have no qualms about searching out Michael's secrets. Still, this was her Nicholas, and she trusted him. "I know you have your reasons."

With a finger hooked under her chin, he pulled her head up. "You see an illusion, Maggie, and I'm flattered. But I'm not as honorable as you think."

"Yes, you are. Maybe you just don't know it. But you always have a choice, Nicholas. Always."

"I made my choice eight years ago."

"Maybe you should choose again." She smiled at him. "I believe in you. You should believe in yourself."

His mouth curled in a gentle smile and he stroked her cheek. "You're very sweet, Maggie."

"I'm right. Besides, you've already made one choice. You're here with me, aren't you?"

"But I'm pretending it's work," he said, his voice teasing. "You're my secret weapon, remember? Ferrington?"

Despite his light tone, for a moment Maggie faltered, wondering if the only reason Nicholas was spending the evening with her was because Michael Ferrington had given her the job. But she pushed the fear away. She'd seen the way Nicholas looked at her, deeper and softer than the way he looked at Angela.

"Is that why you're with me tonight, Nicholas? Because I'm your secret?"

He ran his hands through his hair, then slipped out of his shoes. Bending over, he pulled off a sock. "Take your shoes off and we'll walk to the water."

"Nicholas? Is that the reason?"

Without looking up, he pulled off the other sock.

"Nicholas?"

He straightened up. "No, Maggie. That's not the only reason." He touched her cheek, and her breath caught in her throat. "But we're not going to talk about that. Okay?"

Mute, she nodded. He loved her. It was true. The way he looked at her, the way he touched her. Everything told her that he loved her. Everything, that is, but his words. And it was his words that she needed.

"Do you love Angela?"

"Maggie . . ."

She recognized the warning tone in his voice and chose to ignore it. "It's just a question, Nicholas."

She slipped out of her sandals and followed as he walked to the edge of the surf.

"I'm going to marry her," he said.

Not if she had anything to do with it. But it was probably best not to mention that right now.

"What about you, Maggie? What do you want? Besides your memory, I mean."

You, Nicholas. "I want love." That was true, but there was more. She imagined Deena leaning over her with an eyelash curler, Hoop switching channels on the television, Nicholas holding her close. "I want to be happy. I want a family and friends."

He took her hand, gave it a gentle squeeze. "You have friends, Maggie."

Her heart twisted. That meant so much, and yet in the end, it wouldn't matter if she didn't have Nicholas's love.

"I don't think I have much of a family, though." Even as a cat, she hadn't really belonged. She'd been a stray, fortunate that Old Tom had taken a liking to her and that Nicholas had saved her.

"I'm sorry. I can't imagine being all alone. No matter what, I always had Deena."

She dug her toes into the sand, then pulled her foot up and watched the wet sand ooze between her toes and plop onto the ground. It all came back to Nicholas. As a human, she loved him more passionately and deeply that she ever could have imagined. But she wanted more than just Nicholas. She wanted everything that came with Nicholas, too. Deena, Hoop, the love they all three shared—and were sharing with Maggie—that was so different than the love she felt for Nicholas. Different, but still warm and inviting and special.

"I hope you get everything you want, Maggie. You deserve it."

"Thank you, Nicholas." She hoped so, too, but fear was beginning to nip at her. Her nights were almost half over, and still Nicholas was going to marry Angela. Still, Nicholas hadn't chosen her.

Well, Maggie had him tonight, and that was an opportunity she didn't intend to waste. With a gentle tug on his arm, she urged him closer to the ragged edge of the ocean. "Let's go to the water."

He nodded and followed. The crisp scent of salt water washed over her as the surf came in. She jumped back, away from the advancing waves. She'd learned to love the rain, but now that she was standing in front of the ocean's vastness, she wasn't sure about getting into that froth.

Nicholas laughed. "I thought you were the one who wanted to see the ocean."

She nibbled on her lower lip. "I can see it just fine from here. Thank you."

Grinning, he moved past her into the dancing waves. "I'm not going to be the only one walking back to the car with soggy feet and sand stuck between my toes." He held out his hand. "Come here."

The foam rolled in, and she jumped back again.

"Come on, Maggie," he said, his voice teasing. "Just one toe and the rest will be easy."

She took a tiny step forward, then stopped.

Nicholas laughed. "So far, so good. Now the rest of the way."

Before she could talk herself out of it, Maggie

danced forward into the receding waves, letting the water swoosh back over her feet. Well, that wasn't so bad. She giggled and stepped out farther, until the water reached her ankles. Like a living thing, the ocean pushed and pulled at her, cool and wonderful against her skin, like nothing she'd ever felt before. She kicked her feet in the waves, sending droplets of water flying through the air.

"Fun, isn't it?"

Smiling, she nodded at Nicholas. "Yes. But doing anything with you would be fun."

Their gazes locked, and she recognized the fever in his eyes.

He cleared his throat, turning to look out over the water. "It's getting late. Maybe we should head home."

"Oh, no. Please." She couldn't bear the thought of her time with Nicholas ending so soon. And she had no way of knowing if he'd ever take her out alone again after tonight. She needed more time with him. Especially since her time was running out.

Turning, she ran along the surf, leaving Nicholas and the pier behind her. After a few yards, she spun around, leaning over to splash at the waves with her hands.

"You'll ruin your clothes," Nicholas said when he caught up with her.

She looked down at the little outfit Deena had bought for her. "Won't they wash?"

"You're asking the wrong guy."

Maggie scowled. It seemed silly not to do something just because her clothes wouldn't like it. "Aren't there more?"

His brow furrowed. "More what?"

"Clothes."

The confusion on his face deepened, then cleared as he laughed. "Hell, yes. There are boatloads of clothes."

With a hop, she tried to leap over the next wave that splashed against her feet. She missed, lost her balance, and fell onto her rear. As another wave washed up, the sand shifted beneath her, digging a little Maggie-sized indentation beneath her rump. "It tickles."

His eyes crinkled as he laughed. "I bet it does."

"Are there boatloads of your clothes, too?" she asked, eyeing his soft brown pants, the button-down shirt, and the jacket that fit him so perfectly.

He took a step back, his hands held up as if to ward her off. "Oh, no, you don't."

"Don't what, Nicholas?" she asked, dragging her fingers through the surf.

"Maggie . . ."

She knew he was trying to sound stern, but the warning note in his voice didn't fool her. It was easy enough to see that he was fighting a smile.

"There are boatloads, aren't there? Boatloads and boatloads of your clothes?"

"Maybe there are. Then again, maybe these are the only clothes I can get."

"Hmmm." She licked her lips. "Well . . ." In one

motion, she reached out and caught a handful of water, splashing it up onto him and soaking the front of his pants. She giggled as he jumped back. "I'll trade money that you've got more clothes, Nicholas."

"You would, would you?"

As she nodded, he leaned over and swiped his arm through the waves, sending a wall of water her way. She crawled backwards, but the droplets still found her. She kicked, splashing water toward Nicholas, then scrambled to her feet and ran through the surf.

She heard Nicholas splashing behind her, then felt a tug as he grabbed the back of the loose, flowing shirt Deena had suggested she wear over the tight black clothes. When she stopped, he ran into her, knocking her down through the foam and onto the sand.

Laughing, she rolled over as Nicholas lost his balance and fell atop her. His hands splayed out to land on either side of her, and then he was *right there*, looking down, the intensity of his gaze causing her laugh to catch in her throat. She swallowed, playfulness replaced by passion.

Beneath her, the cool water trickled through the gritty sand, splashing against her body and seeping through her already soaked clothes. She shivered as the ocean tugged at her, but not from cold. Not with Nicholas hovering above her, so close she could feel his heat, so near she could almost hear the thrum of desire running through him. *He wanted her, loved her*. She was sure of it.

She'd tasted his kisses and craved more, so much more. She wanted, *needed*, to lose herself in his arms. She yearned for his caress, the hunger more intense than the pull of waves against her body.

As if reading her mind, he rolled to one side. He propped himself on one elbow, his body pressed close to hers, and his eyes darkened with passion. Slowly, his eyes never leaving hers, he traced the tips of his fingers down the side of her face, leaving a trail of fire in the wake of his touch. Maggie gasped, her breath coming in tiny spurts, her mind reeling under the onslaught of oh-so-wonderful sensations.

His fingers grazed her neck, the gentle caress intoxicating. As his exploration continued, he traced the swell of her breast, his touch both sensual and teasing. Waves of longing crashed through her, setting her body to tingle.

She bit her lip, delirious from the sensation, wanting to cry out and beg for more, for everything, for *Nicholas*. Needing him closer, she wrapped her arm around his neck and urged him near.

"Maggie," he murmured, lowering his face to just above hers. She held her breath, desperate for his kiss, her body humming in anticipation. Then, with a low moan, he pulled back, murmuring an apology. Maggie bit back a cry of disappointment, mourning the distance increasing between them.

Nicholas climbed to his feet, then reached down and took her hand. He pulled her up, looping an arm around her waist to pull her close against him, his breath riffling her hair, their bodies melding together, their heat battling the cool ocean breeze.

For an eternity he held her. And as the surf crashed and swirled around their ankles, she knew one thing for certain—for a few moments, Nicholas had been hers completely. And nothing in her life had ever felt so perfect.

Chapter Fourteen

Strangling a laugh, Hoop watched Nick kick magazines and beer cans out of his way as he cut a path from the television to the sofa and back again. If he'd had a video camera, he'd be recording this for posterity—Nicholas Goodman in a full-fledged tizzy. That had to be one for the history books.

"I spent the entire morning doing nothing but thinking about *her*, thinking about my life." Nick ran his hands through his hair. "I finally just left. Told Larry I had appointments out of the office all afternoon."

Hoop popped the tab on a new beer and took a

long swallow. "I knew our Maggie would get to you."

"*Our* Maggie?"

"What? You wanna claim her all for your own?"

Nick sighed, then gestured for Hoop to pitch him a brew. He snagged the beer with one hand. "I don't know if I want to make love to her or run screaming."

"Bullshit."

Nick sighed. "You win. I *want* to make love to her. I don't know if I should."

"Why the hell not?" Of course, Hoop knew the reason—the Ice Queen. He just wanted to jerk his friend's chain. "I know one sexy, little amnesiac television star who'd love to get cozy with you."

"Cozy we've done already. It's intimate I'm worried about." He dropped onto the sofa and kicked his feet up, then popped his beer. "No, that's not exactly right. It's *not* getting intimate that I'm worried about."

Hoop almost wished Nick would start pacing again. He seemed to make more sense when he was moving. "What are you talking about?"

Standing up, Nick pointed toward the front door. "I have to go out that door, down the block, and into my house. And there she'll be, just waiting for me."

"Lookin' all cute and perky in those little outfits Deena bought for her." Hoop smiled, remembering the odd selection of clothes with which Deena had returned. They were all tight and stretchy. Deena never had been one for subtlety. Thinking about her, Hoop smiled to himself. For the most part, subtlety was way overrated.

"Cute? Perky? Try sexy as hell."

"And she's hanging out in your house. Man, does your life suck." He rolled his eyes. "Doesn't sound like much of a problem to me."

"Maybe you forgot that I'm engaged?"

"How can I forget? It's a nightmare I live with every day. The thought that in just a few months the Ice Queen's going to be living on my cozy little street makes me nuts. I mean, damn, Nick. There goes the neighborhood." He crushed his beer can with one hand, then tossed it toward the kitchen. The aluminum clattered across the tile floor, missing the trash can by a mile.

"I wouldn't lose sleep over it. I doubt Angela's going to want to live in my house. She's been making noises about Brentwood." He ran his hands over his face. "Great."

"Great is right. You get married and I lose my best friend. I've got a sneaking suspicion Miss Angela's not going to be sending me engraved invitations to Sunday brunch."

"Not the formal brunch, anyway." He headed toward the kitchen, stooping to pick up Hoop's can. He pulled up and shot it nicely, sending it soaring in a perfect arc into the can.

"Lucky."

"Not on your life," Nick retorted.

"It's not just my breakfast you have to consider, buddy. It's Deena, too. And Maggie, for that matter. Both Maggies."

"What about Maggie?"

"I just don't think your little woman's gonna be too keen on either me or Miss Maggie dropping by for visits. And you know that girl is not just going to stroll out of your life. For that matter, the Ice Wife's not gonna be too keen on Deena, either. But Deenie's your sister, so she's got a trump card." He kicked his feet up onto the table, vaguely wondering if that might give him a trump card, too. "Not that she'll use it. I don't think your sister's likely to be spending quite as much time at Chez Nick Goodman."

Leaning back, Hoop popped another beer, rather pleased by the look of extreme discomfort playing across his friend's face. Time to add another log to the fire. "And the cat," he said, then paused for effect. "Hell, I'm not even gonna go *there.*"

"What about the cat?" Nick demanded, his befuddled expression morphing into that of his cross-examination mode.

Hoop rolled his shoulder. It was sort of a shrug, but not really. "I just hope she likes living with me, because you know Angela's not letting your furry friend live in her feng-shmeng, color-coordinated, rich-bitch house."

Grimacing, Nick climbed over the back of the sofa, ending up perched atop it with his feet on the cushions and his elbows on his thighs.

"What are you—"

"What?" Nick asked.

Hoop shook his head. "Never mind." If his

friend wanted to join the Loyal Order of Furniture Abusers, so be it. And as far as Hoop was concerned, it was a step in the right, non-anal-retentive direction.

"Anyway, you don't need to worry about Maggie. No way are you going to end up her foster father."

"You say that now, but once you've got that ring on your finger, you're gonna find yourself wrapped around Angela's."

Frowning, Nick shook his head. He certainly didn't intend to be wrapped around Angela's little finger. Now, Maggie's, maybe. That was a different story. He bit back a grin. That possibility had some serious potential. But not Angela. He just wasn't in lo—

"Oh, God."

Hoop stared at him, his face blank. "What?"

"I don't love Angela." The second he spoke the words, he realized he'd known them forever.

"Well, zowie. This is a breaking story. Let me call the news crew; maybe they'll send a van."

Nick ignored his friend, too lost in his thoughts to even acknowledge Hoop. Had he *ever* loved her? Had he ever even thought about it? Or had he just latched onto mutual respect and their shared need to succeed? Hers was to win daddy's love, and his was to keep a full nelson on his security. A week ago, a business marriage wouldn't have seemed at all absurd. But now . . .

Now he couldn't imagine living his life with a woman who didn't share his jokes, who didn't make him laugh. Who didn't look at him with absolute trust, sure that somehow everything would be all right in the end.

"What have I been doing?" he said, mostly to himself.

"I know what you've been doing," Hoop said. "If you were like most guys, I'd say you've been thinking with your *cajones*. But considering we're talking you—not to mention Angela—I'm gonna take a leap here and say you've been thinking with your checkbook."

Using his thumb and middle finger, Nick massaged his temples. "I meant that as a rhetorical question."

"So? I'm right, aren't I?"

Nick held out his hands. "What do you want me to say?"

" 'Yes, Hoop, O Wise Master of the Universe' would be appropriate, I think."

"In your dreams."

"So what're you going to do?"

Nick took a deep breath, then let it out. He let the thought roll around in his head. It was risky. "If I break it off with Angela, I could lose everything."

Hoop snorted. "What everything? Your car's almost paid for, your mortgage is next to nothing. You've probably got more money socked away in stock than Bill Gates. Give me a break."

"I can't go dipping into my savings. That's for emergencies. What if Deena needs surgery? What if she wants to go back to school?"

"So you're telling me you're marrying Angela for Deena? There's some kind of perverse irony thing working there, buddy."

Pacing, Nick tried to gather his thoughts. Hoop just didn't understand. How could he? He lived like a spartan but had a serious trust fund socked away. He'd never known what it was like to be so broke he couldn't buy food or pay rent. "I can't risk Deena's future. Or mine, for that matter."

"Nick, the girl's almost thirty and she's damned independent. Give her some credit for having one or two survival skills."

Nick raised his brow. "We're talking about Deena, right?"

Hoop sighed. "This is about that magic thing, isn't it? That stuff back when we were in college."

"I tease her about it, but she really believes it. And I worry about her."

"No kidding. I worry about her, too. But not because of that. Deenie's got a gift, buddy boy—"

Nick started to interrupt, but Hoop raised a hand to forestall him.

"And I don't mean she's seeing fairies," Hoop said. "Although what the hell do I know? I'm just saying she's got an imagination. Zest and zip, vim and vigor and all that bullshit. She's a hell of an artist, Nick. You ever heard of a *normal* artist?"

He couldn't argue with that. For that matter, Deena's quirkiness was one of the things that he loved most about her. And he'd hate to see it smothered because she had to work some hideous job because he'd failed her. It all came back to the same thing. "Maybe. But when our parents died, I swore that I'd take care of her. I'm not going to break that promise. I'm not even going to risk it."

"What's the risk? You think Dryson's gonna fire you just 'cause you call off a wedding? For cryin' out loud, Nick, who's doing all that kick-ass work down there? You or your wedding invitation?"

"Considering Palmer's practically the only client I've got right now, I'm not so sure. Besides, it's not a question of my talent, it's a question of politics."

"Like hell. You get the job done—you get Vision—and Palmer's not gonna care one way or the other about who marries his little girl."

Nick started to answer, but Hoop held up a hand.

"And Angela's not running the company yet, so it doesn't matter what she thinks, so long as Daddy's happy."

"Maybe."

"Maybe, nothing." Hoop finished off his beer, crunched the can, and tossed it straight into the trash. "Besides, if I'm wrong, you can always go back to the DA's office."

He almost wished Hoop was right. At least when he was working for the DA, he was out catching bad guys. The burps. He smiled as his mind drifted to Maggie, conjuring up an image of her waiting for him in the doorway, wearing his sweatshirt over her skin-tight bodysuit.

That had been another benefit of a government job—the hours. He'd almost always made it home well before dinner. And the idea of spending more time with Maggie certainly qualified as a perk.

He shook off thoughts of the DA's office. That simply wasn't feasible. He couldn't survive on a government salary, and moving to another law firm was out of the question. Not now, not this late in his career.

But Hoop was right. With or without Angela, Vision was the bottom line.

"Well?"

Nick took a deep breath, then let it out slowly. "I'm going to tell her the wedding's off. I can't marry Angela."

"That is going to be one pissed off ice witch." Hoop grabbed the cordless phone off the coffee table and tossed it to Nick. "Tell her now."

"Who are you? My mother?"

"No. I'm your best friend. And I'm with you a hundred percent. So my plan is to make sure you don't screw it up."

By the time he pulled into his own driveway, Nick felt like he'd lost fifty pounds. *This is a good decision. The right decision.*

Since he hadn't been able to reach Angela, he'd paged her. Hopefully she'd call him back while he still had the nerve.

No, nerve wasn't a problem. He was doing this. It was the right thing, and he was going for it. Angela might not understand, but in the end it would be for the best. For everyone. She deserved someone who really loved her.

And so did Nick.

He slammed the car door and headed up the sidewalk, the air somehow smelling cleaner, the sun somehow brighter.

Someone pulled into the drive behind him, and he turned around, expecting to see Angela. Instead, there was Deena in her little red Mustang, the top down, the backseat piled high with boxes, a stuffed giraffe sitting calmly in the passenger seat.

When she waved, he came over.

"What's with the boxes?"

She grinned up at him, then hopped out of the car. "I'm moving in, big brother. You wanna call the Hoopster and get him to help carry in some of my junk?"

Chapter Fifteen

Nick did his best to remain calm as he and Hoop followed Deena back inside, each of them laden with a box overflowing with baubles and knick-knacks, scarves and panty hose.

He dropped his box, letting it land on the tiled entryway with a *thunk*. "Okay. That's the last one. Now do you want to tell me *why* you're moving in?"

Deena plopped down on the far side of the sofa and pulled Maggie into her lap, immediately burying her fingers in the cat's short, black fur. "You mean loving and missing my wonderful brother aren't reasons enough?"

Nick grimaced. Avoidance and the you're-my-favorite-brother speech were never a good sign with Deena. "Come on. Give."

Her gaze shifted to Hoop, who held up his hands. "Don't look at me, babe. I'm just the hired help." He stepped over a box and into the living room. Then he straddled the armrest on Deenie's side of the couch and reached down to stroke Maggie. "But if it's any help, I've got it on good authority that he doesn't bite. So you might as well spill it."

"It's not a big deal or anything. I just had to give up my apartment."

Nick's stomach twisted as he shifted from big brother mode into parent mode. "I'm not sure I really want to know the answer to this, but why?"

Deena shrugged, then leaned back. Nick noticed with mild curiosity that she ended up almost pressed against Hoop's thigh. "It was a money thing."

"That means she is broke."

"Thanks, Hoop. I clued in to that." He fixed his stare on his sister. "Why are you broke?"

"Not having a job had a lot to do with it."

A solid steel ball materialized in Nick's stomach, and for reasons that he wasn't inclined to examine too closely, he thought of Maggie. He swallowed. "How long?"

Deena looked back over her shoulder at Hoop, who laid a hand on her arm. "Three months."

He stumbled into the room and settled himself in his recliner. Almost instantly, Maggie slunk from Deena's lap to his. The cat turned in circles, rubbing her head against his chest and purring louder than a tractor engine as her agitation mirrored his own.

"It's not that big a deal, Nick. Not everyone's as weirded out as you are about money."

"Weirded out? Deena, you don't have a place to live! What would you do if I wasn't around?"

She bit her lip and stared at the ceiling. "I'm not a kid anymore, Nick. Believe it or not, I can take care of myself."

"All evidence to the contrary aside."

"That's not fair. I've been trying to do the art thing because you said I should, that you thought I was good and deserved a shot. If I didn't have you, I'd be doing something else entirely." She waved a hand in the air. "Waiting tables or working in a bookstore or something to pay the bills. Working on my art at night. That sort of thing."

He couldn't argue. Everything she said was absolutely true. When Deena had told him she wanted to try to sell her paintings and jewelry from a cart on the Promenade, Nick had gone out and bought her a velvet banner with her name embroidered in gold. And he'd paid her way until she earned enough to pay her own bills and rent. He snorted. Or until he'd *thought* she'd earned enough.

But most important, he'd promised to always be there if she got into a bind.

"You're right. You can stay here as long as you need to."

He ran a hand through his hair. Backing out of

his engagement with Angela was nothing more than a selfish indulgence that could end up hurting his sister. He knew that, and yet he'd convinced himself otherwise. What had come over him?

The answer flashed in his head like neon. *Maggie.* Maggie had come over him. With a mental shove, he smothered the little voice that said they had found something special and real. Real was food on the table and money in the bank. Real took work, hard work. And it took time. He'd only known Maggie for a few days. What he felt for her was infatuation, nothing more.

It had to be.

And that infatuation was clouding his mind. Making him stupid. Making him actually think that it was in his best interest to break up with Angela and risk everything he'd worked for over the last eight years.

"No way, Nick. Don't even think it," Hoop said.

Nick looked up, confused. Had he been talking out loud?

"Don't think what?" Deena asked.

Hoop ignored her, his eyes locked on Nick's. "You've got a ton of money saved, no one's going to starve, and Deena's very low maintenance."

"Thanks a lot."

Hoop squeezed her shoulder. "I mean you don't have to have a weekly Gucci fix, right?"

"Of course not. I can smell a forty-percent-off sale from miles away. I'm the queen of discounts."

Hoop looked back at Nick. "See. She's a cheap date. Don't do this, Nick."

Deena looked from him to Hoop. "Won't somebody tell me what we're talking about? Do what?"

"Play the martyr to keep you in credit cards."

"I'm not playing anything," Nick said. He stood up, cradling a squirming Maggie as he paced in front of the bookcase.

Deena's forehead creased. "I don't get it."

The doorbell rang. *Angela.* He took a deep breath. He knew what he had to do.

"Shit." Hoop's gaze locked with Nick's. "Come on, buddy. You're on a roll, man. Don't blow it."

The front door creaked open.

"Nickie? Sweetheart, you left the front door unlocked."

Deena's eyes widened. "No way." She looked back at Hoop. "You mean he was going to—"

"Yup."

"Nick, no. I'll get another job. I can flip burgers. I can clean toilets."

Angela rounded the corner into the living room, her nose crinkled. "Why would you clean toilets?"

Deena ignored her, her eyes imploring. "Come on, Nick. It's not about me."

"Hey, hon," he said to Angela as she came over and planted a kiss on his cheek.

Maggie hissed and jumped from his arms to the coffee table. With her eyes locked on Angela, she began to groom herself. If Nick didn't know better, he would swear she was trying to look as polished as Angela in her cashmere outfit and salonified hair.

Angela slipped out of her sweater, draping it over the back of the couch. "I didn't realize when you paged me that I'd be rushing over for a party." She smiled thinly. "If I'd known, I would have brought a casserole."

"They're just leaving." He nodded at Deena and Hoop. "I haven't seen Miss Perdue all afternoon. Would you guys find her and take her to Vision tonight? I need to talk with Angela." He frowned as the other Maggie jumped from the table to the couch and started inching toward Angela's sweater. Great. Just great.

Hoop stood up. "Nick, buddy, I'm begging you here."

"Out." He looked at Deena. "You, too."

"Nick," she said, but she took the hand Hoop offered, and followed as he tugged her toward the door. Then she pulled away and rushed back to give Nick a hug. "I'm a grown-up now, big brother," she whispered. "And you're one of the smartest people I know. So don't start being stupid now."

She planted a quick kiss on his cheek and then ran out the front door after his friend, leaving Angela looking rather bewildered in her wake.

"Whatever was that all about?"

He sighed, recognizing the irony of not being able to share his problems with the woman with whom he was going to spend his life. "Deenie's just being emotional."

"That's not exactly a newsflash, Nickie." She smiled. "But I didn't come to talk about your sister. You paged me, remember? Do you want to tell me why?" Adjusting her skirt, she bent down and sat on the edge of the sofa, ignoring Maggie, who scooted away just in time.

He stood up and began pacing in front of her. Maggie jumped to the ground and began to snake in and out around his legs, frantically rubbing against his pant cuff, her little kitty motor going a mile a minute.

Angela frowned. "Sweetie, I've come to terms with the fact that your feline friend will be living with us, but this is silly. The little thing's acting like she's in heat. Can't we at least get her spayed?"

Almost as if she understood, Maggie hissed, ears flat, and backed away until she was crouched just under the table, a ferocious gleam transforming her cute little face.

"Angela . . ."

"Fine, Nickie. I won't talk about your cat. God forbid I should say something about little snookums."

He cast his gaze toward the ceiling but didn't say anything. She stood up and took his hands, ignoring the low growl that drifted up from under the coffee table.

"What is it, Nickie? You've been so distant lately. Are you nervous? There's nothing to be nervous about. We're going to make the perfect team. And with Daddy behind us, we'll soon be one of the most successful couples in the city."

She was right. He'd never have to worry about money, or finding clients, or whether Deenie could pay her electric bill, or whether she even had a house with electricity, for that matter.

"I *have* been distant, and I'm sorry. I promise it stops now." He glanced down to see Maggie, her belly to the floor, her paws over her eyes. She looked sad and pitiful, and for reasons he didn't understand, his heart wrenched.

Angela kissed him on the cheek. "Darling, we're going to set the world on fire."

No doubt they would, but the thought didn't appease his melancholy. He sat on the edge of the sofa, reaching down to stroke Maggie's head. She opened her eyes but didn't purr, just looked up at him, her green eyes pleading with him to do . . . what?

"Angie, do you love me?"

"Love?" For a moment she looked confused; then her face cleared. "You're turning into quite the romantic, sweetie." She examined her red fingernails. "We're getting married, aren't we? And just think of what a fabulous partnership we'll make."

He nodded. A partnership. That was what it was all about, after all. At their core, he and Angela were the same. He'd spent his whole life trying to succeed, to make sure he and Deenie never went back to the life they'd lived after their parents had died. To make sure Deena was safe. Angela had never lived on the street, but growing up with Reggie Palmer couldn't have been a picnic. The man judged everything and everyone by their profit potential. And Nick knew from the few unguarded moments Angela had shared with him, that Palmer's only daughter was no exception. Succeed, and win Daddy's love. Fail, and stand alone. Angela had chosen to succeed.

And Nick was part of her plan.

Well, she was part of his, too.

The realization ate at him, and he buried his fingers in the thick fur around Maggie's neck, stroking her. His life was a trade-off, a choice. He knew that. But it was a choice he had to make.

With the clarity of a vivid dream, he remembered the way his parents used to walk hand in hand, laughing as Deena and Nick ran after them. Deena's laughter rang in his ears, and he imagined Hoop's gruff voice teasing her.

And Maggie, always Maggie. The sweet ringing of her laughter as she ran through the surf, her soft sigh as she danced in his arms. He didn't have that with Angela; he never would. But it didn't matter. He had a goal. And Angela could help him reach it.

"You're right. We'll make a hell of a team." He glanced around the room, his gaze coming to rest on the oriental box he kept on the mantle. "Let's pick a date. The sooner the better," he said, crossing to the box. He needed to put this wedding behind him, needed to be past this moment so he would quit second guessing himself.

"Really? I've got my planner in the car. We can pick a date tonight if you'd like."

He opened the box and pulled out his mother's bracelet, the one his father had given her the year before their accident. Nothing more than a cheap trinket with fake emeralds, but she'd loved it so much she'd worn it every day.

Without a word, he moved to Angela and slipped it onto her wrist, snapping the clasp before stepping away and admiring the way the green gemstones sparkled in the silver setting.

"What's this?"

"It was my mother's. I'd like you to have it."

Again, her thin smile. "Well, Nickie. It's quite . . . different." With her other hand, she fumbled at the clasp, freeing the bracelet. Using her finger and thumb like a forcep, she dangled it, her nose wrinkling. "But I think it's best that you keep it. I prefer my jewelry to be real. Not worthless pieces of tin and glass. Maybe this weekend we can go shopping for a tennis bracelet."

Nick's chest tightened as she opened her fingers, letting the bracelet slip free. It dropped to the sofa, bouncing off the cushion and falling to the carpet. Immediately, Maggie darted from under the table to the sofa's edge, pouncing on the bracelet and tugging it under the sofa with her.

His heart should be breaking. The woman he was going to marry had just sneered at one of the few material items he truly treasured, the one piece of jewelry he knew that had some bit of sentimentality attached to it.

He should be hurt, irate. His blood should be boiling in his veins and his temper should be spiking off the charts.

Instead, he just felt anesthetized. Numb, and a little sad.

Angela glanced down at Maggie's paw peeking out from under the sofa with the bracelet. "Well, your little beastie certainly loves the thing. Why don't you let little Maggie have it as a play thing?"

"Which Maggie?" he asked, his voice monotone.

She shrugged. "Either, I suppose. It doesn't really matter, does it? I'm sure your fashion-challenged houseguest would appreciate a bauble like this."

With sudden clarity, Nick knew that Angela was absolutely right. Maggie would appreciate the bracelet, both for what it was and for what it meant to him. No matter how many years they shared the same house and slept in the same bed, Angela would just never get it.

He lifted his chin and looked her straight in the eye. "I'm sorry."

Maggie poked her head out from under the couch. Angela blanched.

"Excuse me," she said.

"I can't do it. I'm sorry, Ange. I can't marry you."

She opened her mouth and then closed it again, casting glances around the room as if searching for some tangible explanation. Then her gaze lit upon the bracelet. Swooping down, she grabbed it before Nick could, pushing Maggie out of the way in a flurry of fur and claws and yowls.

"This?" she yelled, waving the bracelet in his face, her blood red fingernails right in front of his nose. "You're breaking our engagement because I don't want a cheap piece of costume jewelry? A piece of garbage like that?" She heaved it across the room, sending it skittering and sliding across the kitchen tile and under the china cabinet. "Have you lost your mind?"

"It's not just the jewelry, Angela," Nick said, measuring each word, as Maggie tore into the kitchen after the bracelet.

"No? Then what?"

"Do you love me?"

"You asked me that already." She stepped backwards, as if his words had struck her. "Besides, what kind of question is that?"

"It's a question you didn't answer."

"Of course I did."

He shook his head. "No, you didn't. The truth is, you don't. You don't love me, and I don't love you." He tried to take her hand, but she pulled it away. "I like you, Angela; don't misunderstand. And you're right. We would make a fine business team. But that's not a reason to get married."

"You son of a bitch. You tell me this now? You've been leading me on." She stalked across the room, then turned back, white-hot anger flaming in her eyes. "Now Daddy will think I'm a fool."

"I'm sorry," he said, knowing the words were

inadequate but meaning them sincerely.

"Sorry? You're sorry," she screeched. "Well, isn't that just perfect?" She plucked her sweater off the back of the sofa and thrust her arms through the sleeves. "You have no idea what sorry means. What do you love, Nickie? This house? Your sister? Your job? Well, we'll see how long you can hang on to any of that when I get through with you."

"Angela . . ."

"I mean it, Nick. Daddy's one of Dryson's biggest clients. I'm sure I can have a little chat with him about letting you go once they pass you up for partner."

Nick's throat tightened. "Your father's not going to insist Dryson fire me. Not while I'm his best shot at acquiring Vision. So don't even think it, Angela."

"Think? Who said anything about thinking? I'm a woman of action, or hadn't you noticed?" She flashed a row of shark-white teeth. "You know as well as I do that whoever snags Vision for Daddy is going to get the partnership. We all thought it would be you. I predict that we were all wrong."

"Don't do this, Angela."

"I don't intend to take this kind of humiliation lightly."

"I'm not trying to humiliate you. I want you to be happy. I want us both to be happy."

She took a step toward him, and Nick stood stock-still as she patted him on the cheek. "I intend to be happy, Nickie," she said, her voice low, the calm before a storm. "Happy as a clam when I see you collecting unemployment. Nobody does this to me. Nobody. But you, Nickie, are lucky. Because you'll get to see the full power of the woman you let slip through your fingers. And when you're crying into your cheap generic beer, you can think about what a wonderful team we could have made, and how it's such a shame you can barely even afford rent."

He stood motionless as she turned on her heel and left, stopping in the open doorway. "Pack up my things and messenger them to me, won't you?" She blew him a kiss. "Good-bye, Nickie. Let the games begin."

Maggie watched the door click shut, her heart beating wildly. She'd won. The words ran through her head, over and over, as she tore out from under the kitchen table and clawed her way up the back of the sofa. She'd won, she'd won, she'd really won.

Nicholas settled on the couch, reaching back to run his hand along her fur. She purred, her head nuzzling his hand, so happy she wanted to roll around on the carpet, so frustrated that the night hadn't yet come. She wanted to celebrate Nicholas's decision in his arms, his lips on her skin, his hands stroking her curves.

"Well, Maggie-cat, looks like I've done it this time."

She hopped from the back of the sofa to the cushions, then snuggled belly-up next to his thigh, purring and rolling side to side as he stroked her fur. Outside the sun hung low in the sky. Still hours before she could celebrate—really celebrate—Nicholas's decision with him. But as soon as she was human again . . .

Writhing in pleasure, she sighed, sure that tonight Nicholas would confess his love for her, sure that after tonight she and Nicholas would be together always.

Three sharp raps on the door echoed through the living room, and Maggie jumped, biting back a hiss and fearing Angela had returned.

Nicholas put a calming hand on her head. "Hey little girl, calm down."

"Yo, Nick?" Hoop's voice filtered through the door, and Maggie sank back in relief.

"In here," Nicholas called as he picked her up and put her in his lap, his strong hands petting and comforting her.

Hoop eased in, and Maggie smiled to see Deena right behind him. He balanced on the recliner's armrest. "The Ice Queen didn't look too happy."

"What were you doing? Hiding in the bushes waiting for her to leave?"

Deena shrugged. "Yeah."

"So give," Hoop said. "What happened."

Nicholas scratched Maggie behind the ears. "What happened is, I just screwed up my career. I broke up with my fiancée—"

Hoop and Deena howled and slapped their palms together in what Deena had called a high-five. Maggie squirmed in Nicholas's lap, wanting to join in the celebration but not sure how.

"—and she's going to make it her mission in life to see that I end up out of a job," he finished without missing a beat.

"Oh, Nick. Don't tell me you're worrying about that." Deena settled herself in the chair, only inches from Hoop. Maggie watched, a pleasant warmth flowing through her, as her two friends moved, almost imperceptibly, closer to each other. "You're the best, big brother."

"I appreciate the vote of confidence, but the fact is that Angela's angling to get me fired. So if I want to keep my job, I have to work twice as hard and get twice the results."

"So forget about the job," Deena said.

Nicholas didn't answer, just scowled as his fingers tightened in Maggie's fur.

"Fine," Deena said, holding up her hands. "Hang on to your security blanket, but don't keep it for me. I can take care of myself." With an exasperated sigh, she pushed herself out of the chair. "I'm gonna go find Mags."

Hoop stood up as Deena left. "She's right, you know."

Nicholas leaned over and straightened the magazines on his table. "We've been over this ground already."

"Just thought you could use a refresher course."

"You didn't find Maggie?"

"Nope. No sign of our girl. At least not in your shrubs, anyway."

Nicholas sighed. "Well, my request still holds. Track her down and take her to Vision tonight."

Maggie growled low in the back of her throat.

"Where you going?"

"I told you. I need to go to the office. If I'm going to stay gainfully employed, I need to make sure I've got a handle on everything at work."

"Nick, my friend, you're just not getting it. The fact is, your sister would live in a dump if it meant you were happy. She wants to spend time with you, buddy, not live on the beach and never see her brother. And Maggie, too, for that matter."

Beneath her curled up body, Nicholas bristled. "What's Maggie got to do with this?"

Hoop fell backward from the armrest into the middle of the recliner. "Oh, come on. Give me a break. If it wasn't for our little Mags, you'd still be heading down the matrimonial path with the Ice Queen. You're head over heels in love with the girl."

Without even realizing it, Maggie began purring, her paws kneading Nicholas's legs. This was it. This was the moment. Her moment. Hers and Nicholas's. All he had to do was tell Hoop the truth—that he loved her—and they'd be together, forever.

"I'm . . . It's not . . ." His brow furrowed. "I couldn't possibly be in love with Maggie."

A thousand little needles pricked her all over as the world shattered into a million pieces. She forced herself to breathe in and out, trying to find some comfort in the simple rhythm.

"Why the hell not?" Hoop demanded as she slinked off Nicholas's lap and moved to the far side of the couch, knowing it was a good thing she wasn't human at that moment, because if she were, she'd surely cry.

"I barely know her. I've had some wonderful moments with her, sure. But I just broke up with my fiancée. I can't just go jumping from one relationship to another. Especially not now, when I need to focus on keeping my job."

"Love doesn't always catch you when it's convenient, my friend."

"You're such an expert?"

Hoop shrugged but didn't meet Nicholas's eyes. "I know a thing or two."

Maggie thought of Deena, and a wave of joy cut through her own despair.

"Well, you don't know this."

"Fine." Hoop pushed himself up out of the recliner. "Do what you want."

Nicholas opened his mouth, but Hoop cut him off.

"And yes, I'll find Maggie and take her to Vision. You go take care of whatever you have to at the office. I just hope that when you finally get your head on straight it's not too late."

"For what?"

"For Maggie. A girl like that's not going to wait forever for you."

Nicholas didn't answer, just stood up and crossed to the little shelves over the short bookcase. As Hoop walked out the door, Maggie wondered if he knew how right he was. Because if Nicholas didn't tell her that he loved her soon, their time really would run out.

Deena perched on the hood of her car, her foot tapping on the fender, absolutely 100 percent positive her brother was going to screw up big-time.

The door opened and she hopped down as Hoop stepped onto the front porch. "Well?"

Hoop shrugged. "Well, what?"

"Did you beat some sense into him?" she asked, following Hoop down the driveway.

"Nick is Nick. When I left he was reorganizing his junk."

"Great. He's regressing."

Hoop laughed and looped his arm around her shoulder. Deena shivered, hoping it was more than a friendly gesture but not sure how to ask.

"He's just being Nick. One problem at a time, and this Vision thing is *numero uno* on his radar screen."

"That's my point. He dumped Angela. Isn't that supposed to be like some big epiphany?" She waved her hand in the air. "Life-changing, earth-shattering, that sort of thing?"

"I don't think your brother downshifts that easily." He pulled her closer. "Nick's just worried about you."

"I know. But I can take care of myself."

"All by yourself?"

She cocked her head, trying to decide what, exactly, she heard in his voice. "What do you mean?"

Hoop swung sideways, dropping his arm from her shoulder and shoving his hands in his pockets. He kicked a rock, sending it careening down the street. "Just that no matter what happens, Nick'll always be there for you." He cast her a sideways glance. "And your friends, too."

Deena couldn't help the grin that took over her face. "My friends?"

"Sure." He took her hand. "Like, if you need a place to crash or anything."

She glanced down at their intertwined fingers. "Thanks, Hoop."

"Yeah, well, we ought to see about finding Maggie."

Overhead, the sun still burned behind the trees that topped the canyon hills. "I don't think we'll find her for at least a couple more hours."

"You know where she sneaks off to during the day?"

Deena shrugged. "I have an idea." An impossible idea, true, but she was willing to bet she was right.

"Lay it on me."

No way, José. "Maybe tomorrow." She needed a little more time, a little more investigation. No way was she going to lay her wild idea on Hoop and be wrong. A dumb-cluck move like that would surely put an end to whatever was finally beginning to develop between the two of them. And end her up in an asylum.

She might have no job and no money, but so far at least, she was pretty happy with the way her personal life was shaping up. And she intended to see that it kept moving in the right direction.

The trouble with office buildings was that once night fell, they became even more tomblike than during the day. The outside world disappeared, lost to the reflected interior of flourescent-lit cubbyholes, as if the powers that be were silently urging the employees to forget that the world went on beyond the windows and to stay through the night working harder and harder.

Nick leaned back in his chair, his art gallery of diplomas reflected in the window along with his desk, his computer, his file cabinet, and his bookshelves. One office of furniture and papers representing everything he'd worked for over the past eight years.

He got up and flipped off the light, transforming the reflective glass into a window on the world. In the distance, the lights of Pasadena winked at him, urging him to go home, to greet Maggie as she burst through the doors full of life and news about her evening at Vision.

Maggie. Was Hoop right? Could he really be in love with her? He frowned at the window. True, she came unbidden and welcome into his thoughts almost all the time, but what did that mean? He didn't know, and he couldn't stop to examine his heart now, not with his professional life crumbling around his ears, not when he wasn't thinking clearly and couldn't trust his own feelings.

If he was wrong, if he hurt her—

The idea of hurting Maggie was too much to bear. He'd hurt Angela today because he hadn't known his own heart. He wouldn't risk doing the same to Maggie.

Besides, she might not love him. Any day now, she could get her memory back, along with a lover, a family, friends. Someone important in her life who would replace Nick. He cringed at the thought, unable to believe it, not wanting to think of Maggie in anyone's arms but his.

He sighed. So much for the argument that he didn't love her. But if it *was* love—true love—it would still be there after she regained her memory and after he got his career back on track. He just needed to keep his focus. If he could just stay on target long enough to acquire Vision for Palmer, then surely everything would fall into place.

"Hey, man. When you leave early for the day, you're supposed to stay gone, you know?"

At the sound of Larry's voice, Nick turned around. Larry was lounging against the doorframe, his wet hair slicked back, jogging shorts and a Dryson & Montgomery T-shirt hanging on his skinny frame, a daypack slung over one shoulder.

"My day took a nosedive, so I thought I'd come back here."

"Must have been some real torture out there in

the real world, if this is an improvement. So when did you get back?"

"About five," Nick said. "I wanted to catch up on some work. What are you doing here so late?"

"Why does anyone work late in Los Angeles? I wanted to use the computers to work on my screenplay."

Nick chuckled. "How's it going?"

"I'm thinking Bruce Willis starring, and the high six figures for me. I figure I'll be retiring from this rat race pretty soon." He grinned. "So, what's the deal with your lovely fiancée?"

"Ex-fiancée," Nick said.

Larry's eyebrows arched. "I guess that explains that."

"Explains what?"

Larry shrugged, his daypack dropping with the motion. "When I was coming up from the gym, I saw her duck into Bullfrog's office and shut the door. Seemed a little weird, what with him not being on your favorite-person list and all. But if you two split the blanket, then I guess it makes more sense." He cast Nick a knowing glance. "I take it the parting wasn't mutual?"

"Score one for your team."

"And now she's a little miffed."

"I'd say a lot miffed, but why split hairs?"

"And she's gonna try to sabotage your Vision deal."

Nick nodded. "Looks that way." And apparently she was going straight for the jugular, trying to get Jeremiah up to speed so he could suck Vision right out from under Nick's nose. In a way, he was glad to know Angela's plan. He could concentrate on getting the dirt on Ferrington. Attack his problems one at a time.

"Your secret weapon found any ammo yet?"

Nick shook his head. "She only got the job yesterday." But she was going to have to double her efforts, that was for sure. Maggie and Nick and Hoop were all going to have to keep their eyes and ears open. More than before, he had to convince Ferrington to sell.

And he needed to do it fast.

Chapter Sixteen

"Now smile for the children and give them the big finish." Michael Ferrington's voice boomed through the studio.

From her vantage point perched on a stool, Maggie looked down at her audience of gizmos and gadgets. Michael had promised that on Halloween, children would flood the studio. But until then, Maggie was supposed to rehearse in front of the appliances. So far, the electric knife and food chopping contraption hadn't been very enthusiastic about her story.

"Come on, Maggie, honey," he said, twirling his arm and then punching the air. "Your audience loves you. Give 'em the old slam-bang ending."

Across the room, Deena leaned against a watercooler. She made a face, then mouthed the words "slam-bang." Maggie giggled.

"Okay, Michael," she said. "But I still feel a little silly without the children."

"Nonsense. An actress works with what she has." He dropped down onto the stage floor, squeezing in between a traveling clothes steamer and some goop that was supposed to remove the hair from women's legs forever. Just looking at the stuff made Maggie cringe. Michael looked up at her and nodded.

She nodded back, then jumped into the finish of her story for the third time that night. "And that's a true story, boys and girls. Once the handsome prince told her that he loved her, she was magically transformed into his princess forever."

Lifting a finger, she emphasized her point for the appliances. "So when you see a kitty on the street, don't assume it's just a cat. For all you know, it could be an enchanted cat, searching out its one true love."

She leaned back, eyes closed, her hands on her knees, her chin held high. It was a wonderful story. All the more so because it was true. Now if Nicholas would only say the magic words.

At the sound of applause, she opened her eyes. Deena and Hoop and Michael were all clapping frantically. Even Michael's assistant, Tony, had set aside his copy of *Variety* and was slapping his hands together.

"It was good? Really?"

"Honey, the kids will love you." Michael stood up, wavering a bit as he tried to untangle his legs from under him. "I swear I'm a genius. A children's story hour. And launching on Halloween." He looked over his shoulder at Tony. "Am I brilliant, or am I brilliant?"

"You're brilliant," Tony said, not even looking up as he went back to flipping pages.

"Well, I am." He flashed a smile at Maggie. "Now we just need to think of a costume." He tapped his forefinger against his lips. "Something Halloweenish, but not too scary or frumpy. Might as well try and bring in the adolescent male viewers if we can." He paused, then held his hands out as if framing her. "I see her as a sexy witch."

"Why can't she be a black cat?"

Maggie looked up to see Deena step forward.

Michael cupped a hand at his ear. "Excuse me?"

"A cat," Deena repeated. "A black cat."

"Oh, yes," Maggie agreed. "That's what I want to be."

"Trust me, man," Hoop said. "You'll be plenty happy with the way our Mags looks in a cat suit." He waved his hand. "Hell, you know. You saw her at the party."

Michael stroked his chin, his brow furrowed. "Well, I don't know . . ."

"Sounds good to me, boss," Tony said.

When Michael looked up at Tony, Maggie thought he looked annoyed. She wasn't sure why. After all, it was her cat suit, not his.

"We've got a cat costume in the back." Tony pointed toward the wardrobe area. "It's in with the other costumes, near the witch's hat." His eyebrows went up and he stared Michael in the eye. "Right near the witch's hat," he repeated.

Maggie thought she heard something odd in his voice but couldn't imagine the cause.

"We can get a few pictures now," Tony went on, "and then Maggie can use whatever costume she wants come Halloween."

A broad grin split Michael's face. "Now, Tony, that's a fine plan. A cat it is, then."

"So, are we all finished here?" Hoop asked from the back of the room. "It's pushing midnight."

"He turns into a pumpkin," Deena said, a grin tugging at her mouth.

Hoop yawned. "I turn into a grump."

"Well, we can't have that," she said.

Maggie watched, delighted with their banter. Near the console, Michael gestured to her.

"Give me a few minutes with Maggie, then you two can take her away."

She hopped off the stool and started to follow him toward the wardrobe room.

Tony waved Michael over as they passed. "Hold up for one second, okay? I need to run something by you."

Michael nodded, and as he and Tony huddled near the console, twisting knobs and pushing buttons, Deena scrambled over to Maggie. "I really need to talk to you," she said, her voice a loud whisper.

From behind her, Hoop yawned again, exaggerated and loud. "So talk in the car."

Deena frowned, then glanced from Maggie to Hoop. "I wasn't talking to you. And it's . . . girl talk." She looked back at Maggie and quirked an eyebrow. "From one sex kitten to another."

Maggie gaped at Deena.

"Great. That means you want to talk about us menfolk."

Maggie glanced at Hoop. Maybe he was right. Maybe Deena did just want to trade flirting tips.

Or maybe Deena had figured it out. She licked her lips, wondering if that would be very good, or very bad.

Hoop crossed the studio, climbed onto the squatty stage, and flopped down on the uncomfortable couch that Michael had explained was designed to look nice for the camera, not feel nice to your body. "I'll be right here."

Maggie frowned, trying to figure out how to ask Deena what she knew without seeming like she was confused, concerned . . . or anything.

"Not that anyone's paying any attention to me, but since I'm driving, I thought you guys might want to know where I'll be." Hoop gestured to the stage, sweeping his arm to encompass the couch he was now spread across. "Here. Right here."

"We got it, Hoop," Deena said. She caught Maggie's eye. "Men. You see what we're up against."

Maggie took a deep breath, nodding. This was just going to be talk about men. That was all.

Deena was just kidding around and Maggie had overreacted. It was silly, really.

"So, can we talk?" Deena asked.

Suddenly, at the console, Michael clapped his hands. "Okay, my dear. I'm ready. Let's go check out wardrobe."

Deena frowned, then mouthed "We'll talk soon," before settling on the edge of the stage, her fingers drumming a rhythm on her knee.

Maggie followed Michael back into the wardrobe area, filled mostly with racks of tailored suits in loud colors that Ferrington had told her "play well to the camera." She followed him through an open doorway and past a mirror lit with over a dozen bare light bulbs, finally ending up at the far side of the dressing room. A black cat costume hung from a hook on the wall, right next to a pointy witch's hat and a thick black cape.

Maggie stepped up to the costume and ran a hand over the mottled fake fur. She wrinkled her nose. "Do you want me to put this on?" She hoped not. The suit was thick and cumbersome, with a plastic mask built in that more or less resembled a big, fat alley cat with an attitude. "It's not very . . . well, sexy."

Nicholas certainly wasn't going to give her a second look if she paraded around in that horrible thing. Besides, Hoop was right. She had a perfectly good cat suit at home. All she needed was a tail and some ears and some fake whiskers. And she'd trade money that Deena could take care of those details for her.

Michael took a step back, looking at the costume. Then he moved forward and leaned against the wall, his hand resting above the suit but under a framed photograph that hung between the costume hook and a shelf.

"Hmmm. No, I suppose it's not very sexy at all." His eyes grazed over her body. "And you certainly can pull off sexy. Would be a shame to waste that." His fingers slid down to the hook with the witch costume, skimming the photograph and sending it swinging back and forth against the wall. "How about a femme-fatale witch?"

Maggie shook her head, her eyes drawn to the now crooked photo. "No, thank you. I think I'd like to be a cat."

He pulled at his chin. "Well, it is a cat story you're telling." Reaching up, he straightened the framed photo.

Something about it looked familiar. She leaned forward, pushing up on her tiptoes, peering at the face in the photo. Then she turned to Michael. "That's you."

Looking a bit like a little boy, he bounced his head from side to side, then looked down at the floor and scuffed his foot along the well-worn vinyl. "Yeah, it is. I'm surprised you recognized me."

Frowning, she leaned back onto her heels. "Why wouldn't I recognize you, Michael? It looks exactly like you. Except that you're wearing a dress." She glanced again at the frilly white dress with the poofed out skirt he wore, along with the matching white cap topped with flowers. "I don't like dresses at all." She cocked her head, contemplating him. From what she'd learned in the past few days watching television, she knew that, for the most part, Michael's wardrobe in the photograph would be considered odd. Since she didn't like dresses at all, she could certainly understand why most men wouldn't like them either.

He swung an arm around her shoulder. "This is the thing, Maggie. The dresses are my . . . well, they're my little secret. Can you understand that?"

She nodded. She knew all about secrets.

"I'd completely forgot that picture was hanging back here, or I wouldn't have brought you into the dressing room. So it's really important to me that you not tell anyone about it. Okay?"

"Okay, Michael." She bit her lip.

"What?"

"It's just that you look fine in the dress. Why don't you want anyone to know?"

He cast his eyes toward the ceiling. "I appreciate the compliment, Maggie. But trust me. This needs to be our little secret. Okay?"

She certainly wasn't going to argue with him. If he wanted to keep it a secret, that was his business. It wasn't as if she was going to discuss his fashion sense with anyone.

"Okay?" he repeated.

"Of course," she agreed, trying to match his somber tone, though she still didn't understand the big deal.

"Great. Wonderful. Well, I suppose we should get you back to your friends."

She hesitated, her hand skimming over the cat costume. "Didn't you want to take pictures of me?"

His face clouded, then cleared. "Right. Of course. Pictures. But we don't have a costume." He looked up and down, scanning the little room.

She followed the path of his gaze, noticing something on the shelf above the photograph. "What about the ears?" She pulled down a headband with built-in cat ears.

"Sure. Fine," he said. "Let's go."

As soon as Tony finished snapping pictures, Deena grabbed Maggie's arm and tugged her toward the break room.

After shutting the door behind them, Deena pointed toward a plastic yellow chair. "Sit."

The door opened and Hoop slipped in. "Listen, kids, I'm not usually one to break up a girl's gab session, but Ferrington wants to shut the place down, and I've got an appointment at seven tomorrow morning."

Deena raised an eyebrow. "I can't imagine you even getting out of bed before noon."

He gave her a look. "I agreed to help out a friend. A weak moment. Sue me."

Maggie stifled a giggle.

Hoop pointed at her. "And I don't want to hear a word out of you. I've never met anyone who was such a night owl."

"Yeah, our Mags is the nocturnal sort," Deena

said, then winked at Maggie before she turned and followed Hoop back out of the room. "Come on, Mags. We'll never have any privacy here. We can talk at home."

Maggie followed them through the studio and toward the car, wondering if Deena meant anything by the nocturnal comment.

Hoop paused at the door. "By the way, Mags, you looked great for the photo shoot. The cat ears were a great touch."

"He's right," Deena added. "You make a hell of a cat."

Maggie nibbled at her lower lip and followed Hoop out the door, trying to ignore her conviction that Deena's "girl talk" wasn't just going to cover the topic of female strategy.

Deena felt like doing a Rocky-style victory dance on Nick's couch. She restrained herself, of course. Blood ties or no, Nick would kill her if she wrecked his furniture. But the sentiment still remained. She was right.

She was absolutely, positively sure that she was right.

That her suspicion had no basis in scientific fact hardly mattered. She'd dropped a few hints, Maggie's eyes had widened, and Deena had just known. If Hans Christian Anderson could dream up a mermaid that turned into a princess, then certainly Deena's little theory couldn't be that off-the-wall.

Well, no matter what, she'd know as soon as she

confronted Maggie. The girl didn't have a dishonest bone in her body.

Thank goodness Nick was still at the office. If she was lucky, they had another hour or so before he dragged himself through the front door.

"Maggie?"

"Just a second," she answered from the kitchen.

"I thought we were going to talk."

"I'm . . . um, making coffee."

Deena fired a disbelieving look toward her reflection in the sliding glass door. "Uh-huh." She climbed over the back of the sofa and tromped off to the kitchen, settling herself on a bar stool and watching as Maggie methodically measured coffee grounds and dumped them into the coffeepot basket.

"Feeling a bit domestic, are we?"

Maggie actually blushed. "I thought Nicholas might want some coffee when he comes home."

"Mags, you've been watching too many commercials. If he drinks that stuff now, he'll be up all night." She tilted her head to the side, considering. "Or are you *hoping* he'll be up all night?"

Managing to look everywhere except at Deena, Maggie filled the carafe and poured the water into the pot. Then she hit the start button and stepped back, pulling the door to the refrigerator open before Deena could jump in with another question.

"Maggie!"

Her head appeared around the door. "Yes?"

"You're avoiding my questions."

Her nose wrinkled. "Well, yes, a little."

"Any particular reason?"

She nodded.

Deena sighed. "Care to share?"

This time, she shook her head.

Well, in for a penny, in for a pound. "Maybe it's because you're a cat?"

For the briefest of moments, Maggie's eyes went wide. Then she met Deena's gaze, her chin high. "Yes. I am. At least most of the time."

Oh, wow. Even though she'd been expecting it—had told herself she really believed it—Maggie's words hit her almost like a physical blow. Her bones turned to rubber, and she started to slide off the stool, catching herself before she broke her butt on Nick's cold, imported tile.

"Okay. Well. Hey." She focused on her sneakers, noticing that the left one was untied. "And here I thought *I* had a unique perspective on the world."

With her lips pursed tightly, Maggie shut the door to the fridge and leaned against it, staring at Deena. "How did you know?"

Now there was a good question. How had she known? "I think I suspected when I saw you eating the kitty snacks. Plus, I know Maggie." She frowned. "I mean you. I know you." Oh, hell, this was way too confusing.

She slipped off the stool and took Maggie's arm, pulling her into the living room, then motioning for her to sit. Maggie complied, curling her feet under her on the sofa, staring at Deena with the same trust she always saw in Maggie the cat's eyes.

Now that she knew, it was so obvious. How the heck had Nick missed it? For that matter, how had Hoop missed it? Wasn't he supposed to be Mr. Observant, hotshot investigator?

"If you knew the first time you saw me, why didn't you say anything?"

With a sigh, Deena flopped on the sofa next to Mags. "I didn't *know*-know. It just all made sense later. And it's not exactly a casual conversation comment—*excuse me, but do you happen to be a cat?*" She shook her head. "That just doesn't work."

Maggie opened her mouth, but Deena's words kept spilling out.

"Besides," Deena added, waving her hand toward the watercolor of Maggie cat that she'd done the summer before. "I spent hours watching that cat—I mean, watching you—before I painted that thing." She paused. "You still move the same, you know. Only bigger, somehow."

Using the back of her hand, Maggie pushed her hair back off her face.

"See! That's exactly what I mean."

She stopped, her hand poised next to her face. "Um . . . what?"

"Never mind. Just trust me. There's still a little bit of cat shining through."

Her brow furrowed. "But I don't want to be a cat anymore. I want to be a woman." She glanced up. "I have to be a woman, because that's what Nicholas wants."

With a satisfying *clink*, all the pieces in her head fit together. "The story, right? The enchanted cat thing. That's all true, isn't it?"

Maggie nodded. "But Nicholas hasn't said he loves me, and I'm running out of time. All Hallow's Eve. That's Halloween, isn't it?" When Deena nodded, Maggie sighed. "I thought so." She nibbled on her lower lip. "Are you . . . Am I . . . Do you still like me?"

"Like you? Don't be a total goon, Mags. Of course I like you. Why wouldn't I?"

"Well, because I'm . . . I mean, I'm a cat."

Deena shrugged. "Yeah, well, everyone's got their quirks." Lord knows she wasn't the most normal of individuals.

"What about Nicholas?"

"I'm pretty sure he's not a cat."

At Maggie's giggle, Deena winked. "If he was, you two wouldn't have any problems at all. Except that I can't see my brother bathing himself with his tongue."

"It is rather hard to go back to. Especially once you've discovered showers."

"But that's not what you were asking, was it? You're wondering if he'll care about your forays into the feline world?"

"Your fairies scare him." She bit her lip.

Deena blanched. "He told you about that?"

Maggie nodded.

"I made a wish. After the accident. I looked up

at the stars and wished for everything to be okay." She felt her eyes well with tears. "And it was. Everything was fine until some third cousin we'd never heard of threatened to take me to Nebraska. So I wished again."

"On a star?"

She nodded. "Right. Both times my wishes came true, and both times I saw a fairy in the garden—and he told me that we'd be just fine."

"Did Nicholas see?"

"He said it was just a butterfly. That magic wasn't real, and I could pretend all I wanted, but I shouldn't confuse fantasy and reality." She shrugged. "Maybe it *was* a butterfly. Maybe it was all my imagination and coincidence. But I want to believe in magic."

"If Nicholas wouldn't even believe in your wish, how will he believe in me?"

"He loves you. He *has* to believe."

Unfortunately, it was in Nick's nature to make sure everything in his world fit in neat, tidy little boxes, not believing in anything he couldn't see or touch. And considering how topsy-turvy his life had suddenly become, his initial reaction might not be exactly what Maggie was hoping for.

At the same time, if Maggie's story was true, she only had a few days to get Nick to admit he loved her. And he *did* love her. Hell, that was obvious. Now he just had to admit it. And it looked like Deena was going to have to see to it that Nick didn't take his usual ponderous, lawyerly route to the truth.

"Deena?"

"Don't worry, Mags. Nick can be stupid at times, but he's no dummy. My same advice still holds: Be yourself. Be yourself to the max."

"But you said I'm still like a cat. Nicholas needs a woman."

Deena made a face and pulled herself off the sofa, tugging Maggie up and off the couch, then leading her into the bedroom. "You need to lay off the television, Mags. Nick needs someone who loves him. That's all. And that's you."

With a hand on each shoulder, she made Maggie face the mirror. "Besides, you *are* all woman. Trust me on that. So you've got a little cat in you, so what? All women have a bit of cat in them. And even as a cat you were pretty darn human. Now you've just got some feline grace. Guys love it. Nick loves it."

As she turned sideways to face the mirror, Maggie's chin lifted, and Deena knew some of her confidence was back.

"Don't worry. You attach yourself to Nick like a burr at night, and I'll work on him during the day. We'll get my brother to admit he loves you—"

"Out loud."

"Right. Out loud."

"And he can't know why. It's not allowed."

Deena nodded. "I know. I heard the story." She frowned, thinking. "Can you tell him?"

"That I love him, you mean?"

"Right."

She cocked her head. "I think so. Old Tom

didn't say that was against the rules."

"Well, there's some heavy-duty ammo for you. What guy can withstand a heartfelt confession of love?" Taking Maggie's hand, she met her eyes in the mirror. "It'll work, Mags. I promise it'll work." And it was a promise she had no intention of breaking.

Hoop ran his hands over the stubble of his beard, hoping the friction would wake him up, at least slightly. Only for Deena would he get up in the middle of the night when he had to be on a stake-out practically by dawn. "You want to tell me again why I'm awake?"

"I told you. I need a favor," Deena said.

He grimaced. "Yeah, you mentioned that when you pounded on the window over my bed. That's a good way to get shot, by the way."

"Sorry," she said. "But you weren't answering the door."

At least she had the good sense to look sheep-ish. *Women.*

"It's two in the morning, Deenie." She shrugged, and he decided to drop the issue. "So what's the favor?"

She sat on the edge of his table, then immediately hopped back up and began pacing. "Can I sleep here?"

Now he was awake. Awake, and thinking about things he shouldn't be thinking about doing with his best friend's sister. *Get your mind out of the gutter, Hooper.*

He coughed. "Wanna run that by me again?"

"I need a place to crash."

Well, hell, that wasn't any better. Did she mean "crash" the way he'd said it when he'd made the earlier offer? Or "crash" the way he'd imagined it? As in, a little bit more than sleeping. Surely number one, right? It was still dangerous turf, but definitely more manageable.

He took a breath. "Last time I checked, my buddy Nick had a nice little house—nearby, too. And from what he tells me, his fridge even has food instead of science experiments."

"Yeah, yeah. It's a great place. But Maggie only has a few days to make Nick fall in love with her, and I figure I'm kind of a third wheel."

Her words spewed out machine-gun fast, and he fell back against the cushions. She was making his head spin, and it was way too early for a Linda Blair impression. Still, it was Deenie who was keeping him twisting in the wind, and he'd put up with just about anything from her. Not that he'd tell her that. Hell, he'd only just realized it himself.

He bit back a grin. If he let her know how he felt, she'd walk all over him. His smile broadened. Not that that couldn't be interesting, too. Actually, it sounded kind of fun.

With a grunt, he forced his head back up and compelled his mind to quit wandering to places it had no business going. "Deen, what the hell are you talking about?"

"I can't tell you. Maggie needs our help. You just have to trust me."

"Seems to me you're not in the best position to bargain, considering I'm the one with an address." He gave her a smug look.

Rolling her eyes, she sprawled out across his couch, her gauzy skirt spreading out around her. She grabbed the edges of her sweater and pulled it tight across her body, practically hugging herself, and looking completely frustrated. Not to mention incredibly sexy.

"You're not going to believe me."

"Why does that not surprise me?"

"I know why Maggie's never around during the day."

He sat up. "I'm listening."

"And she doesn't really have amnesia."

"Just spill it, Deena."

She plucked at her skirt, looking more uncomfortable than he'd ever seen her. Whatever big secret she thought she was onto, it must be a doozy.

"The thing is, you were right."

His mind was a blank. He spread his arms, not one word coming to mind.

"In the mall," she added. "You were right."

"I'm still not with you."

She sucked in a loud, audible breath. "About Maggie. You said she was Nick's cat—"

Oh, Lord, he had a feeling he knew where this was going.

"—and you were right."

Well, now she'd done it.

Now he was really and truly, 100 percent awake.

Nick lounged on the couch, his feet up on the living room table, a cup of hot coffee in his hands, a beautiful woman curled up next to him wearing one of his extra large sweatshirts. Except for the fact that his career was about to be flushed down the toilet, the world was a pretty damn perfect place.

He took a sip of coffee, ready to savor the—

Dreck!

"Nicholas? Are you okay?" She pushed closer, dabbing up the coffee he'd spewed all over his jeans.

Sucking in air like a vacuum pump, he bent forward, holding up a hand and trying to stop choking. "Okay," he gasped. "I'm okay."

Moving to balance on the edge of the coffee table, she kept her eyes locked on his, probably searching for clues that he was going to keel over backward.

He flashed a weak smile. "Really. I'm fine."

"You don't like the coffee."

It was a statement, not a question, and as much as he wanted to reassure her, he couldn't disagree.

"I think you forgot to use a filter, Maggie."

"A filter?" A little crease formed between her green eyes. "Oh. The paper thing."

"It tastes better with the paper thing."

Her adorable nose crinkled. "I'm sorry."

"I promise, coffee grounds are the least of my problems on a day like today." He caught her eye. "I broke it off with Angela, you see."

From her smile, he had no doubt that she'd been well briefed on the whole Angela thing.

"I know. But that's a good thing."

He laughed somewhat resignedly and leaned back against the cushions, tugging her sleeve until she joined him and he could pull her close against him. "You're right. It *is* a good thing." And it was. Just having the opportunity to be close to Maggie—guilt-free—was a good thing. He loved holding her, talking with her, laughing with her. Everything that was a chore with Angela came easily with Maggie.

He sighed. "But now she's a little ticked, and she's trying to get me fired, and that's a bad thing." He tilted his head so he could see her better. "Anything happen at Vision today? Anything at all that might help me convince Ferrington to sell?"

She looked away.

"Is there something?"

Her tongue darted out, moistening the corner of her mouth. "Um . . . no. It's just . . ."

"What?"

"I don't think he wants to sell."

"Maggie, sweetheart, we've been over this. Now it's even more important. If I don't land Vision, I'll probably be out of a job."

"Hoop said you could work for the DA."

He frowned, trying to remember when he and

Hoop had discussed his career options in front of her. "Trust me, that's really not an option."

Shrugging slightly, she chewed on her lower lip.

"You don't look convinced."

"It's just that I love you." Eyes defiant, she caught his gaze. "I know you'll do the right thing."

Love. He'd practically begged Angela for that one little word, then been relieved when she couldn't utter it. And now, now the sound of that one word sent his heart soaring with elation—and with fear. How could she really love him? She didn't really know him, *couldn't* really know him.

"I told you, Maggie, I'm not hero material. Don't make me out to be more than I really am." He stroked her cheek. "We haven't really known each other all that long."

"I've known you forever. And even if I haven't, I know your heart." She pressed her hand against his chest. "You have a good heart, Nicholas."

This was sweet torture. Her hand against his thin shirt was nothing less than a heavenly torment. With a groan, he caught her wrist in his hand, urging her fingertips up to his face. She smiled at him, her thumb tracing the curve of his jaw.

"Don't misunderstand me," he said, hoarse with longing. "There's something between us, and I want to explore it. So help me, it's been killing me not to. But I don't want to rush anything. I can't. Not now. Not with everything I'm juggling in my life."

With the edge of her thumb, she traced his lower lip, and he was pretty sure his heart skipped a beat.

They were so different, and yet she opened up new worlds to him, colored his life with vivid paints rather than dull grays, reminded him of how to laugh, and gave him a reason to come home early.

"Kiss me, Nicholas."

He wasn't about to argue. He leaned forward, sweeping his arm around her waist and pulling her close against him. She moaned—a sweet, innocent sound—and he saw desire flood her green eyes in the moment before she closed her lids, opening herself to his touch. And he knew, in that brief instant, that she trusted him completely, that she was counting on him to make this kiss between them perfect.

He didn't intend to disappoint her.

Softly at first, he brushed his lips over hers, satisfied with her soft noise of pleasure. Holding her close, he let his lips dance on her skin, over her eyelids, along her perfect cheekbone, around the sweet curve of her ear.

He felt her tremble under his touch, and he nibbled at her neck, thrilled with the way their bodies melded together perfectly. Like a man craving nourishment, he kissed his way to her mouth, then feasted on her lips. She opened her mouth for him, and he tasted her, warm and sweet like fine wine.

Groaning, he slid a hand under the back of her

shirt, caressing the soft skin under his hands. She shifted against him, reaching up to bury her fingers in his hair as she pressed closer to him, deepening their kiss.

He wanted, needed her. Self-control was abandoning him, and, conjuring the last remnants of his willpower, he gripped her shoulders and pushed himself back, his determination almost shattering when he heard her little moan of protest.

"We can't," he said, forcing the words out.

"Nicholas," she whispered, her breath caressing his face. "I want—"

He stopped her with a finger over her lips. "I know. I want, too. But . . ." With supreme effort he pulled away, taking her hand as he leaned back against the couch. He took a breath, trying to control his body and his emotions. "So . . . want to watch a movie?"

She stared at him for a moment, looking slightly bewildered. Well, he was a little confused himself. But he wanted to take this slowly, wanted to be sure that the sparks that were igniting between them would light a fire that would burn forever, not burn out in the blink of an eye.

"Like a date," he said. "A last-minute, late-night date, but still a date."

After a moment, she smiled. "Can we have popcorn during the movie?"

He raised an eyebrow. "Sure. I can handle the microwave."

She cast him a sideways glance. "Can we snuggle during the movie?"

This time he chuckled. "You drive a hard bargain, but yeah. I'd say snuggling is definitely on the program."

"In that case, I'd love to watch a movie with you."

As he took her hand to kiss her fingertips, he glimpsed a sparkle of silver on her wrist. Curious, he pushed back her sleeve, revealing his mother's faux emerald bracelet.

She tugged her arm away, hiding the bracelet under her free hand. "I'm sorry."

"It's okay. I was just surprised. Where did you get it?"

"From the floor," she said. "The cat was playing with it. I like it."

And he liked it on her. It looked right somehow, the green perfectly matching her eyes, the deep color of the gems accentuated against her pale skin. Funny, he'd always wanted to give the heirloom to a woman who'd appreciate it. He tried this afternoon and failed miserably, but somehow—despite all of his stumbling about—the right woman had ended up with the bracelet on her arm. And in his heart.

She started to fumble with the clasp. "Do you want it back?"

He put his hand over hers, stopping her. "Why don't you wear it for a while."

Their gazes locked, and, after a moment, she

nodded. He wasn't sure what she saw reflected in his eyes, but he hoped like hell his soul wasn't making promises the rest of him wouldn't be able to keep.

Chapter Seventeen

Hoop guided his car to a stop in front of Nick's house, shifting into park behind Deena's little Mustang. He shook his head, still not sure he believed everything he'd just heard, but at the same time, knowing everything she'd said was the absolute truth.

"Sure you don't want to come with me on this stakeout?"

Deena shook her head. "I'm gonna move my car, get some breakfast, and then go sleep for twenty-five years on your couch. Try not to wake me when you have your next few birthday parties."

"You're gonna sleep? I couldn't sleep if I wanted

to." Which was fortunate. They'd spent the night talking—mostly about Maggie, but they'd veered off onto a variety of other goofy topics—and he hadn't had one bit of sleep since Deena had rapped on his window and finagled her way into his house so she could tell him her so-wild-it-had-to-be-true story.

"I still can't believe it," he said. But for some reason, he *did* believe it. For that matter, he hadn't doubted her for a second. Maggie turning out to be a cat might be bumping up against "The Twilight Zone," but putting all his faith in Deena—well, that was downright scary. Except that it wasn't. Where things like magic and enchanted cats were concerned, there wasn't a person in the world he would believe more. Couple that faith with a few of the images his mind had been conjuring whenever she was around, and he was left with either a damn good relationship or one hell of a way to piss off his best friend.

He sighed. "I really don't believe it," he said, and this time he wasn't referring to Maggie.

"I know, but it's been right here in front of us the whole time."

His mouth went dry. "What?"

"I mean, she's so obviously a cat."

"Right. Maggie. Of course."

"What else would I be talking about?"

He grinned. "Maggie's old news. I meant I couldn't believe that you figured it out before me."

She laughed. "Oh, yeah?"

"Yeah," he said, backing away and trying to

melt into the side of the car, holding out his hands to ward off the tote bag she tried to wallop him with.

"Very funny. You're not the only hotshot investigator on the block."

"Apparently not." Leaning over, he popped open the glove compartment, then dug around until he found what he was looking for. "And for your brilliant contribution to the wide world of detecting, I bestow on you the seal of the loyal order of investigators."

Her grin matched his own as he pinned to her sweater the little button with the cartoon blood drop that he'd kept from the last time he'd donated plasma. So what if it said "I Gave Blood Today"? It was the thought that mattered.

"Thank you, thank you all, for bestowing such a great honor on me." Her hand closed over the pin. "I shall treasure it always." Even though they were just goofing around, he sensed trust in her words.

"Well . . . I should go." She opened her car door, and Hoop realized he was more than a little disappointed that she wasn't going with him on his stakeout.

"You're sure it's okay if I stay at your house?"

"Hell yes," he said, then realized how overeager he sounded. He coughed. "You need a place to stay while Maggie butters up Nick, right? So stay with me. Nick would be furious if I put you out on the street."

She cocked her head, a little smile dancing

around her mouth. He wasn't fooling her one bit, and they both knew it. "But do you *want* me to stay at your place?"

Women.

He let go of the steering wheel just long enough to throw his hands in the air. "Yes. Yes, I want you to stay."

"Well, okay then." Before he even knew what hit him, she slid toward him, planted a kiss on his cheek, pushed open her door, and was gone.

His head was swimming, but Hoop knew two things for sure. First, the morning was definitely shaping up. And second, his buddy Nick wasn't the only guy on the block with females on the brain.

At least Hoop didn't have to worry about felines, too.

Nick stared at his computer monitor, not seeing the black letters against the white screen, seeing instead raven-black hair and smooth white skin. A bright smile, and a warm caress. *Maggie.*

All day, he'd been forcing himself to keep his mind on track as he'd searched the Internet, hoping to find some tidbit of dirt about Michael Ferrington, his family, his former school chums, anything. But always, bits of Maggie slipped in through the chinks.

Finally, six o'clock was approaching. He could cut out, pick up Maggie, take her to Vision, and then take her out on the town. He smiled at the prospect. She hadn't been anywhere to be found before he'd left for work that morning, and now he was going into withdrawal.

Instead of the Maggie he wanted, he'd awakened to find Maggie the cat next to him, and had been sorely disappointed with the situation. In his dreams, he'd held his Maggie tight, her body spooned against him, his breath ruffling her hair. His reality was a hell of a lot less appealing. It was a sad state of affairs when even the press of warm fur against him could make him fantasize about the woman he wanted. But what did he expect? She was on his mind constantly, she'd invaded his thoughts, his head, his heart. Everything he did now came with a bonus Maggie-thought. Kind of like Christmas shopping. Buy one, get one free. Only his little mall perk wasn't an engraved pen in a pretty box, it was an image of Maggie.

At the oddest of moments, he would picture her laughing, or wonder if she'd enjoy trying sushi, or outline in his head all the places he'd like to go with her. He hadn't been to Disneyland in years, had thought the whole theme park thing was pretty much a waste of time. But with Maggie on his arm, a day at the park seemed magical, an adventure.

He hit the intercom button on his speakerphone. "Hey, Larry?"

"Yo, bossman."

"See if Human Resources still has any of those discount Disneyland tickets, would you?"

No Larry. Just the static over the speaker.

"Larry? You there?"

"You? Hanging with the Mouse?" The voice was crystal clear, and not coming over the phone line. Nick looked up to see Larry in the doorway, incredulity smeared all over his face.

"I'm taking a friend."

"Uh-huh."

He closed his eyes. "Just check, okay?"

Larry shrugged. "Sure thing." He leaned back, glancing down the hallway. "But you better go soon. Looks like you might be about to get real busy again." He lifted his hand in front of his chest and surreptitiously pointed down the hall, all the while mouthing "Dryson."

Nick sighed. He really wasn't in the mood.

Not that Mitch Dryson cared about Nick's moods. He marched in and settled himself in one of Nick's chairs, then began tapping his Montblanc pen against his perfectly pressed slacks. Even before he spoke, Nick realized he was gripping the edge of his desk, irritation boiling in his gut.

"I understand your progress on the Vision matter isn't everything we had hoped."

Using every ounce of poker skill in his body, Nick kept a pleasant smile plastered to his face. "I don't know why you'd say that, sir. Everything's going smoothly. I've got a girl on the inside, and I've got our investigator doing some snooping around on the outside, interviewing folks who know Ferrington and his staff. I'm hoping for a break any day now." Even as he said it, he felt a twinge of guilt. Maggie was right—Ferrington didn't want to sell. But ruthlessness was the name of the game, and he needed to beat back this new hesitation before it had a chance to take root. He hadn't joined the corporate department of one of the nation's biggest law firms in order to learn how to be a pussycat.

Dryson tapped his pen against his mouth. "Perhaps I've been misinformed. But I understand Jeremiah thinks he might be able to make progress on the matter."

"I don't have a monopoly on information, sir. We're all a team, right?"

Dryson nodded. "I like your attitude, son. Team or not, though, we're only making one partner this year. Personally, I'd like it to be you. But Palmer and this Vision deal are important to the firm—important enough that we put you on it exclusively," he said. "So you do the math." Standing, he slipped his pen into his breast pocket. "And, of course, I don't have to tell you that most senior associates passed up for partnership tend to leave the firm." His smile didn't do anything toward diminishing the threat in his words. "Just a little food for thought."

Nick's stomach twisted. There it was. An ultimatum.

"One last thing," said Dryson, pausing in the doorway. "Is there something you want to tell me about you and Angela Palmer?"

"No, sir," said Nick, struggling to breathe. "Nothing at all."

For a moment, Nick thought Dryson was going to argue. But then he nodded curtly and walked away. Exhaling, Nick fell back against his chair.

Maggie was his last—his only—chance.

With Tony aiming the camera at her, Maggie pressed the little button on the food processor, sending little bits of basil and oregano swirling madly in the clear plastic cylinder. Delighted, she almost clapped her hands but held back, remembering that Michael had told her to keep her hand on the button, her head held high, and to smile, smile, smile.

From beyond the stage, Nicholas winked at her and her smile broadened. He'd come home even earlier than usual tonight, and Maggie had considered that a very good sign, especially considering how fast Halloween was approaching. Nicholas really wanted to see her, wanted to be with her. The next step was for him to fall in love with her.

No, she corrected. He already was in love with her. She knew that. In her heart, she was sure of it. The next step was to get him to admit it. Soon. Very soon.

"Perfect, perfect." Michael zipped up onto the stage, all energy and bluster. "You're wonderful, my dear. After Halloween, we'll quit rehearsing and run the show live." He swung an arm around her shoulder. "And I want to talk to you about doing the storybook hour every week. I want it to be our Internet launch program."

As he guided her off the stage, she looked back at Nicholas.

"Go ahead and talk it over," Nick urged her. "I'll just wait here."

She didn't want to talk about a job, she wanted to be with Nicholas. But Michael led her to the back, chattering on about how innovative the Internet show would be, and what a boon it would be for children, and wouldn't she just love to dress up as a different character every week and tell a story to an audience of ten or so kids?

"Well, yes," she said. And she did love telling the stories. That was much more fun than playing with the choppers and slicers that Michael kept putting in her hands. But Nicholas hadn't yet told her he loved her, and if he didn't, she wasn't going to be needing a job come Monday.

Her eyes welled with tears, and she sniffled.

"Maggie?"

"I want the job, Michael."

"Wonderful, wonderful," he said, as she tried to block the image of life without Nicholas.

The thought was impossible to bear. Nicholas *would* tell her in time. He had to. She couldn't leave him now, couldn't go on as a cat, knowing she'd missed the chance to be with Nicholas forever. Being human might be confusing, even trying at times, but it was worth putting up with all the awkward, silly things if her reward was Nicholas. And he had to say it soon.

"You haven't told anyone about my photograph, have you, my dear?"

She shook her head. "You told me not to."

"Of course," he said and, for a moment, Maggie

had the odd impression that he looked surprised, even a bit annoyed. "That's good," he finally went on. "Because it's important no one know about that. I'd be extremely embarrassed if the public found out about that photo."

Maggie pursed her lips, sure she was missing something. But in the end, all she could do was nod. "I know. You told me. I won't tell anyone."

With a pat on her back, Michael started to lead her back to the studio floor. "That's fine, then. No taping tomorrow. I'll see you on Halloween, full-costume, raring to go, right?"

"Um, right." She frowned. "Did you need to talk to me about something else?"

He waved his hand as if shooing flies. "Nothing major. It can wait."

"Ready?" Nicholas called from across the room.

Maggie studied Michael's face and sniffed, trying to get a clue as to why he was acting so strange. Nothing. She turned to Nicholas. "I'm ready. What do you want to do?"

When he'd told her he was going to show her the town, Maggie had no idea how much he'd meant his words. A blanket of light spread out below them, flickering and beckoning in the dark.

"Where are we?"

"Mulholland Drive. That's Los Angeles down there, and behind us is the San Fernando Valley."

A lock of his hair fell over his forehead, and she reached up, smoothing it off his face.

"Where do we live?" She asked the question on purpose, and he didn't even blink at the *we.* Without missing a beat, he pointed to a stand of trees. "You can't really see it from here, but it's just past that rise. We could walk there if we wanted."

"Do we want?"

He held a hand out to her and sat on the hood of his car. She stood facing him, his knees pressed against her hips, her fingers locked in his hands.

"No, we don't want," he said. "I've got better plans for tonight than risking our lives walking down dark alleys above Los Angeles." He grinned. "I thought we'd walk down a few dark alleys *in* Los Angeles instead."

Her confusion must have been obvious, because he quickly continued. "Hollywood," he said. "I thought it might be fun to show you Hollywood."

Where television shows were made. She nodded, pleased with his suggestion, but she would have been just as eager if he'd told her they were going to go walking in the sewers. Anything for the chance to spend more time with Nicholas.

Reaching out, he stroked her cheek, making her breath catch in her throat and her skin tingle. "Tomorrow's the only full day both of us have free. I thought it would be fun to celebrate." He smiled. "You missed Deena's spree, so I thought maybe shopping during the day and a nice dinner out tomorrow night."

During the day? She bit her lip, automatically

taking a step backwards. "I'm not . . . I mean, I shouldn't . . ."

"What's wrong?"

"During the day. I can't go shopping. I mean, I—"

"You don't have to walk the streets every day, Maggie." With his forefinger, he lifted her chin until she could look deep into his eyes. Her breath caught as she recognized the passion reflected there, burning hot and pure.

"Your memory will come back in its own time. I promise. And I'll help all I can. But spend the day with me tomorrow, okay? You're on my mind, Maggie. You're in my head and my heart, and I want to show you more of the city. I want to buy you presents and walk with you along the Promenade. Who knows, maybe you'll even have a glimmer of memory."

He spoke words of love, and Maggie memorized every one of them, but he still hadn't said the words she needed to hear. But soon. He would soon. Tomorrow. Surely he would tell her tomorrow. And if not . . . well, she'd still have one day left.

"Maggie?"

Silently, hating that she was lying to him even a little bit, she nodded. She couldn't go shopping with him, not unless he intended to haul around her cat carrier, but if he stayed at home, she planned to be right there, underfoot, every minute of the day.

So maybe that meant her lie wasn't that bad after all.

Nick's stomach twisted into knots as he paced the living room, wondering where the hell Maggie could be. As he walked, he stroked Maggie the cat's fur, letting the rumble of her purr soothe him. He wasn't sure if he was angry or disappointed. Of course, disappointment won out. The truth was, he couldn't be angry at her. Not even when she'd stood him up.

At first he'd been surprised. They'd had such a wonderful evening last night. First a walk down Hollywood Boulevard, a wild place for someone as sheltered as Maggie seemed to have been. Then they went to a retro flick, *Bringing Up Baby,* which Maggie had enjoyed even more then he could have guessed. He'd slipped his arm around her, she'd leaned against him, and they'd shared a bucket of popcorn.

Even now, his body could recall every time their hands met. He'd always thought that feeling sparks was just a saying, a silly romantic notion. He'd been wrong. Just the slightest touch of her hand against his had sent electricity arcing through him. He could remember everything about the way she looked, the way she smelled, the soft, slightly buttery way she'd tasted when he'd kissed her as the credits rolled. But he couldn't remember a damn thing about the movie.

Afterward, she'd practically dragged him to the

ice cream shop. They'd gorged themselves on hot fudge sundaes, drawing stares and applause when she'd leaned over to lick whipped cream off his nose and he'd hauled her over the table for a kiss.

After a night like that, he never would have believed that she would go out and leave him all alone on such a beautiful Saturday. But she had.

And he was sorely disappointed.

As night drew near, he was also starting to get a little worried.

The doorknob rattled, and Nick jumped, practically running to the front door as it opened. "Where've you been? I've been worried—"

Deena.

"Sorry to disappoint you, big brother." She smiled. "But it's nice to know you care."

"I haven't seen Maggie all day."

"She'll show up; she always does."

"I know. I just thought . . ." He trailed off, running his fingers through his hair.

"Feeling a little possessive, are we?"

He tried to glare but couldn't. She was right, after all. "A little." Maggie squirmed out of his arms, dropping down to the sofa and then hopping to the coffee table, where she ultimately perched, her eyes locked on him. He shook off an eerie shiver. "I was looking forward to spending the day with her."

"She's great." Her brow furrowed. "Well? How 'bout it? Anything new and interesting on the romance front?"

No way was he discussing his love life with his sister. Especially not with his sister who had fast become Maggie's best friend. "Deena . . . ," he said, a warning note in his voice.

"Nick . . ." she mimicked, her hands on her hips, her eyes hard. "Come on. Tell."

From the coffee table, Maggie matched her glare. *Great.* He frowned at the cat. "So now all the females in this household are conspiring against me?"

As if she understood, the cat blinked, then aimed her gaze at a random point between him and Deena. With catlike aplomb, she licked a paw and smoothed it across her face. A completely feline gesture that, for some inexplicable reason, made him more than a little nervous.

"Well, I'm glad Maggie's not here," Deena said, but she spoke to the cat, not him. "I want to talk to you alone."

"To me?"

She looked up. "Of course to you. Who else."

"Well, you seem to be awfully concerned that Maggie knows we're about to have a heart-to-heart."

For a moment, she almost blushed, which would vault the day into an entirely new level of bizarreness. Then her face cleared. "Just working out a crick in my neck. Anyway. I'm glad to have the chance to talk to you." She glanced down at the table again. "Alone."

Once again, Nick had the odd sensation that he was the only one in the room who didn't have a clue. Maggie the cat jumped down from the table and trotted toward the bedrooms, casting one final look backward before mewing slightly and disappearing from view.

"This is turning out to be a very strange day," he said, more to himself than Deena.

"Just tell her you love her, Nick. What are you, relationship challenged?"

Nick drew back from his sister's blunt words. "Hell, Deenie, don't beat around the bush. If there's something on your mind, just spill it."

She rolled her eyes, then headed into the kitchen. Nick followed, the thought of a beer suddenly overwhelmingly enticing.

After surveying the contents of his fridge, Deena finally pulled out two beer bottles and twisted off the tops. She passed one to him, and he said a silent thank you that she knew him so well.

"I mean it, Nick. Why don't you just tell her?"

"What makes you think I love her?" He truly wanted her answer. His heart did tell him that he loved her, would love her until the day he died, but his head kept telling him it was too soon. Between his head and his heart, how was he to know for sure?

His sister swallowed, then wiped her mouth with the back of her hand. "Just look at you. It's obvious. It's been obvious from day one."

"That's my point, Deena. How could I have loved her from day one? I didn't even know her.

Lust, sure. But love? This fast? This strong? I want to be sure. I need to be sure."

"Trust me."

He had to grin. His sister, the woman who went on more first dates than anyone he knew, was giving him advice about love. "What makes you such an expert?"

Again, the hint of a blush. "I'm a quick study."

An image of Hoop popped into his mind, the thought both appealing and a little disconcerting. Hoop and Deenie? He never would have made the combination on his own, but he had to admit the image worked.

"Nick, just tell her already. Tell her and then you two can spend all the time in the world exploring what it means to be in love."

Well, that made no sense whatsoever. "Tell her I love her and then figure out if it's really love?"

Deena threw up her hands—including the one with her beer—and sent a shower of foam and brew splattering down on his kitchen. "You *do* love her, Nick. I'm trying to save you years of heartache, here."

"I made a huge mistake with Angela—"

"Yes. And I don't want you to make another one."

"—and I don't want to repeat it." He took a long swallow of beer. "I need to resolve this Vision thing. It's clouding my head, messing up my judgment. I'm worried about my future. About *our* future, Deena. And Maggie. I can't risk hurting her. This thing—it's so intense, so fast, how do I know it's real, and not a reaction to everything else that's going on? How do I know it's real if I can't get a handle on it?"

"For crying out loud, Nick, does everything have to be brick and mortar to you?" She waved a hand through the air. "Can't see the oxygen, can you? But I don't see you keeling over. The world is filled with things you can't see, but that doesn't make them any less real."

He sighed, knowing she was probably talking about fairies. Hell, maybe she *had* seen something magical. Whatever she'd seen—whatever she'd imagined—it had sure helped her get through some rough times. He couldn't knock that. But that was a lot different than being sure he loved Maggie.

He ran his fingers through his hair. "Between you and me, I do think I love her. But I don't know how to tell for sure. I've been wrong before, and I can't be wrong this time. Not with Maggie. I won't do that to her. I need to get clear. Then I can be sure."

Pressing the bottle against her forehead, she sighed. "I'm telling you, Nick. Let the girl know you love her before it's too late."

Sighing, he leaned back against the kitchen table. What was he afraid of, really? That he'd be wrong? That he'd hurt her? All of those things and more. For so long he'd lived his life in compartments, neat and tidy, with things happening in the right order, cause and effect, one after the other. So far it had been working just fine. But what would happen if he took a leap? Chaos, maybe. And Nick wasn't at all sure he was a chaos type of guy.

Then again, Maggie certainly had an aura of chaos about her. It practically floated around her ankles, touching everything she did. And so far, she hadn't done anything to his world except brighten it.

"Hello Nicholas."

He spun around. "Maggie. Where've you been? When did you get back?"

She smiled. "Just a minute ago. I've been nearby." With a tilt of her head, she acknowledged Deena. "Hi."

"Hiya kid. I've got your costume almost finished. I'll bring it over tomorrow."

"Thanks."

Nick nodded. "Yeah. Thanks."

His sister poked him in the chest with her forefinger on her way out. "You think about what I said."

He nodded. He couldn't help but think about it. How he felt about Maggie was pretty much the only thing on his mind these last few days.

"I'm sorry I missed shopping. Are we still going out?"

Suddenly, he realized that he didn't want to share her with anybody, not even a waiter or a valet. "How would you feel about staying in and ordering a pizza?"

Her teeth grazed across her lower lip. "If there's

snuggling on the couch involved, I think that's a fine plan."

Fifteen minutes later, there was no question but that snuggling was definitely on the agenda, as was kissing and stroking and exploring the sweet woman pressed against him. He sat across the couch, his legs spread out, and she fit between his legs, leaning back against his chest, the honey scent of her hair teasing his nose.

She moaned softly, her breath almost sounding his name, as his hand stroked her side, teasing the curve of her breast. He'd be happy to stay that way forever, holding her, letting her presence next to him calm his fears and fill his days.

This had to be love. What else could it be? So pure, so fresh. It was just the words that terrified him—words that, once spoken, couldn't be taken back if he was wrong. They were three little words that could change everything forever.

But he could show her that he loved her. With every look, every touch, ever caress, he intended to let her know exactly how he felt.

Maggie cringed as Deena grabbed some material from above Maggie's tailbone and pinned the cat tail on. "Okay. I think it's tight. There you go. Now you can be a cat twenty-four hours a day."

"I was kind of hoping to go the opposite way."

Deena grimaced. "He didn't tell you, huh?"

Shaking her head, Maggie sighed. "No. And it's Halloween. Deena, I'm out of time."

"He loves you, kid. It'll work out. It has to."

Maggie nodded, trying to keep tears of frustration from welling in her eyes. "I know he loves me. I know he feels it in his heart. But that's not enough to power the enchantment." And Old Tom wouldn't bend his rules. Not even for her. Somehow, some way, she had to make Nicholas tell her that he loved her before dawn.

"Desperate times call for desperate measures, my friend."

"I don't understand."

"This Vision thing. He has to get past it. My brother's a loon about doing one thing at a time. Maybe if he feels like his job's safe, he'll turn to his personal life."

"But Michael doesn't want to sell. And I don't think it's fair to—what's that word?—blackmail him."

"So there is something?"

Shrugging, Maggie avoided Deena's eyes.

"Look, kid, if there's anything, anything at all that you've learned, you need to tell him. It's your best shot. It may be you're only shot."

Slowly, Maggie nodded. She'd promised Michael, but if she had to break that promise so she wouldn't lose Nicholas . . . She sighed, not sure she could do it.

"You have to," Deena said, apparently reading her thoughts. "Just remember, it's only business."

Nodding, Maggie followed her into the living room. A low whistle greeted her.

"Yowza, baby. Mags, you really are one hot number."

She smiled at Hoop, his praise lifting a bit of the cloud around her heart. Next to Hoop, Nicholas just stared, his mouth slightly open. Automatically, her hand went to her hair, and she tried to smoothe it back but hit the headband with the fake cat ears. She lowered her arm, standing awkwardly under his gaze.

"What's the matter, buddy? Cat got your tongue?"

He and Deena exchanged glances, and Maggie realized that Hoop knew her secret. She smiled. If Hoop and Deena were exchanging secrets, then maybe soon they'd be sharing even more.

"Maggie. You're absolutely beautiful."

Nicholas's words flowed over and around her, stroking and teasing her. They were filled with love, with passion, and Maggie knew in that moment that she'd do whatever she had to do to make Nicholas tell her that he loved her.

Chapter Eighteen

"I'm glad you told me," Nick said.

They were in the break room at Ferrington's studio, and Maggie was sitting in a little plastic chair looking miserable. "I only told you because I love you, Nicholas."

His heart wrenched. Because he loved her back, he needed to use the information. That one secret would secure his job, secure their future. His mouth twitched in a halfhearted smile. A future with Maggie, bought with Michael's privacy. The idea sat like a rock in his gut.

She licked her lips. "I'm trusting you with Michael's secret."

He kissed her on the cheek. "You're doing the

right thing," he said, fervently hoping he was right.

"No, Nicholas, I'm not." She paused, then looked up and met his gaze. "But I am hoping that *you* will do the right thing."

He closed his eyes, silently nodding. More than anything, he hoped he was, too.

The door opened and Michael leaned in. "Okay, Maggie, Tony's ready for you."

She stood up but didn't meet Nick's eyes. He felt like a total heel. But he needed to do this.

"Michael, can I talk with you for a second?"

This time, she did glance his way, her eyes pleading with him.

"Sure thing. Maggie, go on ahead. Tony's got everything ready."

"Nicholas . . ."

"Good show, Maggie. I'll be watching from the sidelines."

She opened her mouth as if to speak but closed it without saying anything. Then she slipped out the door, leaving Nick alone with his conscience.

"What's on your mind, Goodman?"

Nick gestured at the chair Maggie had just left. "Sit down."

Michael did, but his eyes never left Nick's.

"I want to talk to you about Reggie Palmer acquiring Vision."

"Not interested."

"Palmer's got capital. With Palmer Enterprises by your side, Vision can really take off. A lot faster than you can get launched without Palmer's backing."

"We've been over this ground, Goodman. My company's not for sale."

Clearly luck wasn't with him tonight. Nick sighed. He'd been hoping to take the easy way out. Digging deep, he pulled out the stops. "Palmer plays hardball, you know."

"I know. And you work for Palmer. But I'm not budging."

"There's this photograph . . ." He trailed off, watching Michael's face. The man didn't seem surprised, and with a start, Nick realized that Michael must have suspected that Maggie would violate his trust. Damn. Guerilla business tactics were one thing, but sucking the woman he loved into the mire . . . well, the thought made his stomach churn.

"What photo is that?"

Nick drew a breath, making a decision. "The one where you're in a dress—"

Michael was out of his chair, his face flushed. "I knew it, you—"

"You need to hide it, burn it, bury it somewhere. Just get it out of here before someone uses it against you." There. He'd done it, and now he was left with an absurd desire to bound around the room. He wanted to swing Maggie around and around, then pull her into his arms and kiss her and kiss her and never stop kissing her. She'd been right. The woman knew him better than he knew himself. He couldn't blackmail Ferrington.

Not and face himself in the mirror every morning. Not and face Maggie.

Michael's mouth was moving, but no sound was coming out.

Nick chuckled, somewhat dryly. "Get a grip, Michael. I'm not airing your dirty laundry. But I am suggesting you hide the photo, because I'm not the only shark swimming in these parts." Except that he was retiring from the shark business as of right now. Deena was right. They'd survive. And he'd rather just survive with Maggie than flounder in wealth without her.

"I was so sure Maggie was looking for things to use against me . . . that she was your spy."

"She was. A reluctant spy. She only told me about the picture because . . ." He frowned. "Wait a second. You *knew?*"

"We suspected."

Well, that figured. Stack another layer of oddity onto an already off-the-wall day. "Then why on earth did you leave the photo out where she'd see it?"

Michael grinned. "It was a trap."

"Excuse me?"

"A trap, bait. It's a complete fake. I mean, really. Me. In a dress? I don't think so."

"But Maggie saw the photograph."

This time, Michael looked so pleased with himself that his already plump cheeks looked ripe. "Oh, it's a real photo. From a charity benefit." He leaned forward, motioning for Nick to come closer. "A benefit that Palmer participated in, too."

"No way."

"Oh, yes. He didn't wear a dress, but he was there."

"Michael, never let anyone tell you that you don't have the stomach for business."

Ferrington's plan couldn't have been more perfect. Leak the photo to Maggie and get Palmer all excited that there was some dirt that would force Michael to sell. Michael would hold fast, and Palmer's lackeys—that would be Nick—would give the story and the photo to the press. Then, when the truth behind the photo came out, and everyone realized there really was no big secret, Palmer would be so embarrassed that he'd crawl away with his tail between his legs and never bother Vision again.

The seeds of an idea took root in Nick's head. It just might work. No, it would definitely work. "You're absolutely positive you don't want to sell to Palmer? No matter what the price?"

"Nick, you forfeited your trump card, remember? I'm not going to sell just because you're a nice guy."

"Then let's fix it. Let's fix it so Palmer never gets Vision."

"I'm listening."

"I'll need to get Hoop and my assistant, Larry, involved." He smiled, imagining the look on the Bullfrog's face when the Vision deal blew up. "And I'll need the picture."

* * *

When the door to the break room opened, Maggie missed a beat on her story.

The little red-haired girl with pigtails held up her hand. "He has to say he loves her."

Maggie nodded. "Right. That's the key to the entire enchantment." She slid back into the tale, but her eyes were on Nicholas. When he smiled and gave her a thumbs-up sign, her heart skipped a beat. He'd done the right thing. Somehow, she knew the thumbs up was for her, and not because he'd convinced Michael to sell.

She finished the rest of the story, then hopped off her stool the second Tony turned the camera light off. Nicholas was right there, at the edge of the stage, and he caught her as she flung herself into his arms and covered his face with kisses.

When he was thoroughly kissed, she leaned back and looked at him, giggling at the little red marks her lips had left all over his face. "You did the right thing," she said. "I knew you would."

He kissed the tip of her nose. "You were right. And it gets better."

Better? She glanced from Nicholas to Michael. "I don't understand."

He explained the plan in the car on the way home. "So we're going to have Hoop take the picture to my office and leave it on Larry's desk, supposedly for me," he said, pulling into the driveway. "Larry will make sure that the Bullfrog sees it, and he'll show it to Angela, and then . . ."

She smiled, knowing exactly what would happen then.

"So. Here we are." He opened his door and got out, then came around the car, opened her door, and helped her out. "Do you want to watch another movie? Go out? Have a glass of wine?"

All of that sounded wonderful so long as she was with Nicholas. But this was her last night. She needed to be bold. "I want you to make love to me, Nicholas."

He stumbled just a bit, then took a little more time than usual getting the key to open the door. But once they were inside, he turned to look at her, his fingers tracing her arm through the skin-tight material of her cat suit.

"Are you sure?" he asked, his brown eyes seeming even darker.

"Oh, yes, Nicholas. I'm very sure."

"Good." The corner of his mouth lifted. "I was going to have to take a cold shower for a year if you'd changed your mind."

He took her hand and led her to the bed, the place where they'd shared so many nights without him even realizing. Now she was here—a woman, and welcome in his arms. She stood in front of him, the mattress pressing against the back of her legs, as he traced her lips with his fingers.

With a whimper, she leaned forward into his touch, wanting to feel his fingers, his lips, his body, pressed over every inch of her. Wanting to experience nothing but the feel of Nicholas, body and soul.

"Maggie, oh, Maggie," he murmured, his breath caressing her ear.

He pulled her close, melding against her, and lightning raced through her soul, a frenzy of sparks that came near to bursting out of her: A shooting star, a sunrise, the sweet music of birds at the dawn.

Their bodies came together, new and yet somehow comfortable, familiar. As if they already knew the secrets they were about to discover. Secrets Maggie craved.

Living fire consumed her, Nicholas's heat both searing and soothing. She opened her mouth to cry out, to beg, but he caught her lips in a kiss, and her cry dissolved into a moan of pure pleasure. Slowly, treasuring the moment, she stretched up on tiptoes and wrapped her arms around his neck, silently willing him to deepen their kiss.

With light, teasing fingers, he traced the curve of her shoulder, finally slipping his finger under the neck of her catsuit. She purred with pleasure, the sound deep and rich in her throat, and flattened her body against him as his fingers wreaked havoc with her senses.

His hand roamed around to her back, his caresses bold and possessive. "My Maggie," he whispered, and she sighed, her heart utterly lost. When he urged the zipper down along her back, she exulted in the cool air that rushed in, providing a small bit of relief to her now red-hot body.

Nothing in her life had prepared her for the

storm raging within her. Part of her longed to quell the surge of sensation—the tingling, buzzing, swirling wonderfulness brought on by Nicholas's touch—to let it heighten and release in a cascade of pure pleasure. Yet another part of her never wanted the feeling to end, and she leaned against his hand, warm and demanding on her back. She arched against him, her eyes locked on his, suddenly awed by the desire reflected in his eyes.

"More," she murmured.

With a low, guttural groan, he slid his hands up and under the material, sliding the stretchy material down to her waist. "You're lovely," he said. He slipped an arm around her waist. With his other hand, he trailed his finger down her arm and she shivered. "Are you cold?"

She shook her head. So was so hot, she was burning up. And she was free-falling even though she was standing on firm ground, held up by the bed against her legs and Nicholas's arm around her waist.

Maggie closed her eyes and he trailed his hand off her arm and onto her belly, running his fingertip under the material that still clung to her hips. With every tiny stroke of his finger, her body melted a little bit more until she wasn't sure where she ended and Nicholas began.

"Nicho—" she began, but he hushed her with a kiss. As his hand wreaked havoc with her stomach, his lips teased and tantalized. First her mouth, then her throat. He trailed feather kisses down her, and she arched her neck back as his tongue traced her collarbone, then lower still until his mouth closed over her breast.

She gasped, dizzy and weak, as his tongue laved her. His hand teased her other breast, his thumb playing with her nipple. Every touch, every caress coaxed her desire into a frenzy. Untamed and reckless.

Nicholas. This was Nicholas, and he wanted her as much as she wanted him. The knowledge aroused her, combining with the sweet sensations swirling within her. She wanted, *needed*, more. She had to have *everything*. She slid her hands up his back, losing her fingers in his hair as she urged his head up, pulling her mouth toward his.

His lips caught hers, wild and feverish. He stroked her hair, her back, and she writhed against him. When he broke the kiss and pushed her gently back, she looked at him, her fear that he'd changed his mind dissolving when she saw the passion in his eyes.

"Maggie," he said, his voice raw. "I want you in my bed."

His hand cupped her face, and she pressed her cheek against his palm. "What do *you* want?" he asked.

Nick held his breath, knowing what her answer would be, but somehow needing to hear it anyway.

"You," she said, simply. Then she looked over her shoulder at the bed. She took one tiny step away from him and peeled off the rest of her lycra outfit until she stood, lithe and naked, before him.

His heart felt like it would burst as he looked at Maggie. So beautiful, so innocent, so *wanting him*. And he wanted her. She amazed him, thrilled him. Made him feel more alive than he had in years.

Without blinking, she watched as he stripped, a little smile playing at her mouth. She was crouched, naked, on the far side of the bed, and he was reminded of their very first kiss. She'd been naked then, too, and she'd pounced on him with single-minded determination. To think he'd actually run from her.

What an idiot.

No more.

Now he needed her. Her touch, her heat. *Her heart*.

Keeping his eyes locked on hers, he climbed into the bed, and rested his back against the headboard. He patted the mattress beside him, fighting a smile.

Her teeth dragged across her lower lip, and he frowned. "What's wrong?"

She looked away, and he tried to bite back the terror rising in him. She couldn't be having second thoughts, not now.

"It's just that I . . . I should tell you something. About me. About us."

He sat up straighter. "It's okay. Whatever it is, it'll be okay."

She smiled then, a real smile, but slightly sad. Then she shook her head slightly and took a deep breath. "It's just that I love you. So much. And I . . ."

"I know," he said, treasuring her words. "You told me." She spoke of love—*of him*—and it thrilled him. He wanted to open his mouth to tell her it was okay, that he loved her, too. But the words caught in his throat. That fear, of being wrong, of hurting her, crashed down on him, striking him mute.

A flicker of something passed over her face. Hurt? God, he hoped not. She was his everything, and if he couldn't tell her so, he'd show her. With every breath in his body, he'd show her.

"You're amazing, Maggie," he said. "Do you know how much I want you? Do you have any idea?"

For a moment, she just stared, then her mouth twitched and her eyes sparkled. "Yes, Nicholas."

He patted the mattress again. "Then come here."

From the other side of the bed, she crawled toward him, her expression both predatory and playful. A lissome beauty. She came nearer, her movements sensual, erotic. He held his breath, savoring the moment, somehow sure that as soon as he felt her touch, coherent thought would abandon him.

Straddling his legs, she eased forward in a sensual stretch, letting her hands slide over his knees, his thighs, up his stomach. And all the while, she was sinking lower, coming closer, until their bodies finally touched. God, she was perfect—warm and supple and delicious. He wanted to taste her, to hold her, to be inside her.

As she moved closer, her breasts pressed against his chest and her hips rubbed erotically against him. He groaned, straining to let this moment last, but nearly overcome just by her subtle movements. She placed a gentle kiss on the end of his nose, then pulled back to smile at him. Sweet. Innocent. Alluring. Sexy.

"My Nicholas," she said with a smile, and he happily agreed.

Catching her around the waist, he rolled them over, trapping her under him. "My turn," he said, then caught her little sigh of agreement with his kiss.

She tasted like some forgotten candy, sweet and tempting, yet comfortable and safe. Like coming home. And she was his. He reveled in the knowledge, exploring her with his lips, caressing her with his hands. With the tip of his tongue, he traced the outline of her ear, her soft sigh of pleasure pushing him nearer to the precipice. His body was tense and tight with anticipation, but he wouldn't rush. Not tonight.

With slow deliberation, he kissed her neck, her breast, her stomach. Then lower still until she opened her legs for him. He teased the insides of her thighs, and she squirmed with pleasure, her body stiffening under his touch. When he dipped his tongue to taste heaven, she sighed his name, "Nicholas," the single word like spoken gossamer.

And in that moment, he knew.

Positively. Maggie was his.

And he loved her.

Maggie sighed, the earth tilting beneath her.

Nicholas was wreaking such wonderful torment. She was completely still and yet her body was spinning out of control. As she writhed against him, the storm built inside her, and she was certain she'd burst.

But not yet. She wanted the feeling to last. At any moment she could break free, and she hung on to the edge of reality, savoring the kaleidoscope of sensations.

But she craved more. Nicholas. All of him. She wanted him on top of her, his body pressed close. She needed him inside her, filling her up.

Her breathing came ragged, and she dragged her fingers through his thick hair, urging him up, wanting his kisses. He came willingly, his lips dancing on the skin of her belly, his body rubbing against hers. She writhed and stretched against him, loving him, loving the feeling. Wanting it to last forever.

She'd almost told him earlier. Almost confessed. And that would have destroyed everything. She wanted him to know the truth, but she couldn't risk losing him. Not now. Not when she was so close.

His mouth closed over her breast and she quivered as his tongue teased her nipple. The hard length of him pressed against her and she closed her eyes, wanting. Silently willing him to take her.

To love her. And he did love her. She was sure of it.

He'd almost said it. *Almost*. And his silence had nearly shattered her soul. But then he'd looked at her, and she'd seen the love in his eyes.

He'd say it tonight. He would. He had to.

She couldn't bear to lose Nicholas.

"Maggie?" His voice was soft. Leaning closer, he placed a tender kiss at the corner of her mouth. "Tell me what you want, Maggie."

Her pulse quickened. *Everything, Nicholas*. "Make love to me."

His eyes darkened and his mouth closed over hers as she pulled him closer, opening herself to him. Then he entered her, and the frenzy inside her escalated. They moved together, Maggie and Nicholas, lost in a haze of passion and love. When she couldn't stand it any longer, she cried out, "Nicholas," sure that every bit of her had shattered into a million pieces.

They made love throughout the night, and Maggie abandoned herself in Nicholas's arms, lost to everything except the rapture of their bodies as one. Finally, exhausted, they lay together, locked in each other's embrace. She sighed. So content, so happy. All the good emotions in the world swirled through her.

There were so many that she didn't even realize, until the sun was already peeking over the horizon, that Nicholas had never actually told her he loved her.

* * *

She'd disappeared again.

Nick couldn't believe it. After their fireworks and starbursts kind of night—the most amazing night of his life—he really hadn't expected that Maggie would roll out of bed at the crack of dawn and go on her daily memory-search walking tour.

Smiling to himself, he stumbled toward the kitchen. He'd never really believed that nonsense about the earth moving, but he was a convert now. With Maggie, the earth had not only moved, it had gotten up and boogied.

Maggie the cat twisted and turned between his legs. He leaned down and ruffled the fur on her head. "Hey there, little girl. Welcome to the best morning of my life. Where's your namesake? Huh? Where'd Maggie go?"

She mewed, then ran into the entry hall and scratched at the door. Well, what the hell. He wasn't going to the office today. Especially since he had no office to go to. "Okay," he said, opening the door. "But just for an hour or so."

She tore out of the house and headed for the vacant lot. Nick frowned, not thrilled with the prospect of spending an hour picking burrs out of her fur.

Well, he'd deal with that when she came back. In the meantime, he'd get some coffee, get dressed, and then go comb the streets, looking for Maggie.

The coffee had just begun to brew when Deena burst in. "Where's Maggie?" she demanded, her face flushed as if she'd run all the way from Hoop's.

"Out there," he said, nodding vaguely toward the street as he poured a cup of elixir.

"You told her, right? You told her that you loved her, didn't you?"

He chuckled. "You win, Deena. I love her. I absolutely, positively, love Maggie."

"But did you tell *her?*"

"Not yet."

"Oh, God." She sank into one of the kitchen chairs and buried her head in her hands.

Alarmed, Nick kneeled next to her. "What? Deena, what is it?"

"And animal control just swept the neighborhood."

Nick blanched, trying to switch gears from Maggie the woman to Maggie the cat. "It's after Halloween. What are they doing sweeps for?"

"I tried to catch the truck," Hoop said, gasping as he stumbled into the kitchen. "But it was too far up the street. They did a sweep. I think they got about six cats from the lot."

"Hell. Then they got Maggie."

Deena took his hand. "That's it exactly, Nick. They got Maggie."

The tingle was back along his spine. "What are you saying, Deenie?"

"Maggie's a cat, Nick," Hoop answered. "You wanna get with the program?"

* * *

"That's the nuttiest thing I've every heard," Nick said. And it was. But nutty or not, he still believed it. All the little pieces—her naivete, her quirks, her funny habits—came together in one complete picture. And that picture was of a midnight black cat with emerald green eyes.

"But it's true, Nick."

"I know." He smiled. Bad enough that it had taken a petite little brunette to bring him to his senses and let him get out there and enjoy life, now it turned out she was a hell of a lot more petite than he thought. "I don't know why I know, but I do." He smiled at his sister. "You were right." *About everything.*

Deena's eyes brimmed with tears, and Hoop laid a hand on her shoulder. "What are we going to do?"

His brow furrowed, the feeling that he was missing something important nagging at him. "We're going to go down to the shelter and get her. It'll cost twenty bucks. No big deal."

Hoop and Deena exchanged glances.

"Okay. Out with it. What don't I know?"

Deena nodded at Hoop, who sucked in a breath of air and looked really unhappy.

"She's not changing back, sport. You missed the witching hour."

The ground shifted under him, and he grabbed the countertop for support. "What?" he said, his voice barely a whisper.

"All I know is that was part of the rules. The old

tomcat said you had to say it out loud or else she'd be a cat forever."

"No. No way." That was unacceptable. And unfathomable. After finally finding a woman like Maggie, he wouldn't—couldn't—let her be ripped from him at the whim of some tomcat. "That's absurd. I told you, I told myself, I showed Maggie. There wasn't any question that I loved her. This is completely unfair."

"So what are you going to do about it?" Hoop asked.

"I'm going to the shelter and I'm going to give that tomcat a piece of my mind. And I'm getting Maggie."

"How do you know the tomcat's at the shelter?"

"He has to be," Nick said, steeling himself. He looked Deena in the eye. "If I'm going to get my Maggie back, he just plain has to be."

He grabbed his keys off the kitchen table and hurried into the living room, Deena and Hoop on his heels.

"Did I hear what I think I just heard?"

Angela. What had she overheard?

He closed his eyes and took a breath. He didn't need this. Right now, he *really* didn't need this.

She stopped in the doorway, the Bullfrog waddling up the sidewalk behind her.

"Can the great Nicholas Goodman really be losing his tiny little mind? A cat, Nickie? I always assumed your delusions would be a little more creative."

He started to respond, hoping that by the time

he opened his mouth, he'd have thought of something a bit more sane-sounding than "Yes, Angela, I'm off to the animal shelter to look for the woman I love."

"Such a pity," she continued, before he could get a word in. "Well, if dropping the Vision ball wasn't enough to kill your career, this little tidbit of information will surely be the last nail in your coffin."

A week ago the threat would have terrified him. Now, all Nick wanted to do was get into his car and get to the shelter. The thought that he actually had to deal with this woman—that she'd entered his house and interrupted his life—angered him more than her cruel words.

"Angela. Move. I need to go. Now."

"We just wanted to stop by and let you know that Vision will be Palmer's within the week," the Bullfrog croaked. "Tell Larry thanks for the tip. And thanks to you, too, Mr. Hooper."

"Any time," Hoop said, but his voice dripped icicles.

"Angela . . ." he said, a warning note in his voice. But still she loomed in the doorway. He sighed. "Fine. Stay here. Gather your stuff, ransack my house, I don't care. Just get out of my way."

When she didn't, he stepped forward, gripped her arm, and pushed her out of the way, ignoring her gasp of surprise. Then he raced down the sidewalk toward his car, Hoop and Deena right behind him.

"You bastard," Angela screeched. "At least now I know that either you're insane, and that's why you left me, or your Maggie really is a magic cat, and she's hexed you into a raving idiot."

For the briefest of moments, the possibility that he'd been enchanted swirled through his head—that it wasn't love, but magic. How much crazier was that than a shapeshifting catwoman? But his heart knew better and he banished the thought. Besides, in a way what they had *was* magic. The best kind of magic.

"You're almost right, Angela," he said, turning to face her one last time. "Not a hex, an enchantment. It's called love. You might want to try it sometime."

"There are only ten cats in the whole place," Nick said, trying to stay calm. In his arms, Maggie snuggled close, her purr almost deafening. "Can't I just pay the fee and take them home with me?"

The kid smacked his gum and shrugged. "Can't do it, man," he said, his eyes drifting to Deena, who was crawling around on the floor peering into each of the cages.

"This is him, Nick. I'm sure." She sat back on her heels, pointing to a cage filled with about twenty-five pounds of mangy, one-eyed tomcat.

"No way," Hoop said. "That guy doesn't look like he can take care of himself, much less cast—"

"Hoop," Nick said, nodding his head toward the kid. He turned to Deena. "Are you positive?"

"All I know is the story. Maggie said Old Tom

had one eye." Her mouth turned up in a half-smile, but her eyes revealed her worry. "If he's here, this is your guy."

"But he might still be roaming the streets," Nick finished, adding the words his sister couldn't.

"It's true, man. We don't even know if he lives in the neighborhood. That cat could be like the Incredible Hulk. You know, goes from place to place, never staying long enough to get any roots."

Nick couldn't let himself believe that. The Fates couldn't be that cruel. He and Maggie belonged together. This old tomcat had to be the key.

"You folks gonna fill out the paperwork, or what?" the kid asked.

"Yes. We want to take those two now. The black one and the one-eyed tomcat."

"Fine. But it's like I told you. You bring me some paperwork that proves you own 'em, and you can take 'em. Otherwise, they gotta stay twenty-four hours—in case their real owners come." He shrugged. "Sorry, rules is rules."

Nick glanced between Hoop and Deena, then back to the kid. "Give me a minute."

"Okay." The kid stood there by the door, blowing bubbles and popping them.

"Alone. Please."

A bubble popped, and the kid used the wad of gum to pluck the little pieces off his face. "Whatever," he said, then he and his gum left, the door slamming behind him.

The second the door closed, Nick stroked Maggie's head. "Are you okay, sweetheart? Can you understand me? I'm so sorry. I didn't know." She licked his fingers and mewed, a sad, tiny sound that tore at his heart.

Deena and Hoop came over, and she licked each of them in turn, her mews so plaintive that Nick was absolutely certain he understood the language of cats.

With a sigh, he passed her to Deena. "I need to talk to Old Tom now," he said. Then he looked up at Deena and Hoop. "I think I should be alone."

They nodded, and Deena put Maggie back in her cage, leaving the little door open. As they left the kennel, he smiled at Maggie, sure that he saw absolute trust reflected in her eyes.

Now for the real show. He squatted in front of Old Tom's cage, trying to remember that this wasn't silly. This was his life. Maggie's life. This cat was the key to their life together.

"You broke the rules," Nick said, and the pupil in the cat's one good eye narrowed. Good. At least he was listening.

"Maggie knew I loved her. So did Deena and Hoop. How would they know if I hadn't said so? The fact is, I did say I loved her. I spoke the words to Deena, and I spoke them in my head. But most important, my heart told Maggie I loved her, and Maggie knew it was true. She's always known it."

The tomcat just sat there, no reaction at all on his face. Outside, beyond the glass, was a different story. The animal control worker was chewing his gum frantically, watching Nick like he might watch a caged psycho at Bellevue. Behind the kid, Deena leaned against Hoop, her lips pressed tight together with worry.

From inside her cage, Maggie watched as Nicholas pled her case. She'd known he would come for her.

"Don't punish Maggie because I was an idiot. I loved her from the moment I saw her. And I've told her so. With every essence of my being, with every breath I take, with every ounce of strength in my body, I've told her I loved her."

Maggie purred, certain that would convince Old Tom. She waited for the tingling, wondering how she would fit into the little cage as a woman. But the tingling didn't come. And though Nicholas kept talking, trying to persuade Old Tom, for at least another hour, nothing ever happened. Until finally, Nick said good-bye, promising to rescue her and Old Tom and the rest of the cats in the morning.

"You are upset with me," Old Tom said.

True, but she kept silent, afraid that if she opened her mouth, she would regret it.

"Did you like being human, Maggie?"

She pushed back her anger and nodded. *"The emotions. I felt things more strongly,"* she said, knowing better than to lie to Old Tom. Her nose wrinkled. *"And at times, everything was very confusing."* Her heart swelled. *"But I loved it. And it was worth it just to be with Nicholas."*

"Your love is as strong as always?"

She nodded. Oh, yes. *"If anything, it is stronger. Before, I loved the Nicholas I saw. Now I love the Nicholas I know. His faults, his strengths, everything. Most of all, I know his soul now."*

She blinked, knowing that if she were still human, she would cry. *"Please. Please don't take away my Nicholas. I love him. I need him. And he needs me, too."*

Old Tom said nothing.

"Shall I beg? I will if it will make a difference."

"Your begging would not persuade me."

No, she hadn't expected that it would. Neither would howling, scratching, or clawing. She dropped to the floor of the cage, laying her head against the cool metal, fearing that it was over and she would stay a cat, without Nicholas, for eight more lives after this one.

"You say that you love him. Are you so sure that he loves you, too?"

Her tail twitched. *"Of course."*

"He did not speak these words of love to you. Not for all the time you were together. Not even when you mated."

The truth of Old Tom's words washed over her, and her heart wrenched. Nicholas *hadn't* told her. He'd said nothing of love, even when she'd said the words to him so openly, even when he'd made love to her. No, he'd been silent. It wasn't until today that he'd told her he loved her. Here, in this kennel.

She flattened her ears, suddenly afraid. Nicholas loved Maggie the cat. Did he love Maggie the woman? Really? Or was it guilt and fear that had ripped those words of love from him?

No! She couldn't, *wouldn't,* believe that. *"He loves me. The words are not important except for your enchantment. He loves me in his heart, and that is what should matter."*

Old Tom stirred, moving about in his cage. *"There is much I have not told you,"* he said. *"Some you do not need to know. But I tell you this now. Your soul, it is not like other cats."*

"I don't understand."

"There is much that is human in you. For that reason alone, I allowed the transformation. And for that reason alone, I give you this choice."

She poked her head out of the cage, glancing over to see the expression on his face, afraid to hope for fear she would be wrong.

"One human life—with Nicholas, yes, but also with all the emotions, pain and joy, that accompany it. Or nine cat lives, with no worries that you have said or done the wrong thing, and without emotions bursting through you. You will have fond memories of your time with Nicholas, but you will not regret.

"Think hard, little Maggie. If you are wrong—if he does not love you—there will be no turning back." Once again he paused. *"Now, how do you choose?"*

The kitchen was a wreck—three glasses in the sink and an empty cereal bowl on the counter—

and Nick stared at the dishes, trying to remember why it mattered if he washed them.

All afternoon he'd been in a daze.

He'd lost. He'd lost Maggie.

The idea was unfathomable, the reality frustrating. No matter what he did or how much he begged, he might not ever see her again. All because he'd been too foolish and scared to look into his own heart.

He turned on the tap and splashed some cold water on his face, hoping Deena and Hoop would hurry back.

The doorbell rang. Thank goodness. As much as he needed to be alone, he couldn't bear the silence in the house. He pulled open the door, and, for the second time in his life, time stood still.

Maggie?

"Hello, Nicholas."

His heart skipped a beat. He reached out and stroked her cheek, needing to feel her skin under his. It was true. She was real. She was human.

And she was naked.

A bubble of joy welled in him and he reached for her. Almost fearing to touch her, afraid she'd be whisked away again, he put his arm around her and ushered her inside. "How did you get away?"

With a smile, she shrugged, then indicted her body with one hand. "If Old Tom can manage this . . . well, those silly cages aren't really a problem."

He nodded at the vacant lot before closing the door. "Is he back over there?"

"Uh-huh. Along with all the others."

"Remind me to invest in some very large bags of cat food. I think it's time to start feeding the neighborhood cats."

"Old Tom really likes tuna."

Laughing, Nick pulled her close, burying his face in her hair. "Oh, Maggie, I love you."

"I know. I love you, too, Nicholas."

He swallowed, almost afraid to ask the question, more scared of the answer. "Are you still going to be here when I wake up?"

She nodded. "After everything I've been through, Nicholas Goodman, you'd better believe I'm not going anywhere."

"Still, I think I'll tell you I love you at least once a day." He kissed the tip of her nose. "Just to be on the safe side."

Epilogue

Maggie dipped the star-shaped sponge into the purple paint, being careful not to drip any of the thick color onto Hoop's kitchen floor. Standing on her tiptoes, she dabbed the sponge onto the now peach-colored cabinets. She stood back, inspected her work, and smiled.

"What do you think?" she asked, calling through the open window.

"Just a sec." Deena's reply floated back to her, soon followed by Deena herself, who stepped through the patio door with an apron full of clean paint brushes. "Hey, that looks great. We'll have this place livable in no time."

Wiping her hands on the oversized shirt she'd

borrowed to paint in, Maggie turned and surveyed Hoop's house. Deena had only been living there for a month, but already the house had been miraculously transformed. Flower-print slipcovers spruced up the sofa and recliner, scented candles topped the newly painted crate-and-board coffee table, a stenciled ivy was just beginning to climb the walls, and Maggie's moon and stars floated on a universe made of kitchen cabinets.

All in all, it was clear that Deena had a new address.

The front door slammed open, followed by the tromping of feet and the familiar male laughter that still made her insides quiver.

Dropping her sponge in the sink, Maggie ran to the living room.

"Ivy?" Hoop said, pointing to the dark green pattern. "Say it isn't so." At Deena's little shrug, he turned to Nicholas. "You see what your sister is doing to me, what I have to put up with?"

"And you love every minute of it," Nicholas said, winking at Maggie, his smile making her heart leap.

"Yeah," he said, dropping his basketball and looping his arm around Deena's waist before kissing her forehead. "But don't tell anyone, okay? It'd ruin my reputation."

Taking Nicholas's hand, Maggie leaned against him. "So who won?"

"I did, of course," Hoop said.

"I think we're due a rematch," Nicholas said, pulling Maggie closer.

"What about tomorrow," she suggested. "Deena and I can cheer you on."

"Can't. I need to work late." One corner of his mouth lifted. "I have to prosecute some burps."

Deena laughed, and Maggie tried to scowl at Nicholas, but she was pretty sure she only managed a lopsided smile. "Are you going to tease me about that forever?

"That's pretty much my current plan," he said, then kissed the tip of her nose.

"Don't you have to work tomorrow night, anyway?" Hoop asked, looking at Maggie.

She shook her head. "Since Michael's company made that deal with the network, he's taking some of his cash and revamping the whole studio." She shrugged. "They're installing new equipment this week, so I've got a vacation."

"After all that effort to stay totally independent, I still can't believe he cut a deal with the highest bidder as soon as his market share skyrocketed." Nicholas grinned, then shrugged. "Oh, well. Good for him."

Deena hopped up onto the back of the sofa and balanced there, her arm around Hoop's waist. "With a kick-ass star like Maggie on his team, it was inevitable."

"Don't you know the Ice Queen and Frog-face are having a fit," Hoop said, a wicked grin lining his face.

"Neither one has time to have a fit," Nicholas said. "Bullfrog's too busy sucking up to Dryson, hoping they won't pass him over for partner again."

"And Angela's been too busy kissing up to big daddy Palmer over losing you," Deena said.

"Hardly. I hear she's traipsing all over L.A. with that actor guy." Nicholas smiled at Maggie and chuckled.

"Enough about Angela," said Deena. "Ick." She slid off the sofa and moved into the kitchen, the clatter of dishes and silverware soon drifting back into the living room. "How about we go shopping tomorrow, Mags?"

"Okay," she agreed, the corners of her mouth curling as she anticipated a full day with Deena at the mall. That was sure to be an adventure.

"Great," mumbled Nicholas as he looked at Hoop. "Now we're both in trouble."

Carrying a plate, Deena stepped back into the room. "Let me put this down for Old Tom, and then we can go get some dinner for ourselves."

"Tuna?" asked Maggie, nodding at the dish.

"Albacore, no less," Deena answered with a wink.

"Only the best for Tom," Nicholas added. "How about Chinese for us?"

"I was thinking MacGuire's," Deena said.

"What about you, Mags?" Hoop asked. "Anything in particular on your mind?"

She licked her lips. "I was thinking that a Big Mac sounded pretty good. I'm in the mood for a grease-fest."

Nicholas gave her a little hug. "Anything you want, sweetheart."

"Thanks, Nicholas." She smiled up at him. "But I already have everything I want."

More Than
Magic
Kathleen Nance